THE ICE QUEEN

THE ICE QUEEN

THE TARRASSIAN SAGA

Aria Mossi

Copyright © 2021 Aria Mossi

The moral right of the author has been asserted.

Apart from any fair dealing for the purposes of research or private study, or criticism or review, as permitted under the Copyright, Designs and Patents Act 1988, this publication may only be reproduced, stored or transmitted, in any form or by any means, with the prior permission in writing of the publishers, or in the case of reprographic reproduction in accordance with the terms of licences issued by the Copyright Licensing Agency. Enquiries concerning reproduction outside those terms should be sent to the publishers.

Matador
9 Priory Business Park,
Wistow Road, Kibworth Beauchamp,
Leicestershire. LE8 0RX
Tel: 0116 279 2299
Email: books@troubador.co.uk
Web: www.troubador.co.uk/matador
Twitter: @matadorbooks

ISBN 978 1800463 189

British Library Cataloguing in Publication Data.
A catalogue record for this book is available from the British Library.

Printed and bound in Great Britain by 4edge Limited
Typeset in 11pt Sabon by Troubador Publishing Ltd, Leicester, UK

Matador is an imprint of Troubador Publishing Ltd

In the memory of my two grandmothers and their never-ending love for storytelling.

"Shelegiel dances,
silently,
upon the house of man,
leaves no trace upon the sleeping land"

Peter Mohrbacher
Angelarium: The Encyclopedia of Angels

PROLOGUE

—

TWENTY-FOUR YEARS EARLIER

The heavy rain hits the small windows as the gloomy London afternoon rolls into an even gloomier evening. The room may be small and dark, but there is no space for gloominess inside. The young mother holds her beautiful newborn daughter. She rocks her gently and the swinging motion of the nursing chair soothes them both. Her other daughter plays on the little woolly rug in front of the fireplace. She is only five years old, but her big grey eyes watch her with a worried look. She knows something is not quite right. She was always too wise for her young age. Mother gives her a bright smile and invites her to come closer. The little girl kneels by the nursing chair and places her head on mother's knees.

"There is no need to be worried, my beautiful flower, I will always live inside your hearts," says the young mother, brushing her fingers through her daughter's long white hair. Her other daughter, only a few weeks old, opens her grey eyes and squirms in her arms. She is perfect. They both are. She may not have long left with them, but they will be well looked after. Who wouldn't want to adopt two exceptionally beautiful little girls? There is no need to worry. She can't let them feel her pain or her worries. She must give them all she has left to give. The memory of her must be one of love and hope. She reaches inside the pocket of her dress to retrieve her beloved brooch.

"Careful with the needle, my flower," says mother with a smile.

The little girl moves her fingers gently over the beautiful pearls of the water lily, then places the brooch on top of her little sister's body.

"You will give it to your sister when she is old enough to understand, won't you, my flower? I know you will keep her safe and I know you will keep my memory alive. My brave flower," says mother with a bright smile.

"Tell us the story of the blue water lilies, mother, will you?" says the little girl, making herself comfortable by her mother's legs.

"Yes, my beautiful flower. We must always keep the stories alive. And you must do it for your sister when I am gone."

Her daughter nods, and mother closes her big grey eyes with a smile.

Once upon a time in a faraway country we nowadays call Egypt, there was an enchanted oasis. Hidden amongst the golden dunes of the desert, away from prying eyes, this was no ordinary oasis. A mysterious purple mist sheltered the most beautiful image. Bewitching palm trees and tall grasses gently swished in the breeze, surrounding a beautiful lake, as blue as the sky. But this was no ordinary lake. Every night, when the moon was full, magic from the skies would descend upon Earth.

The silver moon would lower a magic ladder made of light, all the way to the beautiful oasis. And each night, the stars would take turns coming down to Earth. As their shimmery forms touched the soft sand of the desert, they would turn into beautiful women. Their long white hair reached their feet and their silver eyes glowed in the moonlight. Their long dresses were made of light and a trail of stardust would powder the sand as they stepped on it. Each night, the beautiful stars would dance around the lake, to a tune known only to them. Their laughter would fill the moon with joy, and she would watch over them until the early hours of the morning. Long before sunrise, the magic ladder made of light would lower and all the stars would climb back to the skies. And so, every night they danced and laughed without a worry in the world. Little did they know, every night they had been watched by an old witch, with only darkness in her heart. She would hide her deformed body in the tall grasses and watch them with eyes full of envy. She knew well how to hide her ugliness in the shadows, as she had been doing so for many years. From the safety of the darkness, she used her evil spells to hurt the people in the nearby city. She loved to see them suffer. It made her happy. And yet, these stars dared show their beauty to her! Why should they have it all? Forever young, unimaginable beauty and outfits made of light, while she never had anything more than rags to hide her ugliness. Each day she would make potions and spells against the stars, and each night they would prove useless. The witch's magic could not be compared to the magic of the stars. She couldn't harm them while they were under the protection of the moon. But at sunrise, their magic would perish, and they would be nothing but useless beings. So, the evil witch put all her knowledge into creating the most enchanting music. Its magic entranced the stars as she played it to them. Their feet wouldn't stop dancing and twirling around the beautiful lake, over and over again. As the night sky got lighter, the moon lowered the magic ladder and called for her children to come home. The stars kept on dancing, enslaved by the magical music. The moon called and called again, until one by one the stars heard their mother's voice and broke the evil spell. All except for three... They were further away, and as the witch played her music louder and louder, they couldn't hear the moon's voice. The magic ladder went up and the skies turned pink as the sun opened its eyes. The beautiful stars didn't even notice the bright morning light touching their flawless skin, taking its shimmer away. The evil witch came out from her hiding place and touched them with her magic stick. She took all their youth and beauty and gave them her ugliness. Their long white hair turned dull and tangled, their skin faded into wrinkles and the light died inside their eyes. And yet, they wouldn't stop dancing, the magic music playing inside their minds without the witch's help.

Many years had passed, and the old witch had become one of the most beloved ladies in the city by the river. Long forgotten were her evil spells and her wish to hurt the people. Her unimaginable beauty had brought her fame, riches, and many smiled at the sight of her. She didn't have to hide; she didn't have to repay evil with evil anymore. As the years passed, her heart softened, and the darkness was gone. She understood she was never evil, just hurt, scared and unloved. Each night, she would remember the stars she cursed to dance forever, until the memory of it took her happiness way. She had to do something, even if it meant using magic one more time, or losing her beauty and youth. She travelled to the hidden oasis and there, under the moonlight, she saw them. Three old women in rags, dancing around the lake. Only bare bones left of their feet and only shadows left of their silver eyes.

Her heart cried for them. She had to find a way to give them peace. But how? Magic couldn't turn them back into stars. Magic can only take, it cannot give. Only love can give. So, she used all the love in her heart to cast one last spell. She turned them *into flowers and placed them on their beloved lake. They would close their star-shaped petals under the moonlight to forget their pain and open them under the sunlight. And this is how the blue water lilies of Egypt were born. From the magic of the skies and the magic of the Earth bound together by a spell of love. The beautiful NYMPHAEA CAERULEA.*

1

TARS

Pure frustration, aggression and whatever other things a King shouldn't be feeling plague my sanity. I'd rather be charging like this through an army of vicious Noorranni, taking their filthy heads off. Instead, I'm charging through the gleaming corridors of the Royal Ship Levianha, on my way to meet the Royal Council. Levianha is the jewel in my Royal Fleet and the envy of the Galactic Empire. Despite all that, in the last six orbit rotations, since I became King, I have managed to avoid them all. I'd rather be on one of my warships and I'd rather meet with my Warriors. Thank the Astrals for the wars and all the lowlife scum to kill in the universe. Best excuse to stay away from king duties.

"Whatever happened to all our enemies? Why is there no one left to kill?" I boom over my shoulder at my High General.

"You killed most and drove the rest into hiding, my King," comes the answer in the usual controlled and diplomatic voice of my kingdom's highest general. Even on a good span, Larrssian's platitude and controlled behaviour are hard to stomach. Today is not a good span. And for the love of the Astrals, why is he walking so slowly? I need to get this done and go kill someone. Or fuck someone. Whichever I can get first.

"Speak, High General!" I growl at him as I keep walking towards the Royal Council Cave. "Why is this ship so big? Why do we have to impress anyone in this entire universe? We rule it anyway. I rule it!"

"Please, Tars," comes the unexpected answer. Enough to make me slow down my pace. Tarrassians save the use of our given names for our most intimate moments and for our most treasured people. Otherwise, we address each other by our role in Tarrassian society. For him to use my name it has to be important. Not even my full given name. He calls me Tarsmiamin when he wants to tell me off for my reckless behaviour. And as one of my two oldest friends, he can do that without losing his tongue. But Tars? He hasn't called me that in a while. He looks troubled or tired or… Hard to tell with the constant mask of platitudes and control on his face. I could read more on Tannon's face, despite being covered in scars and the facial fur he couldn't be bothered to trim.

"Say your piece, High General," I say, refusing to address him by name.

"This is your first official gathering with the entire Royal Council attending and…"

"What?" I stop suddenly in my tracks, nearly bumping into him. "Why are all of the boring old ruccuses attending? Don't they have anything better to do? Like run the kingdom or something?"

Larrs lets out a short sigh, as if to calm himself. Stupid of course, as he is always calm and in control. He is even in control when in battle shape. No Tarrassian is ever in control in battle shape.

"You are the one meant to run the kingdom, and don't call them old ruccuses to their faces," he says, once again with a tired look.

I refrain from saying it might be an impossible task and I ask the one thing that bothers me most.

"Why a Royal Council meeting here? On board the Royal Levianha? Why in space and why not back on Tarrassia? Since when do they met in deep space, the old ruccusses?"

Apparently, I had more than one question.

"It's an urgent Council, my King, and there is a very valid reason for meeting on the Levianha. It will all be revealed by your High Elder shortly."

He pauses with what looks like a troubled frown on his stony face, then carries on looking me in the eyes with a silent plea.

"As a race of Warriors, Tarrassians can only follow and respect the King who proves himself in battle. However, in times of sorrow and despair, they need a king, not a warrior. Our great race has millions…" the frown deepens for the sad reminder of our reality, while he corrects himself, "thousands of great Warriors, but only one King. Despite your differences, your father was a great king. In the name of your parents' memory, in the name of the Astrals and in the name of our friendship, I am asking you to walk into that Cave as a King and not as a Warrior."

"My parents are dead, the Astrals and their ridiculous Sign are long forgotten. However, I do treasure your friendship," I summarised, before walking through the mirrored metal doors separating The Old Ways from the new ones.

Despite being one of the most technologically advanced races amongst the stars, we are as stuck in our old ways as it gets. While trying to stay away from Tarrassia and royal prince duties, I met enough races to know that knowledge and technology meant leaving the old ways behind. Not for us though. We are one of the most puritanical societies in the universe. There are only a few other races living on Tarrassia. And even though treated with enough consideration, they are never allowed to mix with us, or to breed amongst themselves. In time, Tarrassia gathered a considerable number of low servants from other races. Not slaves. Never slaves. We combed the Seven Stars and beyond to wipe out the pest of the slavers. All our servants are former freed slaves. They stayed with us because they had no home to go to anymore, or simply because they were grateful. Our morals are as strong as our skills in battle. As the universe's strongest and purest race, it is our duty to protect the weak. Some of the races we saved from extinction consider us their gods. They built funny-shaped domes in our honour and prayed all day. As long as their females keep showing gratitude, I couldn't care less what they were building, or what they were worshipping.

The Royal Council Cave inside Levianha was built to look like every other Council Cave back on Tarrassia, just on a smaller scale. Our Great Ancestors were born in the sacred Caves of Tarrassia, from the Spark of the Astrals and the Circle Nebula. Nowadays, we lived in luxurious homes built to please the senses. However, the most important rituals or decisions were still happening in the Sacred Caves. It is hard to imagine, that outside the dark, gloomy walls of this Cave, there is one of the most technologically advanced ships in the universe. The large oval room is lined with hundreds of torches, shooting out of the walls, dripping the sizzling gaarr oil to the uneven hard floor. In between the torches, the walls have been decorated with sparkling carvings of the long-forgotten Sign of the Astrals. My Council of ruccusses– because that's exactly what they are, despite my General's opinion – are gathered around the large table, carved from the same hard rock. All fourteen of them, plus the two Low Generals and the High Commander of the Royal Ship. What are they up to? They all look as formal as ever, wearing nothing other than the traditional Kannicloth low on the waist and the Swords of the Astrals. There is no room for shinny armour or fancy clothes inside the Caves. Which is really the only reason why I like the Caves. At least no one gives me the look for walking around wearing the traditional Kannicloth and nothing else. Not that I care. I am the King. I wear what I please. Besides, my temper makes my War Beast come to life every so often. I can't really keep tearing through clothes. As I am about to say something to shock the seriousness out of them, I remember my promise to my friend. So, instead, I solemnly initiate our traditional salute. I take a fist to my left silent heart. They all reply with the same salute then bow their heads to me. I take a seat first, then the Elders, then my Warriors in order of age and rank. So many boring rules. Just because I'm the son of the perfect king, it doesn't mean I have to remember them. As I wonder what to do next, the Elder of the Healers stands and opens his personal hollocom device, shaped like the great leaf of the Marni trees. The symbol of his House. The Elder was a great friend to my father. And as far as Elders go, he is probably the least annoying. I feel quite relieved he is the one doing the talking. He runs his claws through his white facial fur, trimmed close to his face unlike some of the other Elders. Their facial fur is longer, reaching their furry abdomens. I try to suppress an unwanted grin as I imagine Tannon's wild unkempt fur at that old age.

"My King, my Elders, my Warriors, I called the Royal Council gathering to discuss the future of Tarrassia," he says with a grim face, and a dark platinum-ore colour takes over his shiny eyes. This time I can't suppress a growl. This is going to be long. I should have definitely stopped on one of the Yellow Planets to fuck a female. Or maybe two. And most definitely should have killed someone or something before coming here.

"This is going to be quick, as urgent action is required," says the Elder, almost as if he can hear my thoughts. I know he can't, because mind reading is not allowed inside the Sacred Caves. "Tarrassians are going to be a thing of the past in no longer than 200 orbit rotations," he adds with a sigh.

A deadly silence descends over the room and I look at my High General. Unlike the other Elders, he seems to know what is going on. My Royal Ship's High Commander, too. Oh, and my other two Generals are definitely in on it. Maybe I can kill someone here and now, after all.

"Get on with it, First Healer," I snap, ignoring the silent warning coming from Larrs.

The Elder doesn't even look at me. Keeps staring at the holographic leaf, as if he can see something we cannot.

"It is no secret the numbers of our great race are falling with every generation. There are hardly any cubs born in our beautiful High City, towns and villages. The sound of happy cubs is dying around us. Most mated pairs have not been able to produce cubs, and there is no record of any pair producing more than one."

He stops and gives a quick glance around. The silence is as sharp as the blade of my Astral Sword. The Healing Elder has spoken of the unspoken. Even though we all noticed, no Tarrassian ever talks about it.

He takes a deep breath and continues.

"The Wise King," he says, reminding me of my father and of everything I am not, "trusted me with an important mission many rotations ago. I have relentlessly researched and fought to bring answers to my King and Council and to save our society. On this rotation of our great sun, I present you with the findings of my research. It is perhaps sooner than I expected, but the timing was pushed forward as the solution was brought to my attention."

He raises his pale, translucent hand and opens the hollocom. Thousands of images start to move fast through the air, but not fast enough for our advanced intelligence.

"Hundreds of subjects have been tested, as well as a long and laborious study of other races with similar problems. Soon enough, a few important facts showed themselves. As the universe hardened and became a more challenging place for life, in many races fewer females were born. Some races have become male only, and artificial cloning devices are all that's keeping them from extinction."

Somehow, what he is saying is very upsetting to me. I don't like my people compared to others. We are superior to all other beings.

"Our females are strong, they are not giving up to the hardships of the universe, First Healer. We have just as many female cubs as males. Your findings are wrong."

I refuse to look at Larrs. I am the King. I say whatever I please.

"A very good observation, my King," says the Elder, quite unexpectedly. "It was the part that didn't match the other findings. Despite our low number of births, there is an equal number of female and male cubs being born. We are not affected by the harshness of the New World. We are not affected by the new viruses sweeping through the galaxies, we are not affected by weakness."

As he speaks, I can feel myself growing out of my skin with pride for my people. Maybe our Astrals are long gone but that is fine, because we are the only Gods we need. Then, his next words fill me with rage.

"We are being killed by our immense arrogance and pride. For as long as we were sentient, we considered ourselves better than all other beings, we refused to mate for procreation with other races, and what is more, we refused to mix in between clans and castes. In time, our blood has thinned and our genetic code has weakened. There is no strength left in us to give birth to new generations of cubs. We are exterminating ourselves," he ends.

"This is an outrageous finding and I contest it," says the Elder of the Caves. And despite him being my least favourite member of the Council, I have to agree.

"Outrageous and offensive," I say, hoping that will be the end of the nonsense. I am itching to leave this Cave.

The Healing Elder rises again undeterred.

"I am not here to challenge or to force change. I am here to offer you my findings and the solution. We need new blood to strengthen our line. We need new breeders to create new, stronger cubs."

"And how is that going to work?" I challenge the fool. "We are the strongest race in this entire universe. We are feared and worshipped as gods. How is the blood of the weaker beings going to strengthen ours?"

Most of the Elders take a fist to their silent heart as a sign of support for my statement. Of course, they do. My statements are never wrong. I am always right. I am the King. And I so desperately need to leave this vexing Cave.

"What weakens the blood is orbit rotations of inbreeding. Not weaker beings," says the Healing Elder. "I stand before you today with the problem and the solution. The fate of our race is in your hands."

"And what is the solution, First Healer?" I boom, making the cave rattle. "Send my Warriors out in the galaxy to spread their precious seed amongst weaklings? Bring the cubs back to be raised as ours? Oh, I know! Shall I go grab some females from the Yellow Planets, bring them round for a dark span meal at your house?"

As I finish talking, I can hear my Low Generals, as well as my High Commander, trying to fight laughter. I can also see Larrs shaking his head at my outburst.

The Elder, however, is unstoppable in his mission.

"That will not work well. We are a race of honour and high morals."

As he says that, Larrs makes a huffing noise, while grinning at me. I return the favour and expose my fangs at him.

"We will not have breeding pleasurers as cub vessels. We will take mates and we will mate them in front of our Astrals and we will honour the tradition of our Mating Sign," says the Elder, while looking at the patterns on the walls with longing eyes.

"Your Astrals and the Mating Sign, are all gone! Stories for cubs and silly young females to believe," I tell him, and I don't care who gets offended.

"That may be so, my King," replies the Elder, "but unless we do something to change our ways, all the Tarrassians will be nothing more than legends soon."

I rise to my feet and smash my fists onto the rock of the table so hard, little sparks of glowing electricity fly into the air.

"Change our ways?" I yell at all of them, feeling the War Beast taking over and making my huge frame grow bigger.

"I have spent a life span watching our 'perfect society' treat my cousin like a feral being. Most, if not all, think Tannon is not even sentient. All because he is Tarrassia's first and only half-breed. He is only good to win our wars and terrify our enemies. Do you think I will let any other cubs be treated like that?"

I finish with a defiant look to my High General. To the pits of fire with all his pacifying nonsense. To my surprise there is a trace of a smile on his stony face and... pride?

"The story of the Great Warrior is a dark page in the scroll of Tarrassian history," says the eldest of our Elders. Nobody can even remember the age of the Elder of the Spark Mountains. His authority is not questioned by anyone in our society. And not only because of his age, knowledge or title. He is the last Tarrassian alive to have seen the Sign of the Astrals or hear the beating of our second heart. The silent left heart. The one awakened by the Sign. His grandparents were the last Tarrassians blessed with that. Personally, I have my doubts. I am smart enough to know sentient beings need legends and hopes to push them forward. The Elders are also smart. So, yes, I do have my doubts. However, because of his blessed ancestry, the Elder of the Spark Mountains is the most revered Tarrassian. He has to give his blessing to every new mated pair on our planet. Hoping his touch would bring back the Marks, the Sign or awaken the silent heart. Honestly, that is a lot of stuff to bring to life. I would really expect more Tarrassians to question this nonsense. However, I am the King and I can question anything I please. The platinum ore in my eyes ignites, sending him a silent warning. No one hurts Tannon. Not in my presence.

"The Great Warrior," he continues with a strong, stubborn voice, "was not responsible for his parents' actions."

"I would choose my words very wisely, Elder of the Spark Mountains," says Larrs unexpectedly. Or maybe not so much. There is a reason why he is Tarrassia's High General and my closest friend. Despite his annoying face, of course.

"I only speak the truth, High General," replies the Elder. "Yes, it was unfortunate what happened to the Great Warrior. Despite that, he was allowed to keep his Tarrassian mother's title and the fortune of the family as the only offspring. It is entirely his choice if he chooses to keep an empty palace for servants to live in while he spills the blood of our enemies across the universe."

"And stay on the Mother Planet for what?" I more or less spit my angry words out. "For every Tarrassian to stare at him? For our females to scurry away when they lay eyes on him? How is that going to be any different for a new half-breed?"

"That, my King, is a question for a different Elder," he ends, and sits again.

As if on cue, the Healing Elder stands, obviously annoyed with the delay.

"I don't need to recall the tragic story of our High Lady Oria," he says cautiously. "The mother of the Great Warrior was not a willing participant in the breeding process. She was just the victim of the mating season rage of a former slave. We have all failed our precious female, while trying to be honourable and offer shelter on our planet to a half-sentient being. As sad as the Great Warrior's birth story is, it was the foundation for my research. According to everything our advanced science has taught us, the Tarrassians shouldn't even be able to create a cub with a different race. If it happened with such a lesser being," he says quickly, trying to avoid my angry eyes, "it can only mean we must be compatible with others in the universe. Sadly, years of painful research has led to... nothing."

"Isn't that great?" I say mockingly. However, the Elder carries on talking and I have to remember my promise to Larrs, to stop myself from removing his head.

"We were never quite able to determine the home planet of the Great Warrior's father. We still don't know where the slavers had got him from. All we know is the creature had been used in the slavers' fighting pits since he was a cub. And it is not important to find out, because we wouldn't use such genetic material to rebuild our great race."

I watch my huge fists squeezing into the hard rock. I can see Larrs' doing the same. The Elder carries on, unimpressed by the spectacle of pure force. I have to give him respect for that. Most, if not all, cower to me.

"It's just frustrating that all the other genetic code I have tested is not compatible with ours. We don't seem compatible with other species."

"Obviously not an issue for the King," mutters Larrs, and there is laughter around the Cave.

No need to get upset with him. Quite happy with my performance on the Yellow Planets. Somehow, I don't think that's what the Elder has in mind. After what happened to Tannon's mother, I was very careful not to spill a single drop of my precious seed into lesser beings. Good to know it wouldn't have worked anyway.

"Until now," he adds unexpectedly, and we all stop breathing for a nanoclip.

"The Astrals have shown themselves in a pure stroke of our Fates."

Not this again, I growl to myself.

"As I visited my son, the High Commander of the Blood Fleet, I couldn't help being intrigued by the information on his hollocom."

I had to take a mental break and analyse what he said. The High Commander of my Blood Fleet is his son? The Healing Elder is the one who sired my most prolific Warrior? Perhaps Larrs is right. I do need to pay more attention and do more king-like stuff. My father, the Wise King, knew the name of every single Tarrassian on our planet and at the time there were millions of us. Now that's not even the case, so my lack of knowledge has no excuse.

"The Blood Fleet was on a mission to rescue more slaves and spill the blood of the slavers. This was meant to be a high-risk mission because of the danger of the location. The slaves were going to be sold in a higher-bidder ceremony, on the filth Planet of Zora 23."

I clench my fangs, almost feeling the taste of enemy blood. The Old Rule of the Seven Stars said any race could keep a planet they claimed first. Unless there was proof of sentient beings already living there, which wasn't the case on Zora 23. The filthy Noorranni didn't have a planet of their own. They spent most of their time on their warships, pillaging and killing the vulnerable. They had hundreds of unclaimed planets spread around the dark corners of the universe. No one lived on these planets, or at least no one knew for sure. However, we all knew that's where all the dirty deals in the galaxy were taking place. That's where the Coalition of the Dark Moon was forging its evil. War in space was always allowed. War against a lawfully claimed planet was not. The Noorranni were making the best of that useless rule. We were fighting an invisible enemy most of the time. Unless we could save the vulnerable while in space, they were lost forever once they reached a planet like Zora 23.

"What awakened my curiosity," says the Elder, "was the price the new slaves were being put up for. The starting call was set at 10.000 old stellar credits, each. And they had four of them."

"What? Why?" My voice was not the only one asking that question.

"Exactly, my King," he replies. "I had to investigate why a female slave would sell for the price of a medium-sized planet, able to support life. These are my findings," he adds as he makes his hollocom come to life. "The slavers' description only said three words: exquisite Human females."

"What's a Human?" I interrupt him.

"I had to investigate, my King, as I also didn't know," he explains as his hollocom brings up an image of a tiny blue planet.

"And of course, none of us is familiar with these creatures, as their home planet is a Red Orbit Planet."

As he says that, I rise to my feet. My anger is itching my skin from the inside, ready to release the War Beast. The fact that even the Elders are angry calms my skin somehow. This is unheard of. The first rule of every galaxy is not to contact a Red Orbit Planet. It was my Ancestors First Rule. And it is being ignored under my watch. Under my reign. This cannot be. A planet was declared a Red Orbit one if it was primitive enough not to support space travel. There were other regulations such as proper lack of healing abilities, short life spans and backward technology. To me such primitive beings were probably not even half-sentient, but nevertheless it meant they were the most vulnerable in the universe. Not even we could protect something as useless and vulnerable, so they were declared forbidden. No contact allowed with the advanced galaxies.

"How is this possible, Healing Elder? Does the High Commander have any knowledge of how it happened?"

"No, my King. The High Commander will leave this knowledge to the Royal Army of Shadows. He is a Space Warrior not a Shadow. However, his rescue mission was a success and that enabled the success of my research. Because Earth is a Red Orbit Planet," he says, rotating the image of the tiny blue planet, "there is of course no sample of their genetic code in the galactic database. After the rescue of the females, the Blood Fleet Healer has successfully extracted a genetic code from all four females. All my tests have proven compatibility with our race."

"How high is the compatibility?" asks the Elder of the Waters.

"There was no such reading, my Elder," comes the unexpected reply. "No matter how many times I ran the tests, the bio MI gave the same reading. It read the Human genetic code as being Tarrassian."

"Show me these Humans," I say, as no one else has any words left. It makes no sense what the Elder is saying. The leaf hologram starts to move at huge speeds through millions of images. Our advanced brains can easily absorb that, but it still makes no sense. Yes, biped of sorts, yes two arms, two legs, one head, no tail, some furry like us... sort of, females with a lot of head fur, unlike our females who have none. At a stretch, their head fur might look similar to our males', but that is the only close-to-similar description.

"Are all these cubs?" I ask. "Can we see a fully grown one?"

"These are the fully-grown ones, my King."

My loud laughter makes the Cave vibrate. Most join in. I only pause to look at the Healing Elder. He is serious! For the love of the Astrals!

"What am I supposed to do with them? Give these tiny females to my Warriors for what? To break them in half, maybe? And what about our females? They can't possibly mate with Human males. Most societies in the galaxies need the protection of their males. Wait, are these Humans like the Hlanni? Where the females rule the men?"

"No, my King, the Human females are smaller and much weaker than the Human males. And yes, you are right, their males may not make suitable mating candidates for our females. Our females need males who can protect them. And in my research with the inbreeding in the galaxies, the genes of the strongest species will be passed on to the cub. Even though stronger than the Humans, our females are weaker than us. In time, such inbreeding will weaken our race."

I look around the room, hoping one of them will point out all the ridiculousness of the situation. No one does, though.

"What about the Rule of the Seven Stars?" I point out the obvious. "We are not allowed to have these females. They are a forbidden species."

"That is true, my King," he replies. "This is something I'll leave to the ruling Elders and my King. I am only a Healer. However, using the same argument, the females cannot be returned to their home planet, as it is forbidden. They belong to us now. I suggest we prove my theory of our compatibility first. We can use it to claim these females."

"Yes," adds the Elder of the Fields. "Once four of them have been taken, we don't know how many more they have, or how safe they are on the blue planet. If the planet is to be invaded, we can protect it and claim their females."

"I don't like this at all," says the Elder of the Waters. More voices join in and others against. I smash my fist against the rock again, imagining it is one or all of their heads. Ideally all.

"Enough!" I say, looking at the Healing Elder. "What do you propose now?"

"Yes, my King," he says, looking me in the eye with the courage of a Warrior. "The reason why I called for the gathering here is because the four females are on board Levianha. The High General brought them here three spans ago."

"Did he now?" I let Larrs feel the heat of my anger.

"Were you part of the rescue mission, High General?"

He simply raises his shoulders, looking as boring as ever.

"I was not. My Generals and I only collected the Humans from the Blood Fleet. Apparently, there's been an incident," he ends with a strange look in his eyes. Is that amusement? The Low Generals are definitely amused by something. The Low General of the Southern Country stands while obviously trying to say something embarrassing.

"We have indeed retrieved the females," he confirms. "Only… the three females that is. The fourth escaped from the Blood Fleet in an emergency pod."

"Zaan lost a female?" comes the shocked voice of the Healing Elder.

On a good span, that would have been my best source of laughter. The toughest Tarrassian amongst the stars has lost a tiny female. However, this is not a good span.

"What do you propose now?" I repeat my question for the last time.

"Now, my King, you will choose one of the three Humans as your mate for life and as the mother of the Royal cubs. I am sure there will be many. Humans are highly fertile and their females are in heat more often than any other female I have studied. Without a doubt the reason for their high price."

As he stops talking, I look around, too rattled to say anything. Except for Larrs, who once again has a strange look on his face, everyone else seems very interested in the grey rock of the Cave's floor.

"You have an offspring, Elder," I say, trying to control my anger. "I am sure you are familiar with what goes where. How am I supposed to mate with such a puny creature? And why me?"

"My King, we raise our cubs by telling them Tarrassians are above all other races and we can only mate amongst ourselves. Nothing my science says can change their minds. The King will have to lead by example. If the Tarrassians have a Human Queen, they will not dare question the council's decision."

"So, are you asking me to sacrifice myself for Tarrassia?"

Once I let out the silly question, I know I have defeated myself. That was the oath I took the day I became King. To live and die for Tarrassia and its citizens. The deed was done and they all knew it.

2

TARS

For the second time in one day, I find myself walking angrily along the mirror-shine tubular corridors of Levianha. The angular glass hubs reveal the darkness of the galaxy as we zoom back to the Mother Planet.

"I don't understand why I had to travel here for four spans to meet the Humans on board. Couldn't it wait until the Levianha returned to Tarrassia?" I shout at my High General, even though he's walking right behind me. I don't care. I refuse to be reasonable. Not that I ever am. Who cares, I'm the King and I do as I please. A treasonous thought reminds me that's not the case. Kings have less freedom than slaves, it appears. I am about to take a mate for life. Once Tarrassians are mated, there is no other for us. So unfair! My people do it in the name of the old stories of the Silent Heart, and the Sign of the Astrals. The legends also say how once you have found the one who unlocks the most powerful traits of our race, one lives and dies for their fated mate. They become one in body and mind. So, I guess it's easy not to want another. But without that, a mate is just someone to share a dwelling with, public appearances and a cub if they are blessed. Some, like my parents, can be really blessed and enjoy each other without the mark of the Sign. Others, like my High General's parents… not so much. They live a life of pain. Once you are in, you can't get out.

"You could have Jumped and got here in a few nanoclips," he answers. "Levianha is too large to do the Jump, but your warship could have easily done that. Then you could have retrieved your own mate from the Blood Fleet."

My pace starts to slow as I try to make sense of Larrs' strange behaviour. Yes, we are more like blood brothers than friends, but it doesn't explain the informal tone. He's too proper and stuck up for that. He seems distracted and angry. Both very unusual for him.

"Besides," he carries on, "the Royal Council wanted you to arrive on Tarrassia with your new Queen by your side. Lead by example and all that."

I let out a frustrated growl.

"I knew I should have stopped for a proper fuck on the Yellow Planets. My last chance gone. How am I supposed to fuck one of these tiny females? What if I get stuck? What if I hurt her? A million blasters of fire! That cursed Elder! And what is wrong with the cursed Humans? Can't they eat more? Can't they grow bigger? And why would they call their useless planet Earth when it's made of water? And why can't you do it instead?" I pause my angry, useless words as I realise, he hasn't heard any of it.

"Larrs?"

"My King?"

"I asked, why can't you do it?"

"I already have a promised mate, my King," he answers as we are about to reach the Humans' quarters on the ship. They actually gave them the Royal Quarters. My quarters. Am I supposed to act on my mate duties straight away?

"You haven't even met your promised mate, Larrs," I sigh, feeling tired and defeated. All by birth right, apparently. "However, I have met your promised mate and she's as beautiful as any proud Tarrassian female. You are a lucky man, Larrs." Something is not quite right. Not that anything is on this cursed span. As we approach the Royal Quarters and the guards salute me silently, I pause to watch Larrs as I have never seen him before. If I didn't know any better, I would say he looks... worried? Larrs doesn't ever break a sweat. Not in battle, not in the Council Cave and probably not in between the furs. He's just not that way. If there was anything normal in the universe, Larrs would be King. Wise and proper, just like my sire. Instead, I am the King. I know very well what my people call me behind my back. Reckless, wild, hot-headed. And I was all that. That's why I couldn't deny my people this sacrifice.

"So, High General, what am I going to find behind these doors?" I ask, watching him with curiosity. His usually blank eyes are staring behind my shoulder at the intricate Royal Symbol carved into the hard metal door. Definitely not blank now. Are those specks of gold in his eyes?

"Larrs...? High General of Tarrassia!" The use of his formal title seems to make the shadow in his eyes pass, and once again the stone-faced Warrior is back.

"The female who was given these quarters is called Jade. And she bites a lot, so I wouldn't go too close, my King," he says with his usual controlled voice.

"She does what? They have blunt teeth and no fangs. What is going on with you this span, Larrs?"

"She bit both my Generals and a few Royal Guards on the way here. The female servants are terrified of going near her," he says with a voice too controlled and impersonal even for him. And he is definitely avoiding my eyes. How very interesting!

"So maybe these tiny, fragile females have made a mockery

of my Warriors?" I say with a grin. "One escaped from the claws of our most prolific Warrior, the High Commander of the Blood Fleet, while another has been biting her way through my Generals. Have you got her teeth marks, General?" I say, unable to contain my growing amusement. Maybe this span wasn't so bad after all. To prove me right, Larrs tightens his huge fists by his side. I watch in disbelief as two dark rust-colour droplets of blood trickle down to the floor. This is a very entertaining span indeed.

"Your claws are damaging the pristine floors of Levianha, my High General," I say as the huge winged guards move away and open the large doors. I haven't been in this room ever since I was a cub. I remember the heavily ornate fabrics my mother seemed to prefer. Her touch is still in the air and I can't help sniffing for her long-gone scent. A deep sense of longing claws at my only beating heart. So many things I never got to tell my parents…

The strange-looking creature in the middle of the room brings me back to the present.

"So, what, I get two *criips* staring now?" the creature says in a voice meant to sound angry, but it is just too funny. That voice couldn't scare a little donian bird. Well, except it could scare my Generals and guards, apparently. With a cautious look at Larrs, who stands behind me, I attempt to move closer to the female. A low growl from him stops me in my tracks. The female reacts with a small jump backwards. Despite her show of bravery, I can smell her fear. Fear smells the same on all creatures. She isn't watching me, she is watching him. She is scared of him. Strange. Normally I am the scary one. I decide to ignore them both and inspect the female closer. I am the King and she is my property. Larrs can growl all he wants. The creature is ridiculously tiny. It seems soft and round and really different. Different, but undeniably beautiful. I can definitely see the appeal. Enough credits to buy a planet and all.

"What's *criips*?" I ask her. "My translation device has left that word out." She rolls her beautiful, strange eyes in an unusual gesture of fake bravery.

"It's not a *criip*," she says. "It's a creep. And that's someone who likes to stare at women and make them feel like they have no clothes on and stuff. Yes, and that too." She points at me, walking around her in circles like a predator. "Creepy dude! Even by alien standards." She says the words defiantly and yet watching my General with a wary look in her eyes. They are unusual. The beautiful green colour reminds me of the feathers of the alini flocks. They turn the purple sky of Tarrassia into green flames of dancing feathers when they are in mating season. And how strange, her eyes have a black circle in the middle and white around the green and the black. Tarrassians have one solid eye colour, in different shades of platinum ore and gold. But three different colours? Very unusual. So is her huge mane of brown head fur. A Human thing, apparently. Tarrassian men have a lot of fur. On our heads, on our faces and a shorter spread of fur covering our bodies. Denser on our chests, lower arms and legs. Some have more fur than others and most keep it trimmed. And of course, there is Tannon, I remember with a sigh. The female pushes her beautiful locks of head fur out of her perfect face. Shaped like a Tarrassian heart. Probably the same size too, I sigh. Her skin is incredibly light in colour and it looks flawless. Like the stone we use for our homes. Her pouty lips look shockingly red on her white face. The bright red paint reminds me of a warning signal I have seen in poisonous species. At least I hope it's paint and not my guards' blood. Which of course is so ridiculous. Everything about the female is tiny. Well, maybe not everything. She wears a traditional Tarrassian female outfit. Her female servants must have adjusted it to fit her short frame. It would look like a short shirt on a Tarrassian female now. However, the low-cut top of the outfit is full to the brim with her soft and plump breasts. What did the Elder say? "Highly fertile". Well, yes indeed. No cubs would go hungry with those. I almost flinch when an aggressive warning growl comes from behind me. What in the name of the Astrals? What's got into him? The female also startles at the noise but seems determined to ignore him this time. Instead she focuses her pretty green eyes on me. Her strange words look enticing on her soft red lips, before the translation device changes them into Tarrassian.

"Are you done staring, dude?" she says like a petulant cub.

"My name is Tarsmiamin, not Dude," I say, "but you can call me King for now."

She puts her hands on her very round and soft hips. The motion pushes her oversized tits up. Our females are very bony. It's the Tarrassian standard of beauty. But all this roundness and softness? It should be a bad thing. Making them vulnerable and all that. Soft and round is intriguing, though.

"I won't call you anything." She points a tiny clawless finger at my chest. "Not until you tell me what you want from me, where are the other women and when can I go home?"

In two long steps, Larrs reaches my side.

"You will respect my King, female!" he threatens her through gritted teeth, aggressively exposing his fangs at her.

"My name is Jade, not female, you creep!" she yells at him. Despite her defiance, her voice is trembling and she takes a small step back. Her fear is intoxicating. In battle mode, the fear of our enemies is like an enhancer for us. I wonder if she knows she is unwillingly scratching at our Beasts. Or more likely at my General's.

"He is not my King!" she says with a trembling lower lip.

"He is now and you will talk to him with respect!"

"Make me!"

"Oh, I will!"

Is he out of his skin? I can see his muscles growing and his shoulders getting wider, his eyes turning golden... Is he turning into battle mode? What in the name of the Astrals? The female is shaking but standing her ground. Good on her.

"Stand down, General," I growl without being able to restrain my anger. Good thing the female doesn't seem scared of me. Our kind just don't hurt females. I step in between them and Larrs finally steps back. He turns his back to us and puts his claws through his head fur, pulling frustratedly at the ends. I decide to ignore him and end this insanity. Despite how enticing this Human is, I can see she already belongs to another. Time for me to act like her King and nothing else.

"Jade, you are on board the Royal Ship Levianha. We are heading towards our home planet, Tarrassia. Needless to say, I am the King of Tarrassia and I vow to protect you as I would any other Tarrassian. I am sorry for what happened to you. I know it's a lot to take in, or to accept not being able to see your home again."

"What are you saying?" she asks, and her big eyes seem wetter. Larrs turns to watch her intensely. I send him a mental warning. He had better not ignore it.

"We cannot return you to Earth, as it is forbidden for us to travel there. You have a chance at a new life and a new home. I know it's not what you asked for but survive we must. I trust you will accept your new fate. We will arrive on Tarrassia during the next span. You will be treated with great honour and I promise you no one will hurt you." As the heat coming from Larrs is burning my back, I am hoping to keep that promise. My words have started to make sense to her and I can feel her sadness. What would it be like to never see Tarrassia again? I couldn't imagine that pain.

"It was very nice meeting you, Jade, welcome to Tarrassia," I say, and I turn on my heels towards Larrs.

"After you, General." I point towards the door.

"My King?"

"No, I insist, you first."

After the guards close the doors behind me, I instruct them and the female servants that the Human is not a prisoner. She is allowed to visit the other females and explore the ship. Of course, with a guard and a female servant companion for safety. I am hoping this gives Larrs enough time to recompose himself. Part of me wants to tease him, make some fun of this cursed span, but it doesn't look like he can take it right now. He seems pained just by walking away from her door. Time for me to act all kingly again. This cursed span. Maybe I could holocom Zaan and tease him about losing a tiny female instead.

"So, what's next, High General? Which female? Actually, Larrs, I will choose the next one, don't bother with the third. I want this over now. Lead me to the female."

He points towards the other Royal Quarters.

"The two females are together in there, my King."

"I see... you only separated that one," I tell him with a grin.

He ignores both me and my grin.

"One of the females in there is very scared and very cub-like. Her eyes water a lot. That's how Humans show distress."

"Cub-like?" I question.

"The Healing Elder confirmed she is of legal mating age, both on Tarrassia and Earth. But only just. So maybe that is why. She seems very soft and fragile, even for a Human. She's quite attached to the other female left. I didn't want to distress her further by separating them. The younger female is called Natalia and she is from a different Earth country to the other two. So is the one who ran away."

It was nice to have a normal conversation with Larrs about the females. For a change.

"And the other female? What's this smell in the air?" I ask as we approach the Royal Quarters.

"I can't smell anything in particular, my King."

Strange, what is it? So familiar, I just can't remember what smells like that.

Once again, the guards move aside and we enter the room. And then time stops. Everything stops.

Pure white hair, gleaming like the peaks of the Spark Mountains. Grey eyes as huge and as still as the waters of Tarrassia. Pale skin, so pale. Almost translucent like the skin of the Elders. Straight back, chin raised in silent defiance. Flowing dress moving like a whisper around soft curves. Delicate. Soft. Defiant. Cold. The smell. I can't separate her scent.

"Separate the females!" My order to my General seems like that of a stranger. I cannot recognise my own voice. Pain. Fear. Hope. Desire.

"Remove the red female!" No more an order. A vicious growl. It shakes the room. The little red female leaks water from her eyes. The other one raises her chin higher. Delicate. Soft. Defiant. Cold.

"My King," a warning in his voice, "the young female is scared. She needs the other one's comfort."

My claws extend, my fangs hurt my gums, my shoulders are growing.

"Remove her!" I say, but it's not my voice, it's the War Beast's voice.

More water-leaking and more chin-raising. Blinding desire shooting painful electricity straight into my cock. She lowers her eyes and looks at my raised Kannicloth. Let her look. Defiant. Cold.

Her voice is touching under my skin.

"It's okay, Natalia, I need you to step aside," she says.

"No, no, no, don't leave me, I'm scared. I'm scared of Monsters. Please, please, hold me," cries the small red female.

"They are not monsters, they are slavers. Please trust me and step aside. That's it, good girl, I am right here. Good, brave Natalia."

Finally. Her scent alone. Mine.

"Look at me!" My voice rattles the floor under our feet. Beautiful eyes. Cold. Defiant. Lifeless.

"Who are you calling a slaver?"

"I am calling you one," she replies without even blinking.

So cold. Silent defiance. Painfully cold.

My steps move closer to the scent. Mine. Prey.

"My King let's talk outside. Please, only for a bit," says Larrs, but his words don't reach me.

My steps take me closer. The scent is everywhere. Her clothes are in my way. Ripping clothes. Defiant. Cold. My Kannicloth is too tight. Painfully so.

"Tars, stop! Out, now!"

If he touches me, he dies. No one stops me.

"Tell me I am a slaver again!"

"Tars, I'm calling the guards, please don't make me do this!"

So close. The scent. My scent. My everything. Only mine. I need to be inside her now! I raise my hand to touch her face. I must touch her translucent face. She raises her hand to block mine. I grab her wrist.

The entire universe goes up in flames. The light itself explodes around us and inside of us. From my fingers the light goes up her arm then back up my own arm. My chest explodes in pain at the same time with the light. The world is screaming. People are screaming. There is excruciating pain in my chest, but the sound of my new beating heart is louder than the pain. My old heart fights for space in my chest. She's screaming, her calm replaced by fear. She tries to push my hand away. Never! Mine! I grab her other hand. More sparks. Light and pain. The bright light pattern of swirls is travelling up our arms, burning our skin on the inside and leaving a trail of blue, purple and white. My body knows what to do. I try to press my forehead to hers. She's too small. I lift her up in my arms. Her touch is like fire on my already painful cock. It can wait. Forehead first. I touch my head onto hers. The light in our arms travels faster. It knows its final destination now. So much pain. We both close our eyes, so the light won't burn them. And then it stops.

My new, awakened heart is louder than the other one. It booms in my chest. It digs like a claw, trying to tear my chest open and reach for its mate. There is burning pain from the tips of my fingers, going up my arms, my shoulders, joining at the back of my head and finally going up to explode in the middle of my forehead. The Sign of the Astrals! I feel humbled it was given to me, the one who believed it was a story of the Elders, a tale for the cubs. I can't see my Sign but I know it's identical to hers. And hers is beautiful. It's the water flower of Tarrassia. The symbol of the Royal House. My symbol. The Elders said the male gives the shape of the Sign, the female gives its colours. And they are beautiful. A swirl of purple, blue and white. Her colours. Mine. Ours. After a nanoclip, when her soft, scented body goes limp in my arms, she's back to screaming and pushing at my chest. She makes me growl as she rubs herself on my painfully erect cock. My loud growl shakes the floor and reverberates off the walls. The tiny red female starts screaming even louder and now she's trying to remove my mate from me.

"Let her go, you Monster! You are all Monsters," she screams with a courage she doesn't seem capable of displaying. "Oh my God, Sia! He's infected you with something! Oh my God! Oh my God!"

Her voice spikes my anger, her attempt at removing my mate from me scratches at my Beast. 'SIA'. My mate is called Sia. The knowledge of her name makes my Sign ignite with swirls of colour. Her chosen colours. Our colours.

"Tars, please put your Queen down," says my General, making my fangs want to remove his tongue.

"You are hurting her. Tars, please! You're drawing blood."

His words penetrate through all the thick layers of light in my head and I look at her. Her eyes are leaking water, her pale skin is now bright pink and it looks inflamed around the marks left by the Sign. But what's piercing with pain my newly awakened second heart is the sight of my claws digging into the soft flesh of her arms. Tiny droplets of red blood trickle down her beautiful skin. I drop her before I can think any better and she collapses in a pile at my feet. Her long gleaming white hair covers her tiny body, almost like it is trying to shelter it from me. Before I can reach for her, the red female grabs her in a protective hug and away from my touch. My whole-body flinches, sensitive to the touch, when Larrs' hand drops on my shoulder, trying to keep me from my female. Does he want me to end him?

"Tars?" He calls my name with a strange softness in his voice. Like talking to a cub. "The Queen needs the Healer. I have sent for the Elder."

"No male touches her!" I yell at him, making both females flinch.

"Your female is in pain, Tarsmiamin," he says, looking me in the eyes with determination. "Her soft skin has been burnt by the Sign. You put your claws in her arms and she doesn't understand what any of it means. It's hard enough even for us to accept the magnitude of all this." His eyes look over my shoulder at the four guards kneeling and bowing their heads in awe.

"The Queen needs space and time to understand. You can't be around her now. You know very well what your instinct wants you to do now. She can't cope with that. Look at her."

My eyes rest on my female. Still in a shaking pile on the hard floor of the room, at my feet. The smaller red female holds her tight in her tiny arms, rocking her like a cub. Painful longing pulls at my new heart. It should be my arms holding her. But she doesn't want me now. I drew her blood.

"Help her," I tell my High General through gritted teeth and I leave the room, before my instinct makes my Beast take over and claim what is mine to claim.

3

SIA

I open my eyes and it takes a minute for my brain to process the facts. Just facts, it can't be the reality. I am naked, strapped to a cold and unforgivingly hard metal table. I try to scream, but my tongue feels huge inside my mouth. I can't move it. And then I realise my eyes aren't open, because I can't move my eyelids either. I can only feel. The table, the cold on my bare skin, the strange device restraining my wrists and ankles to the table. Yes, definitely not reality. Sleep, Sia, I command myself and I do. My willpower never fails me.

Once again, I know I am awake. A woman is crying. She's praying to Jesus. In Russian… Okay, that makes sense. There are models and people from all over the world at London Fashion Week. Some newbie model always cracks under pressure. Or some stylist being treated like crap by one of the 'divas'. But then realisation sinks in. I am still naked and strapped to the metal table. I still can't move any part of my body, but my tongue feels normal again. I don't try to move my lips. I don't pray, unlike the other woman. So, I listen, while pretending not to be awake. She sounds really young, like a child. Maybe she is. My Russian is as impeccable as the other six languages I am fluent in. She speaks of monsters. A chilling thought goes through my mind. I am naked. Would the child be... I remember my big sister, for the first time in many years. No, definitely not reality again. I never remember my sister and I am always in control. I command myself to sleep. Before I do, I hear the clicking noises. They sound low and harsh and there is a pattern. A language. Non-human. This time, I can't make myself sleep again. The little girl prays in Russian but speaks to someone in English. Slightly accented.

"Go away, Monster, don't touch me. I am not here, I am not here, I am not here, you can't see me." They are touching the child, whoever they are. Years of rigorous self-control slip away fast. I can't pretend anymore. Not when another little girl is being hurt right next to me. My sister's face comes out of the fog my brain has covered her in. My eyes are closed but I can see her as clear as I did twenty years ago. I was four and she was nine, saying goodbye to me and promising to come back for me. She never did. She left me at the gas station, with a note I wasn't allowed to read. It wasn't for me. It was for the police. She slipped our mother's brooch into my other hand and gave me one last hug. She turned her back and walked onto the nearby motorway, straight into the speeding traffic.

"I don't like monsters, please, I really don't," says the girl again. I open my eyes. And look straight into the face of... a monster. My brain has had years of training to become smarter, faster and colder than anyone else's. It is working at full speed. For once, I wished it didn't. Not a monster. An alien form of life. Slimy, or maybe just wet, sickly grey skin. No hair, huge head, attached to what seems to be a massive wrinkly body. The forehead sticks out, throwing a shadow over the rest of his wrinkly skin. His eyes are terrifying. Two dark patches of hate as he looks upon me. A chilling, cold, clawed finger pokes my cheek. My nose picks up the disgusting smell coming from his skin. It smells like a combination of putrid leaves and formalin. I stare at him. I think it's a him. My strange light grey, almost translucent, eyes have the same effect on the alien as they do on Humans. He takes a step back and quickly retrieves his finger. His small, lipless mouth is moving fast. Clicks and low hums and some vibrations. My brain knows it's a language and I can almost hear it at work. The more the creature talks, the more I can store information. No vowels. A language of consonants. He is smart. Realisation hits him and he knows I'm learning his language. Fast. Fear. The huge monster fears me. I am strange even by alien standards. Before I get to use it to my advantage, the world seems to rumble and shake and I can feel a welcome source of heat coming from somewhere. The alien takes off like a blur, somewhere to my left, but I still can't move my neck to look around. The noise of their language is filled with a sense of urgency now. The girl is crying and praying again. If she can talk, perhaps so can I. No words come out, though. "Shhh... shhh..." It's all that I manage. The soothing works and she stops crying. She just sniffs quietly. There is an impersonal voice coming from everywhere. Something repetitive and almost robotic about it. AI. Of course, they have AI. They are smarter and stronger than us. The undeniable noise of a fight covers the voice of the AI. There are metallic-like hisses. Not a language, I think they are weapons. I can hear the noise of metal against metal. I can hear the sparks. And growling. Loud and strong. Other words mix with the angry growls. It's another language, I suddenly understand. A powerful, commanding language. I am, however, more worried about the smell that grows stronger by the minute. Even though it doesn't smell like anything else on Earth, my brain can tell it's fuel. And the cold is quickly being replaced by heat. Fire. We are on a ship and it's going down.

A brief moment of peace replaces the noise. Then the noise of heavy footsteps approaching. Really heavy footsteps. Something is coming. Something big. The floor is vibrating. I close my eyes, pretending to be asleep. Is it too much to hope the little girl will be wise enough to do the same? Yes, of course it is, as I can hear her screaming and saying something about monsters. A huge shadow falls over me, blocking the blinding lights above. There is body heat coming from the shadow and a pleasant smell of something clean and fresh. Something is quickly laid over my body. A covering of some sort. I lie perfectly still as another presence joins in and then another. One of the shadows comes really close. It turns my head to the side. I don't know if that is a hand. It's just so big. The touch is firm, but gentle. It gives heat and a pleasant smell of something fresh. Like a forest, or a mountain. As it reaches behind my ear, there's a shooting pain, going straight into my brain. And the world goes dark.

Once again, I am awake, but I don't open my eyes. My brain has learned to process this new reality at fast speeds. I am sitting on a floor, but there's something soft laid on it. It feels like fur. I am not naked anymore. One piece of garment. It covers my body. Soft, very loose and it smells like the shadows from earlier on. Something silky and thick is in my face. It smells like expensive hair products. There's warmth and a soft vibration coming from everywhere. Another ship. Something, no, someone, is hanging on to me. Soft and small. I realise it's the little girl. She's crying softly. Her arms hug my body and her head is on my shoulder. I realise it's her hair that's in my face. I open my eyes. Yes, definitely a spaceship. I feel sick and dizzy as the first thing I see is a small window in the form of an undefined geometric shape. Behind it, there's pitch blackness and occasional flashes of light. Space. Deep space. I turn my eyes away quickly to stop the nausea. We are in a room. It's large enough and the ceiling is really high. The light is soft and there's no telling its source. Other than the window, there are shiny copper metal walls, all around the oval room. And some type of exit in one of the walls. A floor-to-ceiling vertical slit. There is a large square panel next to the slit. Probably to access the opening. There are strange-looking furs laid on the hard floor. Best not to imagine the size of the animals they come from. Or what they might look like. The only other thing in the room is a small legless metal table sticking out of the wall near the window. There's some type of see-through container on it with a clear liquid in it. There are four metal handled cups around it. And a tray with... food? I hope not, because it looks like raw meat... I quickly avert my eyes and allow myself to finally look at the other three Humans. I don't like being around Humans any more than I like being around aliens. As my eyes stop on Gianna Romano, I understand that indeed we were taken from the last location I remember. London Fashion Show. In the middle of hundreds of people and cameras. How is that possible? And there are always people around Gianna and me. We are the highest-paid commodities in the fashion industry. We met many times on famous catwalks around the world. We ran the Victoria's Secret one for the last five years. And we met many times during photo shoots for one famous designer or another. That's about the only thing we have in common. I am British and live in London, she's an Italian African American, from New York. She's a party girl, living up to our high celebrity status. She's also very popular with the men. The tabloids feed like mad on her romantic life. They call her a man-eater. They call me the Ice Queen. So definitely nothing in common. However, that's not why we are not friends. I simply don't have any. I haven't attended a single after-show party or any other social event for that matter. The tabloids have nothing to feed on when it comes to me. Instead of hating that, they all became more obsessed with the strange creature and the whole persona I try to portray. I am the Ice Queen and they get what they expect. Just like the rest of us, Gianna is wearing a bright white long tunic, with a beautiful pattern of swirls twisting around the fabric. It's obviously way too big for her. It looks like it's meant to be a man's shirt. A very, very big man. Gianna is the standard model height, which makes her taller than most women. Well, it makes us both taller. However, the shirt reaches way below her knees. She's bare-footed, like all of us. She paces angrily up and down the room, kicking at the furs. The other woman sitting opposite me is also familiar. She leans against the wall with a pissed look on her pretty heart-shaped face. But then again, she's always pissed and a proper bitch. Even though I have heard her call me that many times, behind my back. I know her name, because I know everything. Details and knowledge mean power. However, I have never spoken to her or worked with her for that matter. A British passport is the only thing we have in common. Luckily, I'd say. She has a vile mouth and a bad attitude. Always arguing with someone. Jade is the beauty industry's most acclaimed hair stylist. Her beautiful chestnut hair is her best advertising. Hundreds of shades of brown, mahogany and chestnut intertwine in her shoulder-length hair, creating a spectacle of light and soft waves. Her skin looks like milk and her eyes are as green as the stone she was named after. And she has makeup on… How is that possible? Permanent makeup, of course. It seems like a good idea now. Her signature blood-red lips look just as lush as ever. Her double EEs and hourglass body fill the shirt better than I do, that is for sure. She gives me a scowling smile and two perfect dimples make her face look even more adorable. How can anyone this beautiful have such a foul mouth…? Eventually, I gather enough courage to look at the little girl holding on to me for dear life. Huge relief fills me as I do. Very young, yes. But definitely not a little girl. Not with those boobs, looking huge on her tiny frame. And tiny she is indeed. The oversized shirt looks comical on her. This girl also looks familiar, but it takes a lot of mental effort to remember.

Yes, of course. The hair product adverts! No wonder, I say to myself, trying to free my face from her mane. Impossible job. Her hair looks bigger than her body. It reaches below her waist, like mine, but probably much longer if she was to straighten it. Unlike my perfectly straight gleaming white hair, hers is a mass of tight bouncy curls. The most astonishing thing about her hair, though, is its colour. It actually looks like fire. Probably a bit unusual for her Russian heritage. No wonder her face is on every hair advert in Ireland. They love her there. Well, everyone loves that hair. I find its touch on my face quite soothing. I am very uncomfortable with being touched. But something about her won't allow me to push her away. Her cute face is covered in freckles and the turned-up nose makes her look like a dolly. Her round blue eyes look swollen from so much crying. Another piece of information enters my brain. The hair-styling contest. Of course, that's why Jade and… I think Natalia were at the London Fashion Show.

"How did they get us in the middle of that crowd?" I find myself asking out loud.

"So, it can speak," says Jade with a dramatic eye roll.

I turn my cold self back on and I am grateful to her for that.

"It doesn't make any sense," says Gianna with a troubled look on her perfect face. Her dark honey, shoulder-length hair and green eyes look beautiful against her brown skin. Her Italian African heritage created the most unusual beauty.

"I don't remember anything after the first day of the show. I know I was going to attend a party after but not sure if I did or not."

"I remember thinking I had to leave quickly before it got dark, at the end of that first day," says Natalia with the child-like voice I remember. "I don't like the dark. There are Monsters hiding in the dark."

"Jesus fucking Christ!" Jade spits her nasty words out and Natalia cowers near me again. "You are fucking nineteen years old, lady," she carries on. "I told you before to stop with the monster shit. Especially when I'm doing your hair and shit."

"You are not doing my hair now," says Natalia, and I feel like smiling. This alien thing is messing with me. I never smile in public.

"I still don't want to hear your bonkers shit. What the fuck!"

Jade is so undeniably British… It takes one to know one.

"Natalia, you looked at these other aliens, didn't you?" I nudge her gently with my shoulder. "The ones who took us from the other ship?" She nods her head in approval, and the mane of curls and fire moves like a halo. "What do they look like? I mean, do they look just as evil as the first ones?" Once again, she nods her head. "Yes, huge Monsters!"

"Go fucking figure," says Jade mockingly. I ignore her. We all do.

"Were you awake the whole time? Actually, how were you awake, Natalia? I am sure I was drugged."

"I think I am cursed." She rushes her words faster and her accent gets stronger. "Monsters always keep me awake."

"Jesus, someone keep fucking Princess Merida quiet. She's doing my fucking head in."

"Did they do something behind your ear?" I ask, refusing to look at crazy Jade.

She touches absently behind her ear.

"Yes, and it hurt. But as soon as they did, I could understand them. One of the hairy monsters said it was a translating device. He said that we were safe, and they were taking us to their warship, away from the Noorranni slavers."

I try to process what she is saying, one thing at a time.

"Hairy? What do you mean?"

"Oh please," says Jade, rolling her eyes. "Of course, she will say hairy. There's fucking monsters everywhere."

"They are hairy," says Gianna.

"You saw them?" asks Jade, a trace of fear in her voice.

"Some sort of explosion woke me up. Naked and strapped to a table."

She squeezes her fists and there is pure hate on her face.

"Then the huge hairy creatures came. They are soldiers. They call themselves Warriors, whatever... I was fighting, trying to escape the binds." She looks with an angry, tormented expression at her bruised wrists. We all had the bruises. Me more than the others, because of my ridiculously pale skin. "Two of them got me up from my restraints. And as I was trying to fight them, I felt the pain behind my ear, going into my brain. I could understand them straight away, like Natalia said. The two who were trying to hold me explained the same stupid story to me. Yeah... right!" She practically spits the words out, kicking at the furs on the floor. She seems like a completely different person from the loud party girl I remember. There is anger and fear and hate rolling off her like waves of bad energy.

"You don't believe they were saving us?"

"Of course, I don't. There are no heroes in the real world, Elsa."

Jade starts laughing and performs an air high five towards Gianna.

I did what I always do when people called me names. Ignore.

"However, you seem sure they are hostile. Why?"

"Because as the two soldiers, Warriors, whatever were holding me, I saw the way their leader looked at me." Her nails dig into her palms and her face is contorted with anger and hate. "Like he wanted to fuck me. Like he was going to fuck me just because he could. Because he is bigger and stronger and it's his right to do so."

What a strange thing to say. Someone with a reputation of jumping from bed to bed. Or maybe the alien looked really disgusting. I vaguely seem to remember her toy boys looking more or less like Barbie's Ken.

"No, no, I can't let them do that to me, I'm a virgin," cries Natalia, pulling at my arm.

"For fuck's sake! Who the fuck is still a virgin at nineteen?"

I wonder what she would say knowing I was still a virgin at twenty-four.

"I can't let the monsters touch me like that."

"Who knows, a monster cock might cure your monster fear!"

"Enough, Jade!"

"You are not my boss, Elsa. I don't take orders from your skinny, famous ass!" She gives me a nasty look, then turns towards Gianna.

"How furry and how big are we talking here?"

"I don't know, who cares? It's more like hairy, not furry, anyway. They have long wild-looking hair and big beards. Their skin is covered in short hair and there's more on their chest and abdomen, going down… well… you know…"

"Shit! Were they naked?"

"Mostly. Except for some sort of white leather kilt thingy. And some leather coverings for their feet. Boots like, I don't know."

"Did you get all these details from the one who wants to fuck you?"

"Fuck you, Jade!"

"Yeah, right back at you, blondie. And how big are we talking?"

"Monsters," says Natalia, making Jade slap her forehead.

"They are huge," says Gianna. "Maybe eight feet tall? Maybe more. They are all pure muscle. Impossible to fight them."

"Wait, was that your plan? Fight some aliens, take their ship and go back to Earth?"

"I have to fight. I won't let him touch me. I will fight. I will die fighting!"

"Good luck to you! Not for me! Last time I fought my way out of shit I got kidnapped by aliens. How is that for fucked-up karma? No fighting for me. Maybe at least I can get myself some monster cock. How about that, Natalia?" she asks with a wink and a disturbing grin on her face.

Natalia starts crying again and I can't help but hug her. Jade is more horrible than I thought.

"I don't want to die like the girl on the ship," she says unexpectedly, and we all stop moving.

"They killed a girl on the ship?" I ask her softly.

"Yes," she says through tears. "Her neck made a horrible noise when they broke it."

I hear a gasp and it could be my own.

"She was having an asthma attack and grabbed at the Monster's robe. He slapped her face and blood splattered all over him. That made him angry and next he broke her neck. It made a horrible noise."

I hug her shaking body close to mine. I am probably blessed to have slept through all that.

"Was it someone we know?" asks Jade, and this time the mocking tone is gone.

"I don't know her name. I think it is… was the pretty Brazilian model. The one with pink hair."

"Yara? They killed Yara?"

Gianna's beautiful lips tremble and she desperately fights back tears. I remember her and the Brazilian girl always hanging out together.

We are all quiet for a long time. Only Natalia's soft crying breaks the heavy silence. I know I shouldn't ask, but I need to know.

"Were there any more women?"

"No, just us four and Yara. There was also the man, but I think they killed him too."

"There was a man?" Jade asks before I get to. One doesn't have to be a genius to understand why they took five beautiful women. But a man?

"One of the models?" I ask.

"No, it was the big scary guy who followed Yara around."

Gianna stops her pacing.

"Her bodyguard? Brian?"

"I don't know."

"It must have been him," says Gianna. "Since her disgusting stalker tried to kill her, Yara wouldn't even go to the bathroom without her bodyguard."

It probably explains why they took the man. He was just unlucky enough to get in the way.

"Did they kill him?" asks Jade.

"He tried to help her," says Natalia, and her big blue eyes seem haunted. "He lost his mind when they snapped her neck. He broke the restraints and attacked them. He killed two of them before they could stop him."

"How? They were huge!" says Gianna.

"He was really, really angry. They couldn't stop him. They kept shocking him with their rods and he wouldn't stop. I wished he did stop, but he kept going for them. His skin was bleeding from everywhere. I couldn't watch so I closed my eyes. When I woke up, he was gone."

There is a sudden vibration in the room, making us all shudder. The vertical slit in the wall opens with a flash, letting through the biggest sentient being I have ever seen. Despite our differences, instinct takes over and we scramble together towards the back of the room, holding onto each other, cowering on the floor.

The slit panel closes behind the alien. He is massive. Not just the height, but everything. The muscles seem overgrown but somehow appropriate for the imposing height. But the most shocking detail of his appearance is that he looks… human. No kilt in sight, as Natalia said. He wears a shirt similar to ours, loosely tucked into a pair of pristine white pants. They look soft and they are fastened with a string at the waist. I quickly move my eyes up, as the soft fabric of the trousers doesn't do much to cover the huge size of his male parts. I feel like covering Natalia's eyes. His hair is black, with a streak of pure white in it. And they call me Elsa… It falls just under his massive shoulders and it probably needs a good brush to keep it out of his face. It looks a bit wild. The lower half of his face is covered in a bushy beard. Very crazy, Viking-like, if there is such a thing. The hard but beautifully shaped lips show in the mass of black curls of his beard. The rest of his body seems covered in a short sprinkle of black hair… fur? Hard to tell. A lot denser in the small neck opening of his shirt, going down his chest. His skin looks like molten copper and his eyes are definitely alien. One solid golden colour. No, copper. Then gold again. Strange. Despite all that, he just looks so… human. How is that possible? His voice, though, is very much alien. Like thunder shaking the room. It has a vibration to it, making Natalia cover her ears. He stops whatever he is going to say to look at her.

"Is the Human in pain?" he asks me, as if I am in charge or something.

"No," I say calmly. "She is only scared."

"No need to be scared anymore, little females."

Jade lets out a huffing noise and he gives her a wary look.

"I am the High Commander of the Blood Fleet. The elite Warrior force of Tarrassia. We are on our way to the Mother Planet. We will arrive shortly, if…" he stops for a second, looking at Natalia, "if we can do the Jump, otherwise it will take four spans. The Jump can be difficult and scary for those unused to it. Will the small female be able to take that?"

Jade ignores his question and asks her own.

"When are you taking us back to our home? Are we prisoners or something?"

"You are not prisoners, female."

"The name is Jade, not fucking Female, dude."

"And my name is Zaan, not Dude, female Jade."

She looks speechless. Probably her first time. He carries on talking and explaining, but without paying much attention to her. His strange eyes are simply glued to Gianna in a very disturbing way. It makes me feel like I want to shelter her from him.

"You cannot be returned to your planet. It is forbidden. You will be taken to Tarrassia and be safe from harm for the rest of your spans. All the former slaves we rescue make good lives for themselves on the Mother Planet. You will be given dwellings, clothing, food and be assigned jobs."

"What? So, we are slaves? Your people get to decide for us?" asks Jade.

"No, you are not slaves. Yes, my people are in charge of your lives now. You belong to Tarrassia."

So, Gianna was right. We are not free. These aliens are all the same. Despite the contradictory words he is saying, one thing is clear. We have no choice. They aren't giving us options, just instructions. So, we must be slaves.

"God, that's just bonkers!" explodes Jade, as expected.

"My name is Zaan, not God and my device can't translate boncars."

"What the hell?"

"Enough, female Jade!" He stops her by putting a huge hand up. They have… claws? "When we get to Tarrassia, the Elders will explain everything to you. I am a Warrior. I don't explain things to females." They are not big on feminism, these aliens, that's for sure. Or is it only this one? He eventually takes his eyes from Gianna and points at the table jutting out of the wall.

"You need to eat and drink, females. Don't your kind eat meat?"

"Jesus! Dude, it's raw!" says Jade, rolling her beautiful eyes dramatically. He gives her a look you would give to an annoying bug.

"My name is not Jesus Dude. It's Zaan. But you can call me High Commander, since you don't seem able to remember my name. Do Humans eat their meat alive? We can't provide that on my Warship, but there are plenty of live animals to eat on the Mother Planet. I will send in some seeds and mountain fruits until then."

His copper eyes stop upon Gianna one more time and turn gold as they do. He watches her like she is dinner or something, and it makes all of us uncomfortable, not just her. As he turns to leave, he warns us, without looking back, "You are not prisoners, but I don't want any loose females walking around my ship, disturbing my Warriors. This door was set to respond to my hand only. My genetic code is the only thing that can make it open. So, I suggest don't try to open it and hurt your tiny hands in the process."

He slaps his huge palm on the left screen, which responds with a bright light, and the slit in the wall opens with a hiss. And then he is gone, before we can even process what he was saying or ask our questions.

"Well, wasn't that interesting?" Apparently Jade always has something to say. "I don't know about you girls, but from my first experience ever with an alien, three things have become obvious. He is very black and white, he put the L into taking things literally and he definitely wants to fuck Gianna."

I don't tell her what I think of her vile mouth, only because she manages to make Natalia smile for the first time since all this started. However, her stupid words act like some sort of trigger for Gianna.

"I am escaping. Anyone coming?" she says, walking to the slit in the wall with a strange look in her green eyes. She isn't well, I think. None of us is well, but she is having some sort of psychotic episode. She doesn't even look like herself anymore. And she is shaking. Badly.

"Gianna, please don't listen to Jade. They look like honourable men... beings..."

"There is no such a thing as honourable men."

"True," says Jade. "However, the options are just as grim. Run-away where? In space, around the ship? Are you sure you want that thing chasing you around his ship? Leaving this room might lead to immediate death."

"I'd rather that than let him touch me. At least I get to choose how I die."

Yes, choice. I know better than anyone how important it is to have choice. I can't tell her otherwise. So, I try to just be practical.

"It doesn't matter anyway, he's the only one who can open the door."

Gianna places her shaking little hand on the massive panel, fit for the alien's size. It lights up straight away and the slit opens, revealing the metal corridor of the ship behind it.

"Well, what do you know?" she says with a crazy look in her eyes. "He thought we were too weak and stupid to question his words. So, are you coming? No? Fine, suit yourselves!"

We all just stare at the slit in the wall for a long time after her exit. We most likely just lost one of us. Another one... We have no words. Not even Jade.

"I am so thirsty," says Natalia, completely out of place. But somehow, what she says makes sense. It makes me remember myself. I stand and walk to the strange-looking container on the table. It doesn't come with opening instructions, but as I touch the top of it, the lid removes itself inside the container. I pour the clear liquid in one of the metal cups. No smell, no colour, just cold and really tempting. Besides, we are all going to die. Maybe drinking this is my choice. The only one I am ever given. I pour the liquid down my throat in one go. Water. Cold, fresh water with a hint of... lavender? Yes, definitely lavender.

I pour two more cups and offer them to the girls. "It's just water. We need to stay hydrated," I say. Natalia takes the cup and drinks it without a question or a doubt. Jade watches me with open curiosity to see if I am going to die or something. "I feel absolutely fine, Jade. It's just water."

"No offence, Elsa, but you're the least human-looking Human I know. Maybe you're one of them after all."

I refuse to rise to that and simply put the cup down. After a few minutes of childish stubbornness, she takes it and drinks it, just like I did. In one go!

"I really don't want to eat anything alive when we get to their planet. And I definitely don't want to be eaten by the Monsters either," says Natalia.

"Do you think there might be something wrong with you, girl? Like maybe your brain is not wired right?"

"That's enough, Jade! Let her be!"

I feel like a hypocrite. The same thought did occur to me. Maybe it's trauma. We have lost track of time. We don't really know how long we were on that ship for. Or what they did to us.

There's a sudden jolt in the room. Then the floor seems to catch fire, as a light pattern like a beacon moves around in a chasing pattern. An alarm. Jade and I exchange a look. Gianna… Did she die in space? Did they get her? Will they ever tell us? Eventually, the flashing stops and everything is quiet again. After a while I realise the soothing hum of the ship is gone. We are floating in space instead of moving towards our destination. What did Gianna do? As if to answer my question the entrance panel comes to life and the slit in wall opens. Is that…? Natalia screams and moves to the far end of the room, looking like she is trying to become one with the wall. Jade also retreats. I put myself unconsciously between him and the girls. Is he bigger? I can feel his rage. It is like a red aura around him. I can feel the heat bouncing off his enormous body. He was big before, but is he bigger now? The shirt, which I clearly remember was loose before, looks like it's going to rip any minute. Underneath his clothes the muscles seem to move like they have a life of their own. His skin shines with thousands of light particles, moving almost hypnotically up and down his body. His eyes glow and the colour is gone. Now they look like white gold with red specks in it. How could I ever think he looked human? He stares me in the eyes and I have to painfully tilt my head backwards so I can hold his stare. It takes me a bit to adjust to all of this, but in the end, I am still me. Humans, aliens, monsters, who cares? They are all the same to me. They all end up more scared of me than I am of them. The cold inside me cannot be defeated by any of them.

"Where is Gianna?"

He ignores my question to ask his own. "How did she get out?" Each word is punctuated and sounds more like growls, scrambled by the translation device. I don't need a translation. Somehow his intense emotions make me understand his words without hearing them.

"The same way you did," I tell him. "She placed her palm on the panel and it opened for her."

He watches me with big white eyes, the red dots in them taking over.

"Do not deceive me, female!" he growls, and finally Natalia starts crying again. "This device only responds to the particles in my blood. I set it that way. It only opens for me. Not for my Warriors, not for the Astrals and not for Humans! For the last time! How did she leave the room?"

"You asked a question, High Commander, and I answered," I say, raising my chin high. The next thing I know he grabs my wrist with only two fingers and starts pulling me towards the slit's panel. I immediately understand he's holding my wrist with two fingers only so he won't break it. I quickly follow willingly, for the same reason. His skin is hot and has a vibration to it. I already know what he's trying to do, so I willingly put my left palm on the screen. Nothing. He removes it, then places it again. Nothing. He tries my right palm. Nothing.

"Tell the females to come here," he says in a less growling voice. Something is troubling him. Well, something other than the obvious.

Jade tries to drag Natalia towards us, but she puts up a fight.

"Come, Natalia, it's safe, I promise," I encourage her, so she does. Jade is nice enough to let her touch the screen first, so she can run back to her safe place, away from him. Then Jade places her left hand, her right and then again, like she's having a blast.

"Jesus, Dude, shall I try my feet, what do you think? Left one? Right one?"

She's playing with fire so I put myself in front of her for no sane reason. God himself, if there is one, cannot protect Jade from the Jade effect. However, he's not getting angrier. Something is definitely troubling him. I can tell the moment when some sort of realisation dawns on him. His eyes change into a beautiful gold. Like golden lava, and the light particles underneath his skin become brighter. He almost glows. He's doesn't shrink back to his normal frame, if anyone can call that a normal frame, but the anger is definitely under control when he addresses us again. He looks at us with more… what is that? Protectiveness?

"The course of action has changed, little females. The High General of Tarrassia and his Generals are on the way to collect you. The Blood Fleet has another destination now. They will take you to Levianha. They will do the Jump and be here in the next eleven nanoclips. Please, don't do anything to put yourselves in danger. You are all precious to us now. Any questions?"

"What is Levianha?" I ask.

"Our Royal Ship."

"What's waiting for us there?"

"Our King!"

Not long after he's gone, the slit opens one more time and more of them come in like they own the room. I guess they do. They own us too. It feels like an army came in, but there's actually only three of them. It's just that they are all so big and they fill the place like an army. We are getting tired. Jade looks like she's about to turn into Gianna and do something silly, and Natalia has given up. She looks defeated. Once again, I step in front of them. These beings are so big, how could Humans have survived this long in this universe? These new aliens have a more official look and they are all definitely older than the ship's Commander. More composed as well. Hard to tell their ages, though. Do they even get old? Do they die? They definitely wear less than the other guy. They are all bare, except for the white leather kilt hanging low on their waist. Swords the size of Natalia are clipped to the belt holding their kilts up. They wear some sort of long black boots and their powerful legs are covered in various dark shades of sprinkled hair, just like the rest of their bodies. It definitely looks trimmed and closely groomed, unlike the Commander's. The wild is well contained here. They all have shoulder-length hair but it's braided neatly at the sides, keeping it out of their faces. Their big bushy beards are also trimmed and less wild-looking. The one in the middle, who somehow seems older, has two braids in his beard. He seems to tame the environment around him as he walks in, flanked by the other two. This is a creature who feeds on control and is used to being in command. His presence is instantly calming and reassuring. He is a man in control and that alone is enough to make me feel safe. As he looks at me, I realise he is like me. He is the alien, male version of me. He watches me with blank copper eyes, then inspects Natalia, then me again, completely ignoring Jade. This one is smart.

"Hanni, females," he says, and I realise it's a greeting the ear device won't translate. He can control the booming voice to make it sound perfectly even and very... human.

"I am the High General of Tarrassia. These are the Southern Low General and the Northern Low General of Tarrassia."

The two giants by his side smash a fist to their chests. A salute, I realise, and I bow my head gently in acknowledgement. But of course, Jade bursts into laughter behind me.

"Really, guys? Is there a middle general?"

He completely ignores her, like she's invisible. For some reason that makes her nervous.

"My Generals and I are here to escort you to Levianha. We will board a small Warship and we will Jump. On board I will instruct you and prepare you for the Jump. It may make you feel unwell. Once on board the Royal Ship, you will be in the care of the Royal Guards and the Royal Servants. Until then, you are in my care. And in my care any sign of rebellion will be punished. I do not care that you are females or that Humans are fragile. Disobedience will be punished drastically. I do not lose tiny females. And now we move."

As he finishes talking, he moves aside as if to show us to walk ahead of him. One of the others moves forward and opens the slit. Apparently, it has been adjusted to react to more than one palm print now. Unless of course Gianna broke it. The other General moves to the far side, obviously trying to walk behind us. They are like a formation. A well-oiled machine. And then, there is Jade.

"I had fucking enough of being hauled like cargo up and down your bloody ships."

"Retrieve the Human," orders the General in charge, without even looking at her. The very second one of his men tries to reach for her she sinks her teeth into his huge hand. Despite the huge size of his palm, she manages to draw blood. I can see a tiny droplet of a shiny copper liquid. Again, without looking her way he gives another short order and walks out.

"Chain her. Separate her. Bring them to the ship."

And with that there are only two of us left.

4

SIA

The last couple of days have been like a dream. I can't sleep even though I am so tired. And when I do, Natalia's nightmares wake me up. They didn't separate the two of us. Except for when they strapped us in the huge chairs on the General's ship. For safety reasons during the Jump, we weren't allowed to hold hands, even though we were close to each other. She cried and screamed and then she fainted during the Jump. It felt like a minute or a year, who could tell. I felt sick, but I refused to show it. I don't show emotions because I don't have any. Natalia makes it harder, though. She makes me soft, I can't be soft. I think we are slaves of some sort. I need to stay strong. I know I need to ask her some questions about this monster nonsense. She seems perfectly normal, except for that. I worry I might not want to know. Somewhere, somehow, her monsters are connected to my sister and I simply don't want to ask. Not yet. We don't know anything about Jade or about Gianna. I think the worst and I know Natalia does too. I refuse to give the aliens satisfaction and ask. Part of me knows it's only a matter of time before they take her away from me, too. We are treated well, too well. The rooms we are in are beautiful. They look like the fairy tale rooms of a palace. You wouldn't be able to tell we are on a spaceship. There's a living room and two huge bedrooms, but we share one. The bed is huge and covered in white furs. The furniture is made of beautifully carved violet wood. It's not painted and it has a soft glow when the lights are dimmed. It's actually violet. Somewhere in the universe there is a forest of violet trees. Would it be on their planet? There are intricate fabrics and beautiful pristine furs everywhere. The bathroom is more like a pool room. Someone fitted a stone pool on a spaceship! There is also some sort of a shower room, spraying powerful jets of hot water at you from hundreds of small orifices. It almost knocked us over when we tried it. Way too powerful for us. Everything smells like some sort of flower. Could it be that flower? I try not to think about the patterns on the door or on the fabrics. I know that pattern. It's all I have left from my sister. I'm not going to think about that. There is light coming from everywhere. It's impossible to find the source. The female servants taught us how to control it. More like how to ask the MI to control it. They call mechanical intelligence what we call artificial intelligence. The MI controls everything. We were asked to choose a name for the MI and use it when needed. Natalia called it Sasha after her childhood favourite doll. She talks to it all day. Occasionally, Sasha replies funny things that make no sense. A bit like Siri back home. There are huge guards outside our chambers. They are not Tarrassian. They look very monster-like, to Natalia's horror. Huge and red and they have straight sharp horns jutting forward out of their foreheads. How do they sleep? How do they kiss? Luckily, we only catch glimpses of them outside our rooms, as the female servants come and go. We have two each, which is really over the top. Except for one who looks a bit like a see-through elf, none of them look humanoid. Obviously, that's a big issue for Natalia. They call them servants, but I think these creatures are slaves. Like us. So, we try not to be difficult. Well, I do anyway. Natalia is too scared of them. I think all their slaves are from different races. Tarrassians believe they are the top dog in the universe. And these slave creatures seem a bit brainwashed. I am worried about what type of slaves we will be. Obviously, not domestic slaves, since we have our own pair of those. I saw the way Commander Zaan looked at Gianna. It's not hard to add up things. Did they separate Natalia and I because we are virgins? Do they know that? I was asleep, but Natalia said they have taken blood from her arm with some strange device. What else have they done? We were given beautiful dresses and ornate pieces of jewellery. The alien women struggle with Natalia's hair, they have no idea how to tame it. I don't let them touch mine. No one ever did. I was Earth's best-paid model, but I never allowed anyone to touch my hair. I don't like being touched. Natalia's the only one who has, in years. We are treated like royalty. When will it be payback time? My stomach is in knots. It has been since morning. The light is automatically dimmed at night, so I think it is morning. Perhaps it's just hunger. The food is a bit strange and we struggle with it. We are told, once on Tarrassia there will be thousands of options to choose from. Until then, we have settled for nuts and seeds to avoid being offered raw meat again. The fruit, however, is way too sweet. We both felt sick after trying a bit of something that looked like a cucumber with spikes. It tasted like a spoon of sugar mixed with honey. The water is nice, at least. A bit addicted to their water. It makes me feel good and at peace when I drink it. Of course, it may contain some type of drug, but we don't really have a choice. We are being looked after like a couple of princesses, but we are not being told anything. We only see the other slaves, so there's no one to tell us anything. How long until we reach their planet? The wait is overwhelming and I feel strange. As usual, no one can tell. Today is just not a good day. Why do I feel so anxious?

I suddenly stand and reach for Natalia. She quickly runs to me and I hug her close to me, watching the heavy ornate doors.

"What is it, Sia?"

"Someone is coming," I say before the guards open the doors from the outside. Two huge beings walk in. White leather kilts and black leather boots. No swords this time. I don't look at him, and only rest my eyes on the one they call the High General of their planet. The one who knows control and self-restraint. The safe one. I can't look at the other one. He is not much bigger than the General, but the chaos inside him makes him feel twice as big. Inside him there is noise and freedom; recklessness, disorder and immense power. And he watches me like a wild beast. I may not look at him, but I am painfully aware of his eyes on me. To him I am prey. A possession. He thinks I belong to him. I defy him using all my years of self-taught restraint. I wait for my coldness to take over and scare this creature back to the hell it came from. But his fire is overwhelming my coldness, so I fake it instead. My defiance does not scare him away like it does everyone else. It angers him, it excites him. It makes me the perfect prey. By the time I realise, it's too late to act differently. Natalia is terrified, but the scariest thing is that so is the calm and collected General. He watches the mad one with a sense of panic. And now I am scared, too. However, no one can tell. No one can ever tell.

"Remove the red female," he orders the General who calls him "my King" and I know my battle is lost. He is their King. The General cannot protect us against his King. I need to protect Natalia. It's the only fight I have left in me. I ask her calmly to walk away from me. She thinks he's a monster and I tell her he's nothing but a slaver. It makes him mad with anger. He seems to grow bigger. He is so unhinged. His muscles are not the only thing growing. His kilt looks like it's going to burst open from the pressure of his huge, growing appendage or whatever that thing is behind his kilt. It can't be what I think it is… can it? He is completely out of control. That is my biggest fear. Without control there's nothing. He moves closer like a stalking predator. I raise my chin, faking a defiance I don't have anymore. His body heat burns my cold skin, his intoxicating scent makes me feel dizzy. I feel his presence with every pore of my body. I feel like falling and I want him to catch me. His presence, scent and body heat are overwhelming. He reaches a huge hand to touch my face. I can't let him. I raise my arm to block his, as if that would ever be possible. He grabs my wrist in a grip of steel and fire and then there is only pain. It's going up my arm, then up the other one as he touches it. He put something inside my body. I'm on fire. He is burning my skin. I lose all control, I lose all reason. I scream and I try to fight him, push him away. But he's already inside my blood, his scent melts inside me. He wants more! He wants my soul. His claws dig painfully into my arms as he lifts me up to his level and presses his forehead into mine. The pain is made of light now. As it reaches my forehead, I have to close my eyes. The lights are blinding. Swirls of purple and blue and pure white. He is taking my soul. He is taking my mind. And as my thighs touch his massive erection, I know he will take my body next. And then, he drops me without any warning and I hit the floor hard. Small arms pull me close in a protective hug. Soft red hair covers my painful face. I shake with pain and fear as a blessed darkness descends on me. Before I let the darkness take me, my last wish is it was him holding me.

5

SIA

For who knows how many times in the last few days, I wake up but I command my eyes to stay closed. His face, his scent, his heat, his voice, his touch. Instead of processing danger and surroundings before I dare open my eyes, this time my mind can only process one thing. Him. The big, crazy, unhinged man... alien, who thrives on being out of control. He's done something to me. He put something inside me. I remember the feel of his hardness against my thighs. Did he put that inside me as well, after the darkness took me? He is so big I would still feel the pain of that. I wait, but there is no pain in between my legs. Just an unexpected, treasonous stickiness caused by the memory of his body against mine. There is no pain anywhere else. Just a faint pulse on my forehead. There's something there. I try to brush it off, but a small soft hand stops me.

"Don't touch it, Sia! Diran put some healing gel on. This gel is amazing. It healed all your burns and... ah... your claw marks."

I open my eyes and look at her red mane of curls. They look a bit tangled and she's got dark circles under her pretty baby blue eyes. I realise she hasn't left my sight. "How long was I out?"

"Not sure how time works here, it's so confusing," she says, trying to push the rebellious curls out of her face. "I think it was noon when… well… you know, when it happened. And now it's close to noon again. So maybe twenty hours?"

"You looked after me," I say, and I remember her fiercely protective hug. She wanted to fight all of them for me. She looks weak, but she is not. I look strong, but…

"Well, yes, but I had help. And a very nice conversation." She smiles and reaches out behind her for… a huge translucent hand? I tense and raise my chin as the huge alien allows her to take his hand and pull him near my bed. What is she doing? Why is she not scared of this one? He is old. Really, really old. Not in the frail, wrinkly way a Human would be. He is only slightly smaller than the rest of them. He wears a white tunic that reaches his knees and loose white trousers underneath. A beautiful golden necklace hangs low, on top of his still powerful-looking biceps. The pendant is a circle containing a glowing leaf. A bit like a maple leaf. His hair is as white as mine, but I somehow know it's the old age that turned it that colour. It reaches below his waist. His long beard is also white. Both hair and beard have intricate braids in them. His skin is not light copper like most of his race. It's almost translucent and I can see strong veins under it. They are copper, like their blood. His eyes glow a soft rose gold colour. And they are… kind? The kindness you get after a lifetime of doing the right thing. All of a sudden, I realise why Natalia is not scared. He's the Tarrassian version of Father Christmas, but with a bulk of muscles instead of fat. He lets go of her hand as he comes closer. He watches me with… is that adoration? Respect? Wonder? Maybe all three. He touches his fist against the left side of his chest.

"My Queen! So, pleased to see you well."

Is he trying to mock me? Like Jade? I choose to ignore it and slowly bow my chin to return his greeting. His hand reaches for my temple and I flinch. He stops.

"I am the Elder of the Healers of Tarrassia, my Queen. I am only trying to check the hotness has left your body. You have been through a great deal of pressure and pain."

"Yes, I recall it was your King who put me through that."

"My Queen, the King had no more control of the Sign, then you did. The Sign of the Astrals cannot be controlled and it doesn't ask for permission. It's the greatest honour a being can be given by the Great Ancestors."

I didn't ask for it and they are not my ancestors. I don't say it out loud. No point hurting an old man's beliefs. The King, however, he will hear what I have to say. I have hundreds of questions, I have unwanted emotions and I feel different. All my senses feel enhanced and I feel too much of everything. I hate feeling. I spent a lifetime trying to suppress all feelings, all emotions. And I was given something that took it all away with a touch. His touch. My eyes are drawn to the patterns on my hands and arms. I try to ignore them, but I know I eventually have to look. Are they tattoos? They look like henna tattoos, but I realise, with an inner flinch, they are not on my skin. They are under it. They start at the tips of my fingers, go up my hands, circle my wrists like cuffs and go up round and round my arms in tiny delicate swirls. They are a mixture of purple, blue and white and seem faded somehow. Like they are dormant. I remember them glowing with light. Under his touch. I look at my now healed claw marks on my upper arms. I also got those under his touch. The swirls of colour go up my shoulders, under my garment and that's all I can see as they disappear behind my neck. I don't want to ask for a mirror. Not yet. I can feel that thing on my forehead. Natalia keeps staring at it. The Elder is staring at it. They both have a revered look in their eyes. I am not ready to look. However, it is time to ask my questions. And I refuse to do it while lying down. As I rise from the bed I wait for pain or dizziness, but they don't come. Someone has changed my outfit to a beautiful lavender blue Tarrassian dress. It's long and floaty, but easy to walk in as it has two long slits going up the sides, all the way to my hips. I try to sit with all the grace I don't have right now and gesture to the other massive violet chair opposite mine. I don't bother with Natalia. I know she likes her corner by the wall, where she can hug the furs, she piled up there for comfort. The Elder looks like he would rather stand in my presence, but as I insist, he takes a seat.

"Where are we going to, Elder?"

"We are on the way to Tarrassia, my Queen. We will get there before the end of the next span."

"Tomorrow?"

"Yes," he confirms.

"Where are the other two Humans?"

"The female called Jade is in the next quarters. She is being well looked after, despite biting the High General's Warriors and the guards."

Natalia giggles from her spot.

"And the other one?"

"Sadly, she is still missing, my Queen."

Not even my efficient brain can understand the fact that she actually got away. From a spaceship, in... space... Definitely misjudged Gianna. She's a force of nature. A strange sense of pride fills my heart.

"Are your Warriors looking for her? She can't possibly be safe on her own!"

"Of course, my Queen. The High Commander of the Blood Fleet is personally looking for her."

"So, he should, since he was the fool who let her get lost in space."

The Elder's translucent face wrinkles under a funny, almost human grin.

"Yes, no one can deny the foolishness of the High Commander. Quite familiar with it, since he is my son."

Natalia giggles again and it is so nice to hear that sound instead of her cries. I was going to apologise but I could tell the Elder was not offended. Just slightly amused.

"Sadly, the fool is also missing now, but have no doubt, my Queen, he will find the female and he will keep her safe."

Before I ask the most important question, I look at the marks on my arms. There is no going back for me. No amount of makeup can hide those and not whatever is now on my forehead. I can feel it pulsing as I speak. It does a lot more than pulse when I think of him. Almost everyone knows my name back on Earth. There is no hiding in anonymity for me. I always stood out, even before fame. I don't have the most common of looks. They make everyone stare. My life as I knew it is over. He decided that for me.

"Will your people return the other Humans to Earth?"

"No, my Queen, the females can never be returned." And once again Natalia is crying. He looks unsure of what to do.

"Let me explain," he starts, addressing both of us this time.

"Your Planet is a Red Orbit planet. It is forbidden to interact, as your people are primitive and cannot comprehend the life outside their little establishment. We don't know how or when the Noorranni slavers made contact or how many others are in danger. We are investigating the matter. Especially now." He points at my forehead and arms. "You and your females are precious to us. We are the most advanced race in the universe. Our blood can heal and preserve life for hundreds of rotations, our minds can communicate silently amongst the galaxies, we are the best Warriors, we have the best technology and our Mother Planet is the most beautiful planet created by the Astrals, our great ancestors. And yet, despite all of these blessings, my species is dying. We have never mixed with lower species and in time, after a million rotations of inbreeding, we have lost our fertility. No cubs have been born on Tarrassia in eleven rotations. We are becoming extinct. The decision was made to use a compatible species to save ourselves. We are giving this great honour to the Humans. What we didn't expect was for the Astrals to bless this new alliance with the Sign of the Spark. We thought it lost to the times of legends. The Elders of our great Elder of the Spark Mountains were the last ones blessed with the Spark. He is the only Tarrassian alive to have seen the marks. Until now," he adds, looking at my forehead. "As a superior race, we travel the galaxies of the Seven Stars and beyond, to free the slaves and protect the weak. It isn't always possible to return the slaves to their former homes, so we keep them. We were never going to return you or the other females to your little planet. But as my tests have proven your species' compatibility with ours, we have decided to keep you as our most treasured mating and breeding females. I have personally asked the King to rule by example and choose one of you as his Queen. What none of us ever expected was for the mighty Astrals to bless us with the Sign. Now, your females are even more precious to us and we will have to protect your tiny planet. In return they will give us their precious females. A great honour to your primitive species."

He ends his little speech with a pleased and peaceful look on his face. I actually thought I liked the man. My hands, covered in their disgusting marks, are nicely folded in my lap, my back is painfully straight, my chin is raised high, my eyes are pools of sharp grey icicles and my frozen smile, meant to offend, are all at work. My weapons never fail me… except for him, I can't help remembering. It doesn't matter. It stops now.

I rise to my full height, which is not much around these giant beings. He stands quickly, completely unaware of what's coming.

"My dearest Elder of the Healers of Tarrassia, thank you for visiting my quarters. Now I am afraid this lower-species female will have to ask you to leave."

He doesn't get my irony nor my mocking tone. Of course, he doesn't. They are too entitled. He expects me to call myself a lower species. Because, to them, we are.

"Yes, of course, my Queen. I will inform the King you have recovered beautifully and he can now join you in the Royal Quarters. I will make arrangements for Natalia to take another room for the rest of our journey home."

"No, no, no, please, I don't want to be alone. Can't it wait until we get to your planet?"

"No, little Natalia, as I explained to you before the Queen woke up, the Sign is claiming its right. Your species is not as affected by the Sign as ours," he says, watching me with a curious look. "The King must be in great deal of physical pain. He has to claim his mate and quiet his new, awakened heart. The King had to spend the night on a warship docked to Levianha, as he didn't trust himself being too close to his Queen. I will send for him now."

"Yes, of course, Elder of the Healers. How do you say an hour in your time?"

He seems a bit confused, as if waiting for his translation device to do a better job.

"I think a rotation of nanos would be the equivalent of a human hour."

"Very well. Can I please have an hour to freshen up and prepare myself for the King? I want him to be proud of his Queen."

This seems to please him immensely. How pathetic!

"Of course, my Queen. Take your time. I will inform the King later, when you are ready. Our King is not a very patient male."

"Don't say…"

After he leaves us, Natalia scurries near and takes my hand. Unlike me she craves constant touch.

"I am not quite sure what he was saying. It didn't sound very nice," she says.

"That's because he wasn't, Natalia. We have to leave. Now!"

I look around as if trying to take things we might need, but there is no time. It's now or never. Besides, we couldn't walk out of here carrying not even as much as a fur. Natalia's plump lower lip starts trembling and she hugs herself. "Go?"

I grab her shoulders and try to look her in the eyes. She is distracted by whatever she's seeing on my forehead.

"These people can call it whatever they want, Natalia. We are their slaves. We don't have a choice as to where to live, who to marry or when, what jobs to do or how to live our lives. They call that the life of a 'precious mate'. I call that the life of a slave." I wish I'd had Jade's colourful language to call it a few other things. Jade. Guilt makes me doubt myself for a minute. But I can't take any chances. She's a wild card. She can't follow instructions for the life of her. She's too unpredictable. I can't take her.

"You heard him. They are a planet of narcs. We cannot let them do what they think is best for us and be grateful about it. We go, now."

"But how, I don't understand. Go where? I am scared, Sia."

"I know you are. I am too. But I am more scared of what's going to happen when he comes for me in an hour." I feel bad for using that, even though it's not really a lie. I am scared of what someone like him could do to someone like me. Even though we are both virgins, I know she's young and far more scared of sex than I am. It's definitely a winning argument. She drops her shoulders, looking defeated and tired. And I remember she hardly had any sleep, looking after me. None of us can sleep here anyway. We have to try.

"I know it sounds crazy, but it can be done. Gianna got off the other ship. If they are still looking for her it means she didn't just fall off in space or something. The old alien said there are warships docked to Levianha. Let's find one, sneak in and then make it to the emergency pods I saw on the High General's warship when he brought us here. We can do this. Now. I don't know how much time we have left before he comes for me."

"We can't fly a spaceship, Sia," she murmurs, without looking me in the eyes.

"I watched everything they were doing when they brought us here. At no point did they do anything other than ask the MI to set the route to Levianha. We can use the MI. Please, Natalia. We'll figure something out. Let's go!" I suddenly stop to look at her, as I understand what I am doing. Yes, I am worried for her, yes, I want to take her away from them, but I am also taking her choice away.

"You don't have to come with me just because I asked you to. Staying or leaving, they are both dangerous choices, but at least we get to make one. You can stay if you like."

I hold my breath for a quick moment.

"I am coming with you, Sia. Their MI seems to like me. You might need my help with that." She gives me a beautiful smile, full of hope and innocence.

I try to find myself, or more likely my inner iceberg, before walking out. We don't even know if the doors are locked or if the guards will let us pass. I know exactly what will give me the strength I need. I also know what I will see on my forehead. Because God, the universe, the alien Astrals, life or whatever else is out there deciding for us, hates me. It wants me to remember I cannot escape my pain and my memories. As I look into the beautifully ornate copper mirror, I see it. The swirls going up my arms meet behind my neck, probably going up my scalp under my hair and reaching their destination in the middle of my forehead.

There, a sign has been carved into my skin like a mark with a hot iron. Just more subtle as it's under my skin and it doesn't look like a scar. It looks like I'm on my way to a summer festival, and instead of gluing face jewels on my forehead, I put them under my skin. Some would say it's beautiful. Like a piece of magical forehead jewellery. I say it's cruel. The sign looks like some artful geometric design, but it's pretty obvious what it contains in the middle of the strange pattern. A water lily. A pale blue water lily, pulsing slightly as I look at my image in the mirror. I look even more alien than all the other creatures around me. I have carved in the middle of my forehead something my sister gave me, before she walked into the motorway traffic. A piece of paper for the police, I wasn't allowed to read, and our mother's brooch.

"Sia?"

"Let's go!" I grab her hand and hold my breath as I open the doors. They are so light. I didn't expect that. The two enormous guards look at each other with a puzzled look, then at me. I stare with my chin high up and they instantly bow their horned heads to me, short of poking me in the head.

"The King has summoned my presence on his warships, in the docking bay. Which way is it?" I have no idea what the translation device is saying back at them. They look unsure, and I find their expression so incredibly human and familiar. I hope they won't be punished for this. They are just slaves like us.

"We will escort you, Queen of Tarrassia," says the one on the right.

"No, as I haven't mated the King yet, I am not allowed to have any males around me. Just tell me how to get there."

The 'when in Rome' approach seems to work. They don't question that. What is more, they take a big step back, away from me. Did I just make up an actual thing?

The same guard gives me a long list of directions and my brain silently repeats everything so I won't forget it.

I walk the strange, undoubtedly alien corridors of Levianha as if I own it. I imagine it is nothing but a catwalk and I definitely own the catwalk. By my side Natalia keeps up with my pace, and her hair bounces up and down. She is calm and composed. My brave Natalia. We run into various types of aliens, all servants obviously, as none of them are Tarrassians. Many guards as well. Also, not Tarrassians. Some look scared of me, some look unsure, but none try to stop me. As we get closer to the docking bay, the ship looks less luxurious, reminding me of the austere Blood Fleet. The stupid sign on my forehead begins to pulse harder and occasionally glows, hurting my eyes. I don't know how I know, but I do. It means he's closer. We have to rush. At the next turn, we run straight into three massive Tarrassians. White leather kilts. And swords. Warriors.

Time to be the Queen. I don't know how to be Queen of Tarrassia. I am no queen of slaves. But I sure know how to be the Ice Queen.

"The King is expecting me, Warriors. Which one is his warship?" Big and stupid never fit better. They are too distracted by my glowing forehead to pay attention. After we walk away and lose sight of them, we take the opposite direction to the one they pointed at. I walk faster and my marks are making me dizzy. If I can tell he is close, so must he. I ignore the choking feeling of longing. Finally, we reach a web of ramps. Boarding ramps. I take one randomly, hoping for luck. Nothing else can help us now. We reach… a wall? The ramp ends abruptly, so it must be the entrance to a ship. There is a massive panel, too high for me to reach. But no door, no slit. I suddenly remember Gianna and the look on the Commander's face when he understood. I know now what he understood and why her palm could open that door. Shouldn't everything on the Royal Ship be connected to the King's genetic code? If his palm print could open this, shouldn't mine be able to do the same? I look at Natalia's tiny frame, wondering how to do this.

"I must touch that panel with my palm. Can you lift me? Only for a bit."

"Yes," she says and grabs my waist from behind. She uses all her tiny body and all her willpower to push me up, and I quickly slap my palm on the panel. It comes to life and the entire wall removes itself, to reveal the entrance to the ship. No sign of life. The corridor lights up as we walk. It's huge! I didn't expect that. It looks complicated and very different from the General's one. Time to try our luck again.

"MI, prepare the closest escape pod for launch."

A green light appears on the floor. It starts to move somewhere to our left.

"Emergency pod, ready to launch in fifteen nanoclips."

"Quick, Natalia. This way." I grab her hand and follow the green light. The emergency pod, which is shaped like a giant egg, is already open and we step in. It closes with a hum and I rush Natalia to the chair as the countdown starts. One chair. Just the one. It's meant to fit a Tarrassian, so we both easily fit in and I ask the MI to strap us in, as I have no idea how to do it. It's all too quick, there is no time to process and I look around with grim realisation. This is too small. The size of an army helicopter. Maybe slightly bigger. One chair, one control panel and a small cubicle as a clean room, without even a door to it. This is too small to reach Earth. What have I done? Too late. Countdown over and my stomach does a somersault as we are catapulted out of the ship at a sickening speed. Natalia's head flops on my shoulder as she loses consciousness. She can't take her G force... It's all very quiet. A small vibration and nothing else. I realise there is no window. That is just terrifying. For some reason not being able to see outside makes me lose myself. The light fades slowly on my forehead. The pulsing is fainter, and a horrible sense of sadness and loss fills me. Is it safe to undo the straps? I don't know...

I feel funny, almost like my life is leaving my body. Natalia wakes up with a whimper.

"Sia?"

"It's okay. We made it."

"This looks scary." She's losing her determination and I can't blame her. I must find a way. I can't give up now. I know the answer, but I have to try.

"MI, set the course for planet Earth." A long pause… "Planet Earth is a Red Orbit planet. Interaction is forbidden," says the impersonal voice. Their MI is adapting to whoever sets it. This one is as stern as their Warriors. Unlike Sasha. At least they weren't lying about Earth being forbidden.

"Hanni, Sasha," says Natalia with a cheeky grin, winking at me. There's a small sound of static and then Sasha's friendly voice takes over.

"Hanni, Natalia." Her smile is so open and full of innocence. Sadness digs at my heart. What did I do?

"Sasha, set course for the forbidden planet of Earth." Clever Natalia.

"Sorry, Natalia, the emergency pod is not fuelled to travel outside the Seven Stars galaxy."

My head is pounding. It's hard to concentrate. I feel so thirsty and faint. I know there must be emergency supplies somewhere in here. I need to drink. But first I need to take Natalia to safety. We can't risk meeting more aliens. They are all hostile, by the looks of it.

"Sasha, what is the furthest non-habited planet you can reach?"

"The furthest non-habited and not planet I can reach is Zora 23."

What kind of an answer is that? Is this thing turning into Siri? It doesn't matter anyway. I am losing strength fast for some reason. And the headache is turning into a migraine.

"Sasha, set course for planet Zora 23."

"Yes, Queen of Tarrassia. Course set for Zora 23."

Why does even Sasha have to remind me of my fate?

"Estimated arrival in two spans. Enjoy your journey."

We ask Sasha to remove the straps. I don't think we're meant to be strapped in for two days. There is limited water and some sorts of pouches. Liquid food? I am not hungry, my mouth is too dry. I just need water. I try to have some, but then I feel sick. It feels like my body is attacking me from the inside. My brain is screaming something at me, my heart is slowing down and I feel faint. I must ignore it. I will ignore it. I make Natalia have one of the pouches. It can't be any more disgusting than the other food we were given. She takes it like a champ. No whining. Without her monster obsession, Natalia is strong, and she has a very no-nonsense approach to everything. There's no forever drama, unlike with Jade and Gianna. Says the woman trapped in a pod in space. Stop thinking, Sia!

"Bozhe moi! This tastes like pancakes with maple syrup!" She claps her hands and her genuinely happy reaction in the middle of all this nightmare is so soothing.

"Try it, Sia!"

"In a minute," I say.

"You have to eat, Sia, you look really pale. I mean... more than your usual pale. And your... you know your marks look really faded now. Are you okay?"

"I will be fine, I just need to sleep." My voice is really small. A horrible idea goes through my clouded brain.

"Sasha, is the emergency pod fitted with a tracking device?"

"Yes, Queen of Tarrassia, our location is being shared with the Mother Ship, every four nanoclips."

Natalia gasps and covers her mouth with her tiny hand.

"Sasha, can you disable the tracking device?"

"I am the tracking device and yes I can disable myself."

"Can the emergency pod continue the journey and land without your help?"

"Yes, Queen of Tarrassia. The autopilot is set. It controls itself."

"Sasha, disable yourself!"

"MI disabled."

I give Natalia an apologetic look. I know she's attached to Sasha.

"It's okay, I know it's only a machine."

Why can't she understand monsters are also not real? Or maybe they are... I am too tired. A different type of tired. I can feel myself leaving my body. My strength, my spirit... all reason left to live is leaving my body. Sleep, I need to sleep. We lay some blankets and a fur from the emergency supplies hatch on the hard floor. Natalia hugs me close to her and starts stroking my hair gently. A memory. Someone used to do that while telling me a story. Was it my mother? After she succumbed to her illness, my sister kept on telling me that story every day. So, I won't forget the mother who died before I could remember her. The story of that flower. His flower. Natalia's sweet scent is so soothing. There's something motherly and protective about her. It helps me relax enough to sleep.

I wake up, but it doesn't really feel like it. The world is dark and cold and everything feels blurred. Natalia is holding me really tightly, too tight. And then I feel it. The pain. A dull pain following the pattern of the marks. It's a deep bone kind of pain. On my hands, arms, going up behind my neck and then exploding in a stabbing pain in the middle of my forehead. I feel really dizzy and thirsty.

"I'm so sorry, Sia," she says, rocking me like you would a child. We're both on the floor and my painful head is resting on her lap. "I'm so sorry I didn't remember what the Elder said. I didn't really believe him, it was just a detail... I don't know..."

I put all my strength into forming words. There is no life in my voice.

"What detail?"

"I was really scared after you lost consciousness. I thought the angry alien, you know, their King, infected you with a virus or something. I thought you were going to die. I didn't want to let the Elder touch you. I didn't want any of them touching you. I still think they might be monsters. The old alien explained their Sign and how it works. After he made your burns better, I asked him if you would die. And he said the Sign only kills mates if they are too far away from each other. Or for too long."

"What? I'm dying because of these marks?"

"I think you're dying of love. We always say that on Earth, but here that can actually happen. This is all my fault, I should have remembered what he said."

I am dying of love?! For a man I met for a few minutes? Not a man, an alien. An angry, scary, wild alien...

There was never a choice. My fate has been decided for me again. And this time for the last time. I am dying and I am about to leave this young, sweet girl alone in a scary universe. What have I done? I can't stop the tears. I don't have enough willpower left to stop them. She hugs me closer. Her hair is like a curtain around me. Soft, scented red curls. Something about her hair can make anyone feel safe. Like it can take the pain away. I hide my face in it. It smells like home and sun. What's going to become of her now?

"How long has it been?"

"We slept for a while. I don't know. It's so dark in here... no windows."

I have no energy to tell her it would be darker outside, in space.

"Please don't hate me, Sia. I can't let you die. You have to go back to him."

I remember the smell of his skin, his body heat, the feel of his arms around me. Safe. Yes, I need to go back.

"Sasha, change course for the Levianha," says Natalia, trying to sound as bossy as she can. Nothing… no response. Just the soft vibration of the pod.

"Sasha? Please!" She's panicking. "You try, Sia, maybe it will respond to the Queen."

I have to put all my energy into talking.

"MI, unable yourself. Change course for the Royal Ship."

Nothing… I have lost this fight, which was never a fight. There was never a choice. Everything in the universe is there to make my choices for me.

I look up at Natalia's sweet face. She's trying to be strong, but tears fall down her freckled cheeks, mixing with my own tears. I know I am dying. She knows I am dying. I gather my last strength to ask the one question I don't want an answer to.

"Do your monsters have names?"

Her lips tremble and she whispers as if they could hear her.

"No names, just Monster faces."

"Do they come to see you often?"

"No, they can't see me. They come for my mother and for my sisters. I hide. Monsters never see me. They can't see me, they can't hear me, I am invisible."

She sounds like a child. I realise, when she talks about her monsters, she is a child again. And she was right all along. Monsters are real. Deep down inside I know Natalia's sort of monsters are the reason my sister took her life. To save mine. We were adopted shortly after our mother passed away. Something was happening to my sister in our new adopted family. She sacrificed herself to alert the authorities, so I wouldn't share her fate. And now, I am dying anyway. Without having done anything useful, other than becoming famous. I wish I could give her one last hug, but my arms don't listen anymore. They feel frozen.

Everything inside me feels frozen. I have spent my entire short life trying to hide behind a coldness I often had to fake. Now it's become real and it's killing me.

"Sia, you are shaking. What can I do? Oh my God, you are so cold. Please, please," she cries, shaking my shoulders. "What do I do? What do you need?"

"I... I need him..." What feels like my last gasp is covered by Natalia's scream as the emergency pod starts shaking and obviously getting faster. It feels as if we're being pulled into a void. My stomach brings bile into my mouth, as there's nothing else in it. Natalia is saying things I don't really understand. She's pulling me towards the chair. Yes... the straps. The last reasoning left in my brain is telling me the pod is travelling through a planet's atmosphere. Landing soon... or crashing. There is no point. I can't help her. She should just leave me. She doesn't give up. She struggles with my limp body, then with the straps and then she's holding my hand so tight, like she's going to break it. She's praying to her god... I can hear sparks igniting the outside of the pod. Will it catch fire? I don't like fire. It scares the cold inside me. There's a boom, or is it his voice? There's warmth on my skin. Is it the fire, or is it his skin on mine? The straps get tighter around me. Or is it his arms holding me again? And then, everything goes dark.

6

SIA

"Sia, wake up, Sia!" Someone is shaking my body. I feel like a lifeless doll. She's slapping my face and I open my eyes. There's painful light coming from the green sky... The sky is green. I must be dead.

"Sia, please, I can't carry you. The pod is catching fire. We have to walk away from it. Please!"

She puts her shoulder under my arm, trying to push me up. I help her by pushing myself up with a strength I didn't know I still had. I put one foot in front of the other as she's pushing me away from the source of heat behind us. I struggle with my long dress, and Natalia almost drops me as she trips over her own. My feet are in Tarrassian sandals. They are made of glittery jelly which makes them sink in the soft blue sand. Is it sand? It's so soft and it's... well... blue. Our feet sink into it, making walking more difficult. I straighten my body to take my weight off Natalia. A strong enough breeze of both warm and chilling air slows us down even more as it tangles our dress slits in between our legs. Natalia desperately tries to push her wild mane of curls out of her face. We almost reach the tree line ahead, when an explosion shakes the soft soil, making our feet sink even more. The pod… We were trapped in there just a few minutes ago… It burns with a soft glow of blue flames. As we get closer to the trees I look behind. The autopilot took us to what seemed like the only available spot to land. The huge clearing seems to be the only one around, in a sea of very alien-looking trees. Is it a forest? A jungle? The air is not humid enough to be a jungle. It's slightly fresh. The breeze reminds me of London if anything. But who can tell for sure? Earth rules may not apply. The trees look really scary. They have willowy white trunks and enormous blue leaves. They are bigger than anything we have on Earth. The size of skyscrapers. Their canopy is somewhere up in the strange fluffy clouds, spread around the green sky. Everything looks a bit fake and cartoonish. Or maybe just that different from anything familiar. We slow our pace as, all of a sudden, the blue sand clearing seems less threatening than the forest. At least here we can see if something is coming. What have I done? How did I think we could survive on a planet we know nothing about? My brain is working again! The realisation hits me suddenly. As my power of reasoning returns, I know exactly why.

"Sia? Are you okay? You look much better."

"Yes, you saved me, Natalia." I give her one of my rare smiles. "You were so brave, back on the pod. I am really proud of you."

She gives me a small smile, but then she looks around with a worried look.

"I think I preferred the safety of the pod. Everything here is so big. What if there are big animals around?" She hugs herself as she looks around. And suddenly covers her mouth as if to stop a scream.

"There could be Monsters here!"

I give her a reassuring hug. It's my turn to look after her once again.

She looks at my arms, then at my forehead.

"Your marks have colours again. And the one on your forehead is glowing a bit. You're not going to die!" She claps her hands with pure joy and hugs me.

"Maybe this planet has healed you. Maybe it's not a bad place after all."

"That's not why I am better, Natalia. It's because he's found me. He's coming for me."

She looks puzzled for a moment, then scared. Her eyes scan the surroundings for an escape route.

"No more running, Natalia," I tell her calmly. "There is no point. Besides, I am happy he is coming. I don't want to see you die on a strange planet, being killed by whatever lives behind those trees. I was so reckless. His madness brushed off on me, or something. This is not like me. I am surprised we survived this journey. Luckily Sasha took us to a planet with an oxygen atmosphere. We can't survive without the Tarrassians, whatever that may imply."

Her shoulders sag, and she grabs my hand without looking me in the eyes.

"Will we get into trouble? Will they punish us for fleeing? The King looks a bit… a bit scary and I think he has anger issues."

I feel like laughing. She makes him sound so human. Maybe that's what I need. Find him some human traits. Treat him like I would any other man on Earth with a macho issue. They call me the Ice Queen for a reason. Then I remember my icy self really winds him up. So maybe not the best approach.

"I am the one who dragged you away. You have nothing to worry about. He will take it out on me only."

"That's not very reassuring. I don't want him to hurt you. And… Sia? Are you okay? Wow, your forehead! It's beautiful! You look like… an alien!"

My insides feel like fire. A feeling of happiness like I have never felt before makes me want to... I don't even know. I feel stronger and free and beautiful. I don't really know this person inside me. A soft rumble breaks the silence and it makes the breeze stronger. I pull Natalia closer to the edge of the trees. I don't know how big this spaceship is. She watches me nervously as I straighten my long white hair with my fingers and remove the dust from my long lavender-blue, silky dress. It's got some extra slits now from the rough landing and Natalia's efforts to pull me out of the pod. There are some patches of blue sand on it, but the dress matches them in colour. Natalia looks at herself for a minute then starts doing the same ridiculous thing to her pink dress. Apparently Tarrassians don't know about redheads and pink. Strangely enough, the crazy colour does suit her. Her cheeks grow as pink as her dress, as the trees start to move, disturbed by something. But there is no ship... I don't understand. Then just like magic there's a massive spaceship, right in front of the clearing. It's got a sleek look, all sharp edges, and it shines like a mirror, reflecting the blue leaves around us. The Jump, I tell myself. They did the thing they call a Jump. So, it took him like... what, one minute to find me? For some reason that makes me very angry. And I am never angry!

"I am scared," says Natalia, and I squeeze her hand. I am also scared; he is so crazy, unhinged and unpredictable. I don't know how to deal with all that. His lack of self-control is unnerving. An equally shiny ramp lowers itself into the blue sand. It looks alive as the sky and the trees reflect on its shiny surface. It starts vibrating under the heavy steps coming down. The spaceship is almost a hundred feet away, but the less sandy soil under our feet rumbles and moves with the same vibration. He is definitely angry. And huge. His eyes are two pits of white gold with red specks swirling around. He is wearing the short white leather kilt, the huge sword and the black boots, like all the other Warriors.

Can he ever be bothered with wearing king-like clothes? Or any clothes for that matter. The more clothes the better.

"Oh my God, Sia!" Natalia whispers close to me, clinging to my hand. "Is he bigger? Do they grow when they are angry?"

How did I not realise that sooner? My brain doesn't ever miss details. That's why their Warriors only wear the kilt. Clothes would tear when they go into battle mode. Or angry mode, whatever this is. He goes down the ramp painfully slowly, like a stalking predator. His glowing eyes on me at all times. His tattoos glow with brighter colours than mine and the Sign on his forehead pulses. His dark hair reaches below his huge shoulders and the breeze makes it look wilder than when I saw him on the Levianha. His beard doesn't mask the powerful jaws almost trembling with anger. His lips are pulled tightly in a severe hard line. One of his huge hands clasps his sword and the other one is in a tight fist by his huge thighs, covered by soft black short hair. Or fur, as Natalia calls it. I know it's like a mixture of both, from the only time I touched him. When he grabbed me in my room… his room, and I tried to push away at his chest. It was like trying to push at a mountain. His pectoral muscles seem even bigger now as they move angrily under the covering of the soft dark hair on his chest. He leaves the ramp, heading straight for me. Painfully slowly. Is he trying to restrain himself or is he toying with me? The whole planet seems to rumble, as an even more massive creature comes from the inside of the ship behind him. I only have a second to register a white kilt and a mass of muscles, scars and fur. A lot of it or… The next thing I hear is Natalia's piercing scream as she pulls her hand out of mine.

"Sia, run! He brought a Monster! Run!"

Before I can grab her, she dashes into the woods on my left at a remarkable speed for her small frame. My heart is frozen with fear as a horrible growl fills the air and the creature runs after her into the woods.

"Tannon? No!" screams the King after the creature, but it is already deep into the forest, as I can tell by the fading growling. I can't stop myself from shaking. The adrenaline is making me dizzy. I can see this huge thing coming towards me but I am more scared for Natalia's life than for mine. I can't even imagine what she must be going through. Sweet, fragile Natalia, who is terrified of monsters, is being chased by one. In the middle of an alien forest.

"Tell your creature to get away from her. She is scared of monsters," I tell him, loud enough for him to hear, but as calmly and dignified as I can. I don't want him to know I am scared. But then I remember they can smell fear. I also remember my cold self drives him even crazier.

My words make him stop in his tracks. I can feel a sharp pang of pain and I know it's his pain, not mine. I have offended him. Badly.

"Creature? A monster?" he shouts, making the large blue leaves shudder around us. He stalks menacingly towards me, but I refuse to run. Never again.

"I keep forgetting we are slavers to you." His words drip venom.

My forehead feels on fire, my tattoos, whatever they are, ignite with a swirl of colour. I am scared, really scared. I want to run. I have to run!

"Do not dare run from me again, Human!" he shouts, increasing his pace towards me.

"You just make sure that... thing doesn't hurt Natalia."

And I know I've angered him even more.

"That thing is Tarrassia's bravest hero and the most honourable male I know. The red female is safe. You? Not so much!"

In lack of anything better to do or say, I turn my back on him.

"Do not run from me! It won't end well for you!"

Without turning, or stopping, I tell him over my shoulder, with my chin held high and my shoulders straight as a board, "I am not running away from you. I am walking away from you."

I step behind the tree line and walking is much easier now. The soil is still blue and covered in a soft moss-like blanket, but no soft wobbly sand anymore. There's no sound from behind me so I keep on walking. An angry growl fills the air and the forest around me is shaking. For a moment I think of running, but I know that will enrage him even more, so I stop suddenly. An even worse idea as an over eight-foot-tall mountain of muscle and sheer force collides with me. All air leaves my body, as two steel arms wrap forcefully around me from behind, in an attempt to stop us both from falling. Dark spots dance in my vision and the forest spins around me. The cracking noise followed by the sharp pain tells me he broke something. My rib cage is on fire and breathing is like torture. He's consumed with anger, his body has increased in size and his claws dig painfully into my waist as he hoists me up and throws me over his hard shoulder like a madman. I hear another crack inside my rib cage and I think I am about to lose consciousness as he strolls with heavy steps through the forest, back to the clearing. My head lolls down his back and I am so high up from the forest floor it's giving me vertigo. Every step he takes is like a knife being twisted in my rib cage. He suddenly stops and there's a huge roar of anger shaking his body and mine. Then blinding pain as he drops me to the ground. My eyes fill with tears and my body shakes with shock. I can vaguely determine the source of his anger. In the middle of the clearing, the ship is gone. The moving sand where it used to be is the only reminder that a huge spaceship used to be there. Another roar of anger shakes the forest.

"You!" He turns with a maddened look towards me, but then he stops. He looks down his torso and his hand touches there, trying to understand where the pain is coming from. He looks at me with pained eyes, as he understands I am the one who's hurt. He runs to me and all anger is gone from his eyes. They are pure gold as he reaches me and kneels by my side. He takes me in his arms and I flinch, waiting for the sharp pain. But it doesn't come. He holds me incredibly gently and he hardly even breathes as he scans my face for answers.

"I've hurt you," he says, and there's so much pain in his voice. I stupidly find myself wanting to reassure him I'm okay. But I know I am not. We have just lost his warship. Thanks to me, we are all four stranded on some forgotten planet and I am in desperate need of a doctor or healer, whatever they call them here. Every breath brings pain and unwanted tears fall down my face. He lowers me gently against the wide trunk of the closest tree. It feels like silk against my back. White silk. He supports my shoulders with one arm as he kneels next to me. The fingers of his other hand touch a wet patch on my cheek. Yes, right. They are too mighty to know tears. He looks around as if scanning for dangers. He tries to contain his powerful voice. I wonder if it's to reassure me or not to attract predators.

"It will be dark soon, my Phaea. We have to find shelter. I don't know what lurks on this cursed planet. But first, you need to heal." This is all too much for me. The emotional rollercoaster of the last days is taking its toll. I don't do emotions. Or maybe it's the pain. Nothing makes sense. He leans me gently against the tree, pulls a curved copper dagger out from the belt of his kilt and then simply cuts himself on his forearm. A wide gash, as long as my thumb, leaks a shiny dark liquid the colour of rust. And as he brings his arm to my mouth, I understand he wants me to drink it. Yes, definitely nothing makes sense. I flinch, trying to get away from his arm and it only makes me cry in pain.

"You have to drink, my Phaea," he tells me with a soft voice, which sounds so unexpected coming from someone so big. "Tarrassian blood has healing powers. It can knit the bones of your supporting cage." The reminder of what caused those to break in the first place gives him a pained look. "Please, my beautiful Phaea, drink it."

I almost feel bad watching his shimmery blood spill down his arm for no reason. But... I just can't...

"I can't just suck your blood, Humans don't drink blood, you know?"

The anger is back. And his ridiculous pride.

"Tarrassians don't feed on blood either." His voice has changed like a hundred degrees and it's full of menace. "We have no need for anyone's blood. Unless it's to spill it. Our blood is precious. But since the blood of your kind is useless and can't heal you, you will drink mine now. Or I will make you. Drink, Sia!"

He shoves his big hairy forearm in my face. A boiling hot drop of it falls down the low-cut dress, in between my half-exposed breasts, disappearing into the fabric of my dress. His eyes travel down my chest, following the droplet of blood. The red dots in the copper of his eyes disappear, replaced by beautiful golden specks.

"Drink!"

And I do, because I don't have a choice. I never do. I try to pretend I am sucking on a slice of orange, as I don't know how else to do this. A huge amount fills my mouth and I almost choke. He pushes my head down on his forearm, holding the back of my head in a grip of steel. I try to set a pace and involuntarily I look up into his eyes. His blood tastes a bit like iron, just a lot sweeter. I remember their ridiculously sweet fruit. No wonder. He watches my lips on his skin and his eyes turn into pools of gold. I can't take my eyes off his. They feel like magnets, holding mine prisoners. How can sucking the blood out of the forearm of a scary being, on some alien planet, make me feel aroused? It feels so intimate and eerily sexual. It has the same crazy effect on him.

The hardness behind his kilt pushes at my thigh. And now it's pulsing, sending my treacherous body into a frenzy of emotions. I try to squeeze my legs together, but I know it's stupid. If he can smell my fear, he can most likely smell my body fluids pooling in between my legs. The thing Tarrassians call panties are useless for that. The fabric of the underwear we were offered reminds me of cheesecloth. Sheer on top of that… Yes, he can definitely smell that. To his credit, he seems a lot more in control than I am right now.

"That's enough, my Phaea."

He removes his arm from my lips and brushes a thick finger over them. Calloused yet soft. And no claws. So, they must retractable, I realise. I also realise there is a pattern I can use to pinpoint his moods. He calls me Human when he wants to kill me, female when he's furious, Sia when he's slightly fed up with me and Phaea when it's all good and stuff happens behind his kilt. I wander what Phaea means.

"Now we need to find shelter. And we need to get away from the trap."

I have no idea what he's talking about, but who cares. He is not giving me choices, just instructions.

"I will carry you and that may hurt for a while longer. But we can't stay here, yes?" His large hand strokes my hair and I feel sleepy. "Yes, my Phaea, sleep. Tarrassian blood can heal quicker when all the senses are asleep."

He picks me up gently and pauses while watching his own arms on my body. One is underneath my knees and the silly dress slits have my entire legs on display, all the way to my hips. His other arm is coiled around my back, long fingers reaching under the underside of my boob, pushing it up. I realise he's not really paying attention to all that. He's just worried about hurting me. He doesn't know how to contain all his force when touching me. I give him a small smile and he stops breathing for a second. His eyes glow and the Sign on his forehead ignites a beautiful shade of purple. Maybe I should smile more often... He picks up the pace and even though he's not running, his long legs cover the distance fast. We both stop breathing or thinking for a second when a horrible sound pierces the air. Then another, then a different one... then silence again.

"What was that?"

It came from the direction where Natalia ran and a feeling of dread fills me. Is that a... No, it cannot be. Natalia won't have a single chance at survival.

"I do not know the name of that beast. Do not worry, my Phaea, Tannon can fight anything. The red female will be well looked after."

I hold one arm around his neck, trying to hold on, but his shoulder is so large and it's a stretch for my painful ribs.

He doesn't seem to miss much. He answers before I ask and he seems to know what I feel or think.

"Keep your arm on your lap, my beautiful Phaea. You don't need to hold on. I would never drop you."

I try to refrain from mentioning he's got a history of doing just that to me, but I know he won't drop me now. My neck hurts from all the physical and emotional stress. Eventually I give up and put my head on his oversized pectoral. I flinch as the beating heart behind his furred chest seems to increase its beating dramatically. I can... I can hear it all around us.

"Is it normal for your heart to beat this loudly?"

"I don't really know, my Phaea. I am the only Tarrassian with two beating hearts. There is no one to ask what's normal."

"You have two hearts?"

"All Tarrassians do, but their left heart is silenced. Only the right one works. I, probably more than most, thought it was a myth. A fairy tale of the Elders."

"And your left heart beats because you are the King?"

He takes his eyes from the darkening forest for a moment to rest them on my face. His look is… adoring?

"No, my heart beats because of you. Only the other half of our Sign can awaken our left heart. My heart only beats because of you, Phaea."

I close my eyes and place my head on his heart. It beats for me. The thought is so overwhelming. The magnitude of all this is too much for… for a Human.

"I would love to reach the mountains," he says. "I can protect you better in the mountains. But you need to rest and it's not safe to travel in the dark. I don't know what awakens here in the dark. We stay here for the night."

He lays me down, gently, on the soft moss. Is getting dark, really, really dark. There's a soft glow coming from the strange white trunks. He points up one of them.

"You will stay here while I knit some vines and make a floating shelter. It's not safe to sleep on the ground."

I look around, panicking a bit. I don't like the dark. I have no control of what's lurking in the dark. There could be snakes on the ground, spiders, or…

"My Phaea, you are safe. I am right up this tree. I'll have my eyes on you at all times."

"But it's almost dark."

"Tarrassians can see in the dark."

"Really? But what if something comes before you can get down?"

"I can smell predators from afar. You are safe." And with that he's gone, somewhere up the silky white trunk, deep in the canopy of blue leaves. My senses are on edge, overpowering even the pain in my rib cage. There is definitely less pain. Perhaps his blood has started doing its magic. I hate feeling this powerless, and I should hate letting him have all the control. But I don't. It feels so good to let someone else be responsible. Someone to look after me. I hear some faint noises coming from above. Leaves ruffling and a branch being bent. He curses his Astrals a few times, and then the planet. Isn't it taboo to curse their Astrals or something? I smile to myself in the dark. This new Sia has turned out to be very smiley. He lowers himself down with a thud. How can someone so big move so fast?

"Ready, my beautiful? Before we go up, I need to release myself, but you go first. Once we're up, I'd rather we stay there."

"What? You need to what?"

He looks at me like I am alien. Well, I guess I am.

"Humans don't...?"

I suddenly feel really stupid as I understand what he means. And now that I remember, I am desperate to go.

"Where do I go?"

I look around and everything looks too terrifying. Anything could be living in that moss.

"You don't go anywhere, Sia, I will turn my back!" Yes, definitely calls me Sia when he's fed up with me.

"Would there be any crawling things, do you think?"

He lets out an exasperated sigh.

"I am here, am I not? Now get it done, unless you want me to help with it." His insufferable grin is all I need to toughen up. As he turns, I try to get it done as quickly as I can, hoping nothing crawls up my vagina in the process. I can tell he's busy doing the same thing nearby, and I feel so relieved when I am done and close to him again. I can't see much around anymore. It's pitch black. The trees cover any moon or stars, if there are any. He takes me in his arms then decides he definitely can't climb up the tree that way.

"I need a free hand to push us up. It's not a good way to carry someone who's hurt. It will give you pain but I will be quick."

I nod silently, bracing myself for the pain. He grabs me with one arm and places me on his hip, on the opposite side of his sword. It looks no different to the way a Human would carry a heavy toddler on their hip, to spread their weight evenly. As we go up, I hold on as much as I can, wrapping my legs around his waist. Not an easy task even for my famously long legs. On Earth anyway. The proximity of his body makes my stomach flutter like mad. What is wrong with me? We don't go as high as I thought before we stop. Despite the dark, I can see the vines, as they are stark white. He has plaited them together in a pattern that looks like the two braids in his hair. I realise what he calls a floating shelter is actually a hammock. It's as long and as wide as his body, which is pretty big, and I am impressed with his skill. Considering he's the King and all that. He has spread loads of blue leaves on top, to make it softer. He manoeuvres both our bodies around the silky branches. "How can you get a grip on these branches? They are so slippery…" I ask out loud without even noticing.

"I can make the tips of my fingers stick to surfaces, if needed."

I almost want to clap, like Natalia does, when something excites her.

"You mean, like Spider-Man?" I find myself ask stupidly.

"No, like myself and like every other Tarrassian. And I will not have you talk or think about other males. Who is this Spider-Man to you?"

I so desperately want to laugh. Let all the worries of the last days go away with a hysterical laugh. Laughing with broken ribs will no doubt end up in crying. So, I refrain from both.

"He's just someone I have heard of. I never met him in person."

"Good," he says with a stern voice and pulls me on top of him. All of a sudden, I realise what's happening. He wants me to sleep on top of him? I can't… I can't be so close to him. I realise he has made it only wide enough for his body. My reasoning brain also tells me he most likely did it to protect me. I could easily roll off in my sleep. And I definitely don't want that. As the darkness has taken over the forest, thousands of creatures seem to have come to life. The noise is so intense. It feels like everything is nocturnal on this planet. Birds maybe? Definitely birds and some sharp screeching noises. And occasionally the horrible sound I heard earlier. I know what it sounds like, but I refuse to put it into words. It's just too scary. Luckily it sounds really far away. More worried about the roars. Guttural roars. And those are not that far. And in the middle of all that noise, there is one my brain is struggling to identify. It sounds like distant whispers. I know I've heard them before. I give up as I am too tired to think or to care. He is very quiet. He pulls me up his body like one would a blanket. He pushes his sword out of the way but doesn't remove it. He does remove something looking like a tube. Some sort of a gun maybe? And the curved dagger he used earlier on himself. He lays them nearby in a makeshift nest of leaves and branches. They are so technologically advanced. Why the swords? And the kilt? No, I definitely can't think about the kilt now. He lays me down on his chest, my head resting on his strong biceps. They feel like pillows under my cheek. The muscle underneath is hard, but his skin is soft and covered in all that soft dark hair. Like silk stretched over steel. His whole body is covered in the fur, more or less. Definitely more on his chest, going down his taut abdomen in a very enticing pattern. Not thinking about that now. It tickles my skin in a soothing way and I can't help nuzzling at it. It smells so nice. He smells nice. Like freshly cut grass, like rain in the mountains and like the pine trees from back home. How can he smell so familiar? He's an alien… As he holds me loosely enough not to hurt but tight enough to make me feel safe, I realise he feels just like a man, not an alien. A really, really big man, but still. Not that I have ever been held by a man anyway. My otherwise long body feels tiny on top of his. His legs are slightly parted and my own are nestled in between his muscular thighs. The white leather of his kilt feels soft and smooth against my very bare belly. The dress is useless. I am still wearing it, but most of it is hanging off my body. I try to lie as still as possible. There's nothing soft under his kilt, that's for sure. He doesn't seem to want to act on it, so I have to trust him. There is something else I have to do. I could feel his pain when I offended his friend earlier. I still feel the bitterness of it. My voice sounds soft and a bit unsure. Is that my voice? What happened to my Ice Queen voice?

"I am sorry for calling your Warrior a monster."

His entire body goes very tense. He cares for that creature, whatever he is.

"Tannon is my cousin," he says unexpectedly.

That huge male is Tarrassian? Almost as if hearing my thoughts, he explains.

"He is a half-breed. His mother was my mother's sister."

I try to look up at him. I can't see his face, but his beautiful eyes glow in the dark.

"Stop moving, Sia!"

"It's okay," I reassure him. "My pain is getting better now."

He makes an exasperated sound as if I'm not very smart.

"That's not why. For the love of the Astrals, stop wriggling."

And indeed, I do feel stupid. I don't even breathe for a few seconds and I can feel his smile, even though I can't see it. I realise I never have. But then I remember something even more important.

"I don't know your name."

"Tarsmiamin of House Tarrassia," he says with pride in his voice. "You will call me Tars. Tannon is the only other member left of the Royal House. Even though he won't use any titles. Tarrassians just call him the Great Warrior." There is bitterness in his voice. And a restrained anger.

"I thought there were no half-breeds on Tarrassia."

"Tannon is the only one. His father was a slave we freed from the fighting pits. We couldn't return him to his home as no one knew of his species."

His body is really tense under mine, and the hold of his arm on my body is getting tighter.

"Some say the male was a huge beast only half-sentient and unable to talk. He forced himself on the beautiful Lady Oria."

Now it's my turn to tense, as his story is just horrible. Stories like this are sadly a common factor on every planet. Even on one as superior and well guarded as Tarrassia.

"The former slave was killed by the guards. Lady Oria took her own life, after she gave birth to Tannon."

I wish I hadn't asked. I don't really plan it, but my hand goes up to his face and I let it rest on his cheek. His beard is a lot softer than I thought it would be. My fingers have a mind of their own and they brush his lips. They are soft and hard at the same time, as if that is possible. My hand moves up towards the sign on his forehead. It glows softly in the dark. I know mine is mirroring the same glow as it throws light patterns on his chest. He grabs my hand and removes it gently from his face.

"I am fighting my instinct with every possible restraint, my Phaea. And I am not a male known for having much self-restraint or patience. No more touching my face and no more moving on my cock. Unless you want me to act on it. Yes?"

"Yes," I agree quickly and remove my hand. I still have one resting on his chest as I don't really know what else to do with it, but I am not moving it.

"I will hunt for you tomorrow and I will find you water, now you have to sleep. My blood can only heal you when you are asleep."

One of his hands moves up in my hair. The touch is incredibly soft. His fingers move through my straight white locks with reverence.

"Sleep, my beautiful Phaea."

And as his fingers gently massage my scalp, I do fall asleep, knowing it will be the deepest and safest sleep I have had since I was a child.

7

TARS

My little Queen is still lost in her peaceful sleep. And despite the raging need to mate her, I am also at peace. For the first time in as long as I can remember. I used to believe killing everything I could get my claws into would bring me peace. That was just calming my rage. For a while. So was fucking whatever alien or Tarrassian female walked my way. Just more craziness to the reputation of the Mad King. If they don't call me that yet it is only because they are all too terrified of my temper. Or because of my father. They still love and respect the Wise King. No other king was ever called wise in our history. Holding my beautiful Phaea and keeping her safe while she sleeps, that is real peace. Especially after the torment of the last spans. I couldn't eat or sleep. I paced up and down the space of Tannon's warship like a wild beast, until he had to force me to stop. And when he tried to take my fire water from me, that's when I hit him. We have sparred together since we were cubs, but I have never hit him out of anger. And then the agony of knowing she risked herself, just to get away from me. The pain of the cursed distance she put between us. As I feel the anger at her actions making my body expand, I try to calm myself down. Instead of anger and fear of losing her, I try to focus on this unknown happiness that makes my new heart flutter like a donian bird. Happiness and a new maddening, cursed kind of torture. Between the feel of her curves laid like an offering on top of my body and my raging instinct to claim my mate, I am left wondering for how long I can stop my cock from bursting all over her sleeping form. I am not sure she will appreciate that. A bit feisty, my new Queen. And from what I have seen so far, it must be a Human trait. So strange for such weak creatures to be that feisty. The sun is up on this cursed planet. A very strange sun. It has an off feel to it. It's increasingly getting warmer, but there's a chilling breeze fighting the warmth. Like two different rotations of nature fighting each other. But then again, the sooner I take her off this forgotten place, the better. If she only knew what kind of danger, she put herself in. And the other female. I try not to worry about Tannon. He can easily fight whatever beast made that deadly sound, the last span. But why can't I connect with him? His mind is clouded and I can't find it. I know him well enough to understand he will take his female towards the safety of the mountains. My people think Tannon is a wild beast, but he's smarter than all of them. He will go the same place I am heading. He understands the Noorranni's trap can't work in the mountains. That's the only place the rescue team can beam us from. For some reason, I can't contact them either. It's the magnetic shield of the slavers, no doubt. Once I mate my Queen, my powers will grow. Nothing will stop me then. And nothing will stop Tannon either. I heard what he said when he dashed after his female. I don't understand what is happening. We have three out of the four Humans we rescued. And all three are blessed by the Astrals. My Queen might be the only one marked by the Sign, but I have seen and heard my brothers. The bond can't be denied, no matter how much Larrs wants to. I stop breathing for a nanoclip as she stretches in her sleep, on top of my body. All the reasons why I shouldn't take her right here and now have left my brain. Probably because it feels like all the blood in my body has travelled to my cock. Nothing else is functioning except that. Her face is as soft as a flower on my chest and her beautiful white hair is spread over both of us. One of her little hands is open, palm down on my chest, over the heart that only beats for her. The other hand has travelled up and is resting on my cheek. She likes touching my face. Small fingers hold onto the braids in my facial fur. After she stretched, she pushed one of her knees up and now it's resting on my abdomen. The cursed motion took my Kannicloth up with it. Now half of my pulsing cock is trapped under the soft skin of her lower leg. I would rather fight an entire army or all the beasts of Neflay than this. I am not an honourable male like Tannon, nor have I the control of Larrs. I may be the King, but I am not a good male. I take my hands off her back and my claws dig at my palms. I can't touch her now. I won't be able to stop. I did stop myself in the long hours of the dark span, because I had plenty of things to kill. As she slept, one too many beasts gathered under our tree. They probably wanted a bite of her sweet body. She doesn't know how to camouflage her sweet scent. I am the only one allowed to taste her blood. So, I went down the tree a few times during the dark span. She slept through it all, my Phaea. She needed to heal. What do I kill now? There's nothing to kill on this planet during the light span. She moves again and I curse out loud. She opens her strange eyes suddenly and looks up at my face. Her little hand on my chest has grabbed at the short fur covering my skin. Big sleepy grey eyes. How could I ever have thought they were lifeless? They are as deep as the bottomless waters of Tarrassia. Just as still and full of mystery. I vow then and there, she will give all of herself to me. There will be no mysteries hidden from me. She pushes up a bit, still sleepy and not sure of her surroundings yet. As she does, the soft fabric of her dress pushes down and the skin of her now bare breasts rests on my chest. Two perfect globes of softness and two hard peaks scrape at my chest. As she realises what has happened, she desperately tries to pull her dress up, while wriggling on top of me. My cock decides enough is enough. I scramble like the madman that I am and grab her, forgetting her fragility for a nanoclip. My sword falls to the ground, so does my fire blaster and everything else. I reach the ground faster than ever, simply lay her shocked little form on the blue moss and disappear behind the trees to release this maddening desire. I want her fully awake and willing when I cover her in my seed for the first time. It doesn't take me long to return to her still shocked form, hugging herself in a defensive gesture that tugs at my hearts.

"I cannot help the mating rage, my Phaea. I don't want you to be scared. I will not act on it. Not yet. And when I do, I will make you ask for it first."

"You will make me what?"

She raises her chin defiantly and just like that my cock is hard again.

"Never mind that," she adds. "And you don't have to apologise for… you know, I understand how biology works. Apparently, males struggle with mornings on every planet."

I am not entirely sure what she means by that.

"I wasn't apologising. I'm the King. I don't have to apologise. I was just explaining the facts, my Phaea."

She closes her eyes and takes a deep breath.

"Yes, of course. I keep forgetting. You're the mighty King. Now, care to explain this?"

I follow her terrified look around us. The ground surrounding us is covered in blood of different colours, and body parts. Pride fills my chest. Yes, I did all that to keep my mate safe.

"You don't have to be scared, my Phaea. They are all dead. I made sure nothing came near you. And you have fresh meat to sustain yourself."

I don't like the way she looks around and I don't like the way she looks at me. Is this how Humans show gratitude? How strange.

She hugs herself and looks really worried at the carnage around us.

"Were these... creatures going to climb the tree?" She points at the body parts but she tries not to look.

"I wasn't going to find out," I tell her, feeling rage scrape at my War Beast. She takes a deep breath, trying to compose herself. But all I can see is the soft globes of her chest inflating and pushing up into the deep opening of her dress. I remember the feel of them on my bare chest. She follows my hungry look and covers herself in a defensive hug. It makes me want to kill those wild beasts again. In two steps I close the gap between us and she nearly falls backwards as she tries to retreat. I grab her wrist to stop her from falling, but despite my rage I make sure not to hurt her.

"You do not cover yourself from me, female! Not ever! No running and no covering from your mate. That will enrage me more than you know."

"More than this?" She uses her free hand to point at the dead beasts on the floor.

"I killed them to keep you safe. Don't Humans kill to keep their mates safe?" The thought of her around Human males makes my shoulders and biceps start to grow. She watches me with a wary look and I try to control the urge of growing my muscles. However, I can't control the lost cause of my growing cock, which is poking at her waist. I don't want to scare her, but she's being very unfair and I refuse to be reasonable. Not sure I know how to be. I can see the moment when she regains control of her emotions and fears. She hardens her eyes and raises her chin. Her voice is cold and composed. I so desperately want to tell her it's useless. I am going to fuck both cold and composure out of her defiant little body.

"No, Humans don't go on a killing rampage to protect their mates."

"Of course not," I say angrily, looking down at her pretty face. "They would rather let precious females be taken away from their planet."

"I don't want to argue, Tars."

She says my name and all anger is gone. I go from feeling the War Beast to feeling as soft and vulnerable as a cub. I press my lips on the inside of her wrists and have a look to make sure I didn't hurt her there. I take a step back, as I can't be too close to her. My forehead Sign pulses and my arms glow. She said my name.

"I am not stupid, Tars, nor unreasonable. I appreciate you had to keep me safe while I was sleeping. I am very grateful for that. It's just…" Once again, she looks around with a horrified look.

"I am a bit worried about your need to overkill things that were just looking for food or being curious. You can't even tell which body part belonged to which animal. You are covered in dry blood, and now I am since I slept in… in your arms. That's all."

She looks at me with a snooty look that makes me want to do all sorts of things to her.

"I didn't overkill anything. I killed each beast once. I don't know what you mean."

"Never mind. I just wanted you to know I don't like unnecessary violence and I find your lack of control quite worrisome."

"Next time I will ask them nicely which body parts they still want to keep, so my Queen won't get offended. Yes, Sia?"

She takes another deep breath but doesn't answer. Good!

"Now we eat."

I grab my Sword and my fire blaster and attach them to my Kannicloth. How did I not notice the blood of the beasts? It's all over me, dried out in most of the fur covering my chest. I can now smell it in my facial fur and it's all over her dress and the pale skin of her arms and chest. A male like Larrs would have never covered his mate in blood like that. Tarrassian females don't like the sight of blood. Cursed blasters of fire! No wonder she's disappointed with me. A painful memory of my father's words makes my hearts bleed. I ignore it and I grab my very reluctant Queen in my arms. She stiffens her body like a tree.

"Would you rather step over the body parts?"

She doesn't answer and I ignore that too. I take her a few steps further and lay her down on a clean patch of moss. The smallest of the beasts I killed for her should be ready to eat by now. I used my claws to dig a nice fire hole and the beast has been there for many nano rotations. I hope it's to her liking. I don't recognise anything on this planet. I don't know if anything other than meat is safe to eat.

"We have a long journey ahead of us this span, my Phaea. You need to eat. I skinned one of the beasts and prepared it for you. I will find water as we journey and to… wash the blood off. I didn't want to leave you alone and go far in the dark."

She gives another worried look at the beasts behind us.

"I really appreciate what you do, trying to keep me safe, and I don't want to sound difficult or offend your people. I really don't think I can eat raw meat. Maybe if I became really hungry."

What is she even talking about? My little Human is rather strange.

"Why would I make you eat raw meat, my Phaea? Unless you prefer it raw, of course, which it doesn't sound like you do."

I point at the hole in the ground. I use my foot to remove the thick layers of leaves, branches and soil. Steam rises from the hole and a very welcome smell with it.

"The beast has been roasting in there for a good while. I don't know if it's soft enough for your little teeth, but it's definitely not raw. I don't eat raw meat either, Sia."

"But we were given raw meat on the first ship, the Blood Fleet. On the Levianha we all asked for nuts and fruit instead."

A smile tugs at my lips.

"The High Commander is a bit of a barbarian, my Phaea. Blood Fleet Warriors don't bother with things like cooking their meat. In the very old rotations, all Tarrassian Warriors used to eat their defeated enemies."

Her eyes grow bigger and I rush to tell her we don't do that anymore. Not entirely sure about Zaan, but she doesn't need to know that. She sits with grace on the forest floor. She gently tries to arrange her torn dress around her long, pale legs, as if it was a royal cloak. Her grace and poise remind me of my mother, the Queen. She was just as perfect as my father. My Phaea acts like that. She was born to be a queen. A treacherous thought reminds me I am anything but born to be a king.

"Thank you for looking after me last night, keeping me safe, and for this," she says, pointing at the food. I offer her a chunk of steaming meat on a blue leaf.

"I will protect you and treasure you for the rest of my spans, Phaea."

Our eyes meet and our Signs ignite with swirls of purple. She lowers her eyes quickly and sniffs at the meat. She tries it suspiciously and then there's a beautiful smile on her lips. She takes another bite.

"This is the best meat I have ever had! It's so soft and a bit sweet. What is it?"

"I don't really know, my beautiful. We have very different-looking beasts on Tarrassia. However, the taste is very similar to our meat. I am happy you find it to your liking. I will make sure you have plenty when we get home."

We eat in silence, disturbed only by the soft breeze in the air.

"What happens now? Is there a way off this planet?"

"We travel for the mountains today. I could reach it in two spans, but maybe four is more like it."

"Because I will slow you down."

"You are only small, my beautiful. It doesn't matter, we will get there soon enough."

She looks a bit worried, despite her perfectly still presence. She can't hide her feelings from me. Not from me.

"Why the mountains?" she asks.

"There won't be any traps, like the sinking sand, to start with."

"That was a trap?"

"There must be many clearings safe to land, but only that one was uncovered by the magnetic shield. For a reason. It was a trap. The rest of this planet is covered by the same shield. For the same reason I can't connect with my people. The signal is blocked."

She looks at my bare hand with a question in her eyes.

"You have a device to connect with your people?"

"Our people, my Queen. And yes, I do. Not a device. My mind can connect with theirs."

Her eyes grow bigger with wonder.

"You have telepathic powers?"

"What is tele…? My device is not translating the word, my Phaea."

"It's when people can talk with each other in their mind, mainly."

"We simply call it a Tarrassian trait."

"Of course, you do," she says with a sigh. "And you think it will be easier in the mountains?"

"Yes, I do. The mountains give us our powers. Tarrassians can connect with the energy in the rocks. Also, it would be easier for one of our warships to beam us up from there. I am sure Tannon will meet us there."

"Can you connect with him? You are both inside the shield so that should work," says my clever Queen.

"It should, but it doesn't. I can't reach Tannon's mind. It's clouded."

She looks worried and everything inside me screams at me to go to her. Hold her close until her worries go away.

"He will protect the little red female with his life."

"Maybe that's exactly what I am worried about," she says, and I have the same fear, despite the strength of my race and Tannon's in particular.

"Do Tarrassians live forever?"

"No, my Phaea. And we may be hard to kill, but nevertheless we can be killed. Many of my Warriors have left us in battle. But we do have some of the longest spans in the universe. A few hundred orbit rotations."

A shadow passes in her still eyes.

"I will die long before you."

"No, my Phaea, you now share my blood and my Sign. It will make you stronger and it will slow the ageing process. And everyone living on Tarrassia will eventually become as powerful as we are. Our water can increase the life span, our air can heal and the energy of our mountains can slow the ageing."

"Is there anything your people can't do?"

"We can't have cubs anymore," I say, remembering the quiet towns and villages of Tarrassia.

"I am sorry, Tars," says my sweet Phaea. My name on her lips is a gift I am not sure I am worthy of.

"The time for sorrow has passed. I have you now and I know you will fill my Palace with my cubs."

"Do you, now?"

"Yes, I do. And the other Human females will do the same for my people."

Defiance is coming off my little Queen like the waves of the High Waters.

"Are you going to invade my planet?"

"Your tiny planet has already been invaded. You are here, are you not? How do you think you and the other females were taken? It's only a matter of time before they will take more and more. And now," I say, pointing at our Signs, "the ones who took you know you are precious to us. They will try to use you against us. I will not allow it. So, yes. I will take your planet. To protect it."

One would think she would be grateful, but of course that's not the case. Are all Humans this difficult, or is it just mine?

"You can't go around deciding who needs what and make their choices for them. If you invade my planet, you are no better than those slavers."

"Then I guess I am not."

I jump to my feet and she does the same. Astrals help me, if she dares to compare me to those slavers again...

"We walk now, female!"

She straightens her back and raises her little chin as she starts walking ahead of me, in the direction I pointed. Silly female, doesn't she know what her little act of defiance makes me want to do to her? As we walk through the strange forest of white trees, I try not to pay much attention to her curves, to the way the light reflects in her hair, the way she touches the back of her neck every time she peeks behind to make sure I am still there. Most of all, I try not to look at those legs. I want them wrapped around my waist for the rest of my spans. Instead I use every enhancement of my senses to look for danger. I can feel none, and that's really, really frustrating. I find myself hoping for the dark span to come, so I can have something to kill. Night span… How am I going to survive another one with her in my arms? And this time there are no broken bones in her body stopping me.

"How are the bones of your cage?" I find myself asking out loud.

She looks at me briefly over her beautiful pale shoulder.

"There is no pain left, just a bruise."

"A what? Show me?" I grab her arm and turn her round to face me. "What's a bruise?"

"It's a dark patch on skin where it got damaged. It goes away as it heals. It's no big deal," she adds, noticing my eyes on the still visible claw marks on her arms. It feels like forever since I gave her those, but it only happened a few spans back.

"If you are in pain you will tell me, Sia."

"Yes, I promise."

We keep on walking and I have all my senses listening for water. I can feel her body losing water. How can Humans survive on their planet? It must be a very friendly place. No wonder they look like cubs. She's stubborn, my Queen. Not complaining, but I know she needs water and probably a rest soon enough.

"Who set the trap?"

I was wondering how long before she asked.

"The beings who own this planet."

She stops suddenly and I almost walk into her. Again.

"There are aliens living here?" she whispers.

"They are not here now. I can't smell them. They own this planet like they own many, but they live in space on their ships. They like moving around."

"Like nomads?"

"I don't know that word, my beautiful. But if these nomads like to move around without a permanent home, then yes."

"Would they mind if we came here without permission?"

"Yes, very much so."

"Maybe if I can explain this was all my fault. I was just trying to escape, not invade their planet."

For the love of Astrals, my female really knows how to push my anger out!

"You do not explain anything to anyone, Queen of Tarrassia! And you do not talk to other males without my permission. And you had better not keep reminding me of your escape! Now we walk in silence, after I release myself. And I suggest you do the same. You haven't since we left."

I don't wait for an answer and leave her there rooted to the forest floor. As I go around some of the trees to mark them, I know she's safe. I can't sense a single predator around. A bit strange but it helps us move faster. I find her in the same spot with her snooty expression in place.

"So, I guess Humans don't need to go that often."

"Not unless we drink a lot. Besides, you go often enough for both of us."

Is she mocking me somehow?

"Well, someone has to cover our scents, since your species seems incapable of doing it. Or anything else for that matter."

She wiggles her tiny nose in the cutest way.

"Is that what you're doing when you… Like a dog?"

"What is a dog, female?"

She seems surprised I don't know. The device didn't translate that word for me. I really dislike her snootiness. Can think of a few ways to remove that trait from her.

"It's a domestic animal on Earth. A pet."

"What is a pet?"

That look again. Maybe if I can show her how hard it makes me, she will stop doing it.

"A pet is a small domesticated creature that follows one around and is cuddly."

"No, we don't have such things," I tell her with a grin as a thought comes to my mind.

"However, it does sound nice. I think I'll keep you as my little pet, Phaea."

She looks at me with wide eyes and her plump lips release a small gasp. She turns her back to me and carries on walking in the wrong direction. Back straight and chin defiantly high. Astrals help me. Once I change her course for the right direction again, we walk in silence. She really didn't like being referred to as a pet. I still like the idea. Very much so.

"We walk this way now, my Phaea," I say, pointing in a different direction. "A small detour, as I can smell water."

As we get closer, I am quite pleased to see it's a running stream. It is forbidden for Tarrassians to bathe in still waters. There are unknown dangers hiding in the stillness. I remember my mate's eyes. Just as still and cold, but that won't stop me. Nothing will. I grab her arm and stop her as she is just about to drink from the running water.

"I drink first. I need to make sure it's safe."

She nods and watches me in silence with those haunting eyes. It will be very much like the Noorranni to poison the water, but there's a huge variety of flora on the banks of the spring and I can smell little scaly creatures in the water. It's cold and fresh and really bland. Unlike Tarrassian water. But it's safe so I allow her to drink. She kneels quickly on the only soft stretch of blue sand amongst the sharp rocks. She takes water into her small hands and replenishes her weakened body. I consider my surroundings, assessing possible dangers. Nothing seems alive or threatening. However, I don't take any chances and make sure I have my sword and blaster as close as possible. I remove my foot coverings and walk into the cold stream. I spot a high flat rock in the middle, perfect for placing my belongings on. By the time I reach for it, the water has removed the dried stains from my Kannicloth, so I take it off and place it on the rock. I turn to look for my Queen. She watches me with wary eyes. The water is deep enough in the middle to cover my private parts. It reaches just under my waist. But if she keeps looking at me like she's prey, my cock will soon reach above the water level. I try not to grin much when I gesture for her to join me. She's not moving.

"I thought you were offended by the blood stains on your garment, Sia. Wouldn't you like to get rid of them?"

She watches me with a cold stare and walks in, as far away from me as possible. She trips on her dress as it gets heavier with water. Before she can fall flat on her face, I reach for her faster than I have ever been and grab her in my arms. She tries to push at my chest. Ridiculous silly female. I hold her tightly to me and only release some of my grip when we are both back in the middle of the stream.

"You will not put yourself in danger anymore!" I more or less shout in her face, making her hair flutter. We are almost at eye level as I keep her up in my arms. She looks... scared. I try to release some more of my grip and she slowly slides down my painfully hard cock. That makes her eyes go wide.

"I did tell you, my Phaea, when you get my cock inside you it's because you've asked for it. Are you asking for it now?"

"Nnn... no," she says quickly.

"Then what are you worried about, my beautiful? Now remove your garment so you can bathe yourself properly."

"I am fine this way, the water is too cold."

I put her down on the rocky bottom and the water almost reaches her shoulders now. Her marks swirl with the same angry dark blue as mine.

"Remove it or I will. It needs to dry before we move. Now, Human!"

I can see her lithe body shivering and I hope it's because of the chill of the water. I desperately try to control my temper but trying never helped before. Her little fingers try to release the dress off her shoulders, but the wet fabric gives her shaky fingers a hard time. I remove it myself, pushing it under the water and down her legs. She's busy covering her breasts with her arms, so she can't stop me from removing her undergarment. I wish I could see through water to rest my eyes on her beautiful cunt. It can only be as perfect as she is. I lay her clothes on top of the warm stone. The leather of my Kannicloth will still be wet for a while, but the heat of the rock can definitely dry her soft clothes. She's not really doing anything, my Phaea. Just standing there, hugging herself with a very defiant look on her face.

"Would you like me to wash your head fur, my beautiful?"

"No, and it's hair, not fur." She's patronising me again but I don't let my rage out to play.

"Would you like to wash mine?" She is definitely considering that one for a moment.

"Tarrassian mates wash each other's fur... hair as a sign of affection. Well, females wash their males' hair, as they don't have any."

"Your women... females are hairless?"

"Yes, but the males can wash other body parts," I tell her with a grin.

"I think we both wash ourselves for now," she says and turns her back to me. Again! My nails extend and the water takes my blood with it as they dig into my palms.

"Human!"

She turns with a startled look.

"Do not ever turn your back on me when I talk to you!"

"Is that a Tarrassian custom?" she asks coldly.

"No, it's the King's custom!"

I start washing my head fur and then my facial fur, without taking my eyes off her for a moment.

"On Earth, it's customary not to stare at people," Her Snootiness says.

"Well, you're not on Earth and I am not people. Besides, I want to make sure nothing crawls up your female parts from the water." I remember her silly words from the other span. Does that actually happen on her planet? Those useless males can't even protect their females from that! Before I even finish my words, she rushes through the water like she's being chased by the beasts of Neflay and throws her little arms around my torso. She presses her body flush to mine, squeezing the life out of my raging cock. She doesn't even notice though. She's more concerned about the crawlers and she scans the water for them. We don't have many crawling things on Tarrassia, but I will make sure to purchase some from another planet. Maybe I can keep one in our sleeping quarters. I pick her up by her tiny waist and she quickly wraps her legs around my hips, desperate to take her feet off the dark bottom of the stream. Cursed blasters of fire! My cock is painfully trapped between our bodies and an unwelcome thought makes me curse again. My cock is pushed up her abdomen, reaching all the way up, in between her breasts and the size issue can't be ignored. I can't help but wonder how it is going to fit inside her body. On the Yellow Planets, I was only given compatible beings so I wouldn't damage the goods. Tarrassians are very big that way and most, if not all, the beings I was denied were bigger than my mate. I push the thought away.

The Sign cannot be wrong. She gave me my marks and awakened my silent heart. The Astrals themselves say she is my mate. She will be compatible, somehow. I hold her away from me with one arm, and remove my cock from between us, while I still have one. Then I hold her close to me. My cock is no different from one of her crawling creatures apparently. It snakes up her backside, pushing at her bottom cheeks. I watch with amusement as she takes notice of our rather interesting position. As I hold her up in my arms, we are at eye level and the Signs on our foreheads glow with need. She looks around for crawling things and seems torn between her options. She closes her eyes and her arms around my neck increase their hold. Obviously, my cock seems less scary than a crawler. I definitely need to purchase some. I press my forehead onto hers. She stiffens as our Signs start vibrating and throbbing. My cock does the same to her backside. I run one hand up and down her back. So beautiful, so soft. I can feel her small bones. So vulnerable and easy to break. How can something so delicate belong to me? She tries to remove her forehead from mine but I grab the back of her neck and keep her still.

"Our Signs need each other, just like our bodies do. I can smell your arousal, my Phaea. Why do you deny it, beautiful?"

"You can smell it?" Her voice is small and she won't open her eyes to look at me.

"I can, my beautiful mate." I rub my forehead gently on hers. She opens her grey eyes and there's wonder in their depth.

"That feels so... intense."

"That's how my people show their desire, their love and their respect for their mates. Tarrassians do it to treasure the memory of the Sign. It feels stronger for us, because we have the actual thing, not just a memory. Do your people touch foreheads, my Phaea?"

"No, we only kiss."

"What is a kiss?" I ask as I nuzzle gently at her neck. It's begging for my fangs' mark. Soon, she will have it.

Her little face moves away from mine to watch me with curiosity.

"Tarrassians don't kiss? But you pressed your lips on my hand and hair and... I thought..."

"Is that what your people call a kiss? Yes, we do that."

"Not exactly," she says, looking at my lips intensely. Whatever a kiss reminded her of it made her arousal intensify. My cock jerks in response, pushing in between her bottom cheeks. She inhales a deep breath and has a panicked look in her eyes.

"Show me what a kiss is."

"I don't think I..."

How very strange of my Queen to lose her words like that. She seems embarrassed and her cheeks have blossomed with a pretty shade of pink. Does it remind her of other males?

I grab her face in between the fingers of one hand, making sure I don't release my claws.

"Did you do this kissing thing with that Spider-Man?"

My question seems to have the opposite effect and instead of getting defensive she just laughs. The most beautiful sound. Like the trill of a bird.

"Oh, Tars, no I haven't kissed Spider-Man. Actually, I haven't kissed any man. I am not the best person to describe a kiss."

"Isn't that what Humans do before mating? We rub our foreheads to show interest." She lowers her eyes.

"I haven't mated anyone either."

I put a finger under her chin and lift her face up.

"Why is that? Are you not of age?"

"I am probably older than the other Humans you rescued. It's just... me. Men are scared of me and I don't really like being touched."

"I am not scared of you, my Phaea, and you will learn to want my touch. You will ask for it. Now show me what a kiss is."

Her eyes are so light they look like the silver in the Spark Mountains. She watches my lips, then my eyes, then again, my lips. The smell of her arousal is intoxicating and her breasts push at my chest with two sharp pebbles I would love to look at. "Show me the kiss!" She places her soft lips on mine and I don't even breathe for a nanoclip. Her lips are so soft and I get a desperate need to bite them. I don't and just let her do her thing. She touches my lips again, this time moving her lips gently on top of mine. Is she trying to make me open my mouth? I ignore the thought of all the appendages I have seen coming from alien mouths in battle and I open my lips for her. She pauses, a bit unsure. Her breath in my mouth feels like fire. And then her little tongue tentatively touches the inside of my mouth. She runs it over my teeth, then over my fangs and then touches my own tongue with hers. Now I am the one on fire. I grab the back of her neck again to steady her and I dip my tongue into her mouth. She tastes like nothing I have ever known before. It's intoxicating and overwhelming. My tongue does to her mouth what my cock wants to do to her cunt. She moans in my mouth and I move her body up and down the length of my painful cock. I will not be able to hold my seed any longer. I feel no better than an eager young Warrior before his first mating. She's nothing like the defiant, cold little Queen she presents to the world. The fire in her kiss makes my insides feel all shattered. Her tongue eagerly meets mine and she rubs her pussy on my length, without my help. Her little blunt nails dig at my back and her legs squeeze me harder. Our Signs are ignited and reflect a maddening display of purple, blue and white on the water surface. She moans again in my mouth and says my name like a prayer. And I am done for. My whole body shudders as my cock throws jet after jet of hot seed up her back. Luckily the water takes it away and I don't drench my mate in my seed. She shakes in my arms and I know she needs to find her own release. I don't stop kissing her as I lower one hand and touch her beautiful cunt. It's so small and covered in short fur. Despite being in water, I can feel her stickiness. I run a finger up and down her slit. Then deeper, then two fingers. As my fingers go up, they brush a little knob and she screams in my mouth. That's all I need. I find her little knob again and grab it in between my fingers. I rub it hard enough to make her squirm in my arms. I press a finger inside her. So small and tight. Sudden resistance meets my finger. She stills her kiss and I go back to rubbing that knob instead. She pushes into my fingers and I rub her harder, faster. I kiss her like I am feeding on her mouth. A hot liquid gushes over my fingers and I hold her tightly as her little body tremors and shakes. My stubborn cock is just as hard as before. It wants her, nothing else will do, so I ignore it. After what feels like an eternity, her body stops trembling and I put a finger under her chin. She resists and doesn't want to look at me.

"Sia?" A warning in my voice and she opens her eyes. She looks vulnerable and unsure.

"I take back everything bad I said about the Humans. Kissing is the best power, ever."

She smiles and all worries leave her eyes.

"You definitely made it feel like that," she says, moving a wet lock of head fur, or hair as she calls it, out of my face.

"Must you be better than anyone else at everything you do?"

"Of course, my Phaea, I am the King."

Her giggle is like a soft breeze on my ears. I look up at the green sky.

"Come, my Phaea, it's time to find shelter and find you some food. We won't go far from the stream, to have fresh water in the next span, when we rise."

I keep her body anchored to mine with one hand and I reach for our belongings with the other. I keep them all above the water as I make my way back to the sandy bank. She clings to me and rests her head on my shoulder. Possession and a choking need for her fill me. I put her legs down but she refuses to let go of my waist. I realise why and I can't help the grin. She doesn't want me to look at her naked body. After what we did… strange creature, my Phaea. I grab her gently by her arms and push her body away from mine. She's probably more shocked about my cock springing up in between us. She closes her eyes.

"I told you, my beautiful, you don't run from me, turn your back to me, or cover yourself in front of me. Your body belongs to me and I will not have you sheltering it from me. Now open your eyes. I want you to watch me when I look at your body."

Only when she does open her eyes do I lower my sight and take in her beauty. She is simply perfect. There are no imperfections on her pale skin. It almost glistens and water droplets add to the illusion. She's so different from our females. Even more different from other species. Yet my brain tells me this is what perfection should look like. And considering how much these females were going to sell for, maybe other species find them just as perfect. Rage fills me at the thought of others wanting what belongs to me. Unlike Tarrassian females, her body is all soft and round. Her breasts are high up on her chest and two pink pebbles on them poke even higher at the air. Her frame narrows dramatically into a waist so small it could fit in my hand. Her body flares into small but beautiful rounded hips. She has the same belly dip as my race. In between her legs, her sex is covered by a small thatch of soft white curls. Very different from Tarrassian females indeed. And then, there are those legs. I watched them like a man possessed by spirits as she walked in front of me all span. I have plans for those legs. The image of them wrapped around my waist while I take her hard has my cock as straight as my sword. Probably not the best time, as she is also inspecting my body. I don't want to frighten her. But then... Arousal. I can smell it again. She's as crazed by me as I am by her. She is my perfect mate. My beautiful Phaea. Her dress is still slightly damp, but the breeze will soon dry it. There is a strange chill in the breeze and then some hot air seems to fight the chill. She puts her dress on while I put my Kannicloth back in place. We watch each other in silence. Our eyes can't leave each other. The swirls on our arms and shoulders glow and our Signs pulse. She suddenly jolts and comes closer to me. Her eyes scan the trees.

"Tars, can you hear that? What is it?"

I try to heighten my hearing to make sure I listen as far as it can travel. But there's nothing other than expected.

"My hearing is much better than yours, my Phaea," I try to reassure her. "It's nothing but the breeze."

"It sounds like whispers and I am very sure I heard my name."

She seems scared, so I take her in my arms and press a kiss on her forehead.

"No harm will ever come to you. There are no whispers in the trees. Just the breeze. Come, my beautiful. Let's find you one of those creatures you like eating."

She smiles at me.

"That makes me sound like a freak."

"What is a friik?"

This time she laughs and it fills my heart with joy.

"A freak is someone who likes to eat creatures on an alien planet."

"That's us, then," I say, reaching for her hand, and she doesn't fight me. I thank again all the crawling creatures in the universe.

8

SIA

He takes my hand in his massive one and I simply follow him. We leave the stream's sandy shore behind us and head back into the woods. The increasingly chilling breeze is making me aware of my still damp dress. Despite my ridiculous nickname, and especially despite the cold inside me, I don't do very well with the cold weather. However, I am anything but cold now. I follow him like… well, I can't help but notice I follow him like an obedient little pet. Just like he wanted me to. I really can't think much for myself right now and my insides still feel like jelly. He's holding my hand with the same fingers he used to give me a mind-blowing, knee-weakening, soul-shattering orgasm. I may not be shaking like a leaf on the outside anymore, but I still am on the inside. My treacherous brain reminds me it was my first orgasm ever. My obsession with not letting anyone touch me included myself. Washing and applying moisturiser was a very clinical experience. Anything else was forbidden by my twisted mind. Whenever I felt aroused, I would simply squeeze my legs together and try to think of something else. Especially in the last few years. Feeling horny was only a mean reminder of my loneliness. There was no man around offering to help with that. No one to hold me, touch me, kiss me or look at me like… like he just did. Of course, I wanted it that way. Kept telling that to myself each night I would go to bed alone. My ridiculously expensive London flat was just as cold and impersonal as I was. A designer chose everything for me. He asked for my input and I said two words: show room. He asked no questions, as he probably didn't expect anything else from 'the Ice Queen'. He delivered just that. A luxurious, pristine and very impersonal environment. No pictures or personal items, other than a huge walk-in wardrobe. Most of my wardrobe wasn't even stuff I bought for myself. I got to keep almost all the designer outfits I had to parade in around the world. The only personal belonging I had in this world was taken from me, the day my sister died. As I watched her walk into the oncoming traffic and the world turned into a blur of screams, metal crushing and blood spattering, my little palm opened and dropped the only two items she gave me. The note for the police and our mother's brooch. The police found the note, but no one ever returned my brooch to me. I try not to remember I now have the same symbol of that brooch encrusted on my forehead. Too much to comprehend. I watch my hand completely engulfed in his massive one. A man is holding my hand. A man gave me an orgasm… he kissed me like he wanted to feed on my soul. A man held me in his arms all night. Not a man… can't help but remembering. An alien. An alien who is not scared of me. After years of training myself to become the person everyone is too scared to touch, I became that person. Even though I never admitted it to myself, I would have given anything for the cold inside me to go away. Even for a day, even for an hour. The cold kept me safe, when I made sure no one wanted to adopt me or to touch me. After years and years of not being touched, the cold had stopped being my best friend. I was hoping one of those women who watched me with envy or admiration would want to talk to me. I was hoping one of those men who watched me with lust would want to touch me. But it never happened. At times, I felt defeated by my own weapon. But then I remembered it was what I had to do to survive. I had to make sure no one wanted to adopt the strange child reminding them of a horror movie. I had to make sure no one wanted to touch the weird teenager. And I had to make sure no one wanted to touch the woman I had become. Until the act became me and I didn't know how to change back. Or maybe I had always been that cold and strange and frigid. Well… I am definitely none of that in his arms. In his arms I am just… me. How did I let that happen? Is it the Sign? I might not be Tarrassian, but it's still embedded in my skin. He says he's in my blood, in my mind… And I feel him there stronger and stronger with every minute that passes. Would I have felt anything for him without the Sign? I realise I hate the Sign more than anything else. It took my most important choice away from me. Love is the ultimate gift any being could ask for. And now I will never know if he wants me for me, or because of some stupid Sign from his ancestors. He has no more of a choice than I do. I bump into his hard body as he stops suddenly. He takes my face in his hands and pushes it up to look at him.

"What is it, my Phaea? I can feel your sadness. I would do anything to make it go away from you."

"Well, you can't!" I say before I can think any better. "You can't take my sadness away, any more than you can take your Sign away. I never asked for sadness or for your Sign. Who cares? I am to keep them both, anyway."

My timing obviously sucks, on top of everything else. I feel overwhelmed by… well, by feeling. I don't know how to do that. I don't know how to feel. It makes me act out of character. In less than a second, every single speck of gold in his eyes is replaced by sharp copper, flecked with red dots. It reminds me of metal being forged in fire. He takes his hands off me and points ahead.

"Walk, Human!"

I don't wait for him to tell me twice and I start walking in the direction he points. Chin high, back straight. Same as I always do. What's not the same is my desperate need to cry. I just want to curl into a ball and cry. Cry until he takes me back into his arms, where there is no pain. Where I don't have to think. Just feel. A ridiculous tear goes down my cheek and I wipe it quickly, hoping he can't smell it or hear it. I glance behind me and I freeze in my tracks. He's gone! Panic takes over, like never before. I feel like I can't breathe. He left me? I don't know what to do. As I consider my options, he reappears from behind a tree dragging some beast behind him. It looks like the offspring of a tiger and a hyena. It's got ridiculous stark white stripes against the light blue fur. Definitely not big on camouflage, for a night creature. Maybe that's why it was around just before sunset. It's covered in blue blood and its head is dangling at a strange angle. He drops the huge creature at my feet and I almost fall on my butt as I take a few steps back.

"See, Queen of Tarrassia? It's got all its limbs still attached. Only killed this one once. Is this good enough for you?" he asks with a menacing voice. He's trying to sound mocking no doubt, but he only manages to sound angry and mad. Can he ever sound like anything else? My stupid brain reminds me he sounds like dripping honey when he calls me Phaea, while his fingers rub my clit. I hate my brain.

I simply stare back at him, in the cursed, quiet, cold way I know he hates.

"We camp here," he says without giving me any more attention. Instead he starts working on the beast, with the same skill and confidence he does everything else. He uses his dagger to quickly remove the fur of the creature, in one fluid move. The skin underneath is bright blue and covered in blood. The smell is not exactly great either. How am I supposed to eat that? But as I ask myself that question, I know I will eat it even if it tastes like Spider-Man himself. I will not act like a spoilt child while he does everything, he can to provide for me and keep me safe.

"Can I help with anything?"

I am secretly hoping he will say no. I don't really want to touch all that mass of raw meat and blue blood. Instead, he says nothing, choosing to ignore me completely. Right... now I get the silent treatment. How very mature. Tarrassians must be proud of their toddler king. I gather all my dignity and sit on a fallen tree trunk nearby, trying not to look his way. Instead I listen for the whispers in the trees. They are gone now, but I know what I heard. There were definitely whispers and two very different voices said my name. As I process the magnitude of what this might mean, I wait for the fear to overwhelm me. But it doesn't come. I don't care what Tars says. The whispers are real and I am not afraid of them. I look at him briefly to see he's finished removing both the fur and the skin of the animal. He cuts parts of the body in smaller chunks of meat, and as I can't see anything gruesome left of its insides, I realise he must have disposed of it. He looks at me a bit troubled by something. Definitely not as angry as before, almost like he's considering his options. Once again, he ignores me instead and grabs a bunch of oversized blue leaves to use them as a cloth. He quickly wipes the blood off his hands and then, in one effortless move, disappears up a tree. Great! Just great! From the now familiar noises, I know he's building a hammock for the night. As I look around the increasingly darkening forest, I take advantage of the last friendly daylight to take care of business behind a tree. As always in this place, I'm grateful and relieved when I finish. Still no crawling creatures up my vagina. I guess that's a job for Tars' fingers nowadays. It takes him less time than previously to return to the forest floor. Again, without a single look my way, he uses his dagger to dig a little hole in the ground. He quickly makes a makeshift pile of dried branches and covers it with moss and dried leaves from the forest floor. And then… he puts his open palms above the branches. As I watch in complete astonishment, the leaves on top start to crunch up, as if affected by an invisible fire, then the branches underneath start to rumble as they catch fire. A beautiful green fire.

"Did you…? How did you do that?" Actually, don't tell me," I answer myself. "Tarrassians can make fire with their bare hands."

"Yes, it appears so," he tells me with an arrogant grin, still without looking at me. Instead of wondering about Tarrassians and their never-ending supply of superpowers, all I can think about is his fingers inside me. What if he put my clit on fire by mistake? My annoying brain reminds me, he kind of did.

He wraps the chunks of meat in leaves and places them in between the branches consumed by the green flames. He runs smaller strips of meat through twigs he sharpens with his dagger and places them on top of the flames. Finally, he looks at me, obviously still upset by my earlier words. Part of me regrets my outburst, simply because I don't do emotional outbursts. And maybe a bit because I can feel his pain. And what if he doesn't want me either? What if he's a victim of this Sign, just like I am?

He reaches out for me and points up the tree.

"Come, Sia, I will take you up to the floating shelter. You will be safe there until my return."

I step back, away from his touch.

"You're leaving me?" I simply can't believe it. And the panic is digging under my ribs, making breathing painful. His eyes soften instantly and his voice becomes calmer.

"I have to make it back to the stream, beautiful. It's getting increasingly cold and I want to clean the beast's fur. Even though I killed it once, this one had a lot of blood. It will be dry by morning, ready for you to use during the light span. I also need to let the skin soak in the water over the dark span. It's a bit smelly now, but it will be ready to turn it into a water pouch by sunrise. I need to keep you hydrated."

All he says is about me and keeping me comfortable on the journey, but all that registers is that he's leaving me.

"But the stream is, like, half an hour walk each way... half a nano's rotation, you say?" My voice sounds whiny and I hate it.

"That's why I am going alone, Sia. It will take me a lot less than that if I go alone. I will be back by the time it's fully dark. You have a rest up there. The meat will be ready by the time I return."

He doesn't wait for my reply and simply grabs me and places me on his hip, like a child. My legs are not worried about any of my dilemmas and wrap around his torso like a vine. Before I get to complain about him, or my legs, we're up in the canopy of thick leaves. He places me on the hammock of white vines and tries to return down to the forest floor. I grab his hand with shaky fingers.

"What if something happens? Please don't leave me alone."

He places his forehead on mine and his hand slowly caresses my hair.

If you need me, you talk to me in your mind and if I need to tell you something, I'll do the same.

It takes a moment to register. He didn't use words. He spoke in my mind. I look at him without knowing if I am relieved or horrified.

Can you hear all my thoughts? I ask him in my mind.

Only the ones you want me to. And you can only hear my thoughts when I allow it. If you need me, you call me. I will always come when you ask for me.

And with that, he's gone. Can't even as much as hear him run towards the stream. He can be really quiet when he wants to be. I sit on the hammock, rather than lie. Without his body weight, the breeze moves the hammock in between the branches increasingly faster. It makes me feel dizzy. And it's definitely getting colder. In the distance, I can hear the forest coming to life as the darkness takes over. I can see glimpses of the green fire through the thick canopy. It makes me feel less lonely. Alone and lonely… that's what I have been all my life. I should be welcoming this. But being without him is terrifying. Is it because I'm scared of being alone on an alien planet, is it because I know my Sign can kill me if I'm away from him? Or is it because I simply need him?

Breathe, Phaea, I'm on my way back. You're safe.

His voice in my head is both overwhelming and soothing.

Talk to me, Phaea! commands his voice in my head. *Why are you shivering? Are you scared? I can't sense any predator near you.*

How can he tell I'm shivering?

I'm okay, just cold. Really cold, I reply in my mind, thinking he can't possibly hear me. And yet… he does.

I'll be there to keep you warm. No harm or cold or fear will ever touch you, while you're in my arms.

I don't reply as I hug myself on the rocking hammock. What can I possibly say to that? That's what I desperately wanted, ever since my sister left me alone in the world. To be safe from harm. Safe from the cold and the fear inside me. To find the one place in the world where I can be free of those. I close my eyes and hug myself as tightly as I can. I try not to think of the passing time, the increasing noises or the cold. I only imagine his arms around me. Strong and warm, and his skin that smells like home. He takes me on his lap and rests us both against the tree trunk. I nuzzle at his chest. The hair on his chest is still slightly humid from the stream and… I open my eyes suddenly. Not imagining. He is here. He came back to me. Our Signs give enough light, so I can see his pleased grin. He looks terribly full of himself. I don't care. I'm back in his arms. That's all I care about. He places a soft kiss on my forehead, over the Sign.

"You feel warmer now, my beautiful Phaea. I'll just be away for a few nanoclips to retrieve the meat. Also, to bury the rest for morning. There won't be anything left by the light span otherwise."

I nod and I move my body so he can go back down. I don't want to be the whiny princess, so I fake a bravery I don't have. It takes him only a few minutes to come back, but I'm already shivering with cold. The breeze is a proper wind now and I try to keep the hammock from smashing against the tree trunk. He built it closer to the trunk this time. I can see how it's easier to get in and out this way and also easier for sitting. However, without his weight to keep it steady, it's like a swing on steroids. He returns carrying steamy chunks of meat wrapped in the blue oversized leaves.

"You're cold again, come here, my Phaea."

He picks me up like I'm his favourite teddy and sits down in the middle of the hammock, placing me on his lap. He leans his back against the silky trunk and opens his legs slightly to allow my body to fit in between his thighs. I feel completely engulfed by his body this way and it's like being surrounded by a furnace. His body is so big around me, acting like a shelter against the wind. His legs hang over the edge of the hammock, meanwhile my otherwise famously long legs can barely reach the edge of it. My cold bottom feels like it died and went to heaven, nestled in his hot crotch. I hope it's the warmth making my bottom happy and not the feel of his throbbing cock. I involuntarily remember the feel of it against my pussy in the stream. And I just want to die as a warm, sticky, unwelcome and unfortunate fluid gushes in between my legs. What is wrong with me? The memory and the feel of his cock going up my backside all the way to my waist should fill me with fear. Probably not even Gianna with all her training could manage that size. No! Not going to think about the size, or about what he looked like naked. I know he can smell my ridiculous leaking issues and can probably read my mind and hear my heart beating like crazy. I'm bracing myself for the grin and the mocking, but none of it comes. Instead he just opens the leaves, grabs a small piece of meat and brings it to my lips. I open my mouth before I get to remember how disgusting the animal looked. I am happy I didn't get to, because the taste is amazing. Unlike the sweet meat of the other creature, this one is a bit smoky and it's got a grilled flavour to it. As he attempts to feed me another piece of meat, I look up at him over my shoulder.

"I can feed myself now. My fingers are not shaking anymore. Feeling much warmer."

"That's not why I am feeding you," he says, and his deep voice makes his chest rumble behind my back. "Open your mouth."

Just like my legs and my vagina, my lips also seem to only do his bidding, not mine. He keeps feeding both of us for a while and I can't help but notice how he takes the time to break my meat into small chunks, which look tiny in his fingers. I also notice how his cock jerks violently each time my lips catch his fingers. Not that I can ignore it. It feels like a crawler on a mission and I know exactly what the mission is.

"I am full, thank you," I say when I can't really fit in another bite.

"You eat very little, my Phaea, you need to eat more. Even by Human standards you are too slim. You may be taller than the other two females, but they are definitely not as willowy as you are."

"That's because you didn't get to meet Gianna. You only compare me to Jade and Natalia. Gianna is more like me and that's what comes with our job, back on Earth."

"Gianna?"

"The one who got away from the Blood Fleet," I explain. He makes a pained sound.

"Please, don't remind me of that fool."

Even though he's not saying, I know he means his Commander and not Gianna.

"I also got away," I say, because apparently all my wisdom has stayed behind on Earth. His arm snakes around my waist and pulls me up against his body, while his lips touch my ear. His soft beard is thick against my skin as he whispers in a menacing voice.

"I told you not to remind me of that, little Human. Not unless you want to unleash my Beast."

Somehow, I know he's not using some figure of speech. It's obvious his kind can become something different and definitely scarier when they are angry. He keeps his arm around my waist, but releases some of the pressure. With the other hand he discards the leftover meat and as soon as it hits the ground, I can hear grunts and shuffling. I tense involuntarily, but Tars pulls me closer to him, without the anger this time. "You're safe, they can't climb. I am pretty sure of it. And if they do, they die. No harm will ever come to you."

I am speechless every time he says that to me. I have longed all my life to hear those words from someone. I just didn't know.

"Drink, my Phaea," he says softly, handing me the strangest thing ever. I think it's a tree branch of sorts, but he has somehow scooped out the inside of it and filled it with water from the stream. "It's not much, but it should be enough for now."

He took the time to make this for me and then carry it while rushing to get back to me? I don't even feel the treacherous tears going down my cheeks. What is he doing to me? *He is undoing you,* replies my brain, even though my question was rhetorical and nobody asked it anything. And of course, he notices my tears.

"Why leaking this salty water, my Phaea?" he asks while gently wiping my tears off with his hands. They probably look ridiculously big on my face. "Have I upset you?"

"No, Tars, Humans cry for many different reasons. I don't normally cry at all."

"Then why are you?"

"Because I didn't expect you to make this for me."

As I look at him over my shoulder, I can tell he's a bit puzzled.

"When we get back to Tarrassia, I will cover you in the most precious gifts. A bit of water in a carved stick is nothing, my Phaea."

I grab the huge palm stroking my hair and luckily, he allows me to manoeuvre it, otherwise I wouldn't be able to. I bring it to my lips and press a soft kiss inside it. There is no hair covering the inside of his palm. It's soft and calloused at the same time.

"It means everything, Tars," I whisper inside his palm. "I had plenty of beautiful things back on Earth. But a carved stick with water in it means more than a gift. It means care."

"You are mine to care for. And one day you will care for me the way I care for you. I won't rest until that day, my Phaea," he whispers with his warm lips in my hair. The guilt is tugging at my heart. I know my earlier words hurt him badly. Especially as I delivered them after being intimate in the stream. But would he just want an apology or would he want me to stop feeling like that altogether? I am too confused to process anything of this new reality. Luckily, he changes the subject. "Why is it that you and the female called Gianna are slimmer?"

His question makes me smile.

"Well, all human females are different. We come in all different colours, shapes and sizes. Different hair and eye colour, too."

"That is most unusual," he says while playing with my hair. Nobody ever touches my hair. It's so soothing and it's dangerously peeling my control away.

"Gianna and I worked as models, so being slimmer than most was kind of mandatory."

"Moudelz doesn't translate," he says, making me giggle. And I never giggle…

"It's probably an Earth thing. A bunch of beautiful women get to wear pretty clothes to make them sell better."

Now that I try to simplify it for him, it occurs to me that's what it actually is. And it sounds stupid.

As if reading my mind, he agrees.

"We don't have this kind of title on Tarrassia. It doesn't make sense why females would want to buy garments based on what they look like on other females. Each Tarrassian female has a hologram fitting device. It uploads their image and as they scroll through garments, they see what they would look like on their own body."

And just like that, my job seems indeed stupid and useless.

"So, good thing your new title is Queen of Tarrassia, my Phaea, otherwise there won't be anything for you to do when we get back home."

"What does the Queen do anyway?" As I ask, I already know what's coming.

"Keep the King happy of course," comes the expected answer. But there's a playful tone in his voice, so I refuse to let him wind me up. The wind picks up and I shiver in his arms, even though I am not exactly cold. Not when surrounded by his heat. "It's definitely getting colder," I say. "Does that mean we're getting closer to the mountains?"

"No, my Phaea, I don't really know what it means. As far as we know this planet only has one nature rotation. A hot one. There shouldn't be any cold at all," he adds with a bit of worry in his voice. "I don't really care about this cursed planet anyway," he adds quickly. "The sooner we leave it the better. If you let me carry you on the next span, we can probably reach the mountains by the end of it. Yes, my Phaea?"

His fingers turn my face gently towards him.

"I will think about it," I say.

"Stubborn female," he says, but doesn't really seem upset with me.

"It's time we rested, Phaea," he says while manoeuvring us both until we reach the now familiar position. Him lying on his back and me lying on top of him like a blanket. His new Human blanket. I try to keep an open mind as the logistics of our sleeping arrangements don't allow for anything else. Unlike the other night, now I can hear the scary beasts roaming under the tree. Occasionally I can also hear far scarier noises. Noises long extinct from my home planet. And some distant flapping of large wings. Like, really large... Luckily, very distant.

He takes a deep breath that pushes his wide chest up and my body with it. His arms hug me tightly to him and he presses a barely-there kiss on my forehead.

"Sleep, my beautiful Phaea. My body heat will keep you warm. No wriggling about and no talking."

I press my face into his chest. His skin is so warm.

"How come you are not cold?"

"Sia!" he says with a pained soft growl. "I said no talking. Tarrassians can regulate their body temperature. Make it cool down in the heat and warm up in the cold. Now keep quiet."

The wind is getting bitterly cold and there's a fresh smell in the air, reminding me of snow. The ridiculous Tarrassian dress I'm wearing floats around me, occasionally getting stuck in the branches. I can hear a lot of sinister noises around me and I wish I could just instantly fall asleep. How am I supposed to sleep when his cock keeps poking at my belly like a knife? Sword more like, considering the size. And just then, my brain decides it would be a good time to remember what he looked like naked, by the stream. As he took in every little detail of my body, I also looked at him. I couldn't take my eyes off him. His body is as perfect as the representations of the Olympus gods. Nothing else on Earth could compare with that pure masculine perfection. It's either that, or I really, really fancy him. Not that much of his body was hidden before. The short leather kilt isn't exactly a lot of clothing. But I tried not to look much, before this afternoon. His chest is definitely a work of art. All those muscles, that don't seem able to stay still, keep moving under the rose gold, almost metallic-looking skin. Most of it is covered in that fine coat of dark hair, which he calls fur. It covers his chest in a wide pattern, then swirls down his incredibly hard abdomen, thinning as it goes down his pelvis, then thickening again as it nests that huge thing, poking at me right now. I probably shouldn't have looked earlier on, but if I am to have that inside me at some point, I might have just as well. My brain took the details in, quite methodically, giving me a risk assessment. Too long, too wide, too many knobs, too hard and definitely too angry looking. And as I was waiting for the panic to sink in, it never came. Instead, my palms were itching to take him in my hand, my mouth was watering to taste him and my vagina was begging to give it a hug. Fluid releasing and all. I stop breathing suddenly as I realise my panties are completely soaked. Again. And what if he…

"Cursed blasters of fire, Sia!"

His booming voice covers the noise of the wind and makes the beasts around us growl in reply. "This is not the best time to ask for my cock, female! Trying to keep you warm and safe through this cursed span."

His arrogance is… I can't believe he's… Obviously, I don't have any thoughts I can carry through.

"I wasn't asking for it!" I tell him with all the dignity people can tell a lie with. He grabs my face in between his fingers and forces my head up, to look at him.

"I am not the one who needs to get that message, your pretty pink pussy is."

His crude words make me want to slap his handsome face, and I never ever want to slap anyone! Maybe I should make an exception for him. He places my head back on his chest, as if I have no will of my own. I close my eyes, ordering sleep to come and take me to a place where my vagina can keep dry. Too much noise around to be able to sleep. The wind, the trees, the animals, his hearts… I realise my head is resting on his left pectoral. On top of the heart that only beats for me. Someone's heart is alive and beating, because of me. Before I can think any better, I place a kiss on top of his beating heart. With an angry growl he grabs me up by my waist with one hand, while the other grips the back of my neck. He pushes my face down on his for a punishing kiss. What he doesn't know yet, and what I am learning myself, is that neither his kiss nor his touch could ever feel punishing to me. I am too crazed for him. I welcome everything he has to give me. I dig my hands in his beard, and my tongue in his mouth gives as much as it takes. Hard to keep up, though. Kissing is definitely something he has mastered quickly. His tongue is as big and invading as the rest of him. Instead of pushing it away I suck on it. He growls in my mouth and pushes me higher, above himself. His hand pulls my dress down and he takes my entire left breast in his mouth the way a starved creature would grab food. Despite the darkness of the forest, our Signs are alive with a swirl of purple and white, giving enough light. I watch him, completely mesmerised by the sight of my entire breast disappearing inside his mouth. He looks starved for me as he sucks on it. A little spark of reasoning in my brain tells me he could bite my breast or tear it off without any effort. Instead of scaring me, it fills me with the most maddening arousal. It goes like wildfire through my body and it comes out as hot stickiness through my vagina. What is he doing to me? I shake like the leaves around me as he releases one breast, only to give the other stroke after stroke with his tongue. Between his licking, the chilling air and my arousal, my nipples look huge. I didn't even know they could get that big. Engorged and hard enough to dent a stone. There's a hint of pain, as they are not used to being sucked and he's not exactly going easy on me. I feel like going into sensory overload. He sucks without mercy on my sore nipples, then gives them a long lick and then rubs his face on them. His soft beard acts like a soothing caress. And then again. Pain, lick, soothe. The cold breeze makes me aware of the increasing wetness in between my legs. I rub on his upper abdomen, desperate to get some friction, anything. He growls in a way that makes me jump and the beasts on the forest floor scatter away. I feel even more worried that I'm going to fall as he lifts me up into the air so suddenly. I desperately try to reach for some branches to steady myself.

"Tars! What are you doing!" I can hear the panic in my voice, as he pushes my torso up then pulls my legs apart, making me kneel above his face. The vines scrape at my knees and the hammock moves around making me feel dizzy. I panic and try to grab at the branches surrounding my head, scratching my face in the process.

"Stop moving!"

He barks the order with a vibrating growl in my panties. God no, not my soaked panties! All of a sudden, I realise what he's trying to do and I close my eyes, unable to watch that. I can hear the sound of my tearing panties and I remember I don't have another pair.

"Tars, you cannot..." My words turn into a moan as his tongue laps at my insides. He grabs me by my waist to position me closer to his face. I simply freeze for a second as the next lap of his tongue starts at the crack of my bottom, over my back hole, in between my folds and over my throbbing clit. It stops there and his teeth pull on my clit and then his lips suck it deep into his mouth. And then he returns to my bottom to start again. Over and over again. It feels invading and overwhelming. The initial shock at his way too intimate touch is replaced by fire. I feel like I'm burning from the inside and my glowing tattoos make me wonder if I am actually about to catch fire. The swirls of the purple, blue and white lights under my skin look like a spectacle of the Northern Lights. The Sign on my forehead pulses and throws a pattern of bright purple on the oversized blue leaves around me. This doesn't feel real. Not this planet, not this forest, not the show of lights coming from under my skin. He doesn't feel real. How can a man make me feel like this? But most of all, I don't feel real. This wild creature arching her body, trapped between his mouth and the canopy above, doesn't seem even remotely familiar to me. My hands grab at the vines above my head, my thighs open as wide as possible for him, my moans are louder than the wind and my body has a mind of its own. It's more or less fucking itself on his tongue, with no shame or self-restraint. Time seems to dilate, the noises disappear one by one, until there's nothing but the ringing in my years and the sound of my beating heart.

Cum for me. Now! he says inside my mind, without taking his tongue out of my core. One of his hands grabs both of my breasts at the same time, squeezing them together painfully. And then... I simply explode. My Sign explodes with light, my soul with wonder and my vagina with a violent squirt in his mouth. I don't even know which is more shameful. All I know for sure is that I can't stop shaking. I just can't stop coming nor can I get enough air. I feel his hands on me, doing things, moving me around, but I don't have any willpower left to process anything. How long have I been shaking for?

"Phaea? Breathe for me, beautiful. Yes? Come back to planet Zora..."

The obvious amusement in his voice is the only thing that penetrates the fog covering my mind. I start breathing slowly and evenly and I open my teary eyes. I am once again laid flat on top of him. His hands support my shoulders to keep my head up. He searches for my eyes. Yep, definitely amused grin on his face. Amusement and something else. Something soft. I just fell apart in front of him, like the weakling he thinks all Humans are. I lost all my control in the most shameful possible way. I can't blame him if he's going to mock me.

"You're back," he says with his typical annoying grin, while stroking my hair. "If this is how your species surrenders, my Phaea, no wonder they don't need to be Warriors. All they have to do is surrender and the entire universe would be at their feet."

His words are miles away from what I expected, and they make me melt some more. I lay my head back on his beautiful chest. I think I may have developed an obsession with his chest. I lower myself a bit, trying to get comfortable. Not easy as my body feels like jelly and I have no control of it.

"No moving still applies, cursed fires!" he says through gritted teeth. Oh my God! His cock is probably going to burn my skin. Why is it so hot? All within less than a second I realise his cock has made its way out of the kilt and now it's a hot rod of both soft skin and throbbing steel, curled up in between my slightly open legs, going up my backside and reaching my waist at the back. Just like in the lake. This is turning into our thing, sort of. I slightly open my legs some more simply to release the squeeze of my inner thighs on his cock. It slaps itself against my bottom cheeks, making me gasp. What the heck?

"Sia! Stop moving! You're killing me, female," he growls, and closes his eyes while fisting my hair almost painfully. He releases it shortly and goes back to gently stroking my white mane.

"Tars? You didn't... do you..."

"Sleep. No more talking and definitely no wriggling on my cock."

"But you didn't..." Once again, he doesn't let me finish and this time the command in his voice is harsher.

"Ignore it, Sia. Go to sleep! Now!"

Maybe I should get him a pet to boss around, because I definitely don't want his bossiness. And I most definitely don't want the job of a pet for myself. I forget all about my outrage, as the last thing I hear before I fall asleep is him calling me his gift from the stars.

9

SIA

Sia kaleyii donaii help! Kenii norrannii davii Assyri help! Sia! Sia...! Sia.

Why does everything have to go so wrong every time I wake up? Without opening my eyes, I try to reach for Tars. My fingers only touch the silky vines of the hammock and some soft fur I am all wrapped up in. My body is warm under the soft covering, but the chilling breeze is hurting my face. It seems the cold stretched into the morning. Despite not opening my eyes I can tell the sun is up, as the bright light reflects onto the white vines and it hurts my eyes. Where is he? Did he leave me? I realise this has turned into my biggest fear. Him leaving me... I can suddenly smell cooked meat and I can hear soft noises on the forest floor. My Sign starts pulsing on my forehead and I know it's because he's close. Both relief and happiness flood me as I try to sit up. I run my hand over the soft, and now very clean, stripy fur of the former tiger-hyena creature. Have I ever been looked after this way?

Sia Assyri, help!

THE ICE QUEEN

So not a dream.

"Who are you? Where are you? Please show yourself."

Help! says a different voice. So more than one. The voices are so close to me, but I can't see anyone or anything other than ginormous blue leaves. What troubles me is the urgency of the voices. There is pain and fear and…

"Sia?"

Before I can understand what's happening Tars' huge body almost makes the hammock turn over and he grabs me to his chest with one hand while the other one holds his menacing-looking sword. He looks around ready to kill whatever walks or breathes his way.

"Who were you talking to, Sia?"

Not sure if he meant to shout, but his voice makes the tree shake around us. As for the other aliens, even though I couldn't see them, I realise I could feel their presence. And now I don't.

"You just scared them away, Tars. And you're hurting me!" I add, trying to free myself from the arm coiled around me. I'm quite sure that's what a giant anaconda's squeeze would feel like. He quickly releases me and I can see the fear in his eyes. He checks my face for pain, so I am quick to give him a small but reassuring smile.

"I am okay, Tars. You just startled me. And them. Whoever they are."

He watches me with a worried look on his beautiful face. Like I hit my head and started to see things.

"Come, my Phaea, let's get you down for your morning meal."

I ignore being talked to like I was a child or being carried on his hip like one. I am quite pleased to see there are no body parts scattered around the tree. He gives me a knowing grin and I really want to roll my eyes like Jade. I go behind a tree to do my morning business and then it hits me! The memory of last night… With the voices and all that, I forgot for a moment. But the lack of panties brings it all back. How did he take all my control and all my reasoning? With a stroke of his tongue, that's how. Why is my brain determined to answer rhetorical questions? And how am I supposed to look him in the eyes now? The stupid Sign is pulsing like mad on my forehead. And as if that is not bad enough my clit is pulsing harder.

"My Phaea? Are you well? You are taking a long time."

"Yes, I'm okay. Almost finished." I rush my words before he comes over to get me. I brace myself before I join him. I have no panties, I can't keep dry for the life of me and I'm a squirter. Despite my lack of experience, I don't think that's very common back on Earth. Or is it? Oh, why didn't I ever watch porn? At least I hope that's normal for Tarrassian women. I walk out as dignified as someone without panties can be. There is a small but welcoming fire and there's steaming meat nicely arranged on blue leaves, waiting for me. His eyes take me in with undeniable hunger as he wraps the beautiful fur around my shaking shoulders. He offers me some sort of a leather pouch. I can see it looks like the leather he stripped off the tiger-hyena. He used some of the thinner vines to hold it together at the top, only loose enough to allow a drink. I can see there are several more pouches resting by the fire. He's already been to the stream and back? I should be grateful for his care, but all I can think of is that he left me alone. I almost drop the pouch, as I don't expect it to be as heavy or as slippery. His grin makes his sharp canines glint in the sun. Or are they actual fangs? Why does he have to find everything I do so amusing? I decide I hate his grin. I pretend not to pay attention and just pour some of the water to wash my hands and my face. I drink some, even though it is not an easy task, and I manage to spill some on my dress. He takes it from my hand, and I don't need to look to know his grin is there.

"Now, my Phaea, let's try not to get you wet first thing in the morning."

The amusement in his voice tells me he's not talking about me spilling water on myself. If he makes fun of how wet I got, I am sure I am going to die of shame. As I try to find my inner iceberg, he pulls me into his arms, lifts me up and crushes his lips to mine. All at once air, shame and icy self leave my body. My legs wrap around his torso, like that's the only reason in the world I even have legs. My arms go around his neck and my mouth meets the fire in his kiss with more fire. After a minute or an hour, who can tell, he moans in my mouth and stops the kiss to press his forehead to mine. Our Signs pulse against each other.

"Ask for it, my beautiful!" he whispers against my lips. His eyes are closed, and his voice sounds pained. I don't need to ask what he means. The hot, steel hardness pressed against my belly is tell-tale enough. I don't say anything. I feel frozen and my body stiffens in his arms. I don't know what to say. Does it matter what I say? As if on cue he reminds me I don't really have a say.

"The bond of the Sign cannot be denied, my beautiful. You may not be as affected by it as I am, but in the end, you won't be able to deny it."

He lets me down and watches me with sad eyes. He seems tired, somehow...

"Come, let's eat, my Phaea," he says while pulling me closer to the fire. Its heat is more than welcoming considering the bone-chilling breeze. I can't help but think I can smell snow in the air. He sits me on his lap and attempts to feed me like that was normal. I consider if this is some Tarrassian custom. I don't want to be rude, but at the end of the day I am not Tarrassian and I don't have to put up with it.

"Is feeding a female a Tarrassian custom?" I ask after I allow him to put a bit of the smoky meat in my mouth.

"It is now," he says with a grin, and I almost choke on the food.

"I can feed myself, you know?" I tell him and try to remove my body from his lap. His arm around my waist instantly turns into steel and I can't even flinch anymore.

"Oh, I do know, my Phaea. I just don't care. I have decided I like feeding you and that's the end of it. I am the King and whatever I say goes."

"You are not my King!"

"I am now! I am your everything."

I open my mouth to protest, but he just shoves another piece of meat in it. I can't fight him so I decide to ignore him and be me. Back straight, chin high, cold eyes… There's a silent warning in his eyes and once again his arm squeezes painfully around my waist. We eat in silence for a few minutes and I try as little contact with the fingers feeding me as possible.

"Do you require the stream this morning, my Phaea? We have enough water to sustain you for the rest of the span, in case we don't find any. Chances are we will run into more streams as we near the mountains. And the sooner we get going the better."

I consider his words. I would really love a nice dip right now. Okay. Maybe it won't be that nice. With the change in temperature the water must be freezing. Or maybe I would enjoy the cold water taking his scent off my body. It's driving me insane with both need and the memories of last night. But then again, the thought of being naked around him, or even worse him naked around me… No, I can't trust myself right now.

"I'd rather we went," I say quickly before I get to change my mind. "How long do you think we have left?"

"Not long. Maybe by the end of this span. I will carry you and we will cover a lot of terrain today."

"I didn't say you could carry me, Tars."

"I wasn't asking permission, Sia!" comes the harsh answer. As he watches me, his beautiful copper eyes start to soften, and golden specks ignite them.

"The longer we are on this planet, the more at risk you are, my Phaea. Something doesn't feel right. The cold weather doesn't make sense. And I still can't reach Tannon's mind. We have to be quick today."

I simply nod in agreement. My years of self-discipline won't allow me to be unreasonable. He puts the fire out and uses some of the vines he cut earlier to attach the two water pouches to his kilt belt.

"Can I carry anything?" I ask, feeling completely useless.

"No, my beautiful Phaea. I can't carry you in my arms, as I need my hands free to reach for my sword. You will travel on my back and I need you to hold on properly. So, no carrying anything. Just keep your arms around my neck and those pretty legs around my waist."

And there it is… the insufferable grin. The man can't help himself and he's not even trying to pretend he can. Once again, I try to be my practical, reasonable self and not let him wind me up. But as he lowers himself in front of me and hauls me up his back, my whole face goes on fire as I remember the small issue of no panties. As I wrap my legs around his bare skin, the issue is definitely not that small. As he starts walking, I clumsily try to grab some of the dress slits and shove them in between my legs. The fabric of the dress is so thin, it does nothing to shelter my aching clit from the scorching skin of his back. As he increases his pace to an almost dizzying speed, the friction becomes unbearable. The thin fabric I managed to put between my legs turns wet and sticky in no time. What is wrong with me?

"I know I said we have to rush, my beautiful, but if you are going to ask for my cock now, I will be happy to stop."

Unbelievable! Even though I don't see it, I know his stupid grin is all over his face.

"I am not asking for anything! Just keep on going."

His laughter shakes my body and it's making my clit vibrate, because why not? Ever since he first put his hands on me, it turned me into a walking bottle of lube. Why not add a vibrating clit to the equation?

After a good while of being tense, my muscles start to spasm, so I just give up and embrace the crazy. I relax around his body and I rest my cheek on his back. It's covered in a fine coat of soft black hair and it smells like fresh pine and clean skin and... home. The belt of his kilt stops my legs from sliding, so I don't need to worry about that. I feel sheltered from the chilling wind, trapped between the fur and the heat of his back. I have lost the battle with my sticky vagina, but everything else is kind of relaxing and almost peaceful. Being looked after is so intoxicating. I nuzzle at his back, as I am a complete sucker for the smell of his skin. He sighs loudly but doesn't slow his pace.

"You will be the end of me, my little Human."

I can't help but smile as I close my eyes, because when I am this close to him, it's safe to close my eyes.

I jolt suddenly and two big hands grab at my upper thighs to steady me.

"I've got you, my beautiful Phaea. I won't let you slide."

I realise I drifted away and probably slept for a while, considering the light looks different, as if the sun is higher in the sky. It's colder than before and the breeze is angrily moving both our manes around. I feel quite tired and I have aches in my arms and legs. Which only makes me feel embarrassed. He is the one carrying me and the supplies, while moving like a blur through the forest.

"I know you are tired," he tells me with a soft voice, yet powerful enough to cover the wind. "We will take a break soon."

Just as I am preparing to tell him I am okay and he doesn't have to fuss over me this much, I hear them. Maybe because I can't understand most of their words, I am more attuned to their emotions. A warning. I think they are trying to warn us about something. I tap on his shoulder and wriggle around, trying to put my legs down.

"Tars, can we stop, please?" He stops so suddenly that my insides feel funny for a second. He lowers me down carefully and steadies me, as my wobbly legs take a while to regain blood flow. I look around, but as expected there's nothing but huge white trunks and blue leaves shaking in the wind, in the canopy above us. The canopy, however, looks less dense as I realise the forest floor is littered by the fallen leaves. Can't even see the soft bluish moss anymore. And most of the leaves look withered and dry. Maybe seasons can change overnight on this planet?

Sia, Sia Assyri, davii lonnii kabarrii fire Sphinnii Assyri n. Lonnii kaffallii herrenii afellii fire, Sia Assyri.

"I am sorry, but I can't understand you," I say to the trees around me, since I can't see anything else. I don't even get to finish my words, before Tars pulls his massive sword out and looks around, growling. That's not the only thing that happens. I can't help the pang of fear as his body starts to grow under my very eyes. It's subtle but nevertheless obvious. His shoulders are larger, his biceps flare out, angry muscles moving under the skin, his thick thighs grow thicker and... Before I let fear rule me, I reach out and grab at his arm. His skin is boiling hot and it starts to shimmer. He is trying to move me behind him, protectively.

"Please stop, you are scaring them! Tars put your sword away. They are no threat to us."

After scanning the forest one more time, his eyes stop on mine. There are specks of white gold in them and I remember the High Commander of the Blood Fleet. Their eyes turn white when the angry beast takes over, or whatever that is. As he watches me, the white specks are replaced by golden ones. He doesn't put his sword away, but he lowers it and his body seems to shrink from giant to less giant... I guess. He gently runs the back of his hand over my cheek.

"There is no one here but us, my Phaea." He states the obvious. I don't know what is more frustrating. Him not hearing them or the worried look on his face. The annoying kind of worried.

"You have been through a lot, my beautiful, in a very short span of time. I know you need to rest, but we have to leave this place and…"

"Just because you can't hear them, it doesn't mean they are not real. Maybe they don't want to talk to you, or to your sword, more like."

"We will rest now, Sia. I will feed you and then we will reach the mountains by the end of this span. No more talking to birds in the meanwhile." His voice is bossy and harsh.

Talking to birds? I am so angry, and I am once again not sure how to deal with such a feeling. I give him a good defiant stare that brings specks of white into his copper eyes. He turns his back to me to do his business right… there? Really? Or is that marking his territory or something? I ignore him and go behind the nearest tree to take care of my own needs. Not an easy task, as it's so cold. My fingers feel numb.

I keep an indignant silence when I return to him. The voices are also quiet. He scared them again. I sit on a fallen log and wrap myself in the soft stripy fur. He is also quiet, maybe because unlike me he is always busy and so annoyingly caring. He's already built a small fire and unpacked some of the meat he roasted in the morning. Before I can even tell he's moving, he's on his knees near me and he takes my feet into his big hands. The dainty jelly-like Tarrassian sandals are barely holding on. And they obviously don't help much in this weather. Only when surrounded by the heat of his fingers do I realise my feet are like ice blocks. I also realise he doesn't miss a thing when it comes to me. Is it because of the Sign? He removes the sandals ever so gently and takes both my feet in between his palms. I don't have small feet by human standards, as I am too tall for that. However, my feet look tiny in his hands. He rubs them and blows hot air over them, making my heart skip a beat. My anger is long forgotten, my Sign and the swirls on my arms ignite with light and I squeeze my legs together, hoping he can't smell my arousal. What is wrong with me? He's not even trying to touch me in a sexual way.

"I would give anything to take you off this cursed planet, right now. It pains me that I can't look after you the way I should, that I can't provide for my Mate."

I take his face in my hands and stroke his soft beard. It's a bit tangled now and I gently remove a few bits of leaves and moss from it. I remember the feel of it on my lips, on my nipples, on my… I close my eyes and mentally scream at my inner ho.

"You have done nothing but care for me, Tars. You provided me with shelter, fire and food, and kept me safe."

I rest my forehead on his, as I know this is how his people show affection. He mastered the way my people show affection, so maybe I can do the same for him.

"I am the one who ran away and stranded us here."

I scream as panic floods me and it takes me a while to understand what's happening. He grabs me so suddenly in his arms that he knocks the air out of my lungs. The sharp claws he obviously doesn't feel it is appropriate to retract this time, dig into my hips and waist as he pulls me up into a punishing embrace of sorts. It's only after that I realise, he isn't trying to embrace me. He gets us both up and takes my seat on the log, placing me on his lap instead. His large fingers squeeze either side of my face, luckily without the claws this time, while staring me down.

"I have told you not to remind me of running away from me, have I not, little Human?"

Wow! The universe has paired me with the shortest-tempered man ever. As Jade would say, he is completely bonkers. A loose cannon.

"Now you eat!" he says while squeezing some more at my jaw to make it open.

"Do you expect me to sit on your lap and eat from your hand after you told me I talk to invisible birds?"

"Yes, that's exactly it."

I gasp at his words and he takes the opportunity to shove a piece of smoky cold meat in my mouth. I involuntary choke on it.

"Easy now," he says, rubbing my back.

So annoying! So, infuriating! I try to compose myself as I slowly chew on the meat. Now that it's cold I find it a bit chewy. He cuddles me closer to his chest and arranges the fur around my shoulders. My lips close over his finger by mistake and his cock under my lap starts swelling and throbbing. He takes a deep breath. I seriously consider using this sort of thing to get back at him. My virgin self, though, thinks it's a terrible idea, so I make sure not to touch his fingers as he feeds me. I also need him as calm as possible to approach the elephant in the room... the voices.

"I think they are scared of you and that's why you can't hear them."

"Sia... not this again." His deep sigh resonates in my shoulder pressed on his chest. I turn slightly to look him in the eyes. As he takes in my features, one by one, like they are some work of art, his eyes turn a blazing gold. I realise I have power over this otherwise very scary man... being. I was never an expert in flirting or wrapping men around my little finger like Gianna. But this is a man I do have power over. Yes, it could be just because a stupid Sign said so, but still. So, I smile. He stops breathing and I try to repress a laugh. My Ice Queen persona nonsense doesn't work on him. It just makes him want to tear my panties off. Well, not want to, he actually did that. The honey trap thing, however, that might work a treat on the big guy.

"So," I start with a smile and a soft touch to his face, "why is it so hard for you to believe me?"

He looks unsure and a bit young all of a sudden. Kind of cute, actually.

"It's not a matter of believing, my Phaea. Voices mean sentient beings and there are none here. I told you the inhabitants of this planet don't live here. They prefer their ships in Space. They only come to the planets they own for business or supplies. If they were to be here now, they would try to kill us, not whisper in the wind. They are not very friendly, I'm afraid."

He pauses while feeding me and hands me the water pouch, helping me with it before I pour it all over myself again.

"I understand what you are saying, but I know what I have heard. Well, not exactly, since my translation device doesn't understand their language. Maybe if they talk more, I can start to understand what they are saying. I have this strange thing like a super brain or something and it helps with things like languages."

"A special brain?" he asks.

I don't know if I want to share much of that. I don't want him to find me as weird as anyone else. Which of course is a bit silly. I already am an alien to him, so it shouldn't matter.

"I am what Humans call gifted, which really is just a better word for extra smart. Despite the useless job I had back on Earth, I gathered degree after degree."

"What is the meaning of that word?"

"Oh, it's something they give you after you studied one thing or another for a long time."

"So, you are a scholar," he says, and he looks at me with pride in his eyes.

"I guess you can call it that. Never got to use any of my degrees. Becoming famous and earning a lot of money made it easier to protect myself. Hide in plain sight, if that makes any sense. Sometimes the people everybody sees are the ones nobody actually does."

I expect him to question my nonsensical words, but he doesn't. He seems to know exactly what I am saying. It brings a shadow to his eyes but is quickly pushed away by a smile. It's my heart's turn to skip a bit. I have seen plenty of his grins. But his smiles? They are just as rare as mine. Maybe we are not that different after all. I probably should let it go, but I can't. My heart squeezes with a new kind of pain. His.

"People can't see you either, can they?"

He seems uncomfortable and kind of vulnerable, which is so strange for someone that big and powerful. He doesn't have to say it. I know he never allowed anyone else to see this side of him before. I don't push for an answer, just cuddle up closer to him. He asks me if I am done with the food and offers me some more water.

"I am the King. I was always going to be the King," he says unexpectedly. I keep as quiet as I can, scared he will stop. But he doesn't. He plays absentmindedly with a lock of my hair.

"Not something people ask you and not something you can choose for yourself. I was the only son of the greatest Tarrassian King ever and that was that. That's what they see when they look at me."

"And you don't want to be the King?"

"But I am the King, my Phaea. That is not a choice. Tarrassians are born into their titles, jobs as you call them. They are also paired at birth with a mate. The reappearance of the Sign might change that. The Sign will choose a mate when the time comes."

My throat feels tight when I ask.

"Do you have someone? I mean, is there someone waiting for you? A mate?"

He laughs and nuzzles at my hair.

"The only perk of being the future King, is that they don't choose a female for you at birth. As Tarrassia's biggest commodity, the Council waited in case there was an important alliance needed at the time."

He jokes about it, but I can hear the frustration in his voice. An unwelcome thought comes to my mind as I remember the Elder's words.

"I was the alliance… Were you upset?" I ask before I can stop myself, because apparently, I am a glutton for punishment.

"I was angry with the Elders, with the universe and mostly with myself for being born into the wrong family." His candid answer is so unexpected. So is the frustration in his voice. And I understand he had even less of a choice than I did. I was kidnapped by some scum alien race to become a slave. My circumstances didn't allow for choice-making. But to be the King, the ruler of an entire planet, and still not have a choice? That really sucks. So does the fact that I was the alliance. His arms pull me closer to his warm chest and he presses his forehead on mine, his eyes closed.

"And then I saw you, my beautiful Phaea, and everything changed. I went from thinking I don't deserve having others decide my life for me, to thinking I don't deserve you and the wonder of the Sign."

Right… the Sign. I now hate it more than ever.

"I might have made fun of it openly and teased the Elders about it," he says with a grin and I can't stop laughing, despite how I feel right now.

"You did not!"

"I did so!" he says with a big grin. The smirk lifts a corner of his lips, making his beard look all sexy and there's a naughty spark in his eyes. I kind of like the grin after all. Well, when I am not at the receiving end, that is.

"I thought they were faking legends for reality to control the people, to be honest. And since I am the King and I can say whatever I want, I told them so. A few times. During the High Council."

I hide a laugh in his chest and shake my head.

"That helped for a while, as they didn't bother me much and let me do what I do best. Go to battle and remove heads."

I am so shocked I don't know whether to cry or laugh. And he is not joking. He means it. Maybe Tarrassian males are naturally aggressive. I answer my own question as I remember the High General. He is probably a very accomplished Warrior to have become first General of their planet. Yet, he is calm and composed and doesn't look like he is into the head-removing business. So, no… It's just mine that's crazy. I decide not to think too much about it, as despite how gentle he's been with me, there's still an element of fear. I feel completely safe when he holds me like this, or cares for my needs. I am even enjoying the stupid feeding ritual. But I never know when he's going to explode next or lose his patience. And I am a bit more than unsettled by his wild passion when… Would he be able to control himself when… I can't think about it now, I just can't.

"So, you don't like being the King," I say to distract myself.

"It could be because I am really bad at it and I hate being bad at anything."

I didn't expect his answer and I look at him, expecting the mocking grin. It's not there. He is serious. He really thinks he's a bad king. But he's so good at everything he does, so imposing and very… very king-like. Despite his anger issues, he looks like someone who should be in charge.

"Why would you say that, Tars? Have the Elders said that to you?" I feel my own anger building up. He laughs at the notion.

"They wouldn't dare, my Phaea. Heads rolling and all that. It was my father who said it. And he was right, so no more talk about it. I am the King and that's that."

He says it like it's nothing, but because I am so deeply connected to him, I can feel it. And now I have more pain to carry around. His.

"It's time we moved again."

He stands suddenly, bringing me up with him. An absurd panic digs at my chest.

"I don't think it's safe to go towards the mountains, Tars. The voices are trying to warn us not to," I say, grabbing one big hand in mine. He looks like he's about to lose it again. He takes a deep breath and then lifts both my hands to his lips, placing a soft kiss on each knuckle.

"Sia," he starts with a sigh, and I realise I am about to be mansplained. I remove my hands from his and take a step back. However, I do put a bright smile on, as the man seems to have a thing for it.

"Tars, can you just listen to what I have to say with an open mind? If you decide it's nonsense, I won't bring it up again."

I lie shamelessly, but I need him to listen. He watches me for a second then lifts a hand in an allowing gesture. I want to smile, because that was definitely very king-like. I have been given an audience with the King and I intend to make the best of it.

"I completely understand that it is hard for you to accept this, as you have knowledge about this planet. We sometimes take the things we learn from a young age for granted. Maybe it's easier for me to accept things as they really are since I don't know anything about this place."

"No, you don't know anything about this place and yet you put yourself in danger by coming here." And just like that, the anger is back on. The man can sure hold a grudge. I need to be reasonable. Honey trap, Sia, I keep telling myself.

"Yes, you are right, and I would have apologised but you won't even let me talk about it because it angers you. For what it's worth, I am terribly sorry."

He nods with a small movement of his chin and invites me to carry on. That is progress and I will take anything positive right now.

"You know this planet is inhabited by some evil creatures

who don't even live here. You also know, or have been told, the weather on this planet is always hot. And it's obviously not the case," I say, looking around. And just like magic... it happens. A big fat snowflake lands on my nose. A few more start to dance around us in the air. Are the voices trying to help me prove a point? He grabs one in between his hot fingers and it melts in no time.

"This is snow," I tell him, because I'm not sure he's seen it before. He looks puzzled.

"We call it the white frost. The tops of the Mountains on Mother Planet are always covered in it. But here...?"

"Yes, and you also said nobody ever comes here because of who owns this planet, so how can anyone know for sure what's really happening here?"

He seems troubled by something. Something upsetting. He looks around with... guilt? Why would he feel guilty?

"If what you say is true, Sia, it can only mean two things. These beings are either here against their will, or they were here before this planet was taken."

"And what does it mean?"

"It means I failed them. If they are to be real, it's no wonder they don't want to talk to me."

"What? No, Tars."

I wrap my arms around his waist because this man's pain, or sadness, is something I don't know how to deal with. My own, yes. But his...? Never. It's a scary thought and I am not quite sure what it means. He lifts me up in his arm so he can hug me back. Our difference in height can make hugging a bit of an issue. He holds on to me like I am his lifeline.

"The King of Tarrassia is also the ruler of the Coalition of the Seven Stars. The coalition is there to keep the old rules alive, restore order and protect the life of the innocent. There are always nations in distress, slavers to be punished, battles to win. I have been so consumed by finding the next battle to win and blood to share, I never stopped to pay attention to the little things. Like how do we know the planets they take as theirs are not inhabited? There are many species, such as yours, we have never heard of. If what you say is true, a planet under my watch was taken and I allowed it. I am indeed a really bad King."

His voice is soft in my hair and I am completely shocked to see this vulnerable side of him. I actually think I prefer the crazy Tars who likes removing enemy heads.

"Tars, how long have you been King for?"

"For six cursed orbit rotations," he says bitterly.

"And for how long have these people, the nomadic ones, had this planet?"

"For 480 orbit rotations. I know what you are trying to do, my Phaea, but that's not going to help. All this kept on happening while I was in charge. It is my job to know what happens under my watch."

"But this also happened under your father's watch and you said he was known as the Wise King."

Good. I have finally got him to listen. He is watching me with something I can't quite put my finger on.

"Your father wasn't perfect, Tars. No one ever is."

"You are perfect."

My words die on my lips as he kisses me. A different kind of kiss. It's light and yet, it feels like it's touching my soul. We keep our lips glued to each other, the way we touch foreheads. After a while, he puts me down and he looks around at the forest. It's not snowing anymore, but the forest looks darker for the first time since we got here. And to be fair the cloudy sky makes more sense, considering the cold weather, than the bright sun from before. It felt fake, somehow.

"Can you ask them if they are slaves or if they are the inhabitants of this planet?"

"I can, but I can't understand their language. My device is not recognising it. But I think they can understand me. Not sure how…"

"Are they here now?"

"I don't know. I can't see them. Do you know of species that can be invisible?"

"Not really invisible, but there are many species who can camouflage or use a shield. A bit like the technology we use to hide our ships."

So, they don't want to be seen. Would they be scared of him? Are they always watching us? Oh God, did they see us last night? Maybe it's best not to think about that.

"Are you here? It's safe to come out. We won't harm you."

I feel a bit silly talking at the trees, but then a voice answers from behind me, making me jump. Tars' hand goes to his sword and I send him a mental plea to stop.

Sia Assyri ravii. Nisilii temarrii kaini safe. Afellii Tarrassian aleii ketennii help.

"Can you hear them now?" I ask Tars but it's obvious he can't.

"What are they saying?"

"I don't really know," I reply, frustrated with the translation device. "I need them to talk more so my brain can get used to their language. I can already understand some words but most are just one big blur."

I turn around and look to where the voice came from.

"Please talk to my… my mate," I say for lack of better introduction. "Maybe he can speak your language."

Sia Assyri, afellii Tarrassian Assyrin, hurt havii doainni safe.

"No, he won't hurt you, I promise you."

Don't make promises on my behalf. I don't trust them. I might hurt them once I find out where their heads are, he says inside my head.

"For once in your life will you listen, King of Tarrassia, and stop being an arrogant prick!"

I realise with dread that I have spoken out loud and probably made the skittish creatures disappear once again. And then I hear it. It's all around us and it's coming from several different voices. It's a light noise that sounds a bit like raindrops. It's laughter! And it's beautiful. It makes the forest come to life. Tars looks around in wonder, then a deep frown sets in between his bushy eyebrows.

"Are they laughing at me?"

"Tars, you can hear them now!" I say with delight. As I notice his hand twitch on the pommel of his sword, I know he can do more than just hear them. He can see them. I don't particularly want to see any heads rolling, so I give him my brightest smile. That's enough to keep him good and docile, at least until we know what we're dealing with here. I take a deep breath and I look around. It takes a while to understand what I am looking at. We are surrounded by them. Whatever they are… To start with, I can only see tall blurred bodies, almost like they are made of fog. I somehow know they are still being cautious and not revealing themselves fully. They are as tall as Tars, but willowy instead of bulky. Their bodies are made of light and mist and they are see-through in a ghostly kind of way. They wear some sort of flowing cloak and even though they're similar to the mass of their bodies, the texture is different. Like air made of silk. Or is it silk made of air? It's a blur of blue mist, surrounding bodies made of… mist. The fashion lover in me can only be enticed by it. I give Tars another smile, to keep him stunned and well behaved, and I take a tentative step towards the one in the middle of the largest group. He, or she, is obviously the leader, as the rest of them gather around him, or her, in a protective way.

"Hanni!" I use the Tarrassian greeting for whatever strange reason. But then I carry on saying even stranger things.

"I think you already know my name. This is Tars," I say, pointing at him. "We are the King and Queen of Tarrassia and we may be here because of all the wrong reasons, but we are very honoured to meet you."

I bow my head slightly and I throw a quick glance at Tars. He watches me with a mixture of pride, astonishment and adoration. His eyes glow, and his fingers caress mine. There's also that stupid 'I am pleased with myself' type of grin, but I can't blame him. With only a few words I have accepted him, my new role as Tarrassian Queen and my fate. He won the game, and he knows it. I give him another smile, just to make his insides shiver, I hope. I take another tentative step towards the alien in charge.

"Sia Assyri, konii Marannii. Marannii belesii welcome Sia Assyri dori Tars Assyrin. Noii derii home. Sketos is our home."

No… it can't be. I turn around to look at Tars, but he watches everything with cautious eyes, and he doesn't seem to understand what they are saying. Another alien with a floating cloud around its head takes over the introduction, and even though I can now understand most of the words, I am only half paying attention. Not all the words make sense, but their bodies are very expressive, and their emotions are like an open book. While she talks to us – I decide she is definitely a she – I try to make sense of all this. I am not superstitious, I don't believe in magic, I don't believe in God, in anything really, and all these coincidences are getting too much for me to process. The Sign, my sister's brooch, my mother's story of the blue water lilies, the cold inside me, these aliens, galaxies away from Earth who live on a planet called Sketos… I really hate my brain right now. Why would my brain know that is the pro-Celtic word for protector? Everything feels so surreal and my head is spinning. I feel dizzy and I am trying with everything I have to keep it together. I feel like I am about to collapse but I know if I do that, all hell will break loose. Tars will think they have done something to me, and he will kill them first and ask questions after. And their language? Should I be able to learn it so fast?

Another one is now talking, and as they do, both fear and tension start to leave the aliens. Their emotions are so strong. Like they are made of feelings and emotions. Their body language tells the same story as their words. Maybe that's why it is so easy to understand what they are saying. As they get more confident, their bodies start to take more shape. They are not transparent anymore, and the more confident ones have solid mass bodies. Or is it the increasing cold helping them change? Now it's snowing again, but the wind has stopped, and despite the bitter cold making my toes ache, there's something incredibly warm about all of us being together. It feels like a family reunion, which is stupid since I don't know what having a family feels like. They are so alien and so beautiful. The most beautiful beings I could imagine. They are really tall and lean and as humanoid as aliens get, I guess. Their bodies, anyway. Hard to tell about the faces, though, as the upper half is covered by some sort of helmet. It's a really strange thing and I am not sure if it's a device or if it's organic. It doesn't have a snug fit, it floats around their heads, like a protective shield, and there is bright light coming from underneath. Maybe to protect their eyes, as I can't see any. They have beautiful faces with a defined jaw line and perfectly shaped lips. Their skin is like marble, gleaming white and flawless. None seem to have any facial hair. They all have wavy blue hair, in different lengths. The males' hair almost reaches the back of their knees and the females' reaches around their shoulders. Their long lean bodies are wrapped in some fabric that must be Earth's equivalent of silk. The strips of fabric wrap around their bodies, from the tip of their toes, going up each beautifully shaped leg, then wrap around the rest of their bodies in a very snug fit. The snugness makes it quite easy to tell them apart by gender. The females have tiny waists and small round breasts and the men are obviously well endowed, even though I took the slightest glimpse. I am well aware of Tars' presence behind me. Last thing I need now is him going feral again. I turn my head and offer him another reassuring smile. He's still watching them with cautiousness and me with confidence. He looks more arrogant than ever, but I can tell it's because, for some reason, he feels so proud of me. He is a quiet, strong presence in the background, allowing me to take charge, while feeling cherished and protected. The sudden realisation makes me feel warm on the inside. My stomach does funny somersaults and my Sign pulses, showing off all its lighting effects. The swirls of light coming from behind me tell me his Sign is responding to mine. I quickly try to push the wave of arousal away before he grabs me in front of these people... beings. The miniature versions of the aliens, I have noticed hiding in the back, come forward to have a better look. Their little voices are full of wonder. Children. A braver one comes really close and reaches his hand up towards my forehead. Even though he is only a child, he is so tall, I don't have to bend much. As he touches my Sign, I ask Tars in my head to keep it together and not do anything silly.

What do I get in exchange, my Phaea?

The man has no shame. I suppress a sigh, as I don't want to scare the child. I can't see his eyes under the helmet, but I know they must be full of wonder, and smile. He likes my Sign. I think they all do. I am probably the only one who doesn't in the entire universe.

"Are you here to help us?" asks the child, and the alien in charge tells him to return to his family.

She steps forward and I cringe on the inside, as I can feel Tars' aggression. The man has trust issues. Amongst other things.

"Lahii, Sia Assyri!"

She gives me her greeting and I nod. All words translate now, so Assyri must be a title. Queen.

"I am Mother. The oldest Mother on Sketos is the ruler of the People. I welcome you and the blessing you bring to us on the day of our freedom."

Ooookay... now I really don't like the sound of that. Maybe she means Tars. Tarrassians seems to be the galaxy's police or something, so I am hoping she means him.

"We have been waiting for you for many rotations and you are finally here, my Assyri."

She raises her long arms in the air and so do the rest of them.

"Lahii Khione, the hope of my people!" says the old woman, who doesn't really look that old to me, and they all reply with the same words. I mentally curse myself for acquiring a very useless degree in Greek mythology. Without that, I wouldn't have known Khione was the daughter of Boreas and the Greek Goddess of Snow. Without that, my head wouldn't be spinning, trying to understand why an alien race, galaxies away from Earth, would share the same myths.

They think you are a goddess! Tars points out the obvious. And even though he's talking in my head, he is also grinning in my head. It must be another Tarrassian special power. Grinning inside people's heads.

Yes, I am aware. And it's really not that funny, I tell him.

Oh, I think it's quite funny, but I would like to get going towards the mountains now and get off this planet. And before you say it, my Phaea, yes, I will return to help these beings, once you're safe on Tarrassia.

Right... back to being bossy. I ignore him and return my attention to Mother. I know for sure he won't hurt them now. They are on his superhero list to save the galaxy or something. So, no need for the honey trap and all that.

"What are your people called?" I ask, and she seems a bit surprised I don't know.

"We are the Ketosii, Khione Sia Assyri."

Why must all beings find crazy names for me? Ice Queen, Phaea, Assyri, Khione? Did I miss any? Yes, of course... I mustn't forget the Disney theme. What is wrong with Sia?

"Can you tell me what happened to your people, Mother? Is this your planet, or were you brought here?"

"This is our planet, Khione Assyri. We have been living here for as long as life and death have been. We do not travel the Stars like we used to in the beginning. We used to have large wings, but we have been hunted for the healing powers of our feathers. In time, over thousands of rotations we have adapted. To survive, we have lost the wings. We never left our planet again and the winds of frost have kept our planet shielded from the outsiders. But we fell prey to the greed of the Noorranni slavers many rotations ago."

She stops and takes a step back as Tars lets out an angry growl. He doesn't understand her language, but he must have heard the name of his enemies.

Can you not do that, please? They are scared enough as it is.

Not sure when we agreed to talk inside our heads in front of these people but considering his anger issues maybe it's for the best.

You will tell me what the female is saying, right now, Sia!

I will not, because I struggle as it is with a language, I can barely make sense of. Last thing I need is to translate for you, just because you said so.

Yes, I am your King and I say so.

Not this again!

Do not try my patience, female. You know I can grab you and take you to the mountains. Your little beings will have to look for a new goddess. Translate!

I look around and they all look terrified of him. Including the men, regardless their size and fit bodies. This is no warrior race. They have no aggression, unlike someone else. The children cling on to the adults and some of them have started to become less visible. No, no, no! I can't let that happen.

Fine, I tell him without looking at him. He gets no smile when he acts like a psycho. He needs to learn that.

I can't translate for you as she speaks. Too complicated. So, you are allowed inside my head when I talk to them. You don't need translation to understand my thoughts. When I stop talking to them, you must leave my head. I mean it, Tars!

I don't wait for him to reply and make my apologies to Mother and her people. Only when I tell her he's upset because he hates the Noorranni is she willing to continue.

"I was only a youngling when they took our planet."

Okay, so she is definitely old. The more aliens I meet the more I wonder how Humans have survived this long. We have nothing on these beings.

"My people don't fight. We just keep the balance of the weather. As you know we are the keepers of the balance and the keepers of the silence."

I want to scream from the bottom of my lungs that I have no idea what she's talking about. But how do I tell her I am not here to save them? I can't, so I just keep on listening.

"The Noorranni didn't even have to kill us. They just turned our Ice Planet into an eternal summer and in time we have started to die anyway. They have tried to take some of us away and sell us as slaves. But we can turn ourselves into mist and become unseen. No one wants slaves they cannot see. So, they just let the hot season kill us slowly. What you see here is all that is left of Ketosii, Khione. We cannot survive without the ice. We have learned to live in mist form, to cool ourselves down as the breeze moves us around. We have survived only to live with the pain of the hot sun on our skin and the sorrow in our weeping hearts. Sometimes we can hear the cries of the slaves the Noorranni keep on our planet. It makes our hearts bleed. We don't like pain."

A slave planet? A painful thought crosses my mind.

Is this the planet the Noorranni were taking us to? When your people saved us? I ask him, and he avoids my eyes. *You knew, didn't you? Is that why you were so angry with me? Because I put myself in danger?*

I will always be angry if you try to run away from me, my Phaea. But I will definitely be less angry if you don't put yourself in danger in the process. Not that you will run from me ever again. I'll make sure of that.

His annoying grin is both on his face and in my head, but the stupidity of my own actions is really the only annoying thing. I did this to Natalia. What if something happened to her? Or to his cousin? What have I done?

It's done now, my Phaea. No need to worry yourself about it. We will find them and leave this planet. Once you and the red female are safe on Tarrassia, I will protect these beings and return their planet to them.

Why are you in my head when you are not meant to be?

You told me to, remember?

That grin...

Now tell them we have to leave, but they are under Tarrassian protection and no harm will come to them from now on. Make it quick, we have wasted enough time.

When he is this arrogant and bossy, it's easy to forget my own faults.

"Stop ordering me around, Tars!"

I probably shouldn't have said it out loud. The Ketosii are scared of him as it is.

"Are you in danger from the Tarrassian Assyrin, our Khione?" asks Mother in a quiet voice. Tars lets out an angry snort behind us and it startles her.

"Can he also understand our language?"

"No, but he can hear my thoughts so he can understand you that way."

I tell them the truth just to spite him. Probably not my most mature moment.

"I am not in danger, Mother, and neither are any of you," I reassure her. "The King is my mate and he would never hurt me."

"He has anger problems and likes violence," says the little boy who touched my Sign earlier. A Ketosii woman, who is probably his mum, pulls him quickly behind her and they are all frozen in fear. But me... I just laugh. And laugh... and laugh. I could kiss that little boy. He sounded so human. Not to mention he got it right. My laughter is making them relax, and they join in, filling the forest with the sound of their strange laughter.

Someone is getting punished for this, my little Human, and it won't be the youngling. I don't punish cubs. You though... I might enjoy punishing you.

His grin is a proper arrogant smirk now, but all I notice is how it's making him look ridiculously sexy.

"Enough of this now," he says out loud in a booming voice. "Now we leave for the mountains so I can contact our people."

"But what about them? There are slaves here. They might be in danger."

I realise a bit too late I spoke out loud. Tars is so infuriating. His lack of patience makes me forget myself.

"There are no slaves or slavers here now, Sia. I have never met a Ketosii, so I was not familiar with their scent. That's why I was not aware of their presence. I am quite familiar with the scents of the slavers and I am telling you there are none here now."

"You need to be patient, Tars. And I need to get my answers from them," I tell him with as much composure as I can. His reaction tells me he misinterpreted that for coldness. Well... tough. I am not here to babysit Tars and deal with his tantrums. These people have lost everything.

"I am not sure I understand, Mother. Yes, it was warm and sunny when I came here, but it's proper cold now." I look down at my toes and they are already covered in soft snow. I try to move them as much as I can, hoping I won't get frostbite. I don't fancy another dose of Tars' healing blood.

"Yes, Khione. You brought the frost back," she says, bowing her head at me. "We felt the change as soon as you stepped on our planet, after the Sphinx Assyrin struck your flying egg down from the sky."

For some reason all I can think of is Natalia's mantra. 'I'm not here, they can't see me.' And maybe I am at home, sleeping in my designer velvet bed and this is just one long nightmare. What shall I tell them first? That I'm no goddess of snow? I doubt my toes would be about to fall off otherwise. Or shall I tell them sphinxes are not real? And why are they taking all our myths? Can't they make their own? And since I am on that, I should also tell them beings with blue hair and helmets growing out of their faces are not real.

"Ask them about the Sphinx, Sia!"

His words are a barked order and I'm about to give him a piece of my mind, but his tension is scaring me. His stupid muscles have started to grow and his fingers are twitching on his blade. So, he also knows what a sphinx is. And what do I ask? What do people ask about a sphinx? What's his favourite colour? What's his favourite food? Oh, not that. I can guess the answer to that one.

"Is the Sphinx around?" Really, Sia? Isn't that the smartest question ever?

"The Sphinx Assyrin lives in the mountains, on the other side of the planet. That is why we were trying to warn you not to go that way. It is certain death. He doesn't come to this side of the planet and we don't go to his. He owns the mountains and the open spaces. He strikes down from the sky all the air-travelling machines. That is what the Noorranni have him here for. That is why no one knows we are here," she says with desperation in her voice.

"The Noorranni have a Sphinx?"

"No one owns or tames a Sphinx, Khione. They brought him here when he was only a cub. Now he is just defending his territory. And he is vicious at it. On this side of the planet, the Noorranni have magic shields of energy and traps keeping strangers away. Their magic doesn't work in the mountains, so they brought the Sphinx. Not only does he keep the planet safe for them, but he would eat whatever poor soul might escape the slavers. They feed him the slaves they have no use for."

Not sure if it's cold, shock or fear making me shake like a leaf. I feel so tired. My brain and body seem to want a break from this crude reality. I can feel him coming to me and his huge arms wrap around my shoulders. He pulls me close to his chest. Warmth and safety. I will never understand how attuned he is to my feelings.

"Can you understand my language, Mother?" he asks her with obvious respect in his voice. It gives her courage to address him.

"Yes, Tarrassian Assyrin. We understand all the languages, but only our kind can understand ours."

Wait a minute... Their kind? But I can understand them. The craziness of her words is also not lost on Tars. He gives me a questioning look and I just sigh. I have no answers for him, or for myself.

"I will hear you, Mother, in my Queen's mind." He gives me a worried look and pulls me closer to him.

"My Queen is tired and needs a warm shelter. The dark span beasts will be out soon. Can we ask for you to house us this span?"

"Yes, Assyrin, it is our great honour," replies Mother. "We used to live in dwellings made of ice then we sheltered ourselves in the canopy to protect ourselves from the night beasts. They only come out at night, as the Sphinx Assyrin prefers to hunt during the light span. As time went by, and the Noorranni forgot about hunting us, we settled in underground dwellings to keep us cool. It is a great honour to have Khione bless our dwelling."

"Your kindness will be rewarded, Mother. Before we go anywhere, I need to know how safe my Queen is."

He gives me another worried look while scanning the surroundings. He hugs me with one hand, but the other one is closed tightly around the handle of his sword.

"The Sphinx King... how can that be, Mother? The Noorranni and the Coalition of the Dark Moon destroyed the Sphinx Planet many hundreds of rotations ago. There are no Sphinxes left. My War Fleet travels the galaxies from one end to another and they have no knowledge of any Sphinxes left."

"That is because the few left are on the planets taken by the Noorranni. No one ever goes there, unless it is to purchase slaves. And the buyers only come with the Noorranni army. They don't wander around and they only see what they are allowed to see."

Tars' body tenses like a bow. I know he feels guilty for every single being in this universe he can't help. I wonder why.

"You are right, Assyrin," says Mother. "They have poisoned their planet and all the Sphinxes died. They used special gases that did not affect the young. After all the Sphinxes died the Noorranni took the few cubs they found and dropped them on the planets they have taken over, to keep any unwanted visitors away."

"But Sphinxes can travel the galaxies, Mother. Why isn't the Sphinx flying away?"

The Ketosii emotions are so intense. They feel everything. Am I the same? Have I become this cold on the inside because I can feel more than most? Right now, their sadness is choking me.

"They broke his wings over and over again, when he was a cub, so they won't heal anymore," she says in a quiet voice. I press my face into Tars' warm chest and inhale deeply. I need his familiar scent and I need his strength to survive all of this. I know bad things happen and all creatures can be cruel, Humans included. But there is something about breaking a creature's wings that really makes me want to cry.

"The Sphinx Assyrin can fly around the planet, but his wings never healed enough to travel in the space. He is stuck on Sketos and he probably doesn't even remember his planet or his own kind."

"Is my Queen safe from him on this span?"

"Yes, Assyrin. He doesn't like to come to this side of the planet. The magic shield hurts his ears. He only ever comes when he sees a flying air machine, like Khione's flying egg. The Noorranni's ships are cloaked and he can't see them."

Tars nods in agreement and I can feel the tension leave his big body. He picks me up and cradles me to his chest. I hide my face in his fuzzy skin and listen to the soothing beat of his heart. The one that beats for me. I don't even care if the Ketosii think I am rude and I am ignoring them. I am just cold and tired and worried about Natalia. I thought the noise I heard from the direction she ran was a dinosaur or some prehistoric creature. Reality is even worse. It was a Sphinx. And I can't even picture such a creature, as my human mind is stuck on the big guy made of stone that tourists gather to take pictures with. But most of all I feel broken on the inside, and all the pain I have tried to suppress for years comes back with a vengeance. All that, because of the thought of broken wings.

10

TARS

She is shivering but it's not just the cold. I know she's tired and hungry and her skin feels as cold as the snowflakes around us. But there is more. Something else upsets her and I fight the urge to listen to her thoughts. She will not like that. I need to get her sheltered and fed, and then she will tell me herself. I don't know if I am pleased or worried, she didn't fight me when I picked her up. I would love nothing more than to rush to the shelter but the strange-looking Ketosii take their time. They don't really touch the forest floor when they walk. It's more floating than walking. And they are so vexingly slow. I adjust my pace accordingly, because I don't really have a choice. This is their home. I fall into step next to Mother, trying at least to ask some of my questions. All I have is questions and that is a good thing. It keeps the raging guilt away. Under my watch, sacred beings are poisoned, inhabited planets are taken, creatures are enslaved and the wings of cubs are being broken. So instead of thinking I ask my questions.

"How often do the Noorranni come here, Mother?"

"Not too often," she says, floating by my side. "They only come to bring more slaves or buyers. But they won't be long now. The Harsallii guardians will no doubt tell them about the change in the weather and they must know about Khione's egg breaching the atmosphere. I don't think they can tell about your invisible air-travelling machine. The one we sank."

The only thing stopping me from killing someone is that my Phaea is giggling against my chest, her breath softly tickling my fur. She thinks this is funny. And I guess it is. I thought they were completely harmless.

"I am sorry, Assyrin, but we thought you were going to take Khione away from us and we need her. Your air-travelling machine is not damaged. We can safely bring it back up from the moving sands."

I stop walking, as sudden hope fills me with joy. I don't have to reach the mountains and contact my War Fleet. I can just fly my own ship back to Mother Planet. I consider doing it now, but I can't leave Tannon and his female behind and my Queen needs to rest. Not that it will be easy to take her away from these people. They think she is a goddess and they need her to get their powers back. Which is annoying, considering I also need her to get my full powers. I don't even know what that means. It's been so long since my people had the Sign. Not even the Elders know for sure. Why would the Ketosii think she's their kind? Yes, I agree with them, my Phaea looks like a deity or a goddess as they call it, and, Astrals help me, she sure tastes like one.

But she is also Human. And Humans... well, Humans are not... What if I am wrong? She did bring our Sign back. And not just her. I know both Tannon and Larrs are about to know the blessing of the Sign, if they haven't already. I have to ask my Phaea when we get alone. There is something she is not telling me. She obviously knows what a Sphinx is and she wasn't that surprised she could communicate with the Ketosii.

Mother thinks the Harsallii would inform the Noorranni about the strange weather or the crashing of the pod. How would they know? I think of the disgusting mutant swarm race working for the Noorranni. Meanwhile some races do their bidding just to survive; the Harsallii are happy to oblige. And they are not the smartest of creatures. If they were to be here, I would know. Their stench travels for lengths.

"The Harsallii are not here now, Mother. I can't sense them."

"They are, Assyrin. You can't sense them, or smell them in this case, as they are in the underground tunnels going to the other side of the planet. The core of our planet is hollow. We used to grow our fruit in those tunnels, before the Noorranni took over them. That is where the buyers come to buy the slaves from."

"There are slaves here? Now?" asks Phaea, and my anger threatens to make my body expand. She was going to be one of them. Kept underground in the dark.

"There are always slaves here, Khione," answers Mother.

I also didn't miss the fact that Sia was familiar with the name Khione. I wonder what it means.

"We are here. Welcome to our home, Khione and Assyrin of Tarrassia."

She points ahead at... nothing. Just a mass of thick white vines and huge branches, already heavy with snow. I hope it's not an invisible dwelling made of mist. One can expect anything from beings missing half their faces. As I'm about to lose my patience, the rest of the Ketosii pass us and disappear more or less behind the vines. Not invisible then, just camouflaged. Which puts me at ease. My Queen will be safe here. It's a tight squeeze for someone my size to make it through the branches and I keep my Phaea close to my chest so she won't get scratched.

On the other side of the vines and trees there's an underground cave. We go through a tight enough passage to only allow one person at a time. Smart. What they lack in strength, they make up in wisdom. And I try not to even think how they sank my ship. There is another curtain of thick white vines and then the passage goes down, following a curved trail of stone stairs. After a good while of going down, the underground cave opens up into a large chamber. The ceiling is higher than I expected and there are vines hanging from it. They have a deep blue colour and there are white fruits of different shapes and sizes growing on it. I don't recognise any of it. All around the circular chamber there is a myriad of tall but narrow tunnels. Even though it's warmer in here than outside, the dirt walls are covered in a thin layer of ice. There is a soft glow coming from the vines and from the water trickling down the walls. It gives enough light for my Phaea to be able to see around. Many of the Ketosii make their way towards the tunnels, especially the females and the children.

Mother gestures at me to follow her to the middle of the chamber. There are large sitting stones arranged in a circular pattern around a very large flat stone. Different types of blue, white and pink fruit are piled on top of it. There is no fire and I don't think there will be one. Unless we want them to go invisible on us. They do not like the heat. I am not exactly upset by this. It means my Phaea will only have the heat of my body to keep her warm. And there is food. I can eat anything, but Humans are fragile and can get sick from strange foods. I will go and hunt for her if needed, even though I would hate to leave her now. She has only moved her face from my chest once, to take a quick glimpse around. Her eyes are closed and her little hands rest in my facial fur she calls a beard. I somehow like that word.

I take a seat with her on my lap. Mother sits next to us and a female is inviting us to try the fruit.

"We do not eat the meat of the beasts and we do not hunt. We have no weapons," says Mother. "But we have plenty of fruit and roots. I hope they are to your liking."

"Thank you, Mother," says Sia with a tired smile. "I welcome it after having only meat for so many days. Which one shall I have?"

Let me try it first, Phaea.

I doubt they have been through so much trouble just to poison us. Relax, Tars. I trust them.

And then she smiles. I am powerless when this female smiles at me. Even when tired and strained, her smile is my undoing. Her little fingers try to unpeel a hard-shelled white fruit, but they are too stiff from the cold to be able to. I open it for her and a delightful smell fills the air. She takes a tentative bite from the fruit and her eyes glow with pleasure. Her plump lips glisten with the pinkish juice inside the fruit and her soft little tongue licks it off her lips. What is this vexing female doing to me? My cock goes mad at the sight and pushes hard against her bottom. I watch in amusement how her eyes go big and her cheeks go red. For some strange reason, her cheeks always turn that colour when she feels my cock against her skin.

"Is it to your liking, Khione?" asks Mother.

"What is? What do you mean?"

She looks embarrassed and the red in her cheeks goes down her neck.

She means the fruit, beautiful, I tell her, amused.

Stop talking in my head, Tars!

The sound of my name makes my cock poke at her even more. Her eyes grow even bigger and she looks around embarrassed. How delightful!

"It is delicious, Mother. It tastes like vanilla ice cream."

I don't know what that is, but I must get it for her when we go back home.

I find the fruit a bit sour. All of them, really, but she makes excited noises with every bite, so I am happy.

"I can see how our Khione is tired and must rest," says Mother, and all of a sudden, I like her more.

"My daughters are getting a chamber ready for you at the back of the cave. It is one we don't use. The water wall is too warm for us, but Khione struggles with the cold."

Mother seems a bit unsure but she asks her question, nevertheless.

"Is it normal for the Goddess of Snow not to like the snow?"

Oh, my Astrals! Is that what Khione means? Do they think she is the Goddess of Snow? I feel like laughing but Phaea pulls at my beard before I get to. I give her a warning growl, but she ignores it.

"I love the snow, Mother, but my skin is very fragile and needs extra protection."

Ever the wise one, my Queen. Mother seems happy with the answer.

"Yes, that is why you will be comfortable in the hot spring chamber."

"There is a spring in the room? For bathing?" she asks with a smile in her voice.

"Of course, it is for bathing. What else would it be for? Don't drink it though. We have sweet water for drinking. My daughters have taken water pouches and more fruit to your chamber. They have also laid furs around. The Sphinx Assyrin leaves many dead beasts behind. He likes playing with his prey. I think he tries to fill his time. We gather the furs and the bones of the beasts and put them to good use. We have prepared many small underground shelters around the planet. We keep them stocked with fresh fruit, water and warm furs. In case any of the slaves escape. Few ever do, and the Sphinx Assyrin always finds the ones that do. But we can't just do nothing. The Ketosii don't like the suffering of any beings."

"That is such a kind thing to do, Mother," says my Queen, and the two of them exchange a warm smile. Two willowy females come out of one of the tunnels and say something to Mother.

"Your chamber is ready, Khione. Rest on this dark span and you will tell us how to restore the balance of the weather in the morning."

"Right… that…" says my Queen in a timid voice and I get up with her in my arms and follow one of the females down the tunnel. Nobody restores anything until my Queen is safe on Tarrassia. I will make sure of it.

It takes a while to reach the chamber and I am pleased to see it is remote from the others. Not only for privacy, but also for safety. There is a curtain of glowing blue vines in front of the chamber, giving enough light for my Queen to feel comfortable. She doesn't like the darkness, because she can't see. She will love Tarrassia. Nature gives a glow at night, so it's never dark. The chamber is small but tall enough for my size. There are plenty of furs on the stone floor for my Phaea. More furs are piled on a bedding of vines against one wall. The opposite wall is covered in dripping water which pools in a deep hole at the bottom of the wall.

"Oh my God, this is amazing! Thank you!" says my Queen to the female, who seems equally pleased. I reluctantly put her down after the female leaves. My Phaea seems to really like the chamber which is nothing but primitive. She is really excited by the water and by the archaic waste removal system in one corner of the chamber. I guess it's better than going outside or doing your business on the floor. I give her privacy as she relieves herself, while waiting on the other side of the vine screen. She is strange about such things, my Phaea. She looks really pale and tired when I return.

"What is it, my Phaea?" I rush to gather her in my arms again. I sit on the furs, with my back against the wall and place her on my lap. She leans against me and rests her head on my chest.

"I am just tired," she sighs. "I know you did all the walking and you carried me all day more or less but…"

"I would happily do that every day for the rest of my spans." I can feel her smile against my chest.

"That is sweet, Tars. Or should I call you Mr Smooth?" She giggles softly against my skin and I don't even bother asking what that means.

"I think all this got a bit much for me. These people, trying to learn their language, having you in my head… I just feel completely drained. My mind can't stretch any further. It needs to rest."

"And that's exactly what you will do. Do you wish to bathe first?"

"Oh, yes!" she says, but I can see the moment when her enthusiasm falters. And I know exactly why. I won't let it get to me. Soon, she will ask for it herself. I know she will. I just hope it's soon enough. Not sure how much longer I can delay taking what is mine to take… I lift her chin to make her look at me.

"I stopped myself from claiming you when I had you all wet and screaming my name, and you think I will do it now, when you can barely stand?"

She lowers her beautiful grey eyes.

"I am sorry, I know you won't ever do anything to hurt me."

"I would rather die before I hurt you." I get us both up and start to remove my kilt.

"What… What are you doing?"

"Bathing. What else?"

I give her my best grin and get into the stone tub. It's hardly big enough for one person to sit but it's deep and the water reaches my chest. Soft steam rises up into the cold chamber. I know she watches me with big questioning eyes, but I don't look her way. I close my eyes and rest my arms on each side of the stone tub. Nothing. She's not even breathing. She must know I am not a patient male. Why is she poking at my self-restraint?

"Are you getting in or shall I come out and help you with the dress?"

"I'm getting in," she says quickly, and I can hear her removing her dress. I try not to smile. When she comes near the tub, she pauses, unsure. I grab her and she gasps in surprise. I place her stiff little body on my lap and can't stop a hungry growl when her tits bounce about. I press her cold back against the warm skin of my chest and I keep her pinned to me, with one arm wrapped around her tiny waist. My arm is too big for her torso and it pushes her teats up over the surface of the water. Two hard pink pebbles poking at the air. I watch in amusement, over her shoulder, how she takes it all in. My cock under her bottom keeps on growing, and my Phaea decides this would be a good time to wriggle about. She straightens herself against my chest but all that does is allow my aching cock to find a gap in between her slender thighs and squeeze itself through. The vexing thing is desperate to find a tight hole to slide into. It presses itself against her soft folds and curls up, the tip of it reaching her waist. She is downright shocked.

"Ignore it, Sia. Just relax."

"But how can I…"

"Leave it, female! I can't stop it from growing or throbbing. All you need to know is I won't act on it. Unless you want me to, of course. Now relax."

I close my eyes and try to do the same. Eventually, the tension leaves her body, and she goes limp against me with a sigh.

Having her in my arms like this is the sweetest torture. I just let her relax in the hot water and try not to touch her. With every nano rotation, my self-restraint gets weaker. She must feel the pull of the Sign. I can smell her arousal. Even now, when all her energy is drained. Does she dislike me that much that she's fighting the Sign? I was so proud when she admitted in front of everyone, she belonged to me. But could it be she only accepted her fate because her Sign is engraved on her skin? That is why I prefer fighting and fucking to thinking. I must find something to fight soon. Especially since she's not giving me the other thing I need.

"How did you learn the Ketosii language so quick, Sia?" I can hear the slight tone of mistrust in my voice but I can't help it. Something strange is going on and I hate not knowing.

Her voice is small and maybe I shouldn't make her talk when she is this tired.

"I don't really know... I have always been able to learn different languages quickly, back on Earth."

"Humans speak different languages?" I ask in disbelief.

"There are about 7,111 languages on Earth. Don't Tarrassians have more than one?"

Such a notion is completely alien to me.

"No, my Phaea. We are one race, one planet, so we speak one language."

"That actually makes a lot of sense," she says with a dreamy voice. "I don't know why I could learn the Ketosii language so quickly though. Maybe because their emotions and body language are like an open book."

"Body language? What a strange notion for someone to talk with their bodies, my Phaea."

"Well, you know... not really talk. But you interpret the way they move, the way they present themselves, their environment, their emotions. You can tell if they are scared, or happy, or... you know, anything. And as you put together a picture of their body language it's easier to understand the things they are saying. And sometimes, even things they are not saying."

She says it like it's nothing. Like that's the easiest thing to do ever.

"I have a Royal Army of Shadows. They go through many orbit rotations of training. They learn how to do something similar to what you have described. I don't think they are very good at it. So, it's a good thing they are really good at fighting. And you can do all that because you have a 'gifted' brain, you said?"

She laughs softly.

"No, all Humans can do that. More or less. It's a human thing, I guess."

"I thought Humans don't have any powers."

She giggles.

"No, not a special power. Just something we do."

"It's not something other races can do, my Phaea. And it's a very useful thing to be able to understand your enemies' intentions. So, it is a Human power. Knowing body language and kissing. Not bad for a Red Orbit Planet."

"I am mentally rolling my eyes, like Jade. Too tired to actually do it," she says with an exaggerated sigh.

"Yes, I am familiar with the Human eye roll," I tell her. "The female with the oversized tits likes to roll her eyes. Especially at my High General."

She almost jumps out of my lap, making water splash over the edge and onto the floor. I grab her by the waist before she gets to do anything else and push her back on my lap. More like on my cursed aching cock.

"Where do you think you're going? Did I say you could leave my lap?" I whisper in her hair, inhaling her dizzying scent.

"I don't need your permission to get up. I am not a lap pet, you know?" She's trying to yell at me and it's quite funny because she has no strength left to do it. She sounds like a wailing newly born cub.

"You obviously don't need my permission to look at other women's tits. You guys are unbelievable!" she says with an indignant huff. "Men are all the same, no matter where they are from! Just ridiculous. Oversized boobs? Really?"

Her back is once again straight and stiff, and she folds her arms over her tits in a defensive gesture. She's covering herself from me and I have told her there would be consequences for that. However, I am willing to let it go, because no male has ever been happier than I am now. My female is jealous. Fiercely so. I push her hands out of the way and grab her beautiful round mounds in my hands.

"These are perfect and they are mine and I will never look at any other female with want again. There is no other female for me."

"Yes, right, a bit hard to explain the Sign to them," she says while trying to remove my hands.

Not sure what she means but my patience is running thin.

"You don't cover from me what is mine, Sia. You should know better." I grab her tits in my hands again, but this time I squeeze them hard and pinch her pebbly nipples. She lets out a pained noise and I release the pressure. I rub her nipples gently and move my hands over her soft tits in a caressing circular motion. She relaxes slowly against my chest and makes cute panting noises. I mustn't forget myself. She is tired and I can't touch her now the way I need to. I will not allow my raging needs to scare or hurt my female. I move my hand to her shoulders and massage her there instead. She sighs and leans more into me.

"There can never be anyone else for me again, Phaea. Only you."

"Have there been any before?"

I really didn't expect that question and I kind of fumble with the answer. Human females are so appealing. I'm sure Human males enjoy mating a lot. Just not sure how much is a lot by their standards. I might have enjoyed mating a bit too much, by Tarrassian standards.

"The ones before you don't matter. They never did matter anyway, my Phaea."

I caress her long white hair, hoping that answer is good enough for her. No such luck. My little female is all of a sudden very alert. Cursed blasters of fire!

She looks up over her shoulder. Her usually still grey eyes are anything but still now. They look like the Great Waters in a storm.

"How many, Tars?"

"Tarrassians live long life spans, Sia. Even though I am very young by Tarrassian standards, I have been around for forty-eight orbit rotations. So, numbers are not that relevant."

"How many?"

This female! I desperately need to kill something on the coming span.

"How many?"

"What does it matter, Sia? And who is counting such things? Do Human males do that?"

"How many females?"

For the name of the Astrals? What is this?

"I don't know numbers. I wasn't counting."

"You can estimate. You know, more or less sort of thing."

"Will you be upset if I tell you?"

She seems to consider my question for a while.

"Of course not, it happened in the past, just being curious," she says, and I am fool enough to believe her.

"There have been many because... well, because fighting and fucking was like an escape from being the King, so I might have done a bit too much of both."

One would think she would appreciate my honesty, but no. She wants her vexing number!

"So what? Are we talking more than a thousand or something?" she asks stubbornly.

"Probably, I said I wasn't counting."

Before I get to grab her, she removes herself from my arm and reaches the other end of the tub, dropping her pretty ass on my lower legs. She watches me in disbelief and something else. She quickly covers her tits with her folded arms when I drop my hungry gaze on them.

"You slept with more than a thousand females?" Her voice is a bit shaky and it tugs at my heart.

"Of course not, my Phaea. Why would you think such a thing? You are the only female I have ever slept next to and the only one who ever slept in my arms. I only fucked the others."

What now? Why does she look so shocked? Enough of this, my thin patience will have no more. I reach for her again and place her back on my lap, on top of my rigid cock to make sure it doesn't curl up her waist again. She doesn't fight me, but that's only because she doesn't have any fight left. I hold her tight to me and press kisses on top of her precious head.

"Ready to come out?" I ask her.

"What happens tomorrow?" she asks instead.

"We leave for Tarrassia."

She turns her tired eyes back to mine.

"I can't leave without Natalia," she says with a sad voice, and I hug her close to me.

"We will try to find them before we leave, Phaea."

"Can you contact your cousin?"

"I cannot," I reply without letting her see how worried I am. "His mind is clouded. Almost as if he can't hear me. He has not passed to the Ancestors!"

It sounds like I am trying to convince myself. Tannon cannot be dead. He is my family, my blood. We have a bond and the bond is still there. But I do think he is badly injured.

"Do you think maybe... the Sphinx has hurt them?"

"No, the Sphinx would have killed them, not just injured them. No one can fight a Sphinx. Not even Tannon. I need you to do something for me, my Phaea," I tell her, and she watches me with those tired eyes.

"Just not now. Tomorrow, after you regain your strength. I want you to talk in your head to the red female."

"To Natalia? No, Tars, I can't. Humans don't have the ability to do that. Like you said I can do it with you because of the Sign."

"Yes, but not just with me. Your Sign connects you with every other Tarrassian."

"Really? That is good... I think. But it doesn't mean I can reach Natalia's mind. She is still one hundred percent human."

I wonder what she will make of the information I am about to give her. But I thought about it and it's the only way.

"I think Tannon has recognised Natalia as his mate."

"What are you saying, Tars?" she asks me with eyes full of worry.

"I think he recognised her scent, ever since we were on board his warship, docked to Levianha. He was acting strange but I didn't pay much attention. I was in too much pain and need for you. And then, when we were trying to find you, I was too worried and too angry to tell. When we landed here and opened the ramp, he asked about the strange smell in the air and I know now he meant his female. When she ran from him, his War Beast took over and his rage was mirroring mine. As I am sure you noticed, our kind don't do well with that. There is no greater pain for a Tarrassian male than to see his female running away from him."

"I'm sorry, Tars, I didn't realise."

Her small hand goes to my face and I lean into it.

"The red female is without a doubt Tannon's mate. But one can have a treasured life mate, without getting the Sign. And without it, you are right. You won't be able to reach her mind."

"I would like to try now," she says softly.

"No, my Phaea. Your mind is too stretched and you need to rest. It's easy for your mind to reach mine, because you wear my Sign. It takes a lot of energy to talk to someone's mind. Our cubs have to practise for many rotations."

"Please, I have to try. She must be so scared. Please?"

I can't say no to my female so I won't even try. I wrap my arms around her small body, much warmer now because of the water. Hold her tightly against my chest and rest her head on my heart. Her heart. Because it will always be hers.

"Close your eyes and picture something familiar about Natalia. Use your senses. The more senses you use the easier it is to reach someone's mind. Use something visual, like her hair or eyes. Use a scent that reminds you of her. A touch. A sound she makes. Picture them all together. And when you have, just pretend she is here with you. It's easier if you talk to her out loud, until you learn how to use the voice of your mind only. Try, my beautiful. I am sure that's no big deal for the Goddess of Snow."

We both share a smile, then she closes her eyes. She is quiet for a while, but I can feel the pressure inside her mind. I am tempted to go inside her head but I want her to do this alone. I want her to know her strengths.

"Natalia? It's me, Sia. Can you hear me?"

She pauses for a while and just as I am about to tell her we will try again on the next span, her body goes really tense and she sits up.

"Oh my God! You are alive, Natalia! No, no, no! Please don't freak out, it's only me! God, your Sign! It's burning my eyes. I know it's strange but it's only me. Please, you have to listen! No! Don't! Natalia, it's me!"

I get us both up, water dripping from our bodies and I quickly grab a fur and wrap it around her shaking body. It's not just the cold. She is having a seizure as her body and mind have reached their limits. I open her eyes with my fingers and hold her close to my chest.

"I shouldn't have let you do that. Come back to me, Phaea. Please come back."

Her big eyes look sore and teary when she looks at me. She goes limp against my body and I pick her up in my arms. I lay us both in the furs facing each other. I lift her little body up for her eyes to be level with mine. I need to know her mind is safe. One thing I have learnt in the many wars I fought: broken bodies can be fixed, but broken minds can't. Not as easily anyway. Many beings only become truly enslaved when their minds have been broken.

She is not shivering anymore, but now her eyes are leaking water. Humans are so alien. I press my pulsing Sign on hers to give her my strength. I wish I could kiss her, but unlike the Tarrassian show of affection, the Human one is a bit dangerous. Especially when we are both naked under the furs and my cursed cock thinks it's about to get wet. Luckily, she is too drained to notice.

"I scared her away," she says with a deep sigh. "She pushed me out of her mind like she does with her monsters. Telling me she couldn't hear me and that I wasn't there."

"Yes, you can't breach her mind without her permission. We will keep on trying. Slowly, until she's willing to understand and accept. Tannon must be hurt, otherwise he would have explained to her about the Sign. Or at least she would be familiar with mind reading."

"So, is she on her own?" she asks, and more tears leak out.

"Was her Sign faded?"

"No, it was really bright and pulsing. I saw it from the inside of her head. It burned my eyes."

"I'm so sorry I didn't think about that, my Phaea. I am learning as you are about the Sign. It has been too long since my people had it. When we talk inside each other's minds, our Signs just reflect into one another. It doesn't hurt us. But someone else's Sign would burn you. You must have your mind eyes closed when you reach her again. The good thing is, if her Sign was that bright and pulsing, it means Tannon was nearby. He may be hurt, but they are together. He will heal faster for her. The need to protect a mate is stronger than anything else. Tannon is the strongest male I know. He will not leave her unprotected. He knows what this planet is. Now will you stop worrying and just sleep?" But as I place a kiss on her forehead, I can see she is already asleep. I lower her little body and rest her head on my chest. I caress the soft skin of her back. I wish I could listen to my own reassurance. But I cannot. Tannon must be badly injured. He would have self-healed by now, otherwise. His tiny female is all alone, left to look after him, on a slave planet, with a Sphinx lurking around. And that female has just barely changed from being a cub. Scared of her own shadow.

I have a painful decision to make, but it has to be done. I will take my Queen back to Tarrassia and only then will I return to look for Tannon, free the slaves and return the planet to their rightful owners. I will not risk my Mate. Tannon would understand. Any Tarrassian male would. The Jump technology is easily disturbed by turbulence. It may not function anymore. But if it does, then I will reach Tarrassia and be back in a very short span. Otherwise, it will take two spans, maybe one at full speed. Would Tannon last that long? I look at the pale face resting on my chest. Her soft breath tickles my fur and my heart beats full of contentment under her cheek. My decision has been made.

11

SIA

I'm awake, but I don't open my eyes. I know how this works by now, ever since I have been taken. Sleeping is safer than being awake. Even a nightmare in my sleep is better than my new reality. But then I can smell his scent, I can feel the warmth of his skin and the safety of his body enveloping mine in a hug. And just like that, reality is better than sleep. The back of my body is pressed to his front, from head to toe. Spooning goes to a whole new level when the person spooning you is this big. My body is completely encased by his. I'm trapped in a cocoon of safety.

One thick arm is under my head and the other one hugs me close to him. His palm rests in front of me on the furs and his fingers push up, keeping his arm at a slightly elevated position. Even in his sleep, he makes sure his arm doesn't crush my body. Even in his sleep, he looks after me. His body heat kept me warm through the night. My breath turns into a mist in the freezing chamber, but I don't feel the cold. His body is a furnace against mine. And... very naked. And... so am I. He is not erect against my back, but when someone is that size, it makes no difference really. I can feel exactly how huge his cock is, pressed against the back of my thighs. And I already know what it looks like since I did have a good look. Maybe it's time I did more than look. There are no windows in the chamber as we are deep underground. The soft glow is coming from the vine screen in front of the entrance. And from our Signs. Especially mine. There is no telling if it's still the middle of the night, or morning. I do feel well rested so it must be closer to morning, I think. A soft steam rises from the water trickling down the wall and pooling into the stone tub. For the first time in as long as I can remember, I feel safe, relaxed, and I have a strange need to have a long lazy morning. Never had that need before. Chilling meant thinking and that was dangerous… It allows nightmarish memories to slip in.

I know I have a difficult day ahead and I want to postpone facing reality as much as I can. I know he wants to leave today, to keep me safe. He is so predictable when it comes to that. My safety is his first priority. My wishes only come second to that. And I cannot leave. Not without Natalia, not without helping the Ketosii and not without freeing the slaves. I can't and I won't. So maybe time to set the honey trap? And besides, I have to do this sooner or later. I have to accept this new reality with grace. I am the new Queen. Amongst other things, apparently. But can I do this? My body screams a big fat yes, before I even ask the question. It would be nice if I could convince myself this is all a necessary sacrifice for the greater good. But it's not. Humans and aliens together can call me whatever they want. Queen, goddess, Disney princess… Right now, I just want to be a woman. And this woman wants this man!

I turn around in his arms, which is no easy task, and he wakes instantly.

"Phaea?" he asks with a sleepy voice, and his hands check me up and down, making sure I am unharmed.

"Hanni, Tars," I say, and I reach up to press my lips to his for an innocent morning kiss. I try not to laugh. He looks completely stunned. An army of Noorranni could barge in and he wouldn't notice. He looks like he has no idea what's going on, or if he's still asleep. His cock is much quicker than he is to get the message. It grows against my belly at a rather alarming rate. And now it throbs and pushes at my skin like a wild animal. I reach out and stroke his face. Every beautiful part of it. His eyes that have turned into golden pools, the ridiculously long lashes, his strong lips, the straight nose, the beard I love more with each passing day. I let my hand travel down his thick neck, his chest, his… He grabs both my wrists in a steel hold. A deep frown in between his bushy eyebrows.

"What are you doing, Sia?"

"I am asking for it," I say, and he stops breathing for a second. I gasp when he pushes me so suddenly on my back and places his body on top of mine. It's my turn to hold my breath, waiting for the inevitable pain. His body is so huge. Could easily crush mine. But of course, he doesn't. Even though completely flush with my body, he keeps most of his weight away, using his knees and elbows as support. He watches me carefully, scrutinising my eyes. I can tell the moment he understands. No, I don't have an aneurysm and no, I am not talking in my sleep. The worry on his face is replaced by his usual smug grin and a predatory glint in those copper eyes, heavily flecked with gold.

"Asking for what, my Phaea?" His voice all smug and amused.

"Well, you know…"

"I don't know, you will have to tell me."

His grin widens enough to allow a glimpse of sharp fangs. That makes wetness pool between my thighs. So, I have a thing for fangs? No idea where I find the courage to do that, but I open my legs wide enough for his body to slide in between my wet thighs. His hard abdomen is pressed against my sticky folds. He inhales sharply and suddenly there's no trace of amusement or grin. His face looks fierce and his voice is a harsh whisper as he places his face close to mine. The hold on my wrists becomes almost painful and he uses it to pin my hands above my head. Both the Sign on his forehead and the marks on his arms ignite with bright purple. Mine mirror it shortly.

"What are you asking for, Phaea?"

I swallow hard and my brain sends danger signals I do my best to ignore.

"I am asking for your cock, Tars," I hear myself say.

"See, my little pet? That wasn't too hard."

Wait! What? When did I agree to the pet calling?

"Now tell me where you want it, Phaea," he says with his lips pressed to mine. I reach up to kiss him, but he pushes me back into the furs.

"Where do you want it? You will be sorry if I have to ask again."

I take a deep breath, but all that does is fill my lungs with his scent. Freshly cut grass, crisp smell of mountain dew and something else. Something that my brain translates as home. I wrap my legs around his torso, as far as they can reach anyway, and his pained growl reverberates around the stone chamber. I think he likes my legs. I have noticed the hunger in his eyes when he looks at my legs.

"I want it inside me, please," I pant against his lips.

My own words turn me into an even stickier mess. "I want your cock inside me. Now, please!"

I can only hope I am this eager so I won't have any time to change my mind or second guess myself.

"And you shall have it, my Phaea. It's yours to ask for," he says, crushing his lips to mine. His hair and beard fall over my face like a caress and his tongue invades my mouth, leaving me breathless. I suck on it and every time I do, it sends a powerful jolt to his cock. It pushes at my inner thigh somewhere above my knee and I desperately want it to push against my aching clit. But as long as he's kissing me it can't, because of our ridiculous difference in height. And he sure likes kissing. Our twinned Signs and swirling tattoos glow like electricity conductors, making the chamber look eerie. There's an increasing sense of raw power coming off him like a magnetic wave, and there's a niggling feeling behind the passion. I think it is fear, but this is my first time so it's probably normal. I know he won't hurt me. The passion increases in his kiss and there's urgency in the way his hands move in my hair. One big hand leaves my head and starts going down the side of my body. When it reaches my hip, it grabs and pulls it up, my entire body slamming into his. The folds of my pussy move against his abdomen with a loud wet sound. It makes him growl in a more feral way than usual. Also, it's not lost on me, he has released his claws and they dig slightly at the flesh of my hip. With a quick move he leaves my lips and moves down my body. The hand on my hip is keeping me pinned to the furs and the other one takes hold of my tits, feeding them to his mouth, one at a time. It does all sorts of things to me. Despite the pang of fear, despite the jolt of sharp pain as he mercilessly sucks on my nipples, I can't stop watching him with hunger. His wildness turns me on more than it scares me. My fingers fist into his hair and I keep his head pinned to me. He moves to my other nipple and a shudder rocks my body as a sharp fang scrapes it. I wonder if it drew blood, because he stops the sucking and his tongue licks tentatively at my nipple. Suddenly he moves back up and presses his forehead to mine. We are both panting and I'm happy he chooses to talk inside my head. Not sure I can feel my lips anymore.

I don't know how Humans mate their females, Phaea... and it probably doesn't matter since you are untouched. Tarrassian mating might be a bit more aggressive, but our females are stronger and can take it. You are so fragile. My need for you, the mating rage and the power of the Sign... I...

Tars, you could never hurt me. I trust you.

I am not sure I believe my own words but I have to say it because he needs to hear.

You must tell me if I hurt you or if you want me to stop. I won't be able to, otherwise. Promise me, Phaea!

I promise, I say, and move my hand up and down his back. The hot skin is covered in a fine coat of hair and I move my fingers through it. He kisses me again. It starts gentle, but it quickly turns into a passionate fight of tongues and lips and his fangs scraping at everything. It's never enough to cause any damage, but enough to keep me on edge. And to keep me wet. I do love the feel and the idea of fangs for some reason.

The scent of your arousal is maddening, my Phaea. But I know the taste of it is better.

He moves down my body so fast it makes me jump involuntarily. His hands pin me down as he settles himself in between my thighs. He moves both his hands under my knees, spreading my legs wider, while lifting them slightly. When his tongue plunges inside me without any warning, light explodes inside my head and my ears start ringing. He makes me come with a single touch of his tongue, deep inside my channel. Not sure what that says about me. Before I get to think about it, he opens my knees wider and licks at my folds, at my inner thighs... Oh God! Did I make a mess? I suddenly take another deep breath as his thick tongue laps at my clit.

You must tell me what this is called, Phaea. All females should come with one, he says while sucking on my clit.

I'll tell you later, much later, I say, and he laughs against my shamelessly widespread pussy. As the sucking on my clit increases, my legs go shakier and without him holding them up they would be a dead weight. I tense slightly as he pushes one thick finger inside me. No claw, I notice with relief. But then the finger rubs my hymen and the relief is gone. He strokes it gently in circular motions, but even that is enough to cause a slight pain. Panic slips into my mind. What if I can't do this? What if there is something wrong with me and that's why I stayed a virgin for so long?

You say the word and I stop, remember, Phaea? I would be happy to just drink your juices for the rest of my spans. If that's all you can give me then it's all I shall have.

His words are probably the strangest words of encouragement ever, but they are my undoing.

My turn to ask for a promise.

Promise me you won't stop, unless I ask you to.

He pauses for a bit and I can feel he's not really on board with the idea. That alone is enough to give me the courage I need.

I promise, Sia.

He says my name and it is not because he is frustrated with me. He knows I need to hear my own name at this time. Maybe he does see me and not my Sign, after all.

He spreads my folds with his fingers and presses a small kiss on my hymen, before lifting himself up on his knees, in between my thighs. He does the most unexpected things. And the sexiest.

He watches me with dark eyes and I curse myself for shivering. I don't want him to know his predatory look scares me. A bit...

He grabs both my ankles in a hold of steel and pulls me lower, towards him. He lets go of my ankles only to grab the underside of my thighs and pull me even closer. His eyes never leave mine, and even though I try to focus on those pools of dark gold, my peripheral view notices his shoulders growing and his muscles bulging.

He rests my feet on his shoulders and I can feel them stretch under my skin. His fangs seem longer. I catch a glimpse of the claws and his facial features seem harder. Like they are set in

The Ice Queen

stone, but so profoundly masculine it makes me shudder with arousal instead of fear. He grabs himself and moves his massive cock up and down my folds. I am so incredibly wet and yet, as he does that, I feel another gush of hotness pooling out of me. I also feel the size of his cock. Not that I wasn't aware before. But having it against my pussy, as I know he is about to push it in, makes it all too real. It's too long and too thick and the large mushroom head is a problem in itself. Yet, what makes me panic is the hardness of it. My brain can only form one word. Impale. It's stupid and I hate it and I am desperate he will ignore his promise and stop anyway and my breathing is… And then I forget all thoughts as there's nothing but pain. Pain like I have never felt in my entire life. The world goes dark around me, a cold sweat covers my body and I think I am about to throw up.

There is more pain as he pulls my body up from the furs and cradles me to his chest. Wave after wave after wave of pain and fire going through my veins. My ears are still popping, as I slowly regain more of my consciousness. The pain is dull, rather than sharp, and I finally take a deep breath of air. I can smell blood. My own. He is deep inside me, but he is not moving. His body is tense and sweaty with the effort of keeping still. He holds me up to his chest, arms wrapped around me, like I am the most precious thing in the entire world. His face is buried in the side of my neck and he is even holding his breath. Eventually, he lets it out and presses a wet kiss to my neck.

I said I wouldn't hurt you but that was always going to be a lie. You are so tight. So small. I am sorry. And I am sorry I had to rush this. I was afraid the more time you had to think about it the more anxious it would make you. I wanted nothing more than to worship your body for many nano rotations, before I go inside you. Do you want me to stop now?

My body relaxes and that makes me slide lower on his cock. He groans in my neck and I just wait for the pain. There is discomfort and the strange feeling of being full, but no pain. I all at once realise I'm not the world's oldest virgin anymore, I have Tars' cock deep inside me and he looks like he will die shortly, unless I say something.

I don't want you to ever stop. I think I want you inside me for the rest of my days.

My legs wrap tighter around his waist and my arms around his neck. At their own initiative, the muscles inside my core start to spasm and squeeze his cock. Tars lets out all the air he was holding and grabs the back of my neck to hold my head still. He gives me a hungry kiss and his cock starts to throb violently inside me, even though he's not moving yet.

"My perfect mate," he whispers into my mouth.

Both his hands go down my spine, caressing my bottom cheeks and then grabbing one in each hand. He starts lifting me slowly up his length.

"A better male would tell you he would go slowly," he says in between kisses. "A better male would go easy on you. But I am no such male," he whispers in my ear.

"I don't want it slow and I most definitely never wanted a better man. There is no better man. Only you."

He doesn't reply, but the heart in his chest and his Sign do. My whole body reverberates with the energy pouring through his. He grabs at my ass, claws and all, but I don't care about fear anymore. He pushes me all the way up to the mushroomed top of his cock, then slides me back down. Again, and again, increasingly adding pressure. I kind of lose myself in his maddening pace. My brain is clouded with pleasure, my pussy gushes loudly with every slide and my mouth desperately tries to feed on his. He pushes me back down onto the furs, roughly enough to make me gasp, and lowers himself above me. This time I don't worry and I don't care. There's only passion and a hunger as consuming as his. He unwraps my legs from around his waist and puts them up on his chest, feet on his shoulders. I push my pelvis into his and meet his powerful thrusts with my own. He grows even bigger inside me and there's a slight pang of pain, but somehow it makes me feel more. Better. Deeper. There's even worse pain in the over-stretched muscles of my thighs as he pushes his body onto them. His hands leave my ankles and go up my legs, over my hips, to the sides of my body and finally they grab hold of my boobs, squeezing my sore nipples. One hand goes up, caressing my throat, my chin and then a thick finger parts my lips, delving inside my mouth. I can taste myself on it and I suck it deep into my mouth.

Cum on my cock, Sia!

His thrusts become more violent and I close my eyes so his Sign won't burn my eyes.

Now, Sia! He barks the order inside my head and my body is quick to obey. My legs are shaking and my toes are curling as I gush all over him, hot liquid trickling out of me with every thrust of his body.

His breathing gets heavier and for a moment his girth becomes wider, stretching me beyond possible, and he releases inside me, something that feels like a huge load of hot lava. Over and over again. And even more surprisingly none of it comes out. After what feels like an eternity, he turns us both to one side, facing each other, and places his forehead on mine. More than half of his hard cock is still inside me and for a brief ridiculous moment I wonder if it's stuck. I think I don't mind the idea.

Mine! he says inside my mind.

Yours! I agree.

12

TARS

The smell of her sweet blood is pulling the fog of pleasure off my brain. She did not complain, but her small body took me deeper than I have ever been inside a female before. She was indeed made for me. My perfect match. My perfect mate. That doesn't mean she's not hurt or in pain. The smell of her blood is proof enough. I may not be able to talk to the Ketosii, but it's a good thing they understand me. I will ask Mother for something to relieve her pain and discomfort. My Phaca is too shy about these things to ask for it herself. I gently pull my still hard cock from her tight channel and, sure enough, it's smeared in her blood. It's also covered in our juices mixed together and it makes me proud. I have never spilled my seed inside a female. This was just as new to me as it was to her. It also makes me proud to remember she asked for it herself. When I least expected it. And despite my smugness and confidence, part of me was thinking she might not ever ask.

I lift us both up from the now very messy furs and take us to the stone tub. I sit and place her on my lap. The contact with the hot water makes her squirm and moan when it touches her sore insides. I try to place her back against my chest, but she turns sideways on my lap. She pulls her knees up and wraps her arms around me, hiding her face in my chest. She's nothing but a small ball of softness curled on my lap. She seems so fragile and vulnerable, and there is this sweet feel of surrender about the way she curls against my chest. I also feel vulnerable when she is like this. Without her usual coldness and snooty defiance scraping badly at my temper, I am completely defenceless in front of this female.

"What does Phaea mean?" she asks so softly I can barely hear her.

"It means water flower," I tell her, and place a kiss on top of her head.

"Of course, it does," she says with a contented sigh.

"They blossom on top of Tarrassia's Still Waters. They are a beautiful pale blue and they glow in the dark moonlight, even though their petals close during the dark span. They are the symbol of the Royal House. That is why one is carved onto our foreheads," I explain. A thought comes to my mind and it makes me smile. "Your grey eyes have the same colour as our Still Waters, your head fur hair is the colour of the frost on the Spark Mountains and your forehead is glowing with the symbol of the Royal House. You look more Tarrassian than any of us."

"I like it when you say head fur hair."

She smiles against my skin, then says something that makes me freeze.

"Your water flower, Nymphaea Caerulea… I should have guessed that's where Phaea came from."

I lift her chin slightly to look her in the eyes. I speak my language, she speaks hers and the device inside our ears translates. That is how it works. But the words she is saying do not translate. They don't have to. I know exactly what they are.

The old language of the Astrals is only spoken by the Elders and not uploaded in any translation device. It is forbidden. I had to learn it as a cub, because I was going to be King one day. No one else is allowed to speak it, but she does it like it's nothing. Like it's normal for an alien from galaxies away to know the sacred language of my people.

"Why is it that you can speak the Sacred Language, my Phaea?"

"Sacred?" she asks with a small voice.

"The name of the blue water flower. You said it in the old language of the Astrals, my Phaea. It is a forgotten language, only spoken by the Elders during the Sacred Rituals. Why would a Human be able to speak it?"

"Why indeed, Tars. I think it's best if I stop asking and just go with the flow."

My device translates that as blind acceptance and I don't really know what she means. Could the Ketosii be right? Is she a goddess? Is she hiding things from me?

"What happens today, Tars?"

"Today we leave for Tarrassia. You will try to reach Natalia's mind again and if you can't, I will return for them once you are safe on Mother Planet," I tell her, and I mentally prepare for battle.

"Okay."

Okay? She's not protesting. Have I hurt her that much during mating she has no fight left? I watch her with a worried look, but she seems happy and content cuddling up to me. It is quite common for Tarrassian females to become very docile once they have been mated. Maybe Human females are the same.

Suddenly I get all tense and get us both out, water dripping everywhere, and I wrap my startled female in a fur. I grab my Sword and prepare to barge through the vine entrance panel. This chamber is too small for battle.

"Tars, what is it?"

"Someone is coming."

"Yes, one of the Ketosii most likely. There is no sign of disturbance in the main cave. No enemy invasion," she says with a smile. "And you are kind of naked and dripping water everywhere. Put your sword away before you scare them. That too," she adds, looking at my erect cock.

If I think about it, what she says makes sense and I do look kind of ridiculous. However, she is back to being snooty and she's telling me what to do and... I don't get to finish my thoughts, because she grabs my hand holding the Sword and places a kiss on my knuckles. Then she smiles at me. And that's that. No more thoughts.

A soft female voice on the other side of the screen says something and pushes a fur wrap inside the chamber. My Queen's eyes go big as she unwraps it.

I smile at her excitement over the garments. I am also pleased with the Ketosii's care for her. Their kindness will be rewarded. I will never allow any harm to come to them or to this planet again. They wear strange wraps around their bodies, which may not even be clothing. They look organic. So, someone must have worked all throughout the dark span to make my Phaea a new garment. She is as happy as a cub when she puts the long leather dress on. Me, not so much, because it covers her beautiful body from me. I decide on the spot I will only keep her naked inside our Royal Chambers when we get back.

"This is so beautiful," she says, touching the blue leather. "I wonder how they managed to make this so soft. It just flows and it fits like a second skin."

I have to admit, the dress looks beautiful on her. Anything would look beautiful on her.

She gets even more excited about the stripy fur cloak. They cut holes for her arms in the big pelt and there's some sort of ribbon made of vines around her neck, to keep the fur nicely wrapped around her. There are also foot coverings made of a thick white fur, and I couldn't be happier knowing my Queen will be warm. Even though I can regulate my body temperature, I have started to feel the increasingly cold weather.

"They are so considerate, I can't believe they have noticed how fond I was of my stripy fur."

"When we go back home you will have the finest furs, my Phaea."

"This one is special. It's the first gift you gave me. It will always be more special than all the riches of the world."

For a nanoclip I watch her and the fur in confusion. Then I remember I killed that stripy beast for her. Does she treasure that? Small things are more important to her than precious gifts?

Something about that makes me feel soft on the inside and my throat feels tight. I feel weak and powerful at the same time.

"Ready to face the world?" she asks, offering me her small hand.

"Yes, my Phaea. I am ready to take you to the safety of Tarrassia."

She laughs and sends a questioning look below my waist. I realise I am still naked and reach for my kilt. I would happily walk around naked, just to hear her laugh.

Outside our chamber and its hot spring, the underground cave is freezing cold. Everything is covered in a sheet of ice. Would they not know how to make a fire?

There is hardly anyone around, except for the cubs chasing each other. Strange. Mother sits where we left her, in the middle of the main large chamber.

We exchange greetings, and Phaea thanks her for the gifts. We are offered more fruit and roots, and I am surprised but very pleased when my Queen allows me to feed her in front of strangers without any fight. Perhaps I should have mated her from the first time we touched and our Signs ignited. When she gets distracted by the curious cub who touched her Sign on the other span, I discretely ask Mother for something to ease Phaea's discomfort. She hasn't said a word of complaint, but I noticed how her lips tightened in pain when I sat her on my lap.

Mother is quick to understand what I need and sends a female to get it.

"Where is everybody this span, Mother?"

No matter how nice the Ketosii seem, I can't trust anyone who is not Tarrassian.

"Our mist form has made mating quite difficult and somehow less pleasant. Now that Khione has restored the balance of the weather and we have our full bodies once again, mating is a lot more pleasant. So, all the couples are busy mating."

My Phaea covers her mouth with both her little hands to suppress a laugh. We both exchange a knowing smile. A female returns with a bowl crafted of animal bone and hands it to my Phaea.

"For your mating pains," she explains.

My Queen's face turns a delicious shade of pink and she throws me a look that could kill. I just shrug and give her a contented smile.

She makes a funny face when she drinks the potion, but I am happy to see she does.

I brace myself for what comes next. I need the Ketosii to bring my ship back from wherever they are hiding it. I may not know how to rule like my father, the Wise King, but I know how to make all beings bend to my will. Mother and her people will learn my protection comes with their obedience. It is how the Tarrassians keep the planets we free safe.

"Mother, I need your people to bring my warship back. I will take my Queen to the safety of Tarrassia and I will return with my Warriors to free your planet. The slavers will be slaughtered, the slaves will be freed and returned to their homes if possible and the Noorranni shields around your planet will be destroyed. Your planet will be under Tarrassian protection from now on and no one will dare disturb your people without the wrath of my Sword."

I look at her, expecting her approval and especially her gratitude. Can't really tell what beings without eyes think, but I don't have to be a body language reader like the Humans to discern her dismissal. She just turns to my Queen, ignoring me like one would a spoiled cub asking for ridiculous things.

"Khione cannot leave us," says Mother, and my hand tightens on the tilt of my sword.

Please, don't, Tars. We need them to get our ship, remember? Be calm and let me talk to her.

I don't say anything because the truth is my female is also treating me like a cub. Yes, what she says makes sense. That's what my father would have done. That's what Larrs would do. I don't trust myself to say anything, so I don't. Not that words are what I need. I need to grab my female, make these creatures return what they stole from me and leave. Sia takes my silence for agreement and returns her attention to Mother.

"Would it be okay to ask a few questions, Mother?" my Queen asks, and her calm and demure manner remind me of my mother.

I feel uncomfortable and the old feeling of not being enough rips at my mind.

Mother nods in agreement.

"We are looking for a female who looks like me, but with bright red hair and a Tarrassian male. We got separated and they might be in danger. Would your people know where to find them?"

Why didn't I think of asking them? Of course, they know where they are. And they had better tell me.

"Yes, we do know, Khione, but that won't help you find them. The Sphinx Assyrin took them away to his mountain."

My heart weeps. There is no hope for them. They are lost to us. My Phaea tries to look strong and composed, but I can feel her shivering on my lap. I pull her close to my chest and she lets me.

"Will it… eat them, Mother?" she asks with a shaky voice.

"Who can tell, Khione. The Sphinx Assyrin does whatever he feels like. He likes playing with his prey and sometimes he lets it go. There is no telling with him. The big Tarrassian male was injured and was not awake when the Sphinx Assyrin took them in his claws and flew away with them."

Why was Tannon so injured he couldn't heal? I will never know… Though he cannot be dead. We have a bond. I would know it, I am sure. And the female is still alive as Phaea could reach her mind the last span.

"Was the female injured, Mother?" asks my Phaea, and it breaks me to see her this worried.

"She didn't seem injured. She was making a lot of noise and throwing moss at the Sphinx Assyrin."

"She was doing what?" asks Phaea, and I think maybe the red female has her mind broken.

"Yes, we thought it was a strange thing to do. I don't think she knew of his kind. She kept calling him this 'Stupid Cat' name, but he is the Sphinx Assyrin, not 'Stupid Cat'."

"Oh, Natalia…" says my Phaea to herself.

I have made my decision. Tannon and the female might be lost forever. I cannot find them on this span.

I can see more Ketosii emerging from their chambers.

"We will travel with you to the location of our ship, Mother. Now!"

I rise and place my Phaea on her feet, only for her to go around me and sit on a different boulder. I let out a small growl and a few cubs scurry away.

"Do you know where they keep the slaves, Mother?" she asks.

Sia, don't worry yourself about the slaves. They will be freed when I return.

Nothing... She is refusing me entry to her mind! On purpose!

"Yes, Khione, we do. They are in the underground tunnels and a span ago when we checked last there were fourteen of them. There may be fewer now, as the Harsallii guards badly hurt a few of them."

My Phaea covers her mouth and hugs herself. Despite my anger, I cannot see her like this. That's why I need her away from here. Humans are too fragile for the cruelty of the galaxy.

"As our bodies were nothing but mist, we could go in and out of the tunnels. But in this form, we can't. Without us, the slaves will not last long. For some reason, the Noorranni haven't had any buyers in a while and they have forgotten about these poor beings. They are at the mercy of the Harsallii. They don't feed them. We left water and fruit for the poor creatures whenever we could. A small Noorranni ship came about nine spans ago. They brought a badly hurt male and two Garrii females and left as quickly as they came. The Harsallii have already killed one of the Garrii females. They are fragile creatures."

"Are there any beings who look like me amongst the slaves, Mother?"

Cursed blasters of fire! This is not going to end well. I have to take her away now. I try to reach for her but the coldness in her eyes stops my hand from touching her. Why is she looking at me like that, after the way she gave herself to me? How dare she?

"There have been many looking like you, Khione, and I am sorry that even some of your kind have lost their powers and become helpless slaves. Now, there are only two females like you in the tunnels. But one may be no more. She has been there the longest and the Harsallii guards like to..." She gives a worried look to the cubs nearby and stops herself from explaining. I can see from my Queen's terrified expression she knows what Mother meant.

"The male they brought nine spans ago might also be of your kind. Hard to tell with his injuries. He also may be no more. They hurt him more than other creatures. He doesn't scream, so they hurt him even more."

Phaea jumps to her feet and the worry on her face looks different. More personal.

"You know this male, Sia?" I try to sound normal, but who am I kidding? The War Beast is not far from taking over me.

"Tars, please. Not now. I know who he might be. We were taken together. At some point he was removed from the Norrannii ship we were on."

"Why were you together, Female? Answer me!"

She just ignores me and keeps on asking Mother about the Human male. No trace left of the smile or of the docile female. Was she deceiving me to get her way? I don't understand the Ketosii's language. All my information comes from her mind. They could be all in this together. My mind is clouded with pain and anger. My body is trying to grow and I know I won't be able to stop it. Since I have spilled my seed inside her, I feel stronger. My powers seem more intense. But this is not a battlefield. There are cubs and females and my own fragile Mate. Is she as fragile as she looks, though? I flinch and my hand goes for my Sword. My Queen is standing in front of me. So close, I can smell her skin, her hair... her salty tears.

She raises her small hands and rests them in my beard. She tilts her head backwards to look me in the eyes. With leaking water pooling in them, her grey eyes really look like the Still Waters. But they are not still, her eyes. They are pained and full of a silent plea.

I don't want to be safe while others die around me. Please, Tars! If you take me away now, my heart will break again. Like it did when I watched my sister die. I was only a little girl, so I had no power to do anything. Now I am not helpless. Now I have you.

I am a foolish male indeed. My father was right to call me that. I find that I don't care about her reasons or about treachery. I just want to give her whatever she wants from me. And she can have my life if that pleases her, but I would never allow her to endanger herself.

I don't touch her back. I need to hold on to the little control I have left.

"I will free the slaves only when the Ketosii bring my Warship up and you are safe on board. From inside the ship, you can communicate with the Blood Fleet, despite the magnetic shield. If I don't make it back to the ship, you will be safe inside until they find you. These are my conditions and you will obey them."

I speak out loud, so the Ketosii can also hear and obey my instructions.

My Queen seems unsure and even more tormented.

"I thought since the Noorranni weren't here, maybe it would be easy to free the slaves. Why would you… not return?"

Her voice is small and I can smell her fear.

"You will be safe inside the ship, Sia. I can promise you that. My Blood Fleet would come for my Queen no matter if I was to be there or not."

"I don't fear for my life, you doofus! I fear for yours! I didn't think it would be dangerous. I just didn't think and I hate not thinking. And I hate crying in front of people and I hate being emotional."

She hides her face in my chest and small shudders shake her body. This time I cannot stop myself touching her and I wrap my arms around her.

"Have you upset our Khione?" asks the little cub who follows her everywhere. I can hear his angry voice inside her head. He must be angry indeed, because a strong light shines from behind his upper face covering.

"I am a very foolish male," I tell him, and he seems to agree.

"No reason to be afraid, my Phaea. I am a Warrior. Fighting is what I do best. It's just that Tarrassians never fight big battles alone. We are stronger together. The Noorranni would have electric shields in place and the guards who fight for the slavers are huge and vicious beings with no honour. There is no telling how many could be there. That is why I need to know you are safe while I fight them."

"There are 200 Harsallii on Sketos," says Mother, and I can feel the panic in my Phaea's mind.

"You will not fight 200 men all by yourself. I will not allow it," she says with determination in her voice, and she hugs me with all her strength. Do I dare hope she is worried for me?

"Perhaps you won't have to fight them, Tarrassian Assyrin," says Mother. "Not all at once anyway. But we must be quick. A slave escaped on the last dark span. They are looking for her, the fools. In the territory of the Sphinx Kallii. She must be of great value to the slavers, because almost all the Harsallii went out looking for her. The frost blanket is making them slow to return from their search. They did not find her. The slaves left behind have little value to the Noorranni. Only ten Harsallii were left behind to guard the tunnels. And we know how to lift the electric shields. But we must hurry."

"No, you take my Queen to the safety of my ship first."

"No, we need Khione! You cannot take her!"

"I can and I will." I know my growl has made the cubs scatter, but nothing will stop me. "She is MINE!" I scream, and the Ketosii start to gather around Mother in a protective circle.

"SHE is not a possession to fight over," I hear my female say over my growl. Her voice is calm and she walks to the middle of the chamber, where Mother and her people stand. She looks cold and composed. No, not cold. I should know better. There is nothing cold about the female I woke up next to this span. She is regal, imposing, wise, and her presence demands respect and obedience. She is the Queen! And to these people she is a goddess. Watching her beautiful face glow with determination I accept she is also a goddess to me.

"Mother, my beautiful Ketosii, I am humbled by your kindness and your efforts to keep less fortunate beings safe. You had everything taken away from you. Your home, your wings, your freedom and even your bodies. Yet, you did not forget how to care for others, or how to hope. You don't need my help to be yourselves. You only need to remember yourselves and that's the one thing the slavers could never take away from you."

Her words are like Sparks from my mountain. They make the Ketosii's bodies flicker between mist, shimmery fog and then back to solid flesh.

"We cannot survive without the cold, Khione. You brought the frost back to us. The frost keeps the balance," says Mother. "Without the balance of the frost many races will be lost. Only because we were enslaved have the Nooranni been able to poison the Sphinx Planet. Without the frost we cannot filter the air of the Stars. More and more Stars will die."

I can see how Mother's words have affected my Queen.

"Is that what this planet does, Mother? It cleans the air in the universe?" she asks.

"How strange that you don't know this, Khione. We absorb the poisonous gases and release the purified air back into the Stars. We keep the balance."

My Phaea seems overwhelmed with emotion and she grabs Mother's hands in hers.

"You are precious to all of us, Mother. I will keep the Ketosii safe, I promise you, and I always keep my promises. You have to trust me."

Mother seems to think for a while then she nods. They all do.

"Good," says my Phaea. "Now let's free the slaves!"

"There is no us freeing the slaves, female, only me," I remind her, trying not to let anger get me.

And then she smiles at me.

13

SIA

In the end, it takes more than a smile to convince him to let me come along. Now more than ever I need to go because I am worried for his life. He gets angry and doesn't think much and needs a cool head to watch his back. Which of course is stupid of me to even think. The man survived just fine before me and was fighting wars long before I was born. But nothing I do or say makes sense anyway. I've just promised an entire race to keep them safe. Maybe I can still turn into Elsa and freeze some trees for them or something. I would turn into anything if I could just to keep these beings safe. Could it be? Can I hope they can keep my own planet safe? Because today is 'no make sense day', I allow myself to hope our ozone layer is not getting damaged by us but because the Ketosii have lost their powers. It sounds mad. But then again, I have a glowing water lily on my forehead.

Most of the Ketosii go to "unveil the air-travelling machine from the moving sands", as they put it. Some come with us to the tunnels. Only Mother stays behind with the children and I don't let that worry me, as they seem to believe their underground cave is safe.

Once we step outside, I am even more grateful for my warm clothes. It's shocking... It doesn't even look like the same planet anymore. All the landscape has changed. The giant trees are gone. Not covered by snow but gone completely. Like there was never a forest there at all. Everything is covered in a thick layer of snow and all is white as far as one can see.

"You are not going to do this to Tarrassia, are you, Khione? he says with an amused grin. Oh, how I missed that grin.

I don't protest when he takes me in his arms. Time is of the essence here. The snow is up to my knees. It will take me a year to get anywhere on this planet. The Ketosii can float above the ground and Tars can run like a blur. Me? I am just human. At least my insides don't feel raw anymore. Whatever was in that horrible drink Mother gave me helped a lot.

Besides, now that he seems less angry with me, he keeps nuzzling at my hair and it feels amazing to hide my face in his hot chest. The wind is biting at my skin and it feels like my nose is about to fall off. All very standard for the Goddess of Snow, I am sure. I realise I have lost track of time when we reach a strange-looking cliff. More like a vertical stone wall. Just that, a wall with nothing behind it. But as we find the entrance, a large slit in the rock, it starts to make sense. We are going deep under the ground level, a steep rocky path unwinding in front of us. A horrible stench reaches from the belly of the tunnels and it's getting increasingly dark. We don't need any source of light, as our Signs and tattoos give a blue and white glow. The light coming from underneath the Ketosii's helmets is also brighter in the dark. I realise with dread we are like a walking beacon. Tars puts me down and hands me something. I almost drop it because of its weight. It's the strange tube he's been carrying attached to his kilt. A weapon. A fire blaster, he explains in my head. He shows me how to aim and how to keep myself safe from its flame.

I am not good with weapons, Tars, I reply in his head. *You need it more. Mother said they have electric rods. You can't just fight them with a sword.*

It is not just a sword. You don't know what you are saying, female. His voice is angry in my head.

You will take the blaster and you will use it if your life is in danger. From this moment, until you are safe back on Tarrassia, you will follow my orders, without a single questioning word. Is that understood?

His eyes have white-gold specks and his body frame has started to grow. There is no point talking to him when he is like this. Besides, I have to trust him on this, so I just nod.

He tells the Ketosii to keep me surrounded and safe at all times. And because he's an asshole he also tells them what he will do to their heads if they don't, and then just turns and walks away without even looking at me. A total asshole!

As we walk deeper into the tunnels, the stench becomes unbearable. To me anyway. No one else seems to notice. Has my sense of smell always been this sensitive? If I think about it, all my senses seem more intense. More alive. I can't see anything, as the Ketosii surround me like a shield and they are much taller than me. I can't even see Tars ahead. The smells grow heavier. I feel a bit nauseous and I do everything I can not to retch, as we have to keep quiet.

The air is heavy with the smell of blood — different types I think — and sweat, vomit, decomposing bodies and something else. Formol. The smell of the Noorranni. I could never forget that smell. As we go forward, there's a new smell. I don't have anything familiar enough to compare it with. It's just disgusting. It makes the air heavy. It must be the Harsallii guards. And then, I hear the noises. Faint weeping and agonised cries. None of them

Human. Not sure if that is a good thing. I can hear chains. And then a sharp scream, like the shriek of a wounded bird. Harsh voices shout something and my translation device picks up scattered words.

"It's your turn, Garrii, you might even like it!" A rhythmic sound makes my skin prickle. Laughter. They are laughing at them... Suddenly, I forget about trying to keep quiet and gasp as the bodies of all twenty or so Ketosii close in on me, like they do when they want to protect Mother. And they are freaking cold. It's like being hugged by an iceberg. I am, however, more worried about the hell ahead. There's screaming and growling and hissing and all sorts of non-human noises. A growl seems vaguely familiar but it's too scary to be Tars'. I hope so, anyway. There are noises like an electric shock touching flesh and I can instantly smell it. I am aware he needs to know I am safe so he can focus, but how can I just not do anything? Are they hurting him? Just as I decide to push the Ketosii away, they release their hold on me and float away. I wish I could do that. The floor is covered in a pool of blood of different colours. Most of it looks frozen, but the orange one is fresh and there is steam rising from it. As I watch in disgust, the pool of blood grows bigger. The noises of the fight have been replaced by soft weeping and occasional desperate growls. Desperate and weak. Slippery, strong arms grab at me and I am pressed to a very wet and smelly chest. I only care he is safe and unharmed.

"Sorry, my Phaea," he says once he notices the state of my once pristine fur. I stroke his beard and give him a brief smile.

"It's okay. I am just happy it's not your blood. Are you hurt at all?"

"Not even a scratch," says the show-off.

Then, I brace myself to look around. It takes a while to understand what I am looking at. Are those heads and littered body parts still twitching? The bodies, or what's left of them, are covered in some sort of shell, similar to a cockroach. There are spikes sticking out here and there, and by the far wall an enormous dismembered arm with pincers instead of fingers. Earwig-like pincers. Eww... The worst to look at are those heads scattered around. A huge elongated scalp with some sort of claws for a mouth. It's hard to tell what they used to look like, as my crazy mate butchered the life out of them. Literally. Is this a Tarrassian custom? Removing heads?

Pain... I feel inundated with pain. I realise it's the Ketosii. A few are gathered above a pile of something on the floor. A flash of my sister's small body scattered by the cars fills my mind. The blood, the screams...

"Don't look, Phaea. The female is dead. Her suffering long gone," says Tars, stroking my hair with a very bloody hand.

But I do look. I have to. I always look.

The rotten flesh tells me this creature has been dead for a few days. Before the frost. She is naked and humanoid-looking, despite the bent-backwards knees and the long tail trapped under what's left of her body. The tip of her tail is missing and so are what must have been her breasts. A raw strip of pink flesh left on her chest. She is not missing body parts because of decomposition. They were cut from her while she was alive. Her face is badly trashed and there are two holes in the top of her head, like missing horns or something.

"Phaea... please, we must hurry now."

Yes, I have to leave this place. It is like a scene from Dante's Inferno. Only this is real.

This side of the tunnel is lined with cells as far as the eye can see. They are nothing but holes dug into the walls of the tunnel, with a live-looking sort of gate in front. It looks like glass, but it shimmers and sparks as the Ketosii put their hands in front of it and make it disappear. An electric shield, I realise. Tars warns me not to move and not to touch anything as they all rush to the cells to release the beings. If they can find any alive, that is. The walls are covered in frost and probably the sudden change in weather took its toll on these already weak beings. As different shapes and sizes of bodies are carried out into the main corridor, I realise that most are indeed dead. Two large and very feral-looking males are dragged out by Tars. He growls a warning at them and one of them tries to attack him. Tars pins him down, sword at his thick bull-like neck. As he does so, two Ketosii stab the male's arm with a small sharp bone.

"Mother said it's safer if we put the slaves to sleep. Their minds might be broken. We will wake them when it's safe," one explains, and looking at the other huge male I understand what they mean. He is not attacking, even though he looks bigger than Tars. He's staring somewhere at something only he can see. His red skin is covered in fuzz and he has horns sticking out from his massive head. Despite the dark blood covering him and the burn marks on his body, he seems incredibly strong. Why didn't he fight them or something? One of the Ketosii stabs his thick arm and he doesn't even flinch. He just softly closes his eyes, allowing darkness to take him.

"His mind is broken, Phaea. Most slaves are lost forever in their heads. Entire planets have been lost this way because the mind cannot accept such pain."

As Tars explains, I can see the damage. Only two females and four males are still alive. But one thing is sure: they all look broken. They are all naked, covered in grime, blood and wounds. I feel relieved as they all fall asleep and I can't hear their pained noises anymore.

Tars pulls me close to him.

"We must rush now, my Phaea. We'll take the slaves to the ship. The Ketosii will carry them. There are only two healing pods on board but they can take turns. And if we can do the Jump, they won't need it. They will be well looked after on Tarrassia."

"The Humans?" I ask with a trembling voice. "Mother said there were three Humans here."

He gives me a sad look.

"There are only two Humans, Phaea. A male and a female. But they are both dead. I am sorry I couldn't save your own kind."

"Where are they?" I ask almost against my will. What I am about to do is also against my will and against my common sense.

"I want to see them. And I want us to take them and all the other dead beings out of here. The snow will give them peace. I refuse to let them rot in this filth."

"Yes, my brave, kind Queen," he says, looking at me with glowing eyes. "We will give the dead the respect they deserve. But I won't let you look at the Humans. I don't want the Ketosii to look either. You are all fragile, gentle beings."

"I want to see my people. Someone has to see. I have to see."

He just nods, and the respect and wonder on his face give me the strength I need to do this. He takes my hand and leads me towards the far end cells. I see her body first. It's lying on the floor in front of one of the cells. I can smell the human blood now. Why isn't it frozen? Has she just died? I could have saved her if only I had arrived earlier.

The blood is frozen though, so not sure why I can still smell it. However, they must have killed her just before the weather turned cold, as there is no sign of decomposition. She looks small and completely emaciated. Matted brown hair of what must have been a bob sticks to her face. She has a massive head wound and a pool of frozen blood shines dark under her head. There is no telling if this girl was taken at the same time as me, or if I might know her. Her face has been punched and kicked and scratched, and it's all an unrecognisable mass of flesh. Like all the other slaves, she is naked and one of her thin legs is bent at a strange angle. There is another pool of frozen blood in between her wide-open legs and it's smeared all over her lower body.

Tars pulls me close and presses my head to his chest. I don't want a hug now so I push him away. He seems hurt, but I can't. A hug would make me weak right now. If I start falling apart, I will not be able to do this.

"Where is the male?"

"Sia... they hurt him badly. The sight of his body would give you bad dreams."

"Where is he?"

Tars is not happy with me and for some reason he looks hurt. But I don't really want to patch up his ego when these people died the most horrible of deaths.

"He is still chained to the wall, inside the cell." He points right in front of us.

Did they kill her in front of him? Did they rape her in front of him? I am pretty sure the dead man in there is Brian, the Brazilian girl's bodyguard. Natalia said the Noorranni broke her neck in front of him. And then, he had to watch this... And I have been complaining because I got shiny tattoos.

The floor of his cell is not grey like the rest of them. It's red. The walls and the high ceilings are splattered with red. I need to vomit. It's choking me, but I am trying to hold it down because I know Tars will get me out if I do.

I haven't paid much attention to Yara's bodyguard. He was just a huge, scary presence, always like a shadow behind her. I do remember his bulky frame and the man chained by the wall is definitely him. What is left of him... He looks like an animal that has been skinned. Everything is raw. From his bald scalp to his bare feet. There's a gash on his forehead deep enough to put two fingers in, his eyes are a purple and green swollen mass, there is a bare bone sticking out of his nose, a hole leaking blood on the side of his neck and...

Oh God... still leaking blood. They have just killed him. How will I live with this guilt? I was too late...

The pain he must have suffered... His thick muscular arms are stretched painfully up by chains so tight they broke his wrists. They dangle strangely where they have been pinned to the wall. All his ribs look broken and his heavily tattooed torso is a mass of blue and green blood clots and bones sticking out. There is one open fracture on his lower leg and Tars was right: I shouldn't have looked. Images of my sister's broken little body clutter my mind and I feel like there is not enough air left in the world. I turn to Tars, ready for that hug. But he is not looking at me. He is just staring at Brian's lifeless body.

"Tars?" I ask with a shaking voice.

"How did he last this long? I saw from outside the cell he was in a bad way, but this?" He points at Brian's horrible injuries. "I remember now Mother said he wouldn't scream or beg like the other beings, so they hurt him more. This was done over spans of intense torture. How did he survive for that long?"

I don't understand, why does it matter anymore? I just want him to take me out of here. But for the first time since we met, Tars doesn't seem focused on me. He is just watching Brian.

"Please, just take him down from the chains," I beg him, and he finally snaps out of whatever trance he was in. I close my eyes like a coward. I don't want to see Brian's broken bones. And then I hear it and I open my eyes. Weak and vague but a moan, nevertheless. Tars hears it too and takes a step back.

He is alive. I don't know how, but he is still alive. I quickly go near him, despite the dread his wounds cause me.

"Brian, you are safe now," I stupidly say to a man with bones sticking out of his body.

He opens one eye in the smallest of slits. The swelling and the cuts won't allow him to open it wider. I can only see a glimpse of green and broken blood vessels.

"Not sure if you remember me, I was also taken from London Fashion Week. My name is Sia. I will explain everything later.

Now we have to leave this place. You have to trust me. We are here to help you."

I stop my words suddenly as I can hear Tars' sword being pulled out. Brian's body tenses involuntarily, making him moan with pain.

"Tars, what are you doing? Is that to cut the chains?"

"Please, look away, Phaea. I will put the Human out of his misery. I will be quick. He won't feel it."

"What? No. What are you saying?"

"I don't understand why he is still alive. But he won't last any longer. His pain must be so great, he would want someone to stop it."

"No," I say, pushing his sword away. "Humans are not like that. It may sound cruel to you, but we don't just kill Humans because they are in pain, or because they will die anyway. Everybody deserves a fighting chance. I can't let you kill him."

"But he will die anyway," he tells me with a frustrated voice.

"Then he will die on his own terms."

"So, your kind let themselves die in pain, rather than die sooner?"

It sounds a bit stupid when he says it like that, but still, we are who we are.

"We don't have the long-life spans of your kind, or the healing powers of… well, of everyone else apparently. So, we make the best of the life we have. Good or bad, painful or joyful, we live it either way."

He looks at both Brian and me like we are a bunch of strange aliens, but that's okay, because that's exactly what we are. He puts his sword away and takes his dagger out.

"I need it to cut his chains and he will struggle, causing further injury. Not sure if he has a translation device. Explain to him he mustn't move. Or better, ask one of the Ketosii to inject him with the sleeping potion."

"No drugs!" Brian's voice doesn't even sound human to me anymore and the effort of saying those words causes blood to pour through his broken lips.

"I stay wake!" he says, and blood spills with every word.

Tars watches him like he is about to grow tentacles. What is his fascination with Brian?

"His mind is not broken," Tars says, and it's not a question. It's a statement. One that for some reason puzzles him.

"Of course, his mind must be broken after what he had to go through," I tell him. "His mind and body are as broken as it gets, but his spirit is not. That is why if he wants to stay awake and fight, we will allow it."

"What is Spirit? All beings have minds, bodies and souls, nothing else. What is a Spirit?" he asks, and I suddenly understand why he is so fascinated with Brian. He is smaller, weaker and more hurt than all the slaves we rescued. Yet, he is the only one unbroken.

"The Spirit is the essence of Humankind. It gives us a fighting chance and as long as we have that, we cannot be broken."

14

TARS

I am trying with every little bit of self-restraint I have to keep my anger at bay and my body from growing. The Elders were right. Once you mate the one who awakens your heart, one's powers increase. Killing ten Harsallii was like cub training. Larrs always says the more power one has the more self-restraint is needed. But I am not him and I don't have much control of anything. I do have to try, because she doesn't like my violence. And with my increased powers, she would like it even less.

I am holding my precious female as we all rush through the endless stretch of white to my warship. Holding her should bring me peace. But it doesn't. I am itching to kill something and soothe my anger. It's not just anger. There is a strange feel of betrayal and the old feeling of not being good enough. And then I am worried and anxious, because there is some information in all this I don't know and she is not telling me. She is being dishonest and it makes my heart bleed. She said she didn't know the Human male. Just someone she knew of, she said. But she knows his name. She is close enough to him to know his name. And she said they were taken together. And to make everything worse, she gave him her fur. The special fur, she said. Because I gave it to her. And then she just gave it to another male. I didn't let my rage out. I kept quiet. My brain can reason. I know I shouldn't feel jealous of a male who may not be alive by the end of this span. I know Humans can't regulate their temperature, he lost a lot of blood and he is in a great deal of pain. He is also being carried by a freezing-cold-to-the touch Ketosii. So, she gave him her fur. The special one.

It shouldn't bother me, but it does. And now she is shivering in my arms, despite being close to my skin. She would rather be cold, just to keep the male warm. I struggle to keep my own body temperature up. But what scratches the most at my skin is the marks on his body. She said Humans don't get mating marks, but despite his injuries and broken flesh, I could see the marks on his arms, torso and back. Strange black symbols. Is he mated? I know with some species the mating marks are different. Either the male or the female get them, instead of both. Could he be her…? No, I can't say it or think it. She wouldn't wear my marks otherwise. And she was untouched by a male. Unless… Could Humans be this deceiving? Could she?

I mustn't let my insecurities cloud my mind. I must focus.

Running in the soft blanket of white frost is not easy. My boots are heavy with water and they slow me down even more. The Ketosii can float above the surface of the frost and they effortlessly carry the slaves we rescued. It angers me to see how they slow down on purpose, so I can catch up. Like I would for a weakling or a cub. To the depths of fire with it this span.

Tars? Are you okay?

"I am good. We just have to rush," I say loudly, so she can hear me over the howling wind. I cannot allow her inside my head when I am like this. I can feel she is hurt by my refusal to let her into my head. Good. She can see what it feels like, not being allowed into your Mate's thoughts.

I refuse to be reasonable. I will keep her safe. I will keep all of them safe, but I can be as unpleasant as I wish.

I can see the large group of Ketosii ahead. They gather around a white hill. I realise with relief it is my warship. Once activated the snow will melt and the shiny copper metal will be visible from great spans of length, without the cover of the trees. We must rush. I hold my treacherous little female with one hand and press my other one on the warship's surface. It comes to life and the white frost disappears instantly. The ramp lowers itself and starts shimmering. To add to my offence, the perfectly smooth mirror shine of my ship is badly scratched after being submerged in the sand. Tannon would rage like a wounded animal. I call it my warship, but this is really his ship. He treats it like a cub. Except for the Ketosii who carry the slaves, all the others keep their distance from the warship, like it's a wild beast. Once inside, the ship is programmed to answer to my genetic code, like everything else that is Tarrassian. If I could only do that to my Queen. Program her to answer to me only. I thought the mating took care of that, but it turns out Human females don't turn docile after being mated. I put her down and pretend not to see she is trying to reach for me. I initiate all the control panels and the only two healing pods on board.

The Human male is still awake. He watches everything through a small opening in one eye. He is much bigger than the Human females, but much smaller than most beings out there. The size of a Tarrassian female. But he is strong. The Warrior in me can only respect such strength. But the male in me is very irritated by this. Is that why she is so protective of him? She admires his strength? She thinks he is a better male? I have to find a way to prove myself to her. And I will.

I know I should ask her to explain to him about the healing pod, as he seems wary of me and of the Ketosii. But I don't want her to talk to him.

He listens carefully while I talk. He is lying on the floor and there's a fresh pool of red blood gathering under his body. And ruining my Queen's fur. A Ketosii is supporting his body as I finish explaining about the pod and how he will be put to sleep in there as he is healing. I know he wants to stay awake.

I wait for a sign of his understanding, but he just looks at the two alien females still sleeping in the arms of the Ketosii.

"They need it more," he says with a weak voice.

"Oh, Brian, cut the macho crap!" says my Phaea, and the way she fights for him irritates my skin.

"They are not as badly injured as you are. And most of these people... aliens can self-heal. Please, let's not do this, okay?" she says, pleading with him... The Queen of Tarrassia begs no one!

I don't let it show. I must control my anger. I must.

After the Human is safely put in the pod, the healing MI starts running its tests. Sia gasps as the machine gives us its findings.

"Damage of biological tissue, 78%; blood loss, 54%; bone and cartilage damage 40%; life expectancy 0.7%. Asking permission to initiate the relief procedure."

"Relief? What is that, Tars?"

"You know, Sia. I have already explained to you this male cannot survive. 0.7% is nothing."

Her little chin is raised in defiance, despite the water leaking from her grey eyes. Her small hands fist by her body, and she shivers with emotion and determination.

"0.7% is something. It is a fighting chance and he will have it," she says, staring at the pod and at the male inside. The male she leaks tears for.

"MI, initiate the healing procedure! Now!"

"Yes, Queen of Tarrassia. Initiating healing procedure."

I am calm. I won't act on my anger. I am calm. She says something to me but I don't want to talk to her. I must stay calm. I go and look at the slaves instead. Before we depart, I need to choose the most injured one for the other healing pod. The males are far more injured than the females. However, they are not right inside their minds and I can't risk waking one. The Ketosii assured me they would stay asleep until given the antidote. It is best to let them sleep. The bigger female is a Kartassii and there is a chance she is mated to the two males who attacked me in the tunnel, since they are the same species. They normally have a mating triad. It might not be a coincidence they are together. It's best I don't find out. So, I ask the Ketosii to wake the other one. No idea what she is. They are all dirty, smelly and grimy but this one is completely covered in it. Mother said the Noorranni ship brought the Human and two Garrii females. They killed the one who tried to run, so this may be the other one. But Garrii females are beautiful and their skin shines with their emotions. And they have long blue head fur hair. Meanwhile, this one has some matted sort of fur glued to her scalp in a disgusting mess of moss, dirt and dried leaves. She also reeks of Human blood. I ask the Ketosii to wake her. As she does, she scurries away from us, hiding under a seat. She is watching us from there with eyes as small as slits. Impossible to see what they look like. Why is she squinting?

"What species is she?" asks Sia, by my side. She is so close, her scent is invading my body. Too close. I take a step away from her and address the female.

"I am the King of Tarrassia. You are no longer a slave. Once you are healed you will be returned to your home planet, if it is permitted. You are safe and under my care."

I can see how she relaxes as soon as I mention my Mother Planet.

"You do look Tarrassian, but no Tarrassian I met had that

on their forehead," she says in that unmistakable happy voice of the Garrii.

"I am mated, it is the Sign of the Astrals. This is my Queen," I add, pointing at my female. But without looking her way.

"That is very pretty. And shiny. I like shiny," she says, coming out from under the seat. She straightens her body and opens her bright purple eyes. Suddenly she looks unmistakably Garrii despite the dirt.

She bows her head to my Queen.

"You are very beautiful, Tarrassian Queen," she says.

"Thank you, so are you. Are you hurt? What is your name?" asks my silly female. What is it with Humans and names?

"I am named Calena, Tarrassian Queen. Where is the painted male?"

I don't understand what she is saying, but she suddenly sees the Human's pod and runs to it.

"Is he well?" she asks, running dirty long fingers alongside the glass of the pod.

She seems worried so I just tell her he is healing, instead of slowly dying. Her loudly expressed relief pokes at my anger. Are all the females attracted to this male? Is it because he can't be broken?

Calm, I must keep calm.

"There is another healing pod waiting for you. We will travel for Tarrassia now."

"Oh, I am not hurt. I don't need to heal. I will watch over him instead. He kept me safe."

I watch my Queen briefly to see if she is jealous of another female watching over the Human. But she just looks a bit lost, hugging herself and watching me warily when she thinks I am not looking. I am always looking at her.

"He kept all of us safe for as long as he could," the Garrii female says, giving the pod an enthusiastic hug. What a ridiculous female!

Maybe she is unwell, after all. The Human was chained and badly injured. He couldn't help anyone.

"What happened, Calena?" asks my female. Her voice is tired and she keeps hugging herself. Is she worried for him?

Calena tells her that after the other Garrii female was killed, the Harsallii came to collect them from the ship. The male told her to keep a low profile and I have no idea what that means. He also told her to camouflage her beauty and make herself look repulsive. As they travelled through the forest, he kept distracting the Harsallii so they would hurt him more. Each time that happened she was to smear herself with his blood, moss and dirt. By the time they reached the tunnels she smelled like the male and not like a Garrii.

"Didn't they notice your change?" I ask, trying to point out how silly the Human's plan was.

"The painted male said they looked big and stupid. Easy to deceive."

I see. Humans thrive on deceiving. Is that what she sees when she looks at me? Big and stupid?

"In the tunnels he kept on drawing attention to himself, making them mad. So, they hurt him more than us. In the end, I couldn't hide my sorrow at his pain and my skin started to glow under the dirt. They knew what I was, but that is when you arrived."

My hand goes for my Sword involuntarily, as there's a lot of activity around me and the Ketosii act strangely, trying to find the exit.

"They are saying the Harsallii are angry. They have returned to the empty tunnels and now they are marching towards Mother and the cubs. We must help them, Tars," she says, reaching for my hand. I allow it but I don't touch her back.

"How would the Harsallii know where your home cave is?"

"They have always known but didn't bother to attack because we were made of mist. They couldn't see us so they didn't come for us. Now they are coming to look for the missing slaves, but they will see Mother and the flurries," one of them replies inside my Queen's head.

"I think he means the cubs. They call them flurries," she explains, watching me with a silent plea in her eyes. She needs me. Not the Human male, not her alien kind and not anyone else. She needs me and I will prove to her I am stronger and braver than any other male.

I contact my Blood Fleet and my Land Warriors from my hollocom. This planet was unlawfully taken, so they are allowed to come to its rescue.

However, Mother and the cubs do not have that long. But that is fine by me, because killing some filthy Harsallii is exactly what I need.

"Thank you, Tars," she says with a timid smile. "How long will they be? Should the Ketosii wait here or return to Mother's cave? She must be so frightened."

"Yes, tell them to go. The Harsallii will not reach the cave. I will get to them before they go anywhere near the cave. You will stay here with the freed slaves."

I am leaving her with him, but that does not matter. She will be safe on board and that is all I care about. I will put the shield up and cloak the ship. No one would find them, except for my Warriors.

"What do you mean, you will get to them? You can't possibly think to fight them alone. Mother said 200. Your Warriors will be here soon, right?"

She thinks I am not strong enough to fight a Harsallii swarm?

"Our Warriors!" She keeps forgetting her place, my female. "They won't arrive soon enough for Mother and the cubs.

After the Ketosii leave, ask the MI to activate the shield and the cloak. You will be safe. Disobey me in this and I will char your little Human planet."

15

SIA

He just left. Gave me one last crazy, angry look and left the ship, without looking back once. I just want to curl into a ball and cry and cry... and cry. Me. Sia. 'The Ice Queen'. The one who doesn't cry and doesn't feel. He has been increasingly acting strange since morning. Since... we made love. Yes, he was upset when I ignored him and refused to leave without freeing the slaves. Was it because I have challenged him in front of the Ketosii? And if that is the case, do I even want a man who doesn't want me to speak my mind? A man who gets offended because I dare not follow his rules.

The answer screaming inside me is YES. Because he is also the man who looks at me like his world starts and ends with me. He is a work in progress, the big idiot, but he is mine, just as I am his. Maybe Tarrassian women are different and I don't match his expectations either. Maybe we are both work in progress and we have to learn how to respect each other's boundaries and how to compromise. A bit. I will make it work. For now, I have to keep him safe.

An idea pops into my mind.

"Calena, do you know how to use the hollocom on this ship?"

"No, pretty name Sia," she says with a chirpy voice. "Can I call you Sia, now that your King is gone? I like your name. Can I call my young Sia? When I get one that is."

"You can always call me that, even if the King doesn't agree."

She laughs at my words, and now that the ice in her matted mess of hair has melted, I can see two long pointy ears. Really, really pointy. Wow, is she an elf? She still stinks to high heaven and I try not to offend her by retching.

She looks over Brian's body inside the healing pod. I don't for several reasons. He is completely submerged in a slushy glittery gel and it gives me sudden attacks of claustrophobia each time I look. The gel cleaned him, so his horrific wounds are on display now. His naked and now cleaned body is also on display. That's enough reason not to look.

"Are these mating marks? Is he mated?" she asks with a less chirpy voice.

It takes me a while to understand she means his tattoos. I explain to her what they are and she seems relieved. And very excited. Now she wants some for herself. Apparently, Brian here has made an impression on the elf lady.

"I knew the King was being silly thinking my painted male was mated to you, but I thought he might have been mated to another."

"What do you mean, Calena? Why would the King think that? And how would you know what he thinks, anyway?"

"Yes, about that... I am sorry," she says, and all of a sudden she reminds me of every other teenage girl on Earth.

"My people can read all minds, but it is forbidden to do so without permission. It's just that I could feel the King's anger at my male and I feared for his life. I had to. Sorry. Now I am content. The King won't hurt him, even though he hates him.

You won't tell on me, will you? My family won't like it. I will get sanctioned and get loads of chores. I do not like cleaning."

I make a quick mental note to inquire about this girl's age before Brian wakes up and we all get into trouble. But for now, I have other things on my mind.

"So, the King thought Brian might be mated to me?"

"Oh, yes, and he thinks you are both trying to deceive him somehow. He thinks you are full of lies and you like my male because he is braver than he is. He mumbles a lot about this fur you gave away and he thinks the Ketosii are very annoying and you also work with them to deceive him. He doesn't like it that you know my male's name or that you worry over him. He wants to prove to you he is a stronger male and he was really happy to go and kill something and then I had to leave his mind as it all became too vivid for me. For some strange reason, the King likes removing heads."

"I see," is all I manage to say.

"Would the Harsallii harm the King? They are vicious when they attack in swarm formation."

"I really hope not, Calena, because I want to kill him first!"

Speechless, just speechless. There are no words to describe the boiling anger inside me. Why couldn't I get a normal alien like the High General? Or anyone who doesn't think with his dick really? Or anyone who isn't a dick? Unbelievable!

The Ketosii on the ship are getting really nervous and look at me like I have the answer to everything. Keep forgetting they think I am a goddess.

I may not be one, but I am the Queen of Tarrassia and their stupid King is not dying on my watch.

"MI, connect Hollocom with the High Commander of the Blood Fleet."

"Hanni, Queen of Tarrassia. The location of the High Commander is unknown."

Gianna's face comes to my mind, but now is not the time to worry about her.

"MI, connect Hollocom to Second in Command of the Blood Fleet."

"Opening connection, Queen of Tarrassia."

I step back, almost tripping on the hem of my leather dress. A moving screen as tall as me appears in front of me and I hear the Ketosii scurrying away.

On the screen, a large Tarrassian male appears. He watches me with open dislike and it's quite refreshing to see not all of them are obsessed with Humans. Like all of them he is big, scary and handsome at the same time, which shouldn't be allowed. Scary beings should not come with that face. Or that body...

"My Queen?" he asks, and it is obvious he hates calling me that.

"Hanni, Commander...?"

He understands my question straight away, just chooses to be an ass.

"Our names are not to be given freely."

I don't want to start my new life by making enemies, so I choose to keep it amicable.

"I need your name in case I have to communicate without the hollocom. My mind reaches beings by name, not by their titles. I hope this is acceptable."

"I am Commander Nodric, my Queen."

"Thank you, Commander. How long before your fleet arrives?"

"We cannot do the Jump, my Queen. The high winds and the disturbances can badly affect the technology."

"How long?"

"A span. Maybe the Ketosii can hide somewhere safe," he tells me with impatience in his voice.

"It is the King who doesn't have that long, Commander. He went to fight a swarm of 200 Harsallii all by himself."

"Why would the King do that?"

There is an accusatory look in his eyes and at the end of the day it is me who caused all this.

Then I remember I only asked Tars to help, hoping he would come up with some sort of reasonable strategy. He is too hot-headed for that. I should have known better.

"Because he decided to prove himself to me, like a petulant cub. He also decided to cut some heads off, because that's what he loves best. After Tarrassia and his Queen, of course," I say with a deep sigh.

An involuntary smile pulls at the Commander's lips.

"We will travel at maximum speed, my Queen." It is all he says, before closing the live feed on me.

Great. I have to do something. I refuse to let him die.

I quickly explain to Calena how to put the Shield up and cloak the ship, and I really hope she is older than twelve.

I grab a clean thick fur for myself as I am no Goddess of Snow, sadly. I could do with some superpowers, right now.

I ask the Ketosii to take me back to Mother's cave and they seem very happy about that. I hate not being able to call them by their names, as they don't have any. Except for Mother, they all call each other Ketosii. Yet, for some strange reason, I know exactly who is who. The one who carried Calena earlier takes me in his cold arms and we float like air above the blanket of snow, getting thicker by the minute. The entire landscape is a stretch of white, only interrupted by the sight of rocky cliffs and a tall mountain in the distance.

I close my eyes, trying to protect them from the icy wind. I brace myself and try reaching his mind. I just know he won't allow it and I don't want it to break my heart. But I have to.

Tars? Will you talk to me? I need to explain. You got it all wrong, you hot...

I stop myself from name calling and aggravating him even

more. I will deal with him when we get home. Home! I said it and I meant it. Tarrassia is home. A planet I have never seen, but my home is wherever he is.

It is important. Please talk to me. Tars?

Nothing. Just the sound of the blizzard turning my stupid tears into painful icicles.

Back at the cave, all the children gather around Mother, and the one obsessed with me wraps his cold arms around my body. His little helmet digs into my chest, but I ignore it and hug him back.

"Will you save us, Khione?" he asks, and my heart breaks some more.

Mother's voice is weak when she addresses me.

"We did not know about the swarm on the other side of the mountain as we do not float into the Sphinx Assyrin's territory. The Harsallii travelled under the mountain to this side and now my people can see them."

What is she saying? A swarm has 200 insects, whatever those horrible monsters are. That is 400 of them altogether. Against one... No, no!

Tars, you must go back to the ship now. There is another swarm coming your way. Tars? Listen, you idiot! Don't you dare die on me! I am only mated to you. I have never been with another and you know it. I have never even talked to Brian back on Earth. He was just someone I knew of. Humans refer to each other by name, not by title. And his marks were done with paint, you idiot! Can you get that into your thick skull?

Nothing. I don't know if he is giving me the silent treatment or if he really blocked me out, like Natalia.

I cannot let him die, I won't let him. But what can I do? The Ketosii are all watching me from underneath their helmets and I am happy I don't get to see the disappointment in their hidden eyes. The penny is about to drop and they will soon understand

I can't save them. I wish I could be a goddess or an ice queen or even have my Tarrassian army here. But sadly, I am only a Human and this is not a superheroes movie.

'A superheroes movie'. My brain keeps repeating that over and over again. Like a scream inside my head. I feel a huge energy pouring through me and they feel it too. Like they were expecting it. It's no superpower though. I am pretty sure I don't have any. It is hope. Humans may not have superpowers, but we have hope. Anyone can have hope.

"Mother, will you remove your helmet for me?" I say, pointing at it. "Just don't look at me when you do it," I add quickly.

She is quiet. Too quiet.

"Mother?"

"It is a casket, I do not know what a helmet is. And it is part of our faces. We cannot remove it, Khione."

"You are the eldest Ketosii, you can remember the wings. What if it was more to remember?"

"I do not know what you mean, Khione."

"What if you try to push it up?" I say tentatively, but she steps back in fear, as if I have asked her to rip her face open for me. They all do. Except for the children. They just listen attentively. I suddenly remember how on Earth it's easier to teach a child a new trick than an adult. Children take things as they are. No lifelong memory telling you, you can't. So, they just do things adults can't. I look at the little boy still hugging me and I lower myself a bit, to be at his eye level, or casket in this case. There is a dim, cold white light coming from underneath.

"Can you take your casket off for me, Flurry? Just make sure you don't look at any of us when you do."

I position him to face the tall wall of the cave.

He grabs the sides of the casket, fingers meeting at the back and pushes up. Nothing happens, he just makes a sound of pain.

I quickly look at the one I know is his mum, but she gives me the vote of confidence and doesn't even flinch.

"Let's try again. This time push it slowly up and let it rest on your head. Don't remove it. And whatever you do, don't look at us." He nods and I move away. Without any fuss, he pushes it up.

Hope. And more stupid tears, but who could blame me. A powerful beam of pure white light shoots out from his eyes. Two fast lasers of light and energy, hitting the cave's wall and leaving a huge crater behind. The stone hisses and trembles until it quietens down. Before I get to react, all the children pull their visors up and start shooting at the wall like it's the best game ever. The cave starts to rumble under our feet like an earthquake.

"Flurries, put your visors down, please," I say as we all rush out, before the cave collapses on us. Out in the open, some of the adults try their new skills. But something is different, even for the ones who don't. The light under their visors is so strong, casting patterns on the snow. There is a strange energy going through all of them. Fear, pain, memories, hope, power. I flinch when I hear Mother's voice right next to me.

"You have given us our powers back, Khione," she says, grabbing my hands in her cold ones.

"No, Mother. Hardship and pain can make all beings forget themselves. We don't need anyone to tell us what we should be. We need someone to remind us who we used to be. Someone to believe in us. And I will always believe in you, my beautiful Snow Angels."

She watches me with flickering lights under her casket. They all do, as they gather around me. I feel surrounded by more emotion and love than in my entire life. The feeling of belonging to them and them to me is so unusual to me. It's family.

"What do we do now, Khione?"

"Now you fight and take back what's yours. And save my reckless King in the process."

"Yes," she says with a smile on her lips. "We must keep your Mate safe. Your flurry would appreciate having a father."

No idea what she is saying but as long as they help... Wait, a flurry?

"Our powers are indeed great. We learn about them with the ticking of time. I can see through beings, I can even see through the belly of the mountain, inside the lair of the Sphinx Assyrin. And I can see the little flurry in your belly. A little speck of growing life."

How can that be? So quick? Is that why I cry myself silly like this? Do Tarrassians' foetuses grow quicker? He needs to know. I must give him any reason I can to return to me in one piece. I prepare myself for more heartbreak and reach out to him.

Tars? Mother can see inside me and there is a cub growing in my belly. Our cub.

There is a what? he asks straight away in my head.

So, he could hear me all along, the bastard! Now is not the time to give him a piece of my mind.

I will not raise this cub alone, do you hear me?

A cub... is this real? he asks.

I keep forgetting you think I am the galaxy's biggest liar. Now I want you to listen and go back to the ship. There is another swarm coming your way. That makes 400 Harsallii. You cannot fight them.

Phaea, I have already killed ten, so not 400.

Is he for real? This man drives me mad!

Tars, this is serious, I cannot lose you! Please let the Ketosii deal with it.

And once again he is angry, temper going through the roof.

What kind of male do you think I am, Human? One who hides like a cub? One who allows fragile beings without weapons to face the Harsallii?

He shouts inside my head like a madman.

The Ketosii are the weapons! And there are 400 enemies coming your way! I shout back.

Yes, I am aware. I can see them just fine. You had better not leave the cave, Sia, like you left my ship. I will take the head of every single Human if you do. And then I will char your little planet.

My turn to block him out. Time to act fast. I want to tell him I love him, I want to tell him a million things, but I could feel something else inside his head. His War Beast. He is already fighting the Harsallii and he needs to pay attention.

The same Ketosii male from before picks me up and I close my eyes as we float at dizzying speed against the icy wind. All the Ketosii follow, children as well. I understand why. They all need this. I don't try to reach his mind this time, not just because I don't want to disturb him. My Sign hurts. So do the swirls on my arms and shoulders. He is injured.

As we travel closer to the mountain, I can hear it and then I can smell it. The noise of battle and the horrible smell of the Harsallii. Even out in the fresh icy air, their stench is sickening. And I can smell blood. A lot of it. All blood smells like blood, apparently. I only have time to see an army of huge, dark grey, insect-like Harsallii. They are so close to one another I can't even see a snowflake in between them. I remember Calena said they fight in formation.

They look a lot more disgusting alive than when they were dead in the tunnels. The head of a cockroach, the body of a locust and all their extremities end in some sort of pincers. Sharp ones, I realise with dread. That is why they don't have any weapons. They probably wouldn't be able to hold them properly. But they don't need them. Their arms are like blades. I can see that when they use them to slash at my man. Even though the Ketosii keep me far enough from the battle I can see him. It looks like the most unreal battle scene ever. And not because I am looking at sentient alien insects. This is an alien planet, so that is expected, I think. It's surreal because one man is fighting an army all by himself. Not a man. He has never looked more alien than now. He is taller than his usual eight feet or so, and his frame is almost doubled in size. It's not in a ridiculous Hulk kind of way. Everything is so proportional and his size matches his strength and his fangs and his growl. An oversized package of pure force. Still, he is just one fighting an army. He retreats as he fights them and you don't need to be a battle expert to know why. As his sword takes off heads and limbs and everything else in between, he leaves huge piles of dead bodies. It slows the Harsallii army down as they try to reach him. In some parts of their advancing formation, the pile is much higher and it takes them longer to make it over it. As they struggle at one end, Tars fights them at the other end and so on. This way, he doesn't get to fight them all at once. He may seem like an unhinged roaring wild beast, but he is very methodical in his fight. And Brian was right. The Harsallii are not very bright.

He is covered in a slush of orange blood and other disgusting things. Despite that, I can see the copper of his own blood. A lot of it. And the Harsallii are gaining on him. He favours his left side and he fights with his right arm. I haven't seen him do that before. This is not good.

"Mother, help him!"

"Tell him to get out of the way, Khione. We are only learning how to use our powers."

I scream with all my powers, both out loud and inside his head. I tell him to run towards me, but he is not listening. He never does when he's feeding his rage. I scream his name over and over again, until my throat feels raw. He can't hear me. I push away the Ketosii who tries to stop me from falling on my knees in the snow. I slap at another hand to leave me alone. Big and clawed and smeared in orange…

"Tars, you heard me," I say, and let myself collapse against his body and the blood covering it. But I don't care. He is alive and in my arms. Or me in his, rather.

"You shouldn't be here! Take her away! Now!"

He screams at the Ketosii who pass us by and advance on the Harsallii army in a formation of their own. A long straight line of floating bodies. The children move in front of them, also in a straight line.

I grab at Tars' slippery hand as he tries to follow them.

"Don't! Stay with me," I say, shivering against his body. I have lost my fur and I'm frozen to the bone. That is enough to make him stop and hold me again. He looks torn and pained, not knowing which one to help. I know he would always choose me. This time he doesn't have to choose.

"They will be fine, Tars. Just watch."

As I say that, all at once, the Ketosii lift the visors of their caskets as they call them. From behind them, all we can see is an explosion of light. Horizontal lines of pure white light reach the first row of Harsallii and simply cut them in half. Then the next one and the next one, leaving a mass of twitching halved bodies in the snow. There is steam rising from their spilled blood, and the air fills with the smell of charred... bugs... I can't describe that smell as anything else.

"What is this?" says Tars, looking at me like I grew another head. I reach up and stroke his beard, despite the blood that has started to freeze in it.

"They were never powerless, my love. And they were never weapon less."

"Why do you call me your love?" he says and takes my face in between his hands, looking me in the eyes. His eyes are almost red. Like metal being forged in fire. But specks of gold shine in it, gaining on the red. I also notice his left hand is shaking badly.

"Because you are my love. You have always been my love, ever since before I met you. Ever since I was born. I was always going to find you."

My tears turn into painful icicles scraping badly at my skin, but I can't stop them. I have for too long.

He is not saying anything, but I know he is just overwhelmed with what I have just told him. And he is hurt. He is still in his battle form or whatever they call it. I think it makes him stronger. But he is hurt because I feel pain in my Sign.

"We will go back to the ship as soon as it's over. The Ketosii will carry you and…"

"Nobody carries me, female. And it's not over yet. I need to go back to the fight."

I grab at him with both hands. I want to slap the life out of him.

"You are hurt!"

"I am a Warrior. I am the King and I do as I please. Now move and don't you dare leave this spot. I will char your little planet twice if you do."

"The Ketosii need to do this. They have to take their own planet back. This is their moment. You cannot take this away from them. Please. For them and for me."

The air seems to leave his body and he slowly starts to lose some of the bulk.

"Can I at least kill the ones the Ketosii miss?"

"They don't miss any. And we seriously need to talk about your passion for taking heads."

Your mate has many anger issues. He is rather entertaining otherwise.

I look at Tars, as I don't know what is happening. The voice in my head is very different from his. It is so strong, but without being loud. It sounds as time itself would sound, if it had a voice. Or God. I am almost scared to move. This thing talking in my head… It's terrifying and fascinating at the same time. And even though it speaks in my mind, I would understand it anyhow. I wouldn't need a translating device either, as it speaks in British English. The posh type, too.

As the Ketosii killed the last of the invaders of their planet, the blizzard instantly died down. Now it's snowing quietly. The silence and the balance have been restored. I try to focus my eyes. I feel him before I see him. His presence is overbearing. And then I can see him. Perched on top of his mountain. The Sphinx.

He is massive. Just as big as the stone one guarding the pyramids. For a brief moment as my eyes focus, I think he is also made of stone. He looks so ancient and completely still. But the wind moves his long hair or fur, or even better both, and I can see he is not a statue. He is alive and watching us with open curiosity. He is not what I expected. Whatever that was. I am looking at the body of a lion three times the size of London Bridge, with the head of a man, probably the size of a bus. An enormous lion tail twitches lazily around his body. He has huge dark brown wings attached to the back of his body. They are folded now, but they look enormous. They have to be, to lift that body into the air. The broken wings... I remember and sadness fills me again.

I find your male's rage a lot more entertaining than your pity, Sia.

You know my name.

I know everything. I am the Sphinx King. Knowledge sounds better than it feels, so don't be too impressed.

I have purposely tried not to acknowledge the very human-like head attached to the lion body. The more he talks, the more I can't ignore that I am talking to a man. An actual man. His face is covered in a huge bushy beard, the same sandy yellow as the short fur covering his lion body. His really long hair is the same dark brown as his wings. Are those dreadlocks? His hair is parted into six thick twists or dreadlocks hanging down his stony face. There are gold bands holding the hair in shape. Many more dreadlocks/twists are perched on top of his head in the coolest mohawk I have ever seen.

The Sphinx has piercing blue eyes that look like blue fires, dreadlocks, a mohawk and a strong British accent. And let's not forget the zebra-like stripes on the back of his body. Is that normal for a sphinx?

Oh please, zebra stripes? His voice sounds bored with my stupidity.

They are sabre-toothed tiger stripes. Zebra stripes… on me? How ridiculous, he says with a big lazy yawn. Oh my God. His canines… They are huge. Tars' body is all of a sudden cutting my view as he steps in front of me. He tilts my head up and watches me warily.

"My Phaea? What are you looking at?"

"At the Sphinx King."

He turns to follow my look. He instantly readies his sword and pushes me behind him in a protective gesture. I slap at his hand and go around him.

"Put that away, Tars. You can't fight the Sphinx!"

"No one can, but I will die trying," he replies.

So dramatic, says the Sphinx inside my head and lets out another yawn.

And he has anger issues. I do find him entertaining. You, however, are boring. And you compared me to a zebra.

Thanks… I guess.

"Phaea, we must go now, while he is not attacking," Tars says and starts retreating while watching the Sphinx.

"He won't attack. He is just curious. You know… like a cat."

"What is this cat thing you and the red female keep referring to?"

"It's a pet on Earth," I say, and I think I have shocked Tars deeply.

"Humans think Sphinxes are pets? Do Humans have pets who could swallow them whole?"

"Some do."

My King has officially up-ranked the entire Human race. There is pure awe in his eyes. And maybe now he won't want me as his pet anymore.

You can be my pet if you are offering, says the Sphinx in my head with a purr.

I'll pass, thank you for the offer. Where is my friend? What have you done with her and her Mate? And there is another Human woman missing. She escaped from the tunnels. Do you have them?

That is for me to know and for you to wonder, Ice Queen, he says and unfolds his wings. As he takes to the skies, his shadow turns the daylight into darkness.

Tars and the Ketosii seem relieved but I am fuming on the inside. Stupid cat indeed!

16

TARS

As my War Beast retreats, my injuries start to get their grip of fire on me. Pain and tiredness bite at me, making my limbs shaky. Especially my left arm. I heard the bone snap in a few places and what hurts the most is I won't be able to carry my Mate. The Ketosii will have to. To add insult, they will have to carry me too. I am losing blood and I have to make it to the warship. I will swallow my big ego, for her safety and for her happiness. She is worried about my wounds. She looks at every single one of my injuries with watery grey eyes and shaking lips. And now she carries my cub. They come first. Even though Sketos is now safe, I am eager to take my female and my cub back home. And not entirely sure how safe a planet where a Sphinx lives can be. He didn't attack and she is not scared of him. The Humans think he is a pet. They are very strange beings, the Humans. I have too many questions for my tired mind. She will answer every single one of them. For now, I will just trust her. She says she is not a goddess, but the Ketosii had no powers before she came, she has mind conversations with the Sphinx King like it's nothing and she speaks the language of the Astrals. She also carries my cub. The first Tarrassian cub in many rotations. The hope of my people. We are not a dying breed anymore. I feel humbled by her. Only a few spans ago I was enraged by the forced alliance with a weakling, a lesser being. Now I feel like I am less. She doesn't look at me like I am, though. And she called me her love. She said she was born for me. Strange words of affection, very different from the Tarrassian words of affection. Humans are better with words.

Before I know it, we reach the warship. My Phaea touches the belly of the ship with her palm before I get to. The warship opens for her. So that is how she managed to gain access to one of my warships and run away. We are two beings sharing one life code. Whatever is programmed to open for me, opens for her. How would she know that? Another question for later.

I allow her time alone with the Ketosii to say their farewells. I know we will have to come back here often enough. They are connected. I heard her calling them her family.

The freed slaves are still asleep, safely strapped in and ready to go. The ridiculous Garrii female is attached to the Human's pod like poisonous vine.

I can feel my Phaea's presence next to me.

"Tars, you are bleeding. We are safe here. Travel can wait until you heal. There is another pod."

"They also need assistance." I point at the sleeping beings. "The Human needs more than just a healing pod."

Against my will, I show my interest in the dying Human. I want her to see I can act normal. He is in my care now and as his King I have to keep him safe.

"MI, run a life expectancy on the Human."

"Life expectancy 2.7%."

The Garrii screams with joy. My female is pleased, but wary of showing emotions, as I acted like an idiot last time she did.

I watch the Human male and his injuries. Mine are nothing compared to his. I watch him until she touches my hand, a silent question in her eyes.

"Resilience! Is that what the Human Spirit is, Phaea?"

"That and other things such as willpower, hope, determination."

"You will explain them to me and to our people. Can non-Humans have the Spirit? A Warrior with Tarrassian power and Human Spirit would be invincible."

She smiles and looks at me and at the other beings around us.

"You already do, Tars. All of you have it," she says, pointing at the freed slaves. You are just not aware of it. Because Humans are weak, can't self-heal and live short lives, we cannot afford to forget our Spirit and everything that comes with it. But I will be happy to remind Tarrassians of what they already have. Just like I did with the Ketosii. No need to be a goddess for that. I am also happy to remind you that you are bleeding and being unreasonable again. So, healing pod for you, my King."

She is trying to put her little cold defiant armour up, but I know better. This female shakes like the belly of a spitting fire mountain when I put my mouth between her thighs. She also leaks like one. That is all I need to remember when my anger takes over my mind. When I don't trust her words, I have to remember her noises when I make her come.

"The healing can wait. Strap in, Phaea. You too, Garrii. Don't forget to regulate your breathing. The Ketosii will keep the weather still for us, so we can do the Jump."

Her little body comes to support mine, as I can't help but lean against the control board.

"Come, I will help you strap in. Please, try to move slower, my love. There's blood gushing out every time you do."

She calls me her love again. I would do anything for her to call me that until the end of my spans.

Pain goes through me, but it doesn't overwhelm. Her scent is in my face as she engages the strap of my seat. Her long white hair falls over my chest.

"I don't understand what the rush is," she says softly with a sigh.

"I want you on my planet, in my palace, in my quarters, in my bed and in between my furs. By the end of this span, that is. It is the King's will!" I say with a smirk. It pulls at the cuts on my face, but my female likes my smirk. She calls it infuriating.

"Oh, why did I bother to ask?" she mumbles to herself as she straps in with her own belt. But I can see her smile.

Everything inside me screams, I need to sleep, I need to make the pain stop, but my duty comes first. I instruct the MI to run the last checks before the Jump. My voice is weak and my words are scrambled. Each time I feel like I can't stay awake, I remember the Human male. But now I understand, it is not because I want to prove myself to her. It is not because I want to compete with him. It is because he is inspiring. If he can survive, so can I.

The Jump only messes me up more and all is very fuzzy once we are back on Tarrassia. I fight it as we dock and we are welcomed by my Royal Guard and Elders. I fight it while making sure the freed slaves are being well looked after; I fight it while telling the Royal Healers I will take their heads off if they let the Human male die, but most of all I fight it while making sure she is well looked after by her servants. They take her to our Royal Quarters and only then do I allow myself to collapse into Larrs' arms.

As he carries me to the Healing Quarters, I use my last strength to threaten the High Elder. He is only to mend my arm, close the deepest of the wounds and clean me up. Everything else will heal while I sleep. With her in my arms. That is all I need. I lose consciousness before he gets to agree, but he knows better.

After what feels like an orbit rotation, I am finally able to walk without aid, back to my quarters. Not that the Healers agreed, but my will is their will.

Halfway through, I can smell her scent. It's stronger now, as it's not covered in blood. She smells like Tarrassian flowers and fresh morri fruit. There is a new scent mixed with hers. Mine. My cub. My cub makes her smell like me.

I get rid of all the annoying guards and servants trying to help.

My beautiful Queen is asleep in my bed. In between my furs, where she belongs. She looks like a cub lost in the vastness of my bed. She must have just collapsed with exhaustion after her bath. She is still wrapped in a blue drying cloth and probably one of her female attendants pulled a soft fur over her sleeping form. It makes my heart grow with happiness to see her safe from all harm. Anything could have happened to her away from Tarrassia. But it didn't. And now she is where she belongs. Her beautiful long white hair shines on my pillows in the soft light of the sunset. Her perfect face looks slimmer than only a few spans ago and there are dark circles under her eyes. She has been through a lot. Her Sign is glowing a soft blue light, just like mine. She sighs in her sleep and says my name. My name! No other's!

I remove my shirt and pants and a cursed injury opens again.

"Cursed blasters of fire! Useless Healers!"

"Tars?" she asks, sitting up and watching me with big sleepy eyes.

"Sorry, my Phaea, I didn't realise I spoke out loud."

"Is that blood?" She points at the injury on my hip and I quickly wipe at it with my shirt, then throw it back on the floor.

"Why are you here? While bleeding, nevertheless. I thought you were in a healing pod, or with the Healers."

"No. I will heal while I sleep. Next to you. That's all I need."

"And your Healers allowed it?"

"I am the King, my troublesome little Human. I do what I please, remember?" I try to give her my best grin, but all I manage is a painful grimace.

She rushes to help me make it to the bed, as if I need to lean on her little body. The instant she touches me, my body goes on fire. My cock doesn't care about my injuries. It only cares about her hands on my skin.

"You have got to be kidding me!" she says, looking at my growing cock with a shocked expression on her face.

"Ignore it, beautiful. It likes you too much. I won't act on it. Unless, of course you ask for it. I can never say no to you when you ask for it, like a good little pet."

"You are lucky you are injured, Tars. You will get my reply to that after you heal. I will just add it to the long list of shit you pulled lately. Now, you stop being a clown and sleep," she says, pulling my good hand towards my side of the bed. How does she know I prefer the left side?

"What is a clown, Phaea?"

"A type of pet that likes to feed on its owners."

"Really? Why would…"

"Sleep now, I will tell you tomorrow."

It feels like forever since I have lain in the safety of my bed. She helps me lie down and fusses over my pillows, over the furs – am I warm enough, am I cold enough, which side hurts less… All her fussing does is make her hands go over my painful wounds and aching cock. But I don't mind. I can see now her care for the Human male was different. It was just her caring nature. Just like her care for the slaves, for the Ketosii or for the Human females. She cares for anyone around her just like a queen would. With grace and gentleness. Her care for me feels different. It is fierce and passionate and makes her act as crazy as I am. She brought an army to my rescue. I wrap my arms around her, and allow sleep to take me, with that last thought in mind.

Pain wakes me up from my blissful sleep. Maybe I should have accepted the High Healer's advice.

A wave of fire goes through my veins and… A smile tugs at my lips. It's not coming from my injuries. Only a dull lingering pain left in those and I remember it well. It means I am almost healed. I can see the soft violet light of the sunrise, behind the window drapes. I must have slept a lot longer than I thought. My wounds are fine enough. I have had worse.

The pain is coming from my cock and I have the cure for that in my arms. She sleeps with her head on my chest, body close to my side. One of those ridiculously long legs for such a small being rests on top of my body. In her sleep, she pushed her knee up, trapping my cock underneath it. Just like the first time she slept in my arms, on the suspended shelter. I try not to move, to enjoy these precious nanoclips, but I know that's a losing battle. My cock pushes so hard at her knee, her whole leg jerks. I rub my hand on it. Her skin is soft perfection.

"Tars?"

Her voice is sleepy and vulnerable at first, then I can hear the worry in it.

She pushes herself up on her knees next to me. She brings her face above mine, white scented hair falling over me. Two long-fingered hands go to each side of my face and start stroking my beard, as she calls it. Our Signs and marks come alive at her touch, mirroring each other.

"Are you in pain, my love?"

"Yes, very much so, my Phaea," I say, running a finger over her lush bottom lip. So soft, so edible…

"Where? What hurts? Shall I get someone?"

She pushes her long hair out of her face, behind her ears and looks over my body. I watch her with amusement. So skittish, my female. A female who can otherwise command an army and talk to a Sphinx. Her breathing halts when her eyes stop on my fully erect cock. The grey turns silver, her long lashes flutter and her eyes go big. Her plump lips part lightly in a rather enticing way and I can't help myself. I push a finger through that little gap, into her mouth. She takes in a sudden breath, causing her mouth to suck my finger deeper. My cock jerks violently against my belly at that.

"You are incorrigible! And I always fall for it," she says, slapping at my hand. "This is not funny, Tars," she adds, ignoring the sight of my cock and checking the now fully closed wound on my hip.

"You almost died on me, you big doofus! Last thing I need is to know you are in pain."

"But I am in pain, my beautiful Phaea," I say as I grab her hand and wrap it around the base of my cock. Her hand is not big enough to close around it, but her touch is more than I need. She doesn't attempt to remove her hand. She looks at it and at my cock which throbs at her touch.

"It does look painful," she says with a voice as soft as a whisper.

I remove the drying cloth, still wrapped around her body, but she doesn't even notice. She is fascinated by the sight of her hand on my cock. That makes two of us. She is slowly moving it up and down in an exploratory way. When her hand is all the way up to the flared tip, she stops tentatively, then she moves her fingers over it and I take in a deep breath.

"Phaea... your touch is the sweetest torture."

"But I shouldn't be touching you. You need to heal."

"Your touch is healing me. My injuries are almost healed anyway. Please, don't stop touching me."

She takes her eyes off her hand stroking me and watches me with an unsure look in her eyes.

"I know you are too stubborn to tell me if you still hurt. We have a lifetime to make love. A long one as it turns out. I don't want you to strain yourself and open your wounds. But I do want to relieve this pain," she says with a shy smile while looking at her hand stroking me. "And I really, really want to taste you."

Just as I am about to caress those beautiful nipples of hers, my hand stops in the air. She is quick to pick up on my reaction and there is an unsure look in her eyes. Probably matching mine.

"Tarrassians don't do that? You touched me that way and I thought..." Her eyes avoid mine.

I reach for her face and make her look at me.

"All males pleasure their females that way, my Phaea, but our females don't pleasure their mates with their mouth. Only alien females who give pleasure as a way of living do that. And only certain species. I have never allowed it, as I have seen some really strange appendages coming out of aliens' mouths in battle."

She giggles and it makes her eyes glow.

"I promise I don't have any strange appendages in my mouth, other than my tongue. I don't think I can kill anything with my small tongue. Will you allow me to do it?" she asks with a timid smile on her lips.

I grab her face between my hands and pull her closer, nanospaces from mine. I lock my eyes with hers.

"Do you want to put your lips on my cock, beautiful? Is that what you want?"

She nods in silent agreement and I pull those lips down to mine for a hungry kiss. Her little tongue is eager to meet mine. Unlike Tarrassian females, her tongue is small, soft and has no ridges. Could never hurt me. Not that I care. Now that she has said that, all I can think of is having her mouth on me, that tongue licking my length. She slows down the kiss and I allow it. I don't know what she wants to do next, so I just let her take control. Her lips move over my face, kissing every single patch of skin and nuzzling at my beard. The trail of soft touches goes down my chin, my neck, my chest, hovering gently over my still visible wounds. She kisses some, gently avoids most and I pull myself up slightly, as I want to watch everything, she does to me. I can't take my eyes off this alien creature, more beautiful than any other being amongst the galaxies. She wears my Sign, calls me her love, but most importantly, she carries my cub. I can't even hear myself breathing. Like she put me under a strange spell and all I can do is lie there and watch. Her lips go down my abdomen and occasionally her tongue licks at my skin, leaving a wet trail on my fur, or hair as she calls it. I am angry at my cock as it decides to jerk up, almost slapping her in the face. She just giggles, so she is not upset, I hope. She stops and looks a bit unsure as to what to do next. She attempts to put a leg over my thighs but then changes her mind and giggles again. I can see she is a bit unsure and maybe a bit shy. However, I try to stay still and not offer to help with anything as I have no idea what she wants to do next. She squeezes herself in between my legs and kneels there, running her hands up and down the side of my thighs. She looks me in the eyes and smiles. My Sign goes mad with colour and my left heart is so loud, echoing in the room.

"The heart that beats for me," she says with a knowing smile.

She pushes her hair out of her face and lowers her lips over my cock, without taking her eyes off mine. A little hand goes back to holding it at the base. When she touches me, I inhale sharply. Her tongue starts at my sacks and slowly goes up the length of my cock. Only when she reaches the top do I let out the air I have been holding in, then desperately inhale more. Her tongue looks tiny as she circles the flared tip. How can something so small give so much pleasure? She repeats the motion a few more times and this time when she reaches the top, her mouth opens wide over it. My head smashes itself against the bed stand and my body tenses.

There is a smile in her eyes and confidence. No trace left of the previous unease or shyness.

I force myself to keep my eyes open and watch her as she sucks gently at my tip. Her small hand keeps going up and down my length and her tongue circles the top of my cock after every sucking motion. My hands are itching to go for her head and fist her hair. But I want her to do this the way she wants to. So, I fist the furs by my side, instead. Her mouth goes lower and lower and she takes more of me in. The eyes pinned on me get watery and now they look just as dangerous and deep as the Still Waters. Her hand rubbing my length is increasing the pressure and her lips suck harder. She keeps doing it until everything compresses in my head and I have the feeling my Sign shines on the inside of my head. My body gets tense and my sack painfully tight. I reach for the top of her head.

"Phaea, I am going to cum, you have to stop... I can't hold it."

Then don't, she says inside my head, without taking her mouth off me.

For the first time ever, I can't talk with my mind, like it's all roasted.

"You want me to... cum in your mouth?" I ask her in disbelief.

Yes, my love.

There is no stopping when she says that to me. I couldn't even if I wanted to. The lights of all Stars explode inside my head. I forget myself and my hands leave the furs to fist her hair instead. My whole body shakes with the power of my release and I feel myself pumping jet after jet down her throat, muscles contracting around my shaft as she swallows.

As the last of my relief leaves my body, I sag against the furs and pull her up on top of me. Her body is shaking slightly and I can smell her arousal. My pleasure gave her pleasure. I arrange her body on top of mine, head on my chest and hug her close to me.

"Tars, your injuries... let me lie next to you."

"No," I say simply. I need to feel her.

She cuddles herself against my chest and nuzzles at my fur.

"I was wrong about your tongue, Phaea. It may kill me after all."

She smiles and I stroke her hair. I want to ask a question, but not sure what she'll make of it.

"Why did you swallow my release, Phaea?"

She lifts her head up and watches me with a worried look.

"Oh, I hope that is not offensive to your kind or something."

"There are no rules about such things as no one ever does it. The few pleasurers who do give mouth-mating won't swallow that."

She seems relieved.

"It's quite common for Humans to do that," she says. "And I am happy my kind does that, as you taste amazing. I might become addicted to it."

I don't know what to say. I am too overwhelmed. And I am starting to think our Astrals are indeed the greatest sacred beings in all the galaxies. They could have made us compatible to any species, but they chose the Humans, who like giving mouth-mating and swallow after.

Her arousal scents the air and she shivers slightly in my arms.

"I know what you need, my Phaea, but I also know you won't ask for it. Not as long as you think I am not fully healed."

"You are the most arrogant male of all," she says with a contented smile hidden in my chest fur.

"I am correct, not arrogant," I say, lowering my hands from her waist, over that deliciously round bottom. "Shall I prove it to you? Shall we confirm how soaked this little cunt is?" I ask her, grabbing her bottom cheeks and pulling them up. The scent of her arousal gets even stronger. She moans and wriggles on top of my cock, getting it painfully hard.

"Oh God! Don't you need time to recover or something?" she says with a cute look on her face.

"No, my Phaea. I am the King, I do as I please, remember?"

She laughs, but then she lifts her head from my chest to watch me with a serious look in her eyes.

"No point denying how much I ache for you, Tars." Her words are melting joy into my hearts. "I just want you to get better. You bled quite a bit before you fell asleep," she says, pointing at one of the soiled furs and the stained covers.

I move my hands back to her waist and remove my eyes from those enticing nipples. I won't be able to leave her side otherwise, and, unfortunately, I have to.

"All my wounds are closed, my beautiful. A slight discomfort left in some, but that's nothing compared to the pain in my cock and the need in my veins. However, I cannot act on it now. The light span is here and I have many council matters to attend to."

"Oh… that's okay," she says with a small voice.

I know she is still a stranger here and I am all she is familiar with for now on Tarrassia. I would love nothing more than to spend this span with her and my unborn cub. But being the vexed King and Protector of the Seven Stars comes with duties I can't ignore.

"Urgent matters need attending to, my beautiful. More so-called non-inhabited planets are being taken by the Coalition of the Dark Moon. After what happened with Sketos, I cannot allow any more beings to become enslaved on my watch."

"I completely understand, my love," she says, stroking my beard.

I pull her up above my face and give her a long kiss. I try to put all my feelings for her in it, so she remembers it later. When I will have to tell her the truth. I get up to prepare for this cursed span and the madness it will bring. She tries to leave the bed, but I tell her not to and tuck her back in.

"It is still early, my Phaea, and you have dark circles under your eyes." And very swollen lips, but for a very different reason. The sight of them and the memory of having them on my cock makes getting dressed difficult. I fiddle with my Kannicloth and I can hear her giggle.

"See what you do to me, my Phaea?"

She laughs and stretches her beautiful body under the covers. I would give anything to be able to join her. Mate her for spans and spans on end, without any worry about the Kingdom. But I can't. That is why I decided not to bathe this morning. Her smell lingers all over me and I want to keep it with me, since I can't have more for now. Besides, it will shock the old Ruccusses.

"A lot of Tarrassians would want to bother you today, my Phaea," I tell her while I attach my Sword and dagger. I should probably do something to tame the head fur hair, but I can't be bothered. They criticise me no matter what I do.

"There will be the Healers, making sure you and the cub are doing well, there will be the Ceremonial Attendants to talk to you about our Sacred Union and some will just come by to stare at your Sign. You can send them all to the pits of fire if you wish. All except for the Healers, of course."

Her laughter fills my heart.

"Oh, Tars, I can't send them to any pits," she says. "It is my duty to attend to them and I will happily do so. I am actually looking forward to it."

"Yes, I know you will, my Phaea. You are perfect, after all. At least the Elders won't moan about the Queen."

"What do you mean, Tars?"

"Nothing important, my Queen. Whatever you do, please don't strain yourself. You have been through a lot and you are with cub. And only explore within the palace this span. The gardens and forests will be too much for you. I will take you to all my favourite places and show you the beauty of Tarrassia. For now, you must rest. The Queen's High Guard Commander and his Warriors will present themselves to you and they will attend to your needs."

I give her another hug and a kiss before I leave. She clings to me and there is a sleepy contented sort of purr in her body. She is happy and content. And I am about to change that.

17
SIA

I am happy, safe, loved and in love. Sure, he didn't use the actual words, but I have a feeling Tarrassians don't quite put love into words. They would rather prove it, which is probably better. Still, it would be nice to hear it.

I am happy, safe and I am about to become a mother. I have to admit to myself, I didn't quite believe it. But this morning, I feel it. I can feel the new life inside me. Maybe Tarrassians' babies grow quicker. I am sure the Healers will be able to answer my questions. Or maybe not. I am their first pregnant Human. Okay, Sia, that is a scary thought. One thing at a time. For now, I just want to enjoy my new reality. Wrap my head around it first. Now that I am not in survival mode anymore, the enormity of everything that has happened threatens to give me PTSD or something. Just over a week ago I had no one. Now I have not one but two entire planets devoted to me and calling me family. That is hoping Tarrassians will be as nice and welcoming as the Ketosii. I have to hope they will be. The second I stepped off that ship, onto the landing pad of the palace, I felt at home. Despite all the rush and Tars' injuries, and worry for the freed slaves, a choking emotion struck me. Home. This was always meant to be my home. I couldn't see much of the planet and I wasn't really paying attention. All I remember is the violet sky and the red forest around the palace. Glimpses of the city on the outskirts of that forest and maybe some huge mountains in the distance, covered in snow. That, and the smell. It's beautiful! Maybe a bit heady and strong. It's like walking through a bath bomb shop. No wonder all the Tarrassians I have met smell amazing. The palace itself looks like an illusion. Like it's not really there. I wonder if birds fly into it, like they sometimes fly into windows on Earth. It was built from the same copper mirror-shine metal as their warships. And their swords. The red forest and the violet sky reflect in it, and without a close inspection it's hard to tell what you are looking at, or its shape. I can hardly wait to explore.

On the inside, the palace is huge. In a way, it makes sense. These are all huge beings. They need a lot of space. The floors and walls have the same mirror effect and copper colour. Like the Tarrassians' eyes and the shimmery shade of their skin. Okay, I will have to enquire about that, especially since I am soon to have a copper baby. A few female servants, some looking very scary, took me to the Royal Quarters after we arrived. The 'quarters' turned out to be an entire separate wing, with huge guards at every turn. We walked forever just to reach Tars' room. Which is made of seven different rooms. Each one bigger than the next. Someone really needs to explain to them what a room is. Why do we need seven rooms? Maybe we can fill them up with copper babies. The Queen's closet, as one of my winged attendants explained, is bigger than my high-end London apartment. And what they call the bathing room is really a pool. And what they call the pressure cleaner is an entire walk-in shower room. Also, the size of my apartment. Not using one of those, though. Last time I tried to, it almost turned Natalia and I into mashed potato. Natalia… Guilt tugs at my heart. I took her to Sketos and now she is there all alone. Well, maybe not alone. She has her mate and the planet is now safe. But there is the small problem of 'Mr Stupid Cat'. I will try to reach her mind soon. For now, I just want to enjoy my new bed and my new bedroom with glowing lavender furniture and the sign of the water lilies carved onto… well, onto everything. The huge windows are draped in gold, heavy fabrics and the gap in the middle allows a soft purple light to stream in. It looks a bit like the purple in my Sign. Is that coming from their violet sky? Too content to get up and investigate. I know I have to start my day, my role and my new life. But this overwhelming happiness is so new to me. I want to roll in it like a cat and purr. I sniff at Tars' pillow because I miss him already. The strange bouncy wonder feels amazing against my skin. Not as amazing as his body feels against mine. Or the way he tastes. Oh God, how am I going to face him after what I did? I don't know what's got into me, and to be fair I can hardly wait to do it again. It was my first time doing that and what a way to learn… His cock is huge and thick and the mushroomed tip a bit more than a handful. And of course, it's totally crazy how hard it gets and how… lively. It smacked me in the face a few times and it was really a challenge having that wild thing in my mouth. Like sucking on a snake probably. But the feel of it, the look on Tars' face, the way he surrendered all of himself to me in that moment and the taste of him… Oh yes, so doing that again.

"Rise and shine, Elsa!" shouts a sultry voice, and straight away someone pulls the curtains away.

"Jade…" I groan out loud, but then it hits me. Jade! I quickly grab a sheet and wrap it around me and get up, almost tripping on it. I give her the tightest, clumsiest hug ever and I discover it's quite interesting to hug someone with double EEs. Her boobs are in a league of their own.

"What the actual fuck, Elsa?" she says, pushing me away. "Despite me not being a Disney fan, I would love nothing more than a hug right now. But, girl? You stink of spunk. The whole fucking room does. I don't want that shit on my pretty Tarrassian dress. Did I tell you I have twenty-three dresses? That is some serious Disney shit."

"Oh, Jade, I have missed you so much!"

"You have?" she asks with a smile on those gorgeous pouty lips. "Actually, I have missed you too. I guess the four of us will forever be connected. My God, look at you. That thing on your forehead... Beautiful, but kind of scary. No offence."

"None taken, Jade. But look at you! Could you look any more Tarrassian?" I say, looking at her in awe. The traditional Tarrassian dress was made for boobs like that! Her green dress is similar to all the others I have seen so far. Made from the silkiest of fabrics, with a deep low-cut sweetheart neckline and held on the shoulders by rows of little glittery beads. Half of her huge boobs spill over and that must be quite a sight for the local Warrior population. Only Jade could pull that off. The corsage is really tight on her tiny waist. Then the dress flares over her generous hips and bottom all the way to the ground. Like all Tarrassian dresses, the lower part falls into a tone of fabric and too many slits to count. Like one of them put their claws through it. I have to admit, it makes walking a very feminine affair. Of course, Jade's curves take it to a whole new level. The colour matches those diva-like jade-green eyes and her intricate makeup.

"Is that real makeup?" I ask, excited. I do like makeup. I wore it for so long because of my job. Got used to it after a while.

"Yes. And thank fuck for that as permanent makeup only lasts that long. Can't live without my bright red lips, sorry. They have an army of servant females that only do pampering. Massages, makeup... you name it. However, they are shit with hair. Because, guess what, I don't look anything like a Tarrassian woman. Those tall skinny bitches have no hair and no boobs. It's the Sinéad O'Connor planet."

I just can't help laughing, until tears pool in my eyes. Jade will always be Jade. And I have missed her foul mouth more than I would like to admit.

"Good thing I have Earth's most famous hairstylist here," I say, looking at her perfect mahogany waves.

"Actually, I would love to get my hands on your hair," she says. "If I remember correctly, you never allowed a stylist to do your hair."

"Yes, I didn't like being touched."

"Oh, man, how times have changed," she says, pointing at the messy bed. "Speaking of that, time for the Queen to take a bath. You stink, man, and no need to rub it in my face. I didn't get any, ever since I got here."

"Jade, you have been here for a week," I point out with a smile.

"Is that so, Elsa?" She puts her hands on her hips and her boobs go up like two huge globes of porcelain. "Let's see what you have done in a week, shall we? Got freaking jewellery tattoos sticking out of your forehead, found lover boy, lost lover boy, escaped in space, lost Natalia, saved a planet, freed some slaves, found Brian, won a war, met a Sphinx, got pregnant, got monster dick, not in that order, obviously."

"Oh dear, if you put it like that…" I say, a bit deflated.

"Come," she says, pulling me gently into the bathroom. "That is a lot to go through. You will shortly be inundated with visitors and shit. Let me show you how your bathtub works. Or more likely the Tarrassian version of an Olympic pool. While you get soaked, I will ask for your breakfast and then I will tell you all the hot gossip on Tarrassia."

"How do you know all this stuff?" I say, almost with suspicion.

"Oh, didn't I tell you? I found myself a superpower, since all these little shits have one. Everyone's business is my business. I am the Goddess of Gossip. I lurk in the shadows and even if they see me, they do shit about it. The servants are terrified of me – might have bitten a few – the hot guys are too scared of their fucking twit General to even look my way, and the rest of the people in the palace are guests, visitors and shit like that. I live here so whatever I do, it's fine by them."

"Still friends with the High General, I see."

"Fuck him!" she says, but this time the insult is real and she is shaking with anger. "Look what he did to me!" She lifts the slits of her dress and I see two beautiful golden bangles on her ankles. Then they flash a green light and now my anger mirrors hers.

"Are those...?"

"Yes," she confirms. "Fucking tracking devices. The servant females put them on me by force. I bit the shit out of them. The fucking coward didn't even have the courage to do it himself."

"This is unacceptable. I am sorry, Jade. I will speak to Tars today about it."

"Thank you. Now go get that spunk off, girl. Freaking Ice Queen gets more dick then I do," I hear her moan to herself as she gets my bath ready.

While soaking in the oval pool, submerged in lavender green water which smells like heaven, I stuff my face on my favourite new thing. Meat. Even Jade notices but blames it on my love for 'alien meat'.

She wasn't joking about her knowledge. She calls it gossip, but her insight on things is priceless. Jade is incredibly smart and a proper survivalist. I can't help but wonder why she is so familiar with all the exit routes, or so obsessed with the word exit. She knows where they keep travel rations and emergency supplies. What? She itches to leave, but there is nowhere safe to go. I need to keep an eye on Jade. Maybe there is a reason for those tracking devices after all. Still, I will make sure they go.

Once you get over the foul language, she is easy to talk to and really, really good with hair and makeup. Maybe I should have let someone do stuff to my hair back on Earth. All of a sudden, I am a sucker for touch. And not just Tars'. Her fingers braiding my hair feel safe and quite relaxing. She did a beautiful milkmaid braid around the crown of my head and braided in some beautiful lavender-blue beads to match my outfit. The rest of my hair is hanging heavily down my back. The same beads cover the corset of the dress. She also insisted on doing my makeup and I let her. For some reason I do feel tired. How fast is this baby growing? I am used to seeing beautiful when I look in the mirror and definitely used to wearing extravagant outfits. But this is different. Maybe because of the alien Sign on my forehead. It's glowing with the same lavender blue colour as my dress. So do the beautiful swirls encircling my arms and shoulders. Or maybe because my eyes are shining brightly and my lips look suspiciously plump. The reason brings a smile to my face and now I really don't recognise myself. I have never seen myself smile in the mirror. No wonder it turns Tars into mush.

The outfit helps with the nerves. I want to make a good first impression with the Tarrassians and I want Tars to be proud of me. I know no one would be able to notice my nerves. They will only see the perfect Ice Queen. But it doesn't mean I can fool myself.

I decide to keep Jade with me throughout the day and I hope she can help herself from insulting them, or swearing like a Brit. She promises to behave, but mischief glints in her eyes as she does.

However, she does behave and mainly keeps quiet. An occasional sad look in her eyes. My personal servants – and I really have to find a better title for them at some point – introduce themselves. All forty... What am I going to do with forty people... beings fussing over me?

Then the Healers come, luckily only two. Both males and that is a bit annoying. I am rather shocked to find out that Tarrassian women are pregnant for... nine months. Not sure why normal feels strange on an alien planet. After two hours of checks, I am happy to see the back of them. Jade looks like she's about to fall asleep on us. One of the servants announces the High Commander of the Queen's Guard – they sure love titles on this planet – and Jade is suddenly alert. Pushing her boobs up and applying even more red lipstick. God, that's bad...

The High Commander is drop dead gorgeous. Even on a planet of handsome men, this one still stands out.

Jade gives me a knowing look, saying, I know, right? Can't really blame her. He is the gorgeous version of handsome. Most Tarrassian men are all bulky muscles and light copper skin shade. He is all lean muscles enveloped in a darker coppery skin covered by a fine coat of dark brown hair. Unlike most Tarrassians I have met, his hair is much lighter, a beautiful chestnut. It is also a lot longer, but not a knot in sight. It falls like a velvet cape around him, reaching his elbows. His beard, however, is kept shorter and trimmed. His smile beams, fangs and all, and he is definitely a charmer. If not for the kilt, boots and sword, I would never consider this one as a Warrior. Polite, charming and kind of sweet. Not that I would let his boyish charm fool me. He's the High Commander of my guard for a reason. I doubt it was charm that got him the job. He introduces his second and third in command and tells me all the safety rules, as he calls them. I am apparently not allowed to go anywhere without one of the Royal Guard members. There are twenty Tarrassians in the Queen's Royal Guard and one hundred guards in the Queen's Guard. The guards are former freed slaves, who couldn't be returned to their homes, or chose to stay. Basically, he is telling me I have an entire army watching every step I take.

Such knowledge should make me feel uncomfortable, or wary, but I just nod in agreement. Maybe it makes all the difference when the guy delivering the news has a smile like that and an easy-going vibe. It takes me a while to notice that his full attention is on me only. Almost purposefully ignoring Jade. A bit rude, and I can see she has also noticed. She seems uncomfortable and on edge. I know he is here to watch over me but still. Maybe Tarrassian social rules are different. He asks me if I have any questions so far and is about to carry on when I say I don't.

"I have a question for you, Commander of Blah Blah," says Jade, ignoring my silent warning.

His smile fades the second she addresses him and he eyes the exit. I feel like laughing. These people are terrified of Jade. Just how many did she bite?

"I have a feeling you are ignoring me and I would like to know why," she says with a really fake sugary voice.

He looks incredibly uncomfortable and for a minute I really think he might bolt.

"Hello? Hanni? Whatever… Earth to tall and handsome?"

"My Queen," he addresses me again, without even looking her way. "The King asked us to deter unnecessary visitors this span. Now that the Healers have…"

His words die on his lips as Jade gets off her seat and walks towards him. I grab her and beg her to behave, but it's not lost on me how he takes several steps back. Are they scared of her? Maybe they are scared of boobs or something. The thought makes me smile. Tars is definitely not scared of boobs.

"Jade is to be treated with the same respect I am, Commander, and I will not tolerate anyone ignoring her. Where we come from that is considered rude," I say in my most icy voice, and I can see he is affected by it. This guy is obviously a crowd pleaser and likes being liked.

"Here it is just as rude, my Queen," he admits with an uncomfortable look on his face.

"So why do it, Commander?"

My simple question has caused a huge debate behind those beautiful copper eyes. He is torn between loyalties and I am about to let it go. Jade can suck it up.

"My pledge has always been to the King, then to Tarrassia's second in command and then to the Elders. We have a very strict chain of command, my Queen." He straightens himself up and looks like he is pleased with his decision.

"Now that has changed, as my pledge to the Queen comes first. The King told me so himself this span."

"He did?" I ask with a silly smile.

"Yes, my Queen, he did."

"So, you won't mind answering my question then?"

"I will be happy to answer and obey my Queen. No male, Tarrassian or freed slave, is allowed to touch, look at, talk or listen to the Human female called Jade."

"What?" Jade and I ask at the same time, and once again I have to stop her from attacking him.

"On whose orders?" I ask.

"The High General's, my Queen," he replies, and there is no stopping Jade now.

"And you all listen to him? Like a bunch of sissies?" she shouts.

"I do not know what a sissy is, but the High General is Tarrassia's second in command, after the King. All beings listen to him."

"Like shit they do!" Jade shouts, kicking randomly at a stack of furs on the shiny floor.

"I promise I will deal with it, Jade. Now, sit down and let it go. Please," I add quickly.

I am getting more tired by the minute and I miss Tars like crazy. We haven't been apart for this long since he came for me on Sketos.

"Is there anything else, Commander?" I ask, and I allow

myself to sit next to Jade. She gives me a soft smile. Didn't know she had one.

"You only have to attend to the High Lady of the Fields, my Queen."

Oh, that piqued my interest despite the tiredness. I have never seen a Tarrassian woman and I want to know what the competition looks like. Just then my stupid brain decides to remind me of Tars' wandering dick and his over-1000 lucky dips. Is this one amongst them? Is she here to gloat? I really can't deal with this right now…

"Do I have to see her, Commander?"

He thinks about it for a minute.

"The Queen doesn't have to do anything," he concludes. "However, I would like to point out, High Lady Umbelina is Tarrassia's only princess. All the Elders have sired sons, except for her sire, the Elder of the Fields. A daughter of an elder is a princess. The daughter of a king is a high princess," he explains, and my head hurts.

"Also, she is to become the Queen's First Lady and she is to organise and assist my Queen with the Sacred Ceremony of Mating."

Does he mean my wedding? I don't get to choose my bridesmaid… I give Jade a guilty look.

"Don't worry about me, Elsa," she says with a wink. "You can have Lady Umbrella."

"It's Lady Umbelina," says the Commander, and I have to suppress a laugh. "And the High Lady has travelled many spans to join your court, my Queen. The Country of the Fields is the most remote one on Mother Planet."

"Very well, Commander," I say with a defeated sigh. "I will see Lady Umbelina. One question, please. Does she have to be my First High Lady because she is a princess?"

"No, my Queen. She is to be your First High Lady because

she is promised to mate the High General of Tarrassia. She has been mated to him since birth."

"Oh," I say, and I sound plain stupid. That's because I can't take my eyes off Jade. She didn't know. 'The Queen of Gossip' didn't know. After the first obvious reaction of shock, now she is just quiet. Too quiet.

I ask the Commander to invite her in on his way out.

"Please, Jade, don't be rude to her. You don't have to be here for this. I hate having to allow a stranger to become my first… anything. Please, don't make this any harder than it is."

"I won't say anything," she says with a quiet voice while avoiding my eyes.

I stand and try to compose myself. My icy, defiant self has never failed me before. Well, except with Tars.

Lady Umbelina walks in and all my prepared speech is gone. Not sure what I expected a Tarrassian woman to look like, but this wasn't it. Are there any ugly people on this planet? Maybe because of Jade's description of "bald, skinny bitches" I wasn't expecting much.

The creature standing in front of me is definitely skinny and completely bald.

She is also utterly, breathtakingly beautiful. She is much shorter than the males, but a head taller than me and would probably tower over Jade. She is incredibly thin and bony, in a very willowy way. It gives her body a certain grace and poise. Like she is floating, instead of walking. I can see what the fuss about Humans' boobs is, since she looks as flat-chested as it gets. It makes you wonder why they would wear such low-cut dresses. But I can see the appeal. There is beauty in those bony shoulders and slender neck. There is also a vague sight of some very erect nipples under the soft fabric of the dress. Her limbs are beautiful and elegant, and her skin is lighter than the males'. It's not exactly copper in colour. More of a rose gold. Her head is bald, but so perfectly shaped. It glows like a globe in the light of the room. Her face is like a work of art. Elegant, beautifully shaped features. Her lips have the same perfect shape as the men's. Like someone took the time to draw them. Despite all that pure beauty, her most outstanding feature must be her eyes. They are huge and their shiny copper is so vast. The more you look at her the more you forget to blink and your eyes start to water. Huge thick black lashes leave shadows on her high cheeks. They flicker with emotion and worry, and I realise I have been staring. I also realise this is no bitchy Tarrassian woman who came to make me feel unwelcome. I believe this might be the Tarrassian version of Natalia.

"Hanni, Lady Umbelina, thank you for coming to see me. I know you have travelled far," I say, and I give her the Tarrassian salute by pressing a fist to my heart. She does the same but then she takes me by surprise and comes to give me a hug and a kiss on the cheek. She smells like a slice of Heaven and her skin is hot.

"I have studied Human greetings on the way here," she says with a shy smile. It reveals tiny, cute fangs. I really have a thing for fangs. Cute? Really?

She looks at Jade, who watches her back quietly without any other reaction.

I make a quick introduction and they both nod at each other. Umbelina seems unsure and one can tell she thinks it's her fault Jade hates her guts.

"Will you move into the Palace until the ceremony?" I ask, trying to distract her. "I don't really know how things work, yet."

She takes a seat in front of me in the most graceful way anyone has ever done.

"Normally, all the visitors to the High City live in the palace as guests of the King and Queen. However, I will be staying in my Mate's residence, as he also lives in the High City."

God, wrong question! Jade's lack of reaction worries me more than her swearing.

"But I will be here for anything you need, when you need, my Queen."

"Please, call me Sia. At least when we are alone. I know it's forbidden otherwise."

"And you can call me Elina. My family calls me that. Humans have very pretty names. And you are both so beautiful," she says, and almost looks embarrassed by her own bravery.

"Once again, I appreciate you travelling for many spans and leaving your life behind for the Ceremony."

"Oh," she says with a shy smile, "I was going to come anyway, Sia. After your Sacred Ceremony, I will have my own. I will live in the High City from now on. I am quite happy to be united with my mate before our own Ceremony. Larrs is what every Tarrassian female wants and he is all mine."

Without a single word or look towards us, Jade gets up and leaves.

I feel terrible and I'm not even a hundred percent sure what exactly is happening here. Jade has an entire planet of hot men to choose from. She can't possibly be infatuated with one who is taken. One who puts tracking devices on her.

I make a quick excuse, blaming Jade's behaviour on trauma and Elina seems heartbroken for her.

We talk for a while and she is excited to hear about the baby, as apparently, she was the last one to know. The Sign on my forehead and the swirls on my arms feel heavy somehow. No pain and they are still glowing, so I don't worry about him. Maybe it's because I am tired and I miss him so much.

Elina is sensitive enough to understand my moods and she is quick to make her excuses.

I really hope they don't make me see anyone else. Another servant female – I must find a way to make them tell me their names – brings me a tray of ridiculously sweet Tarrassian fruit. She tells me it's the King's favourite. I eat one, hoping not to get diabetes, while smiling like the Cheshire Cat. No wonder he tastes sweet… Before I get to wonder over my own slutty self, the large wooden doors burst open. A very flushed, teary-eyed Jade runs in, the Commander of my Royal Guard hot on her trail.

"He is taking Earth!" she screams through tears.

"Pardon?" I say, but I know exactly what she means.

"Your fucked-up-in-the-head lover boy is invading our planet, as we speak."

18

SIA

Jade is shouting the room down. She is getting increasingly frustrated with my reaction, or rather lack of one. The only thing stopping her from shaking the life out of me is the way Commander Sarrian watches her, while looming over me. There is no trace left of his charm, as his brain must have labelled Jade's behaviour as aggressive towards the Queen. I can understand her frustration. It must be quite daunting for a fiery creature like Jade to comprehend why I would be calmly applying a glittery pink dye to my lips or gently arranging my hair and outfit in the mirror. And all that, while my home could be reduced to ash as we speak. While millions of my kind could be taking their last breath. She screams at me, telling me her eight siblings are being exterminated, while I put on lipstick. I didn't even know she had any family, never mind eight siblings. But we are who we are. I can't fight my way through hell, like Gianna and Jade, and I can't even cry my way through things like Natalia. I can't give her the emotion she wants. Her siblings might be dying, her planet might be long gone by the time I even make my way to the man responsible for that. I don't blame her for acting up. She is shaking like a leaf and she's fighting tears. She is my responsibility, because I am still the Queen. I will keep her safe, and whatever other survivor of my kind might be left, any way I can. Obviously, I am not as powerful or as loved as I thought I was. I am not an expert in invading alien planets, but I don't think it happens within minutes. He must have given the orders before returning to our quarters yesterday evening. He held me in his arms all night, he kissed me, he… Did he feel empowered being covered in kisses and having his dick sucked while his army was taking my planet? Who could tell? Obviously not me. My inexperience with men didn't let me see the elephant in the room. Well, if this is my new life not much I can do about it. I wear his Sign and can't get away from him without killing myself and my child in the process; my planet has probably already been taken, and things like Jade's tracking device cuffs might not be a one-off incident. Maybe my own devices are waiting to be fitted. There is not much I can do. So, I do what I always do. Straighten my back, raise my chin up high and pretend there is no pain behind my icy eyes. Damage control. Surviving, the only way I know. It's a win-win situation this time. He may not love me the way I thought he did. Or maybe aliens don't get love the way we do. Or maybe he's just an arrogant asshole who thinks women only exist to look pretty and keep his dick wet. Nothing alien about that. Plenty of those on my own planet. But what I do know for sure, the man does have a thing for me. Maybe it's the Sign, maybe it's a psychotic obsession. Either way, that man wants my smiles, my affection and my legs wrapped around him as often as possible. And he's not getting any of that anymore. Instead, he's about to get what he hates the most: the Ice Queen.

After one last check in the mirror, I approach Jade.

"Where is the King?" I ask as calmly as I have ever been.

"The fucking twat is in the Council's room, cave whatever the shit they call it. What are we going to do about it? Why are you so calm? Has he fucked your brains like he fucked your vagina? Don't you care, Sia?"

"I really wish I didn't, Jade."

I turn my gaze on the Commander of my Royal Guard. I wonder if he knew, but then again, it makes no difference.

"Will you stop me from joining the council, Commander?"

"I am here to protect you not to stop you, my Queen." His reply is short and polite, and whatever personal opinion he may have, it's kept to himself.

"Shall we?" I gesture to Jade, inviting her to show me the way.

I don't rush, there is no point. And as we walk, Jade slows her own pace... We are followed by Commander Sarrian and a ridiculous number of guards. Maybe they are not here to protect me, but to guard me. We walk along huge corridors and pass huge room after huge room. I don't care about the surreal beauty of the place. Only a small part of my brain analyses the utterly alien environment, or the alien light coming through the windows, or the alien beings who are quick to bow to me and move out of the way. A cage is a cage, no matter how gilded.

By my side, the angry Jade turns slowly into a very worried Jade.

"Sia, listen... maybe this was a stupid idea. I don't want you getting hurt," she says with a small voice. "What can you do? We are nothing more than toys to these people and you are all I have left. Maybe they have separated us from Gianna and Natalia on purpose. Maybe they are not even alive. Please, Sia. I really can't be here alone. Don't anger him. He might like his shiny new toy, but he has a really bad temper and you don't want to poke at it. Tarrassians call him all sorts of names behind his back. They are kind of scared of him. He likes violence and blood and taking heads and... For fuck's sake, listen to me, Sia!"

She tries to go for my hand and I stop her before Sarrian decides to act on his dislike of her.

Besides, I can tell we have reached our destination. Two massive doors made of the same shiny mirror metal as the palace are guarded by two of the biggest Tarrassian Warriors I have ever seen. A barely-there slit separates the two doors and it shimmers as we stop in front of it. I see my refection in them. My own image gives me the chills. A beautiful alien creature stares back at me. She has perfect hair, perfect makeup, a beautiful lavender-blue dress, jewellery pulsing with light and colour on her forehead, and alien glowing tattoos on her arms. Her eyes are two icy holes of grey and her heart is broken. But nobody can see her heart, so that's all good. The Warriors guarding the Royal Council Cave look very uncomfortable and they watch Sarrian for instructions. He is not in charge. I am.

"A piece of advice, my Queen, if I may?" he asks respectfully, and I just nod my agreement.

"I am not allowed inside the Sacred Cave and to be fair, neither are you. Females don't attend the Royal Council. No Queen has in the past. However, it is not the Sacred Law. All our Sacred Laws must be written down in The Sacred Book of Conduct and Empowerment. No females in the Royal Council… it is kind of common sense. That's why nobody bothered to make it a law."

There is a light glint of a smile in his eyes and at least I know I can trust my guards, as crazy as that may sound.

I nod a silent thank you and he nods back in acknowledgment.

"I think it's best if you don't come in, Jade," I say, preparing for her screaming, but she is being reasonable. Or just scared.

"It's okay, Sia. I'll listen to everything from my secret hiding place. I have been listening to everything they say in there from my first day on this bloody planet."

I don't say anything and Sarrian just sighs and shakes his head.

And then the guards move aside and the metal doors open with a hiss. Behind, there are two walls made of uneven stone, which open with the unmistakable sound of stone grinding against stone.

My super-efficient brain takes in every detail within seconds. They don't just call it a cave, it is an actual cave. I don't know how anyone can build an ancient cave inside a palace that looks like an alien high-tech illusion. The stone in here must be millions of years old. It smells old too. The cave is huge; can't even make out the ceiling. It has an oval shape and there is no artificial light in sight. The only source of light comes from the huge torches lining the walls. The flames sizzle and hot red oil drips down the uneven walls. The floor is even more uneven and uncomfortable to step on. The only furniture in the cave looks like it's growing from the stone floor. The huge oval stone table, surrounded by equally huge seats shaped like thrones, rises high above the floor. Fourteen seats are taken by the most alien-looking creatures. The Elders. I have already met one of them, the Healing Elder, but he looks young compared to the others. There is a transparent glow to their skin. They are almost see-through and their coppery blood veins look surreal under their fragile skin. There are intricate braids in their really long white hair and beards. Even more surreal, they only wear the traditional kilt and their swords. Despite their age, they still display the typical Tarrassian bulging muscles. Four seats are taken by Warriors, at the opposite end of the table. The High General is flanked by the Southern and the Northern General and there is a fourth Warrior I haven't met. One who is trying really hard to keep a straight face. How strange... No one else seems in a mood to smile. Some feel angry, some puzzled by my glowing blue Sign, some just feel puzzled. As for their King, I don't care what he feels, so I don't look at him at all. I don't have to look to know where he is seated. His seat is made of mirror-shine metal, unlike the others. The backrest is shaped like the corners of a star, or a water lily in this case. Easy to see the pattern, as he stood at my entrance. They all did. He is seated exactly in the middle of the table and there is a large gap between him and the others. On the other side of the table, right in front of him, there are three empty stone thrones. No idea who they are meant for and I don't care. I make my way to the one situated right opposite his. I want him to look me in the eyes when I ask my question. I hope my puny body doesn't block their view. Because this ancient cave comes with a view. A very high-tech view, completely unexpected inside the Stone Age-looking cave. Behind the seat I am about to claim for myself, the entire length of the wall is lit by about sixty screens. They all surround a hologram reminding me of a virtual reality game. A game where hundreds of monstrous mirror-shine spacecrafts float on the outer atmosphere of a planet, ready to descend upon it like hyenas on prey. The blue planet in the distance looks undisturbed and completely unaware. There is a silence about the image. The silence before the storm. The knowledge he hasn't taken my planet yet changes everything. It affects my iciness and it gives me a desperate edge. Like I am about to beg or something. But I won't. The little blue planet is not the only one about to encounter the display of force, from what I can see on the other screens. So, this must be a war council, then. I reach my seat and stand in front of it, bracing myself to meet his gaze. I will probably look ridiculous sitting in the oversized throne, but I intend to do it regardless. My back is board straight, my chin is defiantly raised, all emotion long gone from my icy greys. I expect anger and outrage at my inappropriate behaviour. There is only pain in his eyes. And tiredness. He looks tormented and somehow defeated. I didn't expect that and it almost throws me off. But I won't allow his puppy eyes to do that. I will not learn the same lesson twice. I wait for him to say something before I sit, but he doesn't. I think the Elders also wait for him to take action and there is uncomfortable rustling as he doesn't. One of them is about to say something. I can feel it before his words come out.

"My Queen, females are not allowed in the Royal Council Cave." He has a cold unpleasant way about him, compared to most Tarrassians I have met, and he obviously likes to cut to the chase.

"Elder of the Caves, you will respect my Queen or your body and head will not leave the Sacred Cave together."

Wow, I had no idea Tars was allowed to talk to them like that. He probably isn't, but that won't stop him. And I will not fall for him defending me, just like I won't fall for puppy eyes.

"But, my King, the Sacred Law…"

"The sacred law says no such thing, Elder of the Caves." I interrupt him and give him my iciest look. "The Sacred Book of Conduct and Empowerment doesn't mention such a law. If it is not in writing it is not the law. It is the Tarrassian way and as one of our Elders, I expect you to remember that."

At first there is just silence, then an entire mixture of emotion coming from the room, reminding me of the Ketosii. Tarrassians are very guarded when it comes to displaying emotions, but I think I must have shocked them a bit. Knowledge is power, and I have Commander Sarrian to thank for that.

There is outrage, disbelief, respect, fear and a stupid, adoring look coming from one. Is he faking that? Or does he think he can adore me and break my heart at the same time? There is also amusement coming from the Warrior I haven't met. But I have a feeling that one finds everything amusing. The only one not expressing anything is the High General. Not that I expected the bastard who tagged my friend to have a reaction.

"Now, if there are no other impediments, I suggest you continue. It looks like you are having a very busy span." I address them all as I sit, but I only look at him. He is not looking at me anymore. With the corner of my eye I can see dozens of little orange lights flashing on many of the screens. His Warriors, Commanders, whatever, are requesting to hollocom the Council. He probably doesn't want to talk to them in front of me. Tough!

The Elder of the Healers rises from his seat and his kind eyes smile with genuine joy and pride when he addresses me.

"On behalf of the Royal Council, I express our great joy and our gratitude to the Mother of our Royal Cub."

He takes a fist to his heart. They all do, except for Tars. These people are really hard to kick in the balls and they are really annoying. But I refuse to fall for it. Time to cut the crap.

"You are invading my planet, my King," I say flatly. "Is this a token of your gratitude for the Mother of the Royal Cub?"

I meant to hurt him. I know I did. But his pain is hurting me too and it's just not fair.

His beautiful copper eyes flicker and look dim. I would rather see anger in them. How do you hurt someone you love? I start to think I won't be able to. Unlike him...

If looks could kill, I am sure the High General's eyes would burn a hole in my scalp. His stony face looks grim and a muscle jumps behind those clenched jaws, quite visible, despite being covered by his black beard.

"My King," he says, ignoring me, "Commander Nodric is expecting your order to proceed."

Tars gives him an angry look and I know exactly what the General is talking about. I can't believe it.

"You asked Commander Nodric, who hates Humans, to invade Earth?" I ask Tars, and he finally has the decency to look at me.

"I didn't ask him to do that because he hates Humans, which he doesn't. In the absence of Commander Zaan, Commander Nodric is in charge of the Blood Fleet. This is his assignment and he will keep his personal feelings to himself. He is to harm no Human. This is not an invasion, my Queen."

"What is it then, my King?" I ask calmly, but I can hear the sarcasm in my voice. He does too and there is a little flash of anger in his eyes, quickly replaced by torment and some sort of inner battle.

"I am trying to protect it," he sighs.

"By taking it by force?"

"I am not taking them by force. We have announced our presence and our terms. It's for them to decide now."

I feel like the cave walls are collapsing in on me. It's too late. The Earth governments know...

"My Phaea, are you okay? You are very pale." He attempts to get up and come to me, but I stop him with a look of ice. He dares call me that, while invading my planet.

"Your army is giving its terms to a Red Orbit Planet which is not aware of sentient life outside its borders. How do you think that is going to unfold?"

It is the unpleasant Elder of the Caves who comes to support my argument. Apparently, this was not a popular decision amongst his own kind.

"The Coalition of the Seven Stars will not be pleased with this," he says.

"We can't do something and ask the Coalition for permission after," says another Elder.

I jump in my seat when Tars' massive fist smashes against the table, making the stone ring.

"I rule the Coalition! It exists because Tarrassian Warriors give their lives to protect and enforce its rules!"

"Still, my King," says another, "we cannot act recklessly. There is an order to things and it takes many orbit rotations until such extreme plans are discussed and fully accepted."

"They do not have time for our politics. Their lives hang by a thread. None of them have time to wait for our discussions," Tars says, pointing at all the screens.

"We don't even know if the planets we are about to take are populated," says another Elder, pointing at the screens. "What we do know for sure is they have been claimed by the Noorranni and we are now giving the Coalition of the Dark Moon a reason to strike."

"They don't need a reason for that," says the High General. "They just don't strike in the open. It gives the galaxies the feeling we live in times of peace. But the war is ever present. Our King has shed more blood in this war than anyone else in this room."

"There is an order to things," says the Elder of the Caves. The Wise King would have never questioned such order. It is His wisdom that made Tarrassia great."

Is he for real? I wait for Tars to tell him about what he'll do with his head, but he doesn't. He just avoids looking at any of us.

"Until we have time to investigate wisely," says another Elder, "it is best not to rush things and assume there are enslaved sentient beings on the Noorranni planets."

Tars' fist makes contact with the table again. I know he's hurt it, the idiot, because my Sign hurts.

"Tell that to the Sphinx with the broken wings, tell that to the Ketosii who were so afraid they lived as mist and forgot to use their powers. Tell that to the Human male with only broken bones in his body! Tell that to all the enslaved beings scattered around the galaxies. The galaxies I vowed to protect. I shall fail them no more."

"But is it wise to do it this way?" asks yet another Elder. Tars flinches every time one of them uses the word 'wise'. Bastards. They keep referring to his father on purpose. Why doesn't he give them a piece of his mind?

"My King," says the High General, "the Blood Fleet is waiting."

This fucking guy! As Jade would say…

"You can't take Earth, my King," I say, trying to sound more reasonable. "The second you land a warship they will fire at it."

"For their own good I hope they won't, my Queen," he replies, and as he looks at me his copper eyes glow with specks of gold.

"They have been contacted from outer space and we know our message has been received. However, no response. As a Red Orbit Planet, they would know nothing about our technology. Maybe they are unaware we can even land on their planet, or how easy it would be for my fleet to turn them to dust, if that's what we wished. They have to understand our power, to consider our rules."

"And let me guess, your rules involve endless protection in exchange for willing females. And how convenient, of all the forbidden planets you decided to take Earth, because Tarrassians need fertile wombs and maybe a chance of more Signs."

He gives me a pained, guilty look.

"Our King seems to forget he can't treat Earth like one of his most beloved Yellow Planets," says the Elder of the Caves.

There is an uncomfortable wave going through the council and there is a murderous look on the High General's face. So, he does have reactions.

An Elder stands and introduces himself. Umbelina's father, I realise.

"My Queen, our King has instructed us to put together a very detailed offer for the Humans. The rights of any future mates are at the base of the Alliance. Only females who volunteer will be accepted and they are free to change their minds at all times. Even after being mated to a Tarrassian. The only time they won't be able to leave Tarrassia and return to Earth will be if they get the blessing of the Sign. And only because the Signs cannot be separated.

"In return, the Humans will get protection, cures for their many diseases and resources to develop. Families will be allowed to visit their daughters and they will be welcome to join Tarrassia, if they wish. Of course, these are only a few of the many incentives we are offering. The draft document of the Alliance is vast."

"And you had time to draft all this since yesterday?" I ask Tars with a terrible suspicion in my gut.

"I gave the order on Sketos, when we first returned to the warship," he admits with flickering copper eyes.

"I see…" The bitter taste of betrayal turns my stomach. "Well, since you made up your mind, let me tell you what is going to happen now on Earth." I fist my hands under the table. The stupid pregnancy hormones. I just want to cry and never stop crying.

"Earth is nothing like Tarrassia. There are about 196 countries and they all have their own ideas about everything. Just because one country might agree to your rules, it doesn't mean the others will. This will only encourage disorder and civil unrest, and a lot of the countries would want to fight you, no matter how barbaric their technology might be. And then, there is corruption. There will be individuals and maybe entire governments forcing unwilling women to become 'willing'."

He runs a big hand through his hair, ruffling it wildly. I have a painful flashback of last night, when my own hands stroked his hair as he slept.

"I know it won't be easy. Humans are complicated beings. It will get a lot worse before it gets better. But at least my Blood Fleet will shield the Earth's atmosphere and no more slaves will be taken. They will have to accept in the end."

"So that your Warriors can have the pick of more or less willing females."

"No, that was never my main reason," he says with a sigh.

"Why else would you do such a thing, Tars?"

"Humans are special, I cannot let them perish. The Human Spirit is a great power. I have tried to explain it to the council, but it is hard to understand a power one cannot see."

I have a bad, bad feeling about this. What is he saying?

"Tarrassians have been too preoccupied to save and protect the weaker beings," he continues, without really looking at any of us.

"And maybe the Elder of the Healers was right. We have been too arrogant and not just about our breeding. It is easy to protect the weak. You get nothing but gratitude. Not always easy to protect the strong. But this is how the Coalition of the Dark Moon has taken the Sphinx Planet, or Sketos. We all watched and did nothing. I will not allow Earth to be next."

Is he comparing Humans' 'powers' to the Sphinxes'? Did I put all this rubbish in his head? As I realise this is all my doing, I consider my actions. I can't possibly undermine his authority by telling the council my kind don't have any bloody powers. The Human Spirit is just a thing to make us keep on going against all odds. Definitely not worth an alien invasion.

"Perhaps it is not a coincidence the Astrals have chosen the Humans to be compatible with us and even to rebirth our long-forgotten Sign," he says, looking at me with flickering golden specks in his copper eyes. "The two of us saved a planet against all odds. My Tarrassian strength and my Queen's Human Spirit are two great powers, which become invincible when united. And that is why I am taking Earth on this span. There will be no power amongst the galaxies able to defeat a cub born with Tarrassian strength and Human Spirit. As for the other planets, under the rule of the Noorranni, they will be freed and returned to their rightful owners or to their own ecosystem if there are no sentient beings to be found. I will change the Old Rule of the Seven Stars. From now on, no one can claim a planet just because they got there first, or they felt like it. No planet can be taken, sold or bought. There will be special exceptions for dying planets and their inhabitants in search of a new home."

He ends his speech and it's obvious nothing any of us do or say will change his mind. Not that it stops the Elders from moaning. They do like to bicker. Some keep asking questions, but he doesn't answer them anymore. The three Generals are the ones explaining and answering. Obviously, they were aware of the King's plans. He doesn't look at me either. His eyes take in every screen and he exchanges looks with his General.

"Great wisdom and ruling experience are needed when discussing any rule of our old ways," says the Elder of the Caves. "But to change one of the rules? That is unheard of, and with all due respect to our King, he doesn't have the qualities required to do that."

"The King has ruled, my Elder," says the High General. The look in his eyes is far scarier than Tars at his scariest moment.

"The King's rulings haven't been the wisest in the past," replies the Elder, and I really think Larrs might pull his sword on him.

"The Wise King has ruled for 128 orbit rotations without the need to change our old ways. Our young King should consider that," says another Elder.

I have seen Tars take heads for far less insult. I have seen Tars dismember wild beasts because they dared growl under the tree, I was sleeping in.

I watch him across the table as he tries to focus on the progress of his Warriors, probably making sure they are safe. He is also trying to block the words being said around the table. Trying and failing. Each time one of them compares him to his father a dull pain runs through my marks. Each time one of them says the word 'wise', my Sign pulses with his hurt. I know he won't change his mind on his ruling. But why would he just sit there and let the Elders, or me for that matter, question him, point the finger at him and make him feel like a reckless king who acts first and thinks after? Do I really have to ask? Don't I know it already?

Because he loves us. I am the woman he loves. The one carrying his child and displaying his Sign. These Elders are his people and this is a king who would die for every single one of his people. No wonder he itches to go to war and kill enemies. He is powerless in this room. He will always be powerless against the people he loves. My Sign glows with such a bright purple, the light bounces off the walls, looking kind of ridiculous in the gloomy cave. I stand and they all try to follow, but I invite them to sit.

He looks at me with tired eyes. There is no anger in them. Just pain. He knows he has a duty and he thinks that duty will break my heart. I also have a duty. I have to give this man something no one else ever has. Trust.

"It is very unfortunate I will never get to meet the Wise King. I can only be proud my cub comes from such a great line of Tarrassians." I address the Elders but my eyes never leave his. "I imagine there is nothing better than a Wise King in times of peace. It allows a nation to develop and prosper. Unfortunately, we are now in times of war. And by the sounds of it, Tarrassia has been at war for a long time. The blood of our brave Warriors and the blood of our King has allowed Tarrassians to keep on living their dream of peace. It allowed the Elders to rule from the safety of the Sacred Cave. Such efforts are not enough anymore, as the war takes its toll on the galaxies. It needs to be stopped, before it reaches Tarrassia, and there will be no more peace pretending. There will be no more dreaming of times of wisdom and prosperity. Wisdom cannot win wars. Talking and bickering cannot win wars. There is only one thing that can win wars. Bravery! Tarrassia has indeed been blessed by the Astrals. They have given us the Wise King in times of peace and the Brave King in times of war. The Elders would do well to remind Tarrassians and themselves about their blessings."

I know I am standing as straight as ever and I talk as calmly as ever, but everything shakes inside me and only years of self-control keep me standing. The silence is only disturbed by the sizzling torches and the static of the monitors. Tars looks at me with eyes of melted gold. There is no other reaction and Tars always has one. Just when I think the silence might crush me, the High General stands and presses a fist to his silent left heart.

"To the Brave King!" he says in a booming voice that demands obedience.

We exchange a look and I know I have made a friend for life. The other Warriors and all the Elders stand and repeat the General's words and salute. I do the same when they finish. He doesn't say anything, just watches me with glowing eyes of gold.

"I am deeply grateful to the Royal Council for allowing me to take part in this span. Now if you will excuse me, I would rather not watch when Earth is being taken, no matter how noble or necessary that may be."

They all stand and give their salute to the Queen and I use all my strength to break my gaze from his.

"Please don't keep my King for too long. He still has to recover from his wounds. He also has to explain what his 'beloved Yellow Planets' are."

I hear the room vibrate with laughter behind me as I make my way out.

Once outside, Commander Sarrian gives me a quick check-up from head to toe.

"Still alive?" he asks with that charming smile of his.

"Yes, I am okay. Thank you."

"I wasn't asking about you, my Queen." We smile at each other and make our way back to my quarters. I am desperate for a bath, food and sleep. Also desperate for his arms around me, but that looks like it might have to wait. Jade catches up with us halfway through. She is all flushed skin and swollen eyes, but she is not crying anymore.

"I am sorry about your siblings, Jade. I don't need to tell you what our people are like. They might kill each other while looting or while trying to flee before any spaceship gets to land. I wish I could tell you your siblings will be okay, but I can't."

"That's okay, they are little shits anyway," she says with a sigh. "I am very proud of you, Elsa," she says after walking in silence for a while. "You kick ass, not to mention you used to date Spider-Man and all that shit."

I stop walking and Sarrian almost bumps into me. It's my thing, apparently.

"What are you on about, Jade?"

"Lover boy came to see me this morning. He wanted to know if you might have any feelings for Spider-Man. Oh, my Elsa, I have really underestimated you," she says with a cheeky smile.

Unbelievable! He is just unbelievable! Maybe I should have let the Elders kick his ass.

19

TARS

I trust my Warriors with my life. They don't need watching over. And I owe Larrs yet another favour. He knowingly took it upon himself to command the Royal Army for the rest of the dark span. I will gladly take it from him on the next span. But now? Now I need to be with her and I owe him for making it possible. I don't care how much she will deny it, but she is no ordinary being. She cannot be. The elements bend to her will and summer changes into winter, powerless beings bend to her will and become powerful, the Sphinx bends to her will and doesn't attack, the Elders bend to her will.

I don't think any of them are as ordinary beings as they seem. I have seen some of my strongest Warriors succumb to lesser injuries than the small Human male, the red female is still alive after being taken by the Sphinx King, another one escaped from the most secure warship in the galaxies, as for the female called Jade... I don't even want to imagine how in the name of the Astrals she found a secret passage to the Royal Council Cave.

Mating my Queen has enhanced my senses and I could smell her hiding in the sacred walls. No wonder my Queen was told about my plans before I had the chance to do it myself. She's still there now, like an invisible member of the Council. I decided not to act on it, because I need Larrs' level-headed judgment on this span. There's nothing level-headed left of him when it comes to that female, so I kept her actions to myself. The most extraordinary thing is that one of these unusual beings calls me her love when I act like a jealous, insecure youngling. She calls me the Brave King when I take her planet. She can see the male behind the actions and no one else could before. Not even my parents, despite their love for me. This extraordinary creature can see me.

My quarters smell like her. The entire palace does. I follow her scent like it is my only air. My beautiful Queen is bathing. The dimmed lights in the cleaning room and the soft violet steam rising from the water make her look like a water flower, floating above the mists covering the Still Waters before the sunrise. Her beautiful white hair is piled high on top of her head to keep it away from the water. Soft tendrils have escaped and frame her beautiful face, falling gently on her shoulders. The rest of her beautiful body is covered by the water and that pokes at my anger. I need to see her. I need to taste her. I need all of her. The hot water has flushed her normally pale cheeks and her grey eyes glow as she looks at me. Her lush lips turn into a smile. A snooty one.

"My King, your shit list gets bigger with every span," she says. Her eyes watch me advance on her and then stop on my hands. I remove my Kannicloth and my Sword with slow movements, without taking my eyes from her. I know I watch her like prey and I know my muscles are growing as I step into the water and advance on her. I can't help anything from growing right now and her reaction only ignites my hunger even more. The snooty playful smile is gone as her eyes watch me with a mixture of fear and arousal. She retreats in the pool, without paying attention. As she reaches the far edge, her feet under the water bump into the bottom step and she loses her balance. I catch her in my arms before her bottom makes contact with the stone steps. She clings to me and takes a deep breath. I lift her up, placing her on her back, above the steps. I push a thick drying cloth under her body, shielding her fragile skin from the hard stone, then drag her legs towards me, without breaking eye contact.

"Tars, what are you doing? You are scaring me. Say something!"

I am not good with words like the Humans are. I don't know how to express what I feel for her. But I can show her. My hunger scares her, but her arousal perfumes the air. And now I am going to taste it. She gasps loudly when my mouth makes contact with her wet folds. And it's not only the water causing the wetness. Her beautiful little cunt is coated in her sweet juices. Water could never taste that good. I lap at her and her hands fist in my hair, her body arching under my punishing tongue. I grab the little pleasure knob she calls a clit in between my teeth and pull gently, aware of my fangs. I am desperate to bite her skin and taste her blood, but not here. Her skin would be too sensitive in this spot. She forgets about her fear and her lips let out the most delicious whimpering noises. Under the water, my cock twitches with every noise she makes. I remove one hand from her parted legs and stroke myself under the water. It gives me no relief. Only her sweet cunt can relieve my pain. But for now, I just want to feed on her taste, to inhale her smell and listen to her screaming my name as she comes in my mouth. I push my tongue inside her hot opening, as far as it will go, and I rub her knob with my fingers. Harder, deeper until she begs me to stop. But I don't. She says she can't take any more, but she will. I push her hips into the floor to make her stop squirming and I increase the pressure of the rubbing and my tongue reaches deeper. She comes again with a loud scream, filling my mouth with a hot gush of sweetness. Her legs shake violently and she pants, gasping for air. A better male would let her recover, a better male would hold her until she got her wits back, but I am no such thing. I pull myself out of the water above her and grab her shaky legs. I pull them apart and take her ankles in my hands. I slide into her slick pussy in one fluid motion and only stop when all my cock is buried inside her. I will never understand how her small body can take me the way it does. I only still myself for long enough to take her mouth in a kiss. She's too lost in yet another orgasm to return my kiss. The way she allows me to feed on her mouth makes me lose all sanity. I plunge into her tight little body over and over again, pushing us both higher and higher on the stone floor. A distant warning thought tells me her body is no longer on the cloth and her soft skin is rubbing against the hard stone. Another alarming thought tells me I am pushing too hard and too deep, and that my grip on her ankles is too tight. I am too far gone to listen to any reason and so is she. Her inner muscles clench around my cock, spasming and gripping at my flesh just as violently as I plunge into her. She loses herself into me once again and her body goes limp in my arms. My own release is building and building, making my ears ring. My lips leave her swollen ones and find the softness of her shoulder. I explode inside her shaking body as my fangs sink into her soft skin and the sweet taste of her blood fills my mouth. As the last of my hot seed leaves my body, small glimpses of sanity return to me and I pull us both back into the hot pool. I keep her little body close to mine with one arm and I use the other to remove her now messy hair from her face.

"Phaea, open your eyes! Please, look at me."

Her long lashes flutter and her beautiful eyes open. The silver is swirling with tears and I have to ask her the question my returned sanity demands.

"Did I hurt you? The cub... I didn't think..."

"What? No!" she says, grabbing my face between her little hands. "The cub is in his or her little pouch. You can't touch it. As it grows, perhaps we could be less…" Her cheeks flush as she tries to find an appropriate word.

"Enthusiastic?" I offer, and she hides a shy smile in my neck, using my wet beard to shelter her face from me. I can smell the blood on her shoulder and I inspect the wound. This female of mine is so vexingly fragile. I need to remember this no matter how crazed I get. I wash her wound and then I lick it until the bleeding stops. She squirms in my arms, but it's not because of the pain. My female may be fragile, but she is also insatiable. My cock gets hard again and pokes at her wriggling belly.

I caress her body under the water, letting my hands slide over her shoulders, glowing with the marks of our mating Sign, over her back, her small waist, the curve of her hips and the swell of her ass. As I pick her up by her waist, she wraps those perfect, long legs around my waist. We press our foreheads together, allowing our Signs to connect their pulsing energy.

"There will be no sleep and no rest for you tonight, my Phaea," I whisper against her lips. My dark promise makes her shiver in my arms. I shift her body around in my arms and carry her out of the bathing pool. Back in our sleeping quarters, she lets me dry her skin and remove the pins from her hair, releasing it down her back. Our eyes never leave each other as I take her hand and guide her towards the bed. As we stop by my furs, her little hand goes up to my face and caresses my beard.

"I love you, Tars," she says. Her eyes turn silver and little tears, as she calls them, pool in them. The emotion feels heavy in my stomach.

"Humans say that in words?" I ask her, and she seems a bit unsure, but then a soft smile tugs at her lips.

"Tarrassians do it better. They prefer to show their love, rather than express it with words."

"I like listening to the words, my Phaea. They are beautiful and in a quiet moment such this, words are better than actions," I tell her, stroking her face the way she strokes mine.

"Perhaps there is a time and a place for both," she says. Her little hand goes down my face and opens wide on my chest, pushing me to sit on the bed. I am quick to do as she asks, fascinated by the fire in those eyes. The eyes I stupidly thought to be cold and icy. She straddles me, positioning herself on top of my lap. Her knees go either side of my thighs and her own thighs are spread wide open, trying to accommodate the size of my body. Her beautiful cunt is fully exposed to my hungry eyes and the scent of her arousal fills my nostrils. My cock grows even harder and twitches, pressed in between our bodies. She wraps her arms around my neck and brings her lips to mine.

"Tell me," she says, her breath hot against my mouth.

"Ask me nicely," I tell her, licking her lower lip.

Of course, she doesn't ask me nicely, instead she rubs her wide-open folds against the base of my cock, then rubs her belly against the rest of my length. This is not the sort of battle I can win, so I just tell her.

"I love you, Sia." I use her name because she needs to know I see her, the way she sees me. The words feel light on my tongue, as if I have waited all my life span to say them.

I inhale sharply as her hand grabs my cock. She lifts her body higher, positions it at her wet entrance, then slides on it all the way down. My hands grab those perfect globes of her ass and I push her up and down my cock, trying to remember to be less 'enthusiastic'. Her round tits rub against my face each time I push her higher and I grab a juicy nipple in my mouth. Her inner muscles grip me so tight I forget all about my thoughts of self-restraint. I grab her hips and feel my claws dig into her skin. I am once again too far gone to even command my own claws to retract. I use my grip on her to push her body faster and harder.

My lips lick the spot on her neck where her pulse throbs wildly. She stills for a nanoclip.

"Are you going to bite me again?"

"Do you want me to bite you again, my Phaea?"

"Yes," she says.

And I do, because I would never refuse this female anything.

As my fangs dig into the soft skin of her neck, her pussy clenches around my cock, coating me in the juices of her orgasm, my own release not far behind.

We held each other for a long time after our soul-shattering orgasms, trying to stop our bodies from shivering with lust. My cock is still trapped inside her and her head rests on my shoulder. Her lips are pressed against my neck and I love the way she inhales my scent.

"Is the bite a Tarrassian thing or is that the King's thing?" she asks softly.

"A male would mark his female with his fangs during their first mating. It's a sign she belongs to him. When lacking the Astrals' Sign, my people learnt to treasure the bite."

"You didn't bite me during our first time," she says with a contented sigh against my neck.

"I thought I had made you bleed enough on that span. I saved it for the next time."

"What about the second bite?" she asks.

"That's just the King's thing."

She giggles and pinches my arm.

"You are incorrigible, King of Tarrassia."

"Yes," I agree. No point denying. "I have something for you, my Phaea," I say, lifting her off my lap, and she makes a delicious sound as my cock slides out of her. It is enough to make me hard again. She watches me grow under her eyes, with a shocked expression.

"I did say you would have no sleep or rest tonight," I tell her with a grin. I place her on the furs and retrieve her presents. Her eyes light up as she sees the first one. It's too big to be disguised.

"My fur," she says full of excitement and happiness. "I thought I lost it on the warship. And it's all cleaned. Thank you, Tars," she says, hugging the stripy blue and white fur to her chest. She inhales the clean scent of the fur and a shadow passes over her face.

"There was so much blood on it," she says with a small voice.

I lift her chin up and look her in the eyes.

"I have just checked on the Human male, my Phaea. He has a lot more than a fighting chance now. His vital signs are strong and his bones have started to knit themselves. He will live."

She acknowledges my words with a beautiful smile and places the fur on the bed next to her, like it's the most precious gift ever. I lie next to her and pull her into my arms. The small box in my hand catches the light and shimmers. She looks at it, then at me with a questioning look. I push her white head fur hair behind those tiny ears, too small to hold it in place for long.

"I did get you a present for giving me a cub and it wasn't invading your planet."

"Tars, I shouldn't have said that to you in front of everybody," she says, and her grey eyes shimmer with tears.

"No, I deserved that, my Phaea," I say as I brace myself to tell her the truth. No more hiding and no more doing things behind her back. "And you were right, taking Earth won't be easy. Humans are very confusing. When I left the Royal Council Cave, there were about ninety-seven different answers to our terms," I admit to her.

She sighs, but there is no accusation in her eyes. Just sadness.

"I can't fully accept the magnitude of your decision, my love, but I will trust it with all my heart. I cannot deny that we were taken, or Brian's wounds, or the horrible death of the Human female in the tunnels. Who knows how many more there have been in the past? I understand you are only trying to keep them safe. I just don't know how my people will survive the change. Or comprehend a world too vast for their knowledge. What if they forget who they are and what they used to be?"

"My Phaea," I tell her with a smile, "it took me a while to understand why beings from a Red Orbit Planet, without strength, powers, or decent life spans, would be so resilient. There may be things about the Human Spirit I still don't understand."

"However, the one thing I do understand is Humans don't forget who they are and most of all, they don't forget who they used to be. You don't let your stories die, like we let ours perish. We are learning with every span about how our Signs work, because the details have been long forgotten. And the Sign is the most important thing to my kind. It should have never been forgotten. Humans will never forget themselves! They treasure their stories. Their past keeps their present alive."

She watches me with glowing eyes full of pride for her kind and love for me.

"So, as I was saying before you decided to interrupt the King, I have a present for you. A present to show my gratitude for the cub you are carrying. I ordered it for you back on Sketos, when we returned to the ship. Tarrassia's High Master of Stones has worked on it ever since."

I open the shimmery box and reveal the beautiful piece of adornment inside. The High Master has outdone himself. He used our most precious metal, the Platinum Ore our swords are made of, to craft my Queen's adornment. It is shaped like the Circle Nebula that gave birth to our Astrals. It is the shape carved onto our foreheads. In the middle of the inner circle, he used the precious stones of the Still Waters to craft a water flower. They are very rare and only once every 500-orbit rotation, one or two would wash onto the shores.

She watches it with something I can't quite understand. She might be an alien, but all beings are able to admire beauty and perfection. She must like it. Her shoulders, tremble and her Sign vibrates. Something makes my marks hurt and it must be her strong reaction to my gift.

Maybe she doesn't understand what it is. Pins are not very common pieces of adornment amongst the galaxies. Most would have pendants or bangles, cuffs and body chains. The pins are very much a Tarrassian thing. Is she shivering? Her body shakes in my arms and she watches the pin like it is about to come alive.

"My beautiful Phaea, this is a pin I have ordered for you. You wear it on your garment, rather than on your skin like other pieces of adornment. It secures itself onto your garment and you can wear it to remember my love for you and for our cub."

Why is she crying? Big blobs of salty water fall down her face and onto my chest. She raises her eyes to look at me. The light in them is so strong, I involuntarily remember the Ketosii, and for a nanoclip I consider shielding my eyes. But no, it's just emotion and something else giving them an alien glow. It must be a Human thing.

Her voice trembles as her fingers brush over the pin.

"I know what a brooch is, Tars. And I know what this is. This is my mother's brooch, the one I lost the day my sister died. And now I have found it."

EPILOGUE

SIA & NATALIA

I rub my belly through the soft fabric of the dress. I know it's silly, but each time I do it I wait for a kick back. The baby is too small for that. I smile to myself in the mirror as I brush my long white hair. My baby. Our baby. I find all this happiness too much to deal with. It sounds crazy how pain and loneliness were less overwhelming to me. Not that I want them back. Maybe I am strange after all. My eyes stop on the blue pearls of my brooch. It looks beautiful against the lavender colour of my dress. I promise myself, one day I will allow myself to understand and process all these strange coincidences. I know Tars wants answers I simply don't have. He thought I didn't like the brooch, so I had to tell him it was mine all along. I dropped it at a gas station when I was four years old and it was given back to me by the man I love. Well… yes, twenty years later, on a different planet, but I really can't deal with all that right now, so I postpone the reasoning. Apparently Tarrassians don't function that way. Tars decided the High Master of Stones had some answers to give and his head might not survive the process.

Managed to change his mind for now. My King has a soft spot for my smile. And for other things I can do with my lips. My newfound power brings a glint to my eyes. Maybe this is my superpower. I can put my lips to good use. The thought makes me laugh out loud in my bedroom. Luckily there are no servants around. I won't mention it to him, though. Let him think I am Queen of this and Goddess of that, when all I really have going for myself is skilful lips...

I know the sacrifice he makes, commanding his armies from the Royal Council Cave. He will always be a warrior first and a king after. I know it's not the kingdom keeping him from the battlefield. It's me... It's been four days since he gave me my brooch. Four days of happiness, anxiety and anguish, for both of us. And I think there is also guilt on his side. He does not say it, but I know he needs to be close to his Warriors. He needs to fight by their side. He is not the sort of king who gives orders from the safety of his palace. He is the Brave King and I have to be worthy of him. So, I intend to toughen up, grow some faith and let him go to war. According to the Elder of the Spark Mountains, now that our bond is stronger and we are about to have a cub, the pain should be less when separated for too long. Tars, however, thinks the Elder is faking a knowledge he doesn't have. We will have to find out, I think. I have decided, I will let him join his Warriors after our Mating Ceremony. Despite my irrational fear of being without him, or even worse, losing him, I refuse to be the whiny woman who wants her man safe and away from danger. Tars is not that kind of man and I have to accept it. He will be fine. I know he is reckless and wild and... No, not going near that list. I think he will treasure his life and do everything he can to come back to me. To us. I still have six days until the Mating Ceremony. Six days when he is all mine. Well, not entirely. He is always busy in the daytime, but he comes to me at night and that is all I care for. We make love for hours on end and I am quite grateful for my new Tarrassian self-healing properties. My King doesn't like to go easy on me. Not that I want him to. Besides, he always kisses it better after. The thoughts of last night make me squirm in my seat. Nope, not going to last until tonight, or lunchtime for that matter, so maybe it's time I called him. Mind-talking has its perks.

I also have an increasing number of things to do and people to meet. Luckily, sweet, shy Lady Umbelina turned out to be a real treasure and quite hands-on. She would make the best project manager ever on Earth. She handles everything with grace and doesn't seem too overwhelmed with organising a huge royal wedding. Sadly, because she is always around me, Jade keeps her distance and it breaks my heart. It's bad enough I cannot have any of the other Humans I was taken with at my wedding. Brian is recovering well, but he still has months of healing in the healing pod before he can be allowed out, Gianna is still missing and Natalia… I have asked not to be disturbed this morning, to focus on Natalia. I haven't tried to reach her mind since the disastrous first time. The longer I have left it the more scared I have become of what I may find. I have to try. For them, for me and especially for Tars. Tannon means a lot to him. His only blood family left. He cannot reach his mind and I could see the shadows in his eyes when he tried and failed.

I have to try. I close my eyes, hoping my mind eyes will also be closed. Natalia's Sign almost blinded me last time. I regulate my breathing and try to picture her. It's not hard. Despite her fears, Natalia is light and joy and giggles. She doesn't have to fake bravery, unlike me.

A soft pink light floods my mind and I can almost smell her bouncy mane of red curls. They smell like cake and childhood dreams. The pink gets brighter and I can see the shape of her Sign. Impossible to tell what it is from the inside of her forehead. But one thing is for sure, it is very pink… What would a being as big and scary as Tannon look like, with a bright pink sign on his forehead? Only Natalia could have managed to do that. And stay alive. Because she is definitely alive and aware, I am in her head. I can feel her fear, but it's not as overwhelming as last time. She is trying to let me in.

Keep your eyes closed, Natalia, and don't look at my Sign. It will burn your eyes from the inside. I know you are telling yourself I must be a monster and I can't see you or hear you. But I can, because I am not a monster, I am your friend Sia.

It doesn't work like that anymore, comes the unexpected answer. I try to contain my happiness and tread carefully. She allows me in and talks back, so at least I know she is not injured.

The Monsters can see me and hear me now. I am not safe anymore, she says, and I can feel the tears on her cheeks from the inside. It feels very surreal.

I promise I am not a monster, Natalia. It's only me. Well... us. A lot has changed since I saw you last. I have a baby growing inside me.

You do? she asks, unsure, and even inside her mind, her voice sounds wary.

Yes, I do, and all I need now to be completely happy is to have you back safely. I know it's hard to understand what's happening, but you have to try. I promise I will explain everything to you. For now, I just need to know you are safe. I can hear you talk out loud, but you don't have to do that. It's safer if you do it in your mind only. I will hear you, I promise.

There is no one to hear me talk to you, she says, and my heart drops.

Are you alone? Is Tannon...? I can't even bring myself to say the words.

Who is Tannon? she asks, leaving me completely puzzled.

Tannon is your mate, Natalia. You have his Sign on your forehead and his mating Marks on your body. How can you not know his name?

Oh... him. I just call him Monster, she says.

God, no! Please, don't. People have hurt him in the past because of the way he looks. He is not a monster, Natalia. His name is Tannon and he looks a bit different from the others because his dad was a different species. That is all. How come you don't know these things? Natalia, where is Tannon?

Here, with me, she says, and I can feel her sadness.

Where is here and is he okay?

We are in a cave and it is freezing. He is not awake. His brain is bleeding.

I can't help but cover my mouth with both hands to stop a cry. What is she saying?

Natalia, please tell me what happened. I have friends on that planet who could help. They can come and get you and Tannon out of there. Is the… the Sphinx there? I ask while my mind is at work, trying to fit the missing pieces.

No, he is not here, which is good. He is very annoying and I don't trust him around my Monster. He is the one who hurt him in the first place, she says, like her words should make perfect sense.

Can I ask the Ketosii to go against a Sphinx? Would that endanger them?

She answers my dilemma before I get to act on my idea.

My Monster… I mean Tannon, cannot be moved. The blood could inundate the rest of his brain. The Sphinx says he put him into a healing sleep. I think he means an induced coma, but I don't trust him. I don't like cats too much. I prefer dogs.

God, what do I do? Shall I tell Tars? He will run to Sketos to fight something no one can fight. A Sphinx!

What shall I do? How can I leave you alone with the two of them, in the middle of an Ice Planet? I ask in her mind without realising.

It's okay, Sia, please don't worry for me. It turns out Monsters are more scared of me than I am of them.

THE TARRASSIAN SAGA

The Tarrassian Saga is my praise to Humanity and to everything that makes us special. In an alien world of powerful beings who come with a long list of superpowers, our weaknesses become our strengths. Our resilience, our willpower, our determination to carry on, and especially our obsession with love, turn out to be the only superpowers that matter in the end.

Writing The Ice Queen has been the most rewarding, magical experience. Somewhere around Chapter Five, the story felt like it was writing itself. There were moments when my characters' actions were quite unexpected and they simply used me to write their story.

The Tarrassian Saga will unfold over five books, The Ice Queen being the first in the series. All five human characters introduced in this book will have their own stories. The books are better enjoyed when read in order, but there are no cliffhangers. Each story can be read on its own.

As hinted in the epilogue of The Ice Queen, Natalia's Story will be next. Her book is called The Queen of Monsters because when one is as terrified of monsters as she is, there is only one thing to do: own it!

A labour of love and support made this book happen, and I would like to say a huge thank you to my husband and my beautiful children.

An equally big thank you to my talented illustrator, Dave Hill. He caught the essence of my characters in a way I didn't even think was possible.

Thank you to the very supportive team at Troubador Publishing and everyone involved in this adventure.

I hope my wonderful readers will enjoy The Ice Queen just as much as I enjoyed writing it. Don't forget to look out for the next books in the series, and don't forget to leave a review. Good or bad, the reviews help me understand my readers and grow as a writer.

Loads of love and carry on!
Aria